SOMEBODY KNOWS

a novel

PAMELA UNGASHICK

Somebody Knows
Red Adept Publishing, LLC
104 Bugenfield Court
Garner, NC 27529
https://RedAdeptPublishing.com/

---

1.   http://StreetlightGraphics.com

For Mark, Stacia, Troy, and my mom, Shirley.

A grandfather was teaching his grandson about how to live. He explained that inside everybody is a terrible fight between two wolves. One wolf is evil: he is anger, envy, sorrow, greed, arrogance, self-pity, guilt, resentment, inferiority, lies, false pride, superiority, and ego.

And, the grandfather continued, the other wolf is good: he is joy, peace, love, hope, serenity, humility, kindness, benevolence, empathy, generosity, truth, compassion, and faith.

The grandson thought about this for a while then asked, "Which wolf will win?"

His grandfather replied, "The one you feed."

—traditional Cherokee story

Part I

CHAPTER 1

Audrey
July 1943

By the middle of the afternoon, the day was so hot that Audrey's only relief was to suck on a chunk of frost from the freezer and let the cold stream of water dribble down her neck. She was lazing on an old chair on the back porch, dressed in shorts and a light-blue tee, her feet tucked under her sticky thighs as she watched Harry. At six, her little brother seemed oblivious to the sultriness. He was happily playing one of his make-believe games in the parched grass.

Shifting uncomfortably, she considered engaging Harry in a game of hide-and-seek. That would be something to do, anyway, to alleviate her boredom. Despite their four-year age difference, they had fun together and were pretty much each other's only friends. Whenever they played the game, Harry liked to hide near the Ritters' house next door, but Audrey always made a beeline for the thick woods behind the field that abutted their backyard. Whenever Harry took too long to find her, she would caw like a crow, and he would follow the sound only to brag later that he'd found her all on his own.

She never minded, though.

Audrey eyed the lush treetops of the faraway woods, knowing the air would be much cooler under their leafy expanse. She felt the familiar tug to seek their comforting shelter, to get far away from their house and the woman inside. Her eyes shifted to the screen door.

Only a few weeks ago, Mother had ordered her and Harry to keep out of the woods, Audrey's favorite place in her small world.

"I ain't raisin' no clodhoppers," she'd said. "You both stay out of them woods from now on."

Audrey didn't know what clodhoppers were but, being so poor and all, figured maybe they were just that. She knew not to question Mother about why they couldn't play in the woods anymore or about anything else, either. Worse yet would be complaining to her daddy. That would only lead to more trouble.

Mother's demand had come the day after Grandmother Hamilton moved away. She'd just up and left without a word of goodbye, off to live with a friend somewhere else, leaving them to live in the house she'd owned forever. But instead of being happy, Mother had been ornery as a bear, much worse than her normal surly self. Audrey figured she was mad because her own mother had not said proper goodbyes to everyone. Mother was big on good manners although she had none herself to speak of.

Audrey couldn't have cared less that the old lady was gone. Her grandmother had never paid any attention to her or Harry, and now, at least, the only yelling that went on was between Mother and Daddy. Even better, Audrey and Harry had their own rooms up on the second floor.

She swiped the sweat from her top lip and stretched out her tanned, gangly legs, still deciding if standing was worth the effort. Sighing, she unstuck her bottom from the chair, blew the frizzy bangs off her forehead, and pulled herself up. She pressed an ear to the screen door. Quiet—only an electric buzz from their old fan hummed in the kitchen. When she ambled into the yard toward Harry, he was examining a ladybug as it crawled around the tip of his finger.

"Hey, wanna play hide-and-seek with me?" Audrey twirled curly ponytail strands while she admired the way his golden hair glinted in the sunshine. Her own locks were black as night. "C'mon, you can count first."

After ensuring the bug had crept unharmed onto a blade of grass, Harry looked up at her, his face grimy with a mixture of sweat and dirt, and sniffed. "Okay. But Mama said no woods. Remember?" He eyed her with suspicion. "You can't go there. You know how Mama gets when you don't do what you're told."

Audrey snuck a glance at their dreary clapboard house, a two-story shack, really, that people pointed at when they drove by on Illinois Highway 6. She always pictured the motorists shaking their heads, saying things like *"Do people really live there?"* and *"What a damn shame."* But everyone in Willowdale knew Clarence and Edith Scott and their kids lived in the place. The town's three thousand residents never gave their house a second glance. Most of the paint had peeled off, but just the other day, Daddy had said nobody could afford to take care of such things with a war going on, except for the rich folks.

Audrey tapped Harry on his head while calculating the risks of disobeying their mother. "I'm sure Mother won't care," she said, keeping a straight poker face.

His long stare meant he was not convinced, but Audrey wagged a finger at him.

"Let's say Mother comes outside. You holler somethin' loud, like 'Here I come,' and I'll run back through Mr. Ritter's yard like I'd been hidin' behind one of his trees *near* the woods."

Mother did not approve of Alfred and Gertrude "Gertie" Ritter, but she at least allowed Harry and Audrey to play in their yard. They had been a young couple back when Mother grew up in the house and had never had children of their own. Mrs. Ritter and Grandmother Hamilton had been lifelong friends, and Audrey figured Mrs. Ritter might be the only person who actually missed her grandmother.

Harry still looked skeptical, but he bounced to his feet, looking adorable in a Superman T-shirt. When he stretched his arms out, his belly showed. "You hide first," he said with a grin that revealed two missing teeth. "I'll count to a hundred. Don't go too far."

As Harry covered his eyes and began calling out numbers, Audrey ducked under a sagging clothesline and scurried behind their dilapidated toolshed, careful to avert her eyes from the woodpile as she passed. That was a superstitious habit she'd fostered years back. When Mother whipped her, those long, spindly branches hurt the most, and she didn't want to acknowledge their existence. Unfortunately, Daddy kept plenty of chopped wood to feed their fireplace and kitchen stove—one of the few things Mother had said he ever did right.

Across the yard, Harry was counting, but Audrey slowed, unable to resist glancing at the sticks. She reconsidered whether playing a game was worth the risk of another lashing. Mother never tolerated any form of disobedience—unless Harry was the one disobeying. Audrey lifted her gaze to the woods, where dense foliage blocked out the blazing sun's rays, and she mopped her face with the neck of her shirt.

Mother was in the house. She would never find out.

Within minutes, Audrey had crouched behind a fat oak tree that shaded her like a giant green umbrella. Five minutes went by. She swatted a fly and waited some more, but after ten minutes, there was still no sign of Harry. Cupping her hands, she called out, "Caw, caw," feeling like one of those Army buglers playing reveille. After cawing two then three more times, Audrey figured chances were good that actual crows were winging their way to her spot. If Harry had decided it was too hot to play, she would fix him good for that, leaving her waiting.

Audrey got to her feet and wiped her sweaty brow.

She wouldn't have been surprised if her brother was playing a trick on her. Harry was smart for a kid.

Then she froze, holding her breath.

Snap. Snap. Twigs were cracking loudly under someone's hefty footsteps—too heavy to be Harry's—and the sound was coming from behind her, from the deeper part of the woods. She shivered. A pair of eyes was on her back. She could feel them.

Whirling around, Audrey saw Mother quickly advancing, snapping young saplings as she sure-footedly tromped over them, so close that she would reach her within seconds. Her eyes darted to the long switch tightly clasped in Mother's plump right hand.

She screamed.

Despite tree limbs scraping her arms and legs, Audrey ran as fast as she could through the trees then sprinted across the field and into her yard. Mrs. Ritter was kneeling in her flourishing garden, a floppy hat covering her face. If only Audrey could fly into that sweet old lady's arms and be wrapped in her protective embrace while inhaling the calming scent of her lavender water. But she knew better. Mother always said that Mrs. Ritter and her husband were dirty Krauts and that because America was fighting them in Europe, she could not talk to either of them.

Audrey raced up the porch steps and scurried through the kitchen. On her left, the stairway door was ajar. She threw it open and blasted up the stairs, barely noticing Harry and her daddy chatting in the small living room, what Mother called a parlor. The blaring RCA radio drowned out their words. Daddy liked to listen to the big bands on the afternoons he wasn't drinking down at Lucky's.

Once upstairs, Audrey frantically surveyed her room—a rocking chair, nightstand, washbasin, the narrow closet draped by a flimsy yellow curtain. Her eyes swerved to the space under her bed and then back to the closet, both places she'd hidden before.

She hugged herself and shut her eyes, knowing her hiding place didn't really matter.

Mother always found her.

An hour passed.

Audrey was propped up in bed, pretending to read a library book. Suppertime was near, and her stomach was growling, but she'd seen no sign of her mother. She tiptoed to the bottom of the stairs, where she'd left the door open, and eavesdropped. Mother was rattling around in the kitchen.

"Get in here and sit, Audrey. We're about to eat supper."

Like always, Mother had sensed her presence, an uncanny ability that unnerved Audrey. But her voice was pleasant enough, so Audrey slid into one of the four empty chairs tucked under their wobbly kitchen table. She always sat with her back to the far window, which faced the rest of the house, while Harry claimed the seat opposite her—putting the stairway, parlor, and hallway directly behind him.

Mother had pinned her gray-streaked tendrils into a bun and slicked them into place, her preferred old-lady look, which stretched her rough skin taut. Daddy had told Audrey that when he wed Mother, she'd been real pretty, with hazel eyes that sparkled, ebony hair like Audrey's, and a teensy waist "just perfect for dancing." If Mother had a figure, it was hidden under baggy house dresses, but a person could still detect the rolls of fat that Daddy called "her spare tires."

As Mother stirred a frying pan on the stove top, Audrey pressed old crumbs scattered on the table onto her thumb. They rarely had enough food to eat, so she felt no shame in licking them off like a hungry mouse. Harry and her daddy lumbered in to join her, and Audrey shot her brother a look, but he acted as though nothing had happened. Soon, the four of them were slurping vegetable soup and dipping bread crusts into their bowls. Harry chatted away, and her parents grunted one-word responses—all perfectly normal—and Audrey felt her shoulders and stomach relax, tension melting off her lithe frame. She emptied her bowl and kept herself from licking it clean.

For the rest of their evening, Mother did not speak to her, which was fine by Audrey. After she and Harry visited the outhouse, they headed upstairs even though the night was still too hot for sleeping. Daddy had said warm air was lighter than cold, so the heat rose to the rafters and baked their bedrooms long after sunset. Audrey did not beg to sleep in the parlor, where several windows meant a better chance for soft breezes. Distance between her and Mother seemed wise, just in case.

Alone in her room, Audrey eagerly scanned a few chapters of *The Ghost of Blackwood Hall* and let Nancy Drew's cleverness and antics buoy her spirit. One of the few joys of her summer was walking to the Willowdale town library. Inside those walls, the surroundings seemed so much cooler, with dozens of fans blowing in different directions, whooshing the tantalizing, musty smell of old books across marble-floored aisles.

Her eyelids drooped. Audrey set the book on the floor, turned off her bedside lamp, and yawned, happy that her stomach was full. Clad in a thin nightgown, she stretched then rolled over to face the open window overlooking the backyard. She'd never had a screen, but the arrival of an occasional June bug did not bother her. The night was clear, and she could see the stars and the lightning bugs floating about in their carefree way, with no worries at all except for when to glow.

Audrey's skin prickled then, with the odd sensation she was being watched.

She twisted her head, expecting to see Harry, who often snuck into her bedroom when he got scared, and her eyes widened. Still in her daytime frock, Mother had just closed the door behind her and was approaching Audrey's bed. She said nothing, just opened her palm to reveal two long, narrow strips of yellow ribbon.

Puzzled at first, Audrey pushed up onto her elbows. "What are you doing?"

"Lie down and put your arms over your head."

Half of Mother's face was cast in moonlight, the other half lost to the shadows, which made her features seem distorted, even disfigured. But before Audrey could ask why, Mother grabbed one of her arms and pulled it above her head, quickly wrapping one of the strips around and around her wrist. Confused, Audrey thrashed about, bouncing and kicking, swinging her other arm wildly. But Mother was larger, stronger, and quicker. She tied that wrist to Audrey's wrought-iron headboard as fast as any cowboy could rope and tie a calf. Audrey sobbed, pulling against the cloth handcuff to loosen it, trying to ease her wrist through.

It held firm.

"Be still, Audrey," Mother ordered.

She would not—could not—be still.

"Please, please, Mother, is this about the woods? I won't go there again. I'm sorry. Mother, don't." Snot flowed like lava from Audrey's nostrils. Tears rolled off her cheeks and trickled onto her neck.

The room was too dark to see well, but Audrey scanned her mother's face to help her understand what was happening, to find an emotion that explained the casual cruelty of what she was doing. Mother's eyes were black and as cold as those of any dead carcass Audrey had seen flattened along the highway in front of their house.

Then Mother put a finger to her lips. Audrey lay still, her cheeks streaked with tears and her heart drumming like a tiny bird's. She gave up the fight. If she screamed, Harry might come to her, but he would be terrified at seeing her like that. Daddy would do nothing to intervene. He never did anything. Her mother stepped back to study her handiwork.

Suddenly, Audrey understood Mother's behavior at dinner. She'd been luring her into feeling safe, deceiving her until later. Audrey wanted to scratch her, slap her, kick her square in her big fat gut, but she knew Mother's reaction would be far worse than what she herself could dish out.

"Hush. You believin' you got away with going against me?" Mother whispered, low and sinister like some gangster in a movie. "Think again." She whisked the sheet up to Audrey's chin and tucked it loosely around her shoulders. "Might get chilly tonight, so let's get this on you right now."

The bedsprings squealed as Mother settled onto the mattress. Audrey turned her head away. Only moments before, she'd been enjoying the moonlight, imagining what being a firefly was like. With her luck, someone would drop her into a glass jar and not bother to poke air holes into the lid.

"Listen." With her fingers, Mother tipped Audrey's head back toward her.

Audrey did not resist, but she kept her eyes closed.

"How many times have I told you not to disobey me?" Mother asked. "I've told you and told you since you was little." She sighed as though the ordeal was hers, not Audrey's. "It's important to never question me. You hear? Ever. Don't care how old you get."

For as long as Audrey could remember, Mother had insisted on obedience from her—which was never the case with Harry—and told her that one day, they would be rich if she did what she was told. That would be her reward.

The springs groaned with relief, giving way as Mother eased off the bed. Audrey knew what she had to say. "I'm really sorry. I p-p-promise I'll be good."

But her pledge was met with silence.

She opened her eyes to find the door had been closed and she was again alone. Immediately, Audrey tested the tethers, which were loose enough that she had some slack but tight enough that she couldn't break them. She managed to turn the lower half of her body onto one side, and she inched closer to the headboard to give her arms relief. Then she curled her legs to her chest to form a ball, just like a roly-poly poked into submission.

The bedroom was as quiet as the hushed evening outside her window. The katydids and tree frogs had ceased their incessant, jubilant concert. Audrey took several shuddering breaths and closed her eyes, letting her arms sag into the restraints. She allowed her head and shoulders to go limp and wished that somehow she could go numb both inside and out. Sniffing loudly, she pinched her lips together and blinked furiously.

Her mother did not love her. That was the ugly truth Audrey had never wanted to face.

She had her own awful truth too. She hated the woman. Working to earn her mother's love was useless as that had always been reserved for Harry—such love didn't even include her daddy. Audrey's body stiffened as her heart hardened, chiseled into a block of ice.

Mother thought she could control her. Mother did not think Audrey would ever fight back.

But Mother was wrong.

She might've been only ten, but Audrey was determined that she would control her own life one day. She would. She had to.

Mother would see—she would show her, no matter the cost.

CHAPTER 2

Edith

Two years later

Late in the afternoon, Edith was staring out the back screen door, spying on her children as they sat next to each other on the porch, busily shucking corn from the garden. She was proud of the green thumb she'd developed over the years. It was just as good as Mrs. Ritter's, next door, not that anyone would pay Edith such a compliment.

When Audrey gave her brother a sideways smile, Edith studied her daughter's features—the heart-shaped face, high cheekbones, and perfectly shaped lips. Their rosy-pink hue might've been painted by an artist. Audrey's blossoming beauty was satisfying to see, but her attitude needed work. With her wisecracking mouth, the girl stepped out of line far too often.

To Edith's dismay, whippings had become ineffective on her daughter. She frowned at the thought. Perhaps she should lock Audrey in the outhouse for a bit the next time she disobeyed, just as Mrs. Hamilton had done at times to punish her. The experience had been disgusting and unforgettable and might work quite well on her daughter.

Mrs. Hamilton—Edith had used the formal address for her mother since she was fourteen—had come up with a few useable ideas. As a child, Edith herself had been quite compliant after such punishments. The problem was her mother had stopped using them far too soon and had given up on Edith rather than keeping up with the necessary discipline she needed.

The result of such poor mothering was obvious. Edith was still living in the very same shithole with her idiot husband, only a few feet from the bedroom where she'd been born.

She stared hard at the back of her daughter's curly head, at the natural waves that spiraled down the middle of her back. Audrey was such a moody child, angry and sulking one moment, then happily playing with her brother the next. The girl just didn't get it, that everything Edith did—even if she seemed overly stern at times—was for her daughter's own benefit. Being firm with Audrey was necessary, just like making sure she learned to read or attend school. Edith had begun teaching her daughter discipline early on, starting when she was about five years old.

That first lesson, that day, was so easy to recall.

Edith was pressing her nose against the storefront window of McClain's Mercantile in downtown Willowdale, clutching Audrey's small hand. A large cardboard cutout of the modern housewife—wearing chunky high heels and a ruffled pink apron—had drawn her to the advertising copy for a fancy, newfangled washing machine. After seeing the price, Edith balked. She could not afford a new, modern appliance. That day was March 12, her twenty-eighth birthday, but she expected nothing. In that way, she would not be disappointed.

She'd taken Audrey with her to pick up free blocks of cheese, but the government truck had not shown up. Leaving empty-handed had put Edith in a foul mood. There would be no cheese, no birthday cake, no fine meal, and certainly, no adoring husband to greet her at home—just her ignorant, disappointing one.

Her spouse, Clarence—or "Red," as everyone called him—was known in Willowdale as "the dimwit with the head injury." The newspaper had even published an article about the mining accident where Red had been injured when he was twenty years old. After that, Bell and Zoller Mining had offered him steady work, and he'd kept it up for a while, only to become too damn lazy or dim-witted to show up every day and earn a decent wage.

Because Edith was an old maid at twenty-two and the daughter of penniless Chester Hamilton, she'd had nothing to offer a groom except her good looks. The old biddies in town might've felt sorry for her at first, having to resort to marrying Red, but their sympathy was short-lived. Those busybodies always counted the days from a young couple's wedding to their first child's birth, and Edith had fallen quite short in that regard.

Edith noticed the proprietor glaring at her from inside the store, so she lurched away from the window and marched down Main Street, squeezing her daughter's hand. Audrey's tiny feet were pedaling fast to keep up. When they passed the Daily Standard building, a headline, "Germany Invades Austria," blazed from the sidewalk newspaper stand.

Edith scoffed, not giving a whit about problems in other countries. The Great Depression might've been easing up, but Edith was still scratching around for feed like a starved hen.

The spring breeze kicked up, suddenly morphing into a cold, bitter wind. Their home, where Mrs. Hamilton was begrudgingly babysitting Edith's sweet one-year-old son, Harry, was a good two-mile walk. They hurried by the weatherboard houses common to Willowdale's middle-class neighborhood. Audrey trudged next to her mother, quietly hugging her own tiny frame as they both braced against the fierce wind.

Edith's head was bent low, but she heard spirited laughter and high-pitched giggles coming toward her and Audrey. She peered up and instantly recognized their faces. The three women were getting closer, each snuggled into fine wool hats and coats the pastel colors of dyed Easter eggs. They'd been a few years behind her in high school.

Their voices blended together, smooth and modulated, sophisticated and without a trace of the hick twang common among lower classes in southern Illinois.

Those women lived on Victorian Row.

The trio looked like models who'd dropped right off the pages of *Good Housekeeping* magazine. Edith set her jaw and slowed her pace, her heart pounding faster because one woman in particular raised her hackles. Of all the people to see on her birthday, it had to be her, the tallest of the three. She was willowy and graceful, with naturally rosy cheeks and bouncy blond hair that cascaded from below a pale-yellow hat onto her shoulders.

Mrs. Somebody. That was what Edith called her even though she damn well knew the younger woman's name.

Instantly, Edith felt self-conscious in her faded, frayed pants, which were too short on her. They revealed her scuffed-up moccasins with holes. And without a coat in the cold, she looked ridiculous. By her side, Audrey looked like a sad ragamuffin in ill-fitting hand-me-downs with matted hair resembling a bird's nest.

Their chattering stopped. Two of the young women linked arms then moved in tandem off the sidewalk to cross Highway 6, which eventually rolled past Edith's house on up the hill. Mrs. Somebody, however, motioned toward Edith and jabbed one of the other women with her elbow, pointing and making an attempt to move her way. But her girlfriend pulled her away with such force that they both tripped, then the three of them crossed the street in a rush of rainbow colors.

Edith's cheeks burned at the intentional slight, as though she and her daughter were offensive. She wanted to spit on their expensive coats. Instead, she yanked Audrey's arm to get her to walk faster. Edith stole furtive glances at the child's blue eyes and admired her long, dark lashes—just like her father's—and the fresh ivory skin.

It had always been critical that she be beautiful.

With a quarter mile left on their walk, Audrey started to whine, but Edith scolded her and refused to pick her up. Audrey dashed away from her side, running fast and shouting over her shoulder, "I'm cold! I'm running up the hill to home!"

Several times, Edith bellowed into the wind, shouting at her daughter to stop and wait. Of course Audrey could hear her—she simply chose to ignore her command. The girl continued up the grassy path when the sidewalk ended, following it along the highway as it curved up the hill toward their house, just outside the town limits.

Catching up to her was easy enough. Audrey's legs were short. Edith grabbed her child's arm and slapped her flushed cheek. Audrey stumbled sideways and burst into tears before she crumpled onto the wet ground.

"Don't you ever—and I mean *ever*—ignore what I say to you, Audrey Mae. Do you hear me?"

Her little girl shrank back, her eyes wide and frightened. For Edith, the moment had been less about her daughter's safety than ensuring she understood the golden rule of obedience.

That had been the first serious lesson, and Edith resented the need to continuously correct her stubborn child.

She pushed through the screen door to the porch, causing her two children to become mute as doorknobs. Audrey turned halfway around and stared at her mother, wrinkling her nose with disgust as if she'd eaten a nasty grasshopper. In response, Edith shoved her hands onto her ample hips and glared back. Her daughter's contemptuous expression was not surprising at all, but it pissed her off to no end. Audrey's behavior would not do.

For everything to work out the way it was supposed to, she would have to get tougher on her daughter—much tougher.

CHAPTER 3

Audrey

October 1948

Two months into Audrey's sophomore year at Sauk Indian River High School, her English literature teacher asked to see her after class. The last thing Audrey wanted was attention directed her way, which was why she always sat in the back of any classroom, but she couldn't avoid feisty Mrs. Patton.

"Audrey, do you like to write?" Mrs. Patton asked as she pushed her desk chair back and stood.

Audrey nodded, staring at her shoes.

"I have something for you, then."

Mrs. Patton handed her two green spiral notebooks and two pens, which Audrey accepted cautiously, knitting her eyebrows. She stared at them, wondering what she'd done wrong to earn extra assignments.

The teacher crossed her arms nonchalantly, rested a hip against her desk, and smiled. Her hair was ratted into a fashionable teased pouf like ladies on magazine covers wore, making her seem much taller.

"Let me explain. I think you have a wonderful way with words, a talent for expressing yourself in your assignments. I think keeping a diary and writing every day will help you become an even better writer."

Audrey felt the teacher's penetrating stare and looked up.

"You can write about anything you want, get out what's going on inside you. And a diary is private, too, meant for your eyes only."

Audrey did have a lot going on in her head that she'd never shared. Pretending to be normal had become her normal, especially in front of her mother. That was a survival technique because Audrey had read once that a predatory animal could smell the scent of fear.

Then an awful thought occurred to her. Mrs. Patton probably knew all about her family because she, too, lived in Willowdale, and this was her sly way of helping. Audrey's cheeks felt hot, and she looked away. That didn't stop Mrs. Patton.

"Many women earn a living as writers—for newspapers, magazines, radio, even books. If you're good, that is, and have a passion for it."

Audrey let the words sink in. Then she said, "My mother says if a woman works, it shows she's lower-class. Like how she has to work because my daddy is such a terrible provider." She stole a glance at Mrs. Patton to gauge her reaction.

The teacher's mouth had dropped open. "Well, I work, Audrey, and my husband is a great provider. I don't agree with your mother because I think things have changed. I like working. It doesn't mean that I'm lower-class." Mrs. Patton looked thoughtful and seemed to be picking her next words with care. "What I mean is this. In America, women can do whatever they want now. It's okay to be a housewife, and it's okay to work. And people who come from poor circumstances—say, like Abraham Lincoln—can better themselves by learning a skill they enjoy. During the war, I daresay many women figured that out."

"Poor circumstances" had to be a synonym for "the wrong side of the tracks," meaning people like Audrey's family. Regardless, the wheels in Audrey's mind were churning. At fifteen, she'd already spent many years dreaming of the day she could escape her mother's fists, her taunts, and her unrelenting orders. Mrs. Patton was possibly showing her a way.

"What do you like to read?"

"Nancy Drew books," Audrey blurted. They were still her favorites.

"Readers make good writers. Keep reading." Mrs. Patton turned and nodded to some students entering the classroom.

Audrey scooted through the doorway, baffled by her teacher's sudden interest in her. Then for one fleeting moment, she let herself dream of becoming a writer.

A month later, when the November air was crisp like a ripe green apple, Audrey grabbed her coat, a pen, and her scribbled-in notebook and made haste for the woods. That was a forbidden choice that could mean trouble, but Audrey had convinced herself to take the risk on a clear, cool day. Mother was out of the house, running Saturday errands.

Once she passed through the tree line, Audrey clipped over mounds of crunchy fallen leaves. The last time she'd dared enter the woods to sit in her Indian Trail Tree had been late in the summer. She missed the solitude, her private communion with nature. Moving quickly, Audrey finally spied the clearing and the thickest, broadest trunk of any tree around, and her chest squeezed with the sheer delight of its existence.

Only her special tree could give her solace and keep her mind off the upcoming holidays.

In fourth grade, Audrey had told her teacher, Miss Jackson, about the tall, weirdly shaped tree she'd discovered in her woods, with its low, heavy branches and trunk that together formed an *S* shape. Miss Jackson had explained that early Native Americans in parts of America often twisted select saplings into unusual shapes.

At first, the stems were weakened, and some wouldn't survive, while other saplings grew but lost their intended shapes. The healthiest would grow tall, she'd explained, keeping their bent contours to later become trail markers for native travelers. Such trees—purposely mangled when small—were celebrated, even revered, for their survival and strength.

Audrey dropped her supplies to the ground and swung into her tree. She breathed in the musty scent of wet bark and ran her hand over the impermeable wood.

Like her, the tree was an oddity, an outcast that stood out as a curiosity within its surroundings. They were connected in that way, and while in the tree's presence, she didn't feel as alone. She brushed the bark, hoping to absorb the tree's strength through her skin. She wanted to tap into the mysterious power her tree had forged from its roots upward. Somehow, her special tree had overcome its difficult beginning.

And she stayed there, neglecting the hour, breathing deeply and not writing a single word.

CHAPTER 4

Audrey

Daddy did something completely unexpected.

On Christmas Eve morning, Audrey had looked around the house for her father then panicked because he was nowhere to be found. She couldn't think of a single place he would have gotten off to except Lucky's tavern, and that spelled trouble.

That was when butterflies lit in her gut and began their frantic dance, crashing into one another in such wild abandon that Audrey struggled to breathe. Good sense and experience prevented her from asking Mother about his whereabouts. Instead, she and Harry kept vigil from the window in her brother's bedroom, which overlooked the highway, careful to be as quiet as corpses in their graves, tiptoeing over floorboards known to creak loudly.

After a few hours, they glimpsed Daddy's stout figure emerging in the distance, walking toward their house and growing larger as he plodded along the vacant, snow-packed road. He was carrying what looked like an ax. When Audrey realized he had a rope slung over his shoulder and was dragging a small fir tree, she gaped at her brother in amazement, and they both squealed. Three years had passed since their little family last bothered with a Christmas tree.

Later, Daddy stood the tree up in a bucket of water in the parlor corner, near the front window, and right away, three feet of live greenery filled the room with piney freshness. "Let's decorate it, kids," he said with a smile, and she and Harry gleefully clapped their hands.

Her father and Harry were draping ribbons on tree branches while Audrey did her best to draw angels on construction paper he'd managed to supply. Mother sat on the couch and brooded, watching her family with a sour face, refusing to utter a single thank-you to Daddy. Audrey shot looks at her mother, wishing she understood what went on in her head. She doubted her grandparents had ever celebrated the yuletide with their only child, and Mother had probably added that grudge to her long list of grievances. Frankly, Mother had shared little about her childhood, so that was just a guess.

In the late afternoon, temperatures outside dropped while their old furnace was sputtering in rebellion. The house was frigid. Audrey bundled up in layers, concerned that she would see her frosty breath hovering in the air at some point. After covering her feet with three pairs of socks and donning a hat to warm her ears, she strode into the kitchen to prepare hot tea or broth, depending on what might be in the cupboard. She paused when she heard a quarrel erupt in the hallway outside her parents' bedroom.

Mother's and Daddy's voices were rising and falling like a storm-fueled tide, constantly interrupting each other. They hadn't missed a Christmas Eve yet without a bitter knockdown argument, and this one would be no different. Her stomach lurched. The butterflies flapped into her throat, and she began to tremble. Even so, Audrey inched closer to the end of the counter to hear better.

"You know I hate the holidays," Mother spat, clicking hard on the *t* in *hate*. "Especially Christmas Eve."

Daddy, who was a soft-spoken man and a slow talker, responded in an unusual quick-fire burst. "Sorry you hate our anniversary, Edith. Hate me too? You knew 'bout my head when we got hitched. You got nobody to blame but yourself. It's not like I forced you into marrying me."

Audrey cringed at their harsh words. She shouldn't have been eavesdropping, but her body seemed rooted to the spot.

Mother's reply was as tart as her lemon pie. "Every year, I just think, dear God, let this day go by just like any other. There's nothin' to celebrate."

At the mention of their anniversary, Audrey frowned. In her entire life, neither parent had mentioned their anniversary date, that it was on Christmas Eve.

"I'm sick of this, Edith. You don't wanna be married? Then leave."

"No, you leave."

"I ain't the one kicking up a fuss all the time. Maybe it's you not right in the head 'round here. Lord, Edith, we got two young'uns to raise. Ever think o' them?"

"We'd be better off without you."

Audrey had heard their brutal arguments before, but her folks' threats were new. Sure, Daddy didn't work much, but the cutting comment was just mean. Mother knew he couldn't help his head injury.

"Wanna know why I stay, Edith? It's not cuz of you. I worry about them kids, mostly Audrey. I can't stand what you do to that girl."

Audrey's heart cartwheeled under her layers of clothing. For the first time, she was hearing her father acknowledge that Mother was cruel. That made it worse somehow, knowing he'd never bothered to step in when Mother was whipping her. Or when Mother pulled Audrey's hair or held her to the ground and kicked her. Or when she refused her soap or shampoo because it pleased her to make Audrey beg.

If Daddy was her ally, he was just a cowardly one. Audrey stared down at the counter. But he was kind to her—made her jelly sandwiches and snuck them to her room.

Then the bedroom door slammed.

Alarmed, Audrey shuffled to the window. She pressed her forehead on the icy pane and waited, but nobody came into the kitchen.

Whatever had gone wrong between her parents had always been a mystery. They'd never celebrated their wedding day, and to hear Mother actually despised that very day was crushing. She swallowed hard. *And also to detest your very own flesh and blood?* But not Harry. For some reason, Mother hated only her.

Her parents had been married on December 24, and she'd been born in late May the following year. Audrey performed the math in her head.

Her eyes flew open, and a gasp blew through her lips and fogged the glass.

The reason Mother took everything out on her suddenly made sense.

CHAPTER 5

Edith

Edith stomped into her bedroom and slammed the door, shutting Red out.

If he didn't like how she treated Audrey, then to hell with him.

He knew nothing—less than nothing.

Edith twisted the door's lock and walked brusquely to her closet. She pushed the curtain aside and flopped to the floor on top of their soiled clothing. She dug around, found her old winter boots, retrieved a folded piece of stationery from inside one of them, and flattened it against her thigh.

The letter was dated October 29, 1932. The blue ink had faded but was legible. Edith could easily make out the elaborate cursive, partly because she'd memorized the words a long time before. As she read to herself, Edith pressed two fingers into the arch of her eyebrow to ease the growing, painful throbbing.

His handwriting was pretty, almost feminine, and perfectly scrawled:

> *I am sorry for how I reacted a few days ago, not responding to your news the way you had hoped I would. Then I left you alone and crying in the woods, in your special place, which is unforgivable. I can only say that my surprise, and fear, took over my sensibilities, and I needed time to think.*

After scanning the remainder of his note, her eyes fell off the page.

Edith sat still for a minute, not for the first time considering how nice the first part of his letter had been.

That he'd needed time to think, she understood.

That he'd decided to ruin her whole life, she had not understood—and never would.

CHAPTER 6

Audrey

On Christmas morning, the space below their pretty tree—where luckier children would have pounced upon colorfully wrapped presents with bows—was barren. Audrey had expected that, but Harry looked crestfallen even though he should have known too.

She and Harry were sitting cross-legged on the floor and staring up at their tree when Daddy came to them with his arms outstretched and tears shining in his eyes. He fell to his knees. Audrey welcomed his embrace, then he nestled Harry into their fold, all the while mumbling that he was sorry. For what, Audrey was not sure—maybe for how they lived, for his boozing, or even because he'd married their mother. Most likely, he was just sorry no presents were there for her and Harry.

Wrapped in his burly arms, Audrey made a wish, a Christmas wish, that her daddy would start staying home every night, away from Lucky's and random town gutters. His gift to her was his love, of that she was certain, and she wanted him around all the time. Audrey couldn't find the words to tell him she didn't need anything else, just him and Harry, and she hugged him as tightly as she was capable.

New Year's Eve had been uneventful, which was as good as it got in the Scott household, and Audrey was glad the holidays were finally over. January 1, 1949, dawned cold and draped in a cloudy granite gray, matching her dreary mood.

She was sitting at the kitchen table, grazing on a stale sodium cracker, staring at nothing, eager for the next day, when she would at last be back at school. Not only was that huge brick building warmer than her home, but it had indoor toilets and bright, welcoming neon lights, and she could disappear into the mazes of chatty, clueless classmates.

Audrey had read once that each new year was a reminder of renewal and hope, and she was holding onto that belief like a life raft. She was one step closer to graduation and charting a new path, maybe moving to St. Louis or Chicago, climbing out from under her mother's thumb. After all, she would be sixteen in May and could make decisions for herself. A few months before, she'd overheard a boy at school make that claim, saying he planned to drop out to join the Navy.

Audrey began to hum along with Perry Como, then Bing Crosby, her daddy's favorite crooner, as the RCA radio cranked out tunes in the parlor. Music would ease the tension in the air, just like soft lullabies could calm cranky babies. Her parents—who Audrey believed mostly acted like toddlers themselves—were not speaking, and she wouldn't have cared all that much except the house was chilly enough without their frosty demeanors.

For days, the four of them had dressed like Eskimos to keep warm. They didn't have money for more coal, and Daddy was shoveling sparse amounts into the furnace to make their limited supply last as long as possible. The woodpile was also waning, shrinking before their eyes, so they no longer used the fireplace to help warm the parlor. Baking in the woodstove was out of the question too. The nights were so bone-chillingly cold that Audrey slept fully dressed under a heavy mound of whatever clothing or blankets she could find. Harry would sometimes sneak into her bed once the house was quiet, their combined body heat helping to stave off the chill.

The worst part of the winter, though—and what had started the latest fight between her parents—was Mother's refusal to use the outhouse because marching through the bitter wind and snow was too difficult. She tossed yellow pee from her chamber pot right out the door whenever she felt like it, which was not often enough for Daddy. When he yelled at her to put her coat on and do her business in the outhouse like everyone else, Mother screamed back that if he were any sort of provider, the house would have an indoor toilet. Audrey was certain Mother left her pee pots around the house to upset him. They all knew how much the stench of urine nauseated Daddy. She didn't like it much either, but he was particularly offended.

Despite Audrey's layering of thick wool socks, her toes had gone numb, so she rubbed them like she was vigorously twirling sticks to spark a fire. Gumming another cracker with her tongue, Audrey savored the salt then let it gradually melt in her mouth. She'd taken four but wanted to save the remaining two for Harry.

The one positive thing about her holiday break had been spending more time with him. Even when deep snow covered the ground, he could cajole her into playing outdoors, and they would make snow angels or roll the powder to make snowmen. She always made sure to add rocks for eyes and a wide smile of pebbled teeth because that final result delighted her brother so much.

The fact was that Audrey was jealous of her brother and had been most of her life. That wasn't his fault, though. Mother was to blame. Despite her feelings, she and Harry continued to forge a special bond. They were the only two who knew what their homelife was like, even if they chose not to speak about it whenever they were alone. And when they goofed around outside, they had a silent agreement to remain together in the frosty air as long as possible.

Audrey padded into the parlor to see if Daddy wanted to listen to orchestra music with her, only to find him asleep in his chair and Harry conked out on the couch. The scene was pleasant somehow, even sweet. She frowned and darted her eyes around the room, a realization striking her like a thunderbolt. She checked her parents' bedroom—empty. Mother had not likely gone to the outhouse, given her stubbornness.

But she could have gone to Audrey's room, where her latest diary was hidden under her bed so that she could write into the night. She'd never told her mother about it. Mrs. Patton had said Audrey's words were hers alone, private, belonging only to her. Mother would never understand that.

She headed for the stairway and placed a foot on the bottom step, stopping cold when she heard the squeaking of bedsprings above. Audrey's heart skipped then vaulted into her throat.

If Mother had found her diary, she'd been in Audrey's room, reading stories that would infuriate her, like the one when Audrey was twelve and got her first period.

She'd been curled up on the couch while her abdomen cramped in a relentless, painful rhythm. Finally scared enough to tell her mother, Audrey stood up, and blood gushed into her underwear and ran down her leg. She screamed, terrified she could be dying, and Mother came to her. After Audrey had explained through tears what was wrong, her mother guided her to her bedroom dresser and handed her a bunch of clean rags.

"Put one in the crotch of your underwear to hold the blood," she said, "and wash it out when it's full, then keep using clean ones until the bleeding stops."

Audrey wanted to ask questions, but her mother cut her off with a dismissive wave, finished with the encounter.

And that was that. Audrey hadn't known why she was bleeding or where the blood came from each month until a year later when her period started at school. A sympathetic teacher suggested she read about it in the *Britannica*, which was far more helpful than what Mother had offered, which had been nothing.

Rooted in place, Audrey imagined Mother's reactions to the tales in her diary. She had to get it back.

Climbing the stairs with wobbly legs, she prayed for a miracle. There could be a God, and He could be listening. When Audrey reached the top, where she could peer into her bedroom, her hand flew to her chest. Mother was sitting on Audrey's bed with her back to the doorway, holding the notebook she had hidden.

"Why are you in my room?" Audrey asked, gulping, keeping her tone light. Her legs had turned into tree stumps.

Mother rose and looked at her with fiery eyes, anger smoldering behind them.

"I don't answer to you, now do I? *Your* room? This is not your house. It's mine."

Audrey bit her tongue and clamped her mouth shut.

"You hid this from me... under there. Don't deny it," she said, pointing at Audrey's mattress.

One of Mother's favorite debates was whether Audrey actually had a right to privacy, but Audrey did not want to continue that argument. The weather was too cold outside to risk her wrath.

"I don't have a lot of room to store things, you know, and I didn't want Harry or Daddy to read my personal stuff." Her voice was quivering. But if she could explain, tell the truth, Mother just might understand. She blurted, "It's just that I'm hoping to become—"

Mother stepped forward and flapped the pages of the notebook in Audrey's face, creating a breeze between them.

"I don't care what you want to become." She held up the diary. "This notebook is filled with lies about me." Mother's ample chest was heaving.

"Nobody is supposed to see it. My teacher said so, not even you. I'm sorry if your feelings are hurt, but—"

Mother sputtered and tossed her head back. "You're sorry? What if this notebook gets stolen? Someone in Willowdale reads your filthy trash? People around here might think your lies are true."

Audrey made a face. They were not lies. She lowered her eyelids in a scowl, framing her mother's face inside an oval. "Please. You know I'm telling the truth."

Mother's eyes sparked, the fire building, which was a bad sign. "Lies," she repeated. "You're a damn liar. I'm a damn good mother."

That was a lie Audrey had heard many times before. She set her jaw and swallowed a lump, buying time. Mother was still much bigger, broader, and meatier than she was, but Audrey had strong legs, if she could only steady herself, and could run much faster. She inhaled sharply.

"It's a lie that I'm your lackey? That you want me to do whatever you say for the rest of my life? That's just weird, and I won't." She stomped a foot. Audrey had never confronted Mother so adamantly before, despite her desire to do so, because she'd always chickened out. But seeing her mother's face, she knew it was too late to back down.

Mother's hazel-green eyes had darkened to a glossy deep brown. Audrey stared at the diary in Mother's hands and briefly pictured herself strangling her, cutting off precious air. She lifted her head and stretched to appear taller and locked eyes with her.

"I'm not staying in this town, Mother. I want to have a job. A career. Be a writer."

The whack of the notebook against her arm came fast, and although the blow did not sting, Audrey retreated to her doorway. Mother's face had gone scarlet, and her chest was heaving up and down, air whistling through her nose. A voice inside Audrey's head warned her to be careful, to stop talking. Mother was gripping the diary like it was her hostage, a ransom held for control of her daughter's life.

Audrey plunged ahead. "You know what? Other people have great mothers or good mothers. You're not even close. You're not a mother at all. You're just—" She drew in a breath, frightened by the wild look in Mother's eyes, her jutting jawline and tigress sneer.

When the blow came, Audrey slammed into the wall. But instead of attacking her further, Mother barreled right by her and flew down the stairs. Audrey chased after her, wishing she had the guts to push her so she would fall and break something—a leg or maybe her neck.

In the kitchen, Mother was standing at the sink with the notebook in one hand and a book of matches in the other, and Audrey rocketed into her, attempting to pry the spiral from her hands.

"It's mine! Give it back!" she shouted, gripping the notebook and pulling as hard as she could.

Their tussle lasted only a few seconds. Mother kicked Audrey in the shins, and she fell against the table, yelping. When she looked up, Mother struck a match and lit a corner of the notebook while she held it over the sink.

Audrey watched in horror as the flame grew bigger and glowed brighter, consuming her treasure.

"No. Stop it!" Audrey's work—her private, personal reality—was shriveling before her eyes.

When Audrey heard a sob behind her, she swung her head around. Harry and Daddy were huddled together at the bottom of the stairway, and Harry was blubbering, cowering. Daddy was stooped over Harry as though to shield him, but Audrey only saw him as a lump of henpecked timidity.

Mother twisted the water faucet on, and Audrey watched while her mother drowned the remains. The silver spiral glinted at the edge of jagged, burned cardboard. Mother's expression was smug, even delighted, and she tossed her gaze at each of them one by one. When her eyes landed on Audrey, she sat back on her heels with a look of anticipation, apparently expecting an apology.

Audrey would never give her one.

Across the kitchen, Harry was sniffling, and Audrey drifted over to her brother.

"Stop crying now. It's all okay. I'm okay," she murmured to him. She scratched his head and ruffled his hair before trudging up the stairs, her heart still beating wildly.

Audrey collapsed onto her bed.

Her home had always been like one of those bullrings in Spain that she'd learned about in history class. She was the poor bull who'd never wanted to be part of the entertainment yet was confined to be used, observed, taunted, and forced into combat. Everyone knew the bull always died in the end.

Audrey bit her lip and crossed her arms over her chest.

No.

She was no longer the ten-year-old girl Mother could tie to her bed. She was old enough to fight back, to fight dirty.

She wiped her eyes to clear them.

With Mother, you live by the sword or die by the sword.

She would live.

CHAPTER 7

Edith

Edith donned a long wool coat and belted it across her thick middle then stuffed her bun into the back of her felt hat. Since the Jesus holidays were over, she needed to see Pastor Dressler about getting back to work at the church.

The family had been surviving on soup, canned fruits, and canned vegetables that Edith had put up the previous summer. With those and the awful government-issued cheese regularly brought to town on big trucks, they'd had enough to keep from starving, but like usual, it was up to her to keep the money jar filled.

She scoffed. Red was useless.

Edith slid her hands into a pair of gloves, pulled her hat brim over her eyes, and snatched her pocketbook from the kitchen counter. She had to remind herself that all of this—her eyes swept over the room—would be a thing of the past soon enough. She was grooming Audrey to marry into the wealthiest family around, and the stupid girl had no choice in the matter.

She glanced at Red, who was snoring in his chair, either hungover or just snoozing his way through another day. The kids had left for school an hour before. Her sweet boy, Harry, had been in high spirits, but Audrey had been acting strangely, as though she had something up her sleeve. Edith knew such things. She planned to keep an eagle eye on her and inspect every room in the house for any notebooks, even the shed and under the porch, anywhere that girl could think of to hide a diary. Audrey—a rebellious teen, to her mind—would be testing the waters.

Edith had been the same age when she had valiantly defied her mother.

She waddled down the front stoop steps, thinking back to her own teen rebellion against Mrs. Hamilton. Edith had won. When she became a master at deception, her mother no longer cared what might happen to her, her only child. In plain terms, she'd given up on Edith.

She'd let her stumble and fall.

And fail.

Edith still hated her for that. Her mother had been weak. She could remember the exact day when Mrs. Hamilton let go.

The year was 1926.

Edith was sitting on her front stoop, caressing her knees and fidgeting, imagining the moment her mother would arrive and confront her. The autumn day was chilly, but the sky was clear, and warm sunshine had tinted Edith's cheeks to a high color that complemented her dark locks. She patted her new, short hairstyle.

Several days before, her mother had scolded Edith when she mentioned her intention to get a fashionable hairdo called a bob. "Those damn flappers wear their hair like that to seduce men," she responded. "Them women drink and have sex with anyone who'll take 'em. I'll be damned if my daughter's gonna go around lookin' like some floozy."

The words did not deter Edith from wanting the cut. Frankly, they made the whole idea seem more alluring, daring. So she did the deed and walked home with her head high, feeling brazen and more alive than ever. But at home, Papa told her that gossipy Mrs. Ritter next door had seen her in Fanny's Beauty Parlor and rushed home to tell Mrs. Hamilton, who then rushed downtown to stop her daughter.

Edith shuddered. It had been a blessing that they didn't run into each other.

Wringing her fingers, she mulled over how she could appease her mother. Edith could say she'd simply misunderstood her direction or explain how the hairdo hadn't cost a cent. Sweet old Fanny had touched Edith's hand, tender-like, and said she could do chores in return for the cut and styling. Fanny had been so nice to her that Edith came close to bawling, something she would never let herself do in front of people.

Edith didn't understand why Mrs. Hamilton cared so much about her hairstyle, anyway. It was her hair to do with what she pleased.

She scanned the lawn, for the thousandth time taking a mental inventory of the scattered junk that made up her family's circus of crap. *Ladies and gents! Step right up, and visit Mr. Chester and Mrs. Louise Hamilton's flea market of useless things*—broken chairs, pots and dirty jars, a rusty wheelbarrow, metal pipes, a wobbly table, chicken wire. *Junk.*

When she was just eight years old, Edith had overheard a parent tell a teacher that people who lived like the Hamiltons deserved what they got, which was nothing. The teacher stole a glance at her, obviously concerned she'd overheard. Humiliated, Edith had turned beet red.

Too nervous to sit still any longer, Edith meandered through the patchwork of remnants her parents were hoping to sell. Nothing in the yard was worth a plugged nickel. A few months earlier, a tornado had ripped through several states, touching down just ten miles from their house, destroying homes, and killing many people. Papa had said Edith should be grateful because they'd been spared. But she wasn't. If her house were ever smashed to smithereens and their things got sucked into the sky, she would just be grateful it was mercifully gone.

Edith was rubbing the lid of a mildewy stew pot when she heard fast footsteps approaching. She froze, her eyes glued to a chair, afraid to look elsewhere.

"Just look at you. That hair. And after I told you not to do it," Mrs. Hamilton fumed aloud, walking closer. Her hair bun was so tight that her eyes slanted up at the corners. "You a slut, Edith?"

Edith pondered the question. She wanted people to notice her whether Mother liked it or not. She despised being an outsider, the girl hanging out in the school library to avoid being teased about her clothes. As far as Edith was concerned, nothing was wrong about wanting to fit in.

"Answer me, girl. You flashin' that new do so's boys can get into your pants?"

Hearing her mother talk that way was revolting. But Edith's throat had gone so dry that she couldn't speak.

"What's that, Edith? Cat got your tongue?"

Mrs. Hamilton circled Edith as though she were her next delicious meal. "You think you're better than us. That's your damn problem. I've got news for you, Edith. You're in the muck with the rest of us pigs. Just po' white trash."

They were a few feet apart when Mrs. Hamilton spat on Edith then wiped her mouth with the back of her hand. "People gonna laugh at you puttin' on airs, and that's the same as them laughin' at me. I won't stand for it."

Even though Edith stood her ground, her legs were trembling. She liked her hairdo and did not regret for one second that she'd gotten it, no matter what Mrs. Hamilton said. She was attractive and would appeal to the better sorts of boys, the wealthy, popular ones a girl ought to marry. The time had come to make a stand. She gathered her courage.

"Oh, they already laugh at you. But not because o' me," she said. "It's all you."

Mrs. Hamilton's mouth fell open.

"Why don't you want me to amount to anything, Mother? Be like other people? I don't want to live here forever."

Mrs. Hamilton charged Edith like a bulldozer, grabbing two handfuls of Edith's short curls.

"Let go!" Edith screamed. She broke free but stumbled to the ground.

Mrs. Hamilton seized a metal pipe rusting near a bush. Edith was not quick enough to scramble away, but she blocked the blow with her left arm. Pain radiated like shock waves through her forearm and elbow. When the pipe hovered over her body again, Edith drove both feet into Mrs. Hamilton's thighs as hard as she could, and her mother tumbled to the ground. For once, Edith's youthful vigor counted for something. She was fast and nimble compared to her shorter, portly mother.

"Stop it! Stop it!" Mr. Ritter was yelling and running toward them, his black hair flying. In one swift motion, he pulled Edith to her feet and locked her in a protective embrace, which she endured for his sake. Then he loosened his grip and turned to Mrs. Hamilton.

"I've had enough of this, Louise. You're going to end up truly hurting this girl. Does Chester see you doing things like this to her? Approve?" His German accent was thick, yet he'd been in America since he was twelve. "I'm making this girl's welfare my business now, whether you like it or not. Shameful what you do. You leave her be, or I swear..." He wiped his brow with the collar of his jacket and left his words dangling in the air.

Pushed up on an elbow, Mrs. Hamilton glared at him from the ground. Edith whispered a thank-you into Mr. Ritter's ear and hugged him, wishing he did not smell like his stinky pigeon coop. Then without looking back, she strolled toward the back of their house. She needed to stay out of sight for a while, at least until Mrs. Hamilton had calmed down or Papa was around to intervene.

But she felt charged. Everything had changed.

After that victory, and with the realization that Mr. Ritter had her back, she would do whatever she wanted when she wanted and with whom she wanted. Plenty of boys around Willowdale desired her. One thing Edith knew for certain was that she could just as easily fall in love with a rich man as a poor one. And she'd already set her sights on several older boys—men, frankly.

Edith rubbed her arm, which was bruised and aching, and sat down on a stack of logs in their woodpile. A battered arm was a small price to pay for freedom.

When the time came, she would go on to bigger and better things, leaving Mrs. Hamilton behind, right where she belonged. Their family's shithole, with its leaky roof and squawking chickens and junkyard, was all Mrs. Hamilton would ever deserve.

That was how Edith had figured things would go for her future, with all the wisdom of her sixteen years, pretty close to the same age Audrey was.

But that had never happened.

Pulling back from her memories, she bristled as she trudged down the path. She'd always been a better mother than Mrs. Hamilton. And she would see to it that Audrey got away with nothing.

CHAPTER 8

Audrey

At three o'clock in the afternoon, the bell rang, and teenagers poured out of classrooms with earsplitting babble, racing to their lockers or afternoon activities. Audrey, happily sheltered in anonymity, flowed along with the throng until almost everyone pushed through the school's main doors like slow-moving cattle.

She'd been glad to be back in class. In the morning, her pulse quickened when the imposing three-story structure loomed into view. Built on top of Brickner's Hill, the school overlooked the town of Penshaw, slightly larger than Willowdale with amenities such as a hospital, restaurants, and fancy boutiques she'd never visited.

Breaking free of the pack headed for home, Audrey raced down another flight of stairs and zipped along the school's first-floor corridor. She had no time to dally because the bus going to Willowdale would be leaving soon, and if Audrey missed it, she would need to find a ride home or take a late bus.

She was focused on a classroom door at the end of the long hall when, without warning, she was body-slammed hard against a locker. Audrey's armful of textbooks launched into the air then skittered across the floor tile like runaway marbles. She landed with a thud on the floor.

On the opposite side of the hallway, the two culprits, with overcoats tossed over their shoulders, chortled and fist-bumped each other, ogling her. Audrey knew they were sophomores like her, but they ran in far different social circles, not that she belonged to one.

Behind Audrey's collapsed frame, a voice bellowed over her head.

"What the hell is wrong with you two fatheads? You knock a girl down, and you think it's funny?"

The pair stopped prancing about and shifted their eyes to whoever was looming behind Audrey. She took that moment to adjust her skirt back to its appropriate length then looked up at Cliff Elliot, a well-known ruffian, the one who'd knocked her over.

"C'mon, man. We didn't mean to knock her down. But look..." Cliff lowered his voice as if to reveal a secret. "It's just Audrey Scott. Get me? No big deal. She's like one of them colored girls, always keeping to herself. She'll just go on her way." He sniffed and jerked his chin in Audrey's direction, and her jaw dropped at his words.

Audrey wondered if they thought she was deaf. She felt as small as a mouse and wished she could scurry away into a hole. Cliff snickered and poked his leather-patched elbow into the side of the other boy, Johnny DeDecker. Girls considered Johnny's blue eyes as dreamy as Frank Sinatra's and were always flirting with him, hoping to be his next girlfriend. The fact that his father was the wealthiest man for counties, even states, around did not hurt his popularity either.

Audrey's embarrassment was so profound that she looked away, hating that she'd been thrust into this unwanted spotlight. Even though Negro girls seemed to be treated like third-rate citizens in her school, farther down the social ladder than she was, at least they had each other. Audrey had no one.

Johnny spoke up, sounding indignant, as he rubbed a hand over his cropped blond hair. "What's it to you anyway? You the hallway patrol?"

Audrey felt movement behind her then at her side. She looked down at a pair of brown-and-white lace-up saddle shoes topped by checkered argyle socks. She glanced upward to find a tight-lipped

Freddie Littleton, annoyance clouding his face. He crouched down and collected Audrey's books into a small pile then crossed the deserted hallway to face the snickering pair of jerks.

"Say you're sorry, assholes," Freddie said with such assuredness that Audrey blanched, gaping at him. He was easily a foot shorter than the other two. His red hair was longer than the current style demanded and messy, like a tangled mop head.

"Um, it's okay. I'm fine." Audrey's voice was firm as she folded her books to her chest and got up.

"No, it's not okay," Freddie said, his back to Audrey. "You guys apologize to her, and then take your two little dicks in hand and waddle on out of here."

He had to be crazy to talk that way. Freddie was just a lanky freshman, younger and smaller than the pair he was confronting. They could stuff him into a locker or worse in no time. To defend someone like her seemed risky.

From the corner of her eye, Audrey spotted someone walking toward them and realized it was Mrs. Patton, looking svelte in black boots and a long, gray-striped coat.

The boys went mum as the teacher strolled by, but she offered Audrey a friendly wave and raised her eyebrows in surprise at seeing her. After she disappeared down the hallway, Freddie started up again.

"So, Cliff. I guess I'll have to tell your mom about how buzzed you've been getting before class, about that little bottle of gin you keep on you all the time." Freddie paused and placed a palm over his sweater vest as though his comments were heartfelt. "How do ya think that'd go over?"

After putting his hands up in a sign of defeat, Cliff coughed. "Hey, Freddie boy, I—"

"Both of you are assholes. I've known you too long to waste my time on your shit. It's a damn shame you gotta be hog-tied into doing the right thing. Didn't your mamas teach you manners?" Freddie gave Audrey a sideways glance and winked. "I'm quite sure yours did, Cliff. Should I tell her how rude you are? And maybe your mom too, Johnny?"

Cliff sighed, and when he turned his gaze on Audrey, she lifted her eyebrows in anticipation of more rude remarks.

"Say, well, I'm sorry, there, um, Audrey. Didn't mean to plow you over. Shouldn't have said what I did, either. Johnny and I was just rushin' to get to detention, and you got in the way."

When Cliff said "detention," Freddie howled and slapped his knee.

Cliff looked irritated but poked Johnny on the shoulder with his finger.

"Yeah, uh, I'm sorry too." Johnny grinned at Audrey and bowed from the waist like a charming prince greeting his fair lady. Something changed in his eyes then, and he cocked his head slightly, staring at her as though he'd never really seen her before.

Audrey looked away, aware her flesh was tingling and her heart was beating more quickly. The only time Johnny had ever spoken to her was when they were children, and that had been to tease her.

"Good boys. Now, go on. Nuts to you both," Freddie said as he waved his arms to shoo them away. The pair raced off.

Audrey clapped a hand over her mouth. Mrs. Patton had left already, so getting new notebooks was out of the question, and her bus was probably long gone too. A late bus might not have even been scheduled on the first day of school after the holidays. Some teachers lived in Willowdale and drove the ten miles to school, but she would have to find one of them quickly. Her stomach churned.

Without a word, she dashed down the hallway.

"Wait!" Freddie shouted after her.

Audrey ignored his fast-approaching footsteps until his firm hand gripped her shoulder, pulling her to a stop. She looked at him.

"I wanted to say I'm sorry about those goons. I hate seeing them get away with the stupid shit they do." His eyes were earnest. "Our families have hung out since we were all kids, so we're friends, just in case you were worried about me." He offered her a toothy grin that smooshed his freckles together. "Honestly, they're just stupid and spoiled. Are you okay?"

Audrey nodded and hurried away. Freddie was on her heels then walking beside her. Curious about the boy, she pushed thick curls behind her ear while simultaneously peeking at him. He had blue eyes like her, but Freddie had light-reddish eyelashes and a pale complexion. Audrey could admire his smile, those perfect teeth, and pinkish lips.

His choice of friends was another matter.

"Where's the fire?" he said.

"I missed the bus. I have to find a teacher with a car or see if there's a late bus. I have to go," she said, panic rising in her voice. He was like a pesky insect buzzing around her ear, refusing to fly away.

"Stop." Freddie jumped in front of her, almost getting run over. "Calm down, okay? Yes, there's a late bus. But listen. My mom is outside to pick me up in our car. I know you live in Willowdale, so go get your shit from your locker, and I'll get mine, and meet me at the doors."

Audrey couldn't just accept a ride from Mrs. Littleton. Of the many women her mother despised, Freddie's mom was at the top of the list. She frowned, averting her eyes.

"Look," Freddie said, tapping her arm, "it's just a car ride, my way of making up for those idiots. Seriously, you can trust me. I see you eating alone all the time, and then I find you laid out on the floor, and they're laughing. It just pissed me off."

Audrey studied his expression and concluded he was being sincere. She was desperate for a way home. She smiled politely and nodded her agreement.

"You'll love my mom too," Freddie said. "She's the best there is."

Audrey was startled by his assertion. *Liking your own mother?* She'd never liked her own, and Grandmother Hamilton had been no prize.

When they parted ways to scurry to their lockers, Audrey was beaming, wondering if she'd made a friend. That seemed preposterous, though. Freddie's father owned the only bank in Willowdale and was well-known and very wealthy. Audrey could only imagine what he would say about his son hanging out with a lowly Scott.

At her locker, Audrey quickly grabbed her coat then sprinted to find Freddie waiting by the door. With a cheerful smile, he led her down the snowy steps to a waiting black Packard and opened the door for her like a gentleman.

Audrey glanced into the car, hesitating until a lighthearted voice from the driver's seat greeted her with a melodious "Hello." The voice was as welcoming and warm as the car's interior, so she took a deep breath, smiled back at Freddie, and jumped inside.

CHAPTER 9

Audrey

Pink and red paper hearts of all sizes swayed on strings attached to the cafeteria ceiling, and Audrey dodged the lowest ones before taking her seat beside Freddie. In the past month, she'd become comfortable sitting among his friends, but even so, she preferred to listen rather than share anything about herself.

Freddie's fiery hair was newly cropped, which made his ears seem to stick out farther, and he wore their school colors of orange and black. He gestured wildly with his hands as he told an amusing story to the two boys eating across from them while his bowl of tomato soup remained untouched.

Audrey opened her lunch sack and pulled out a peanut butter sandwich and a peach, enough to sustain her through afternoon classes. She chewed slowly to savor every bite, at the same time admiring Freddie's easy manner and confidence among his peers. Since he ushered her into that small group of friends, Audrey had experienced a taste of what belonging felt like, but the feeling evaporated whenever he wasn't with her.

The gang had been slow to warm up to her, a person they'd only previously gawked at and gossiped about—especially Cliff, who would not acknowledge her presence even if she was sitting right next to him. His conceit was bothersome, but Cliff's attitude toward her was likely more honest than the others' polite acceptance.

Once, she'd overheard Freddie whispering to his buddies that she was shy, which was true, and that he would "punch the living daylights out of anyone who's mean to her." For weeks, he'd met her between classes and walked with her like he was her bodyguard, giving the stink eye to anyone who shot a questioning look his way. Freddie was amusing and kind. Even if she was his pity project—which Audrey suspected she was—she was happy to be with him.

Mother would strongly disapprove of her having a boyfriend, and Audrey believed she would go ballistic that he was a Littleton to boot. For as long as she could recall, Mother had detested the Littleton family and spat their name from her mouth like it was poisonous. But Audrey didn't care. Valentine's Day was a few short days away, and she was excited to see what Freddie might do to help her better understand the nature of their relationship.

Biting into her sandwich, she watched him tear into a corn muffin and slurp his cold tomato soup, still chatting. That someone could wear their skin so effortlessly seemed impossible, but Freddie did.

Audrey heard rustling behind her, then a body dropped into the chair on her other side. Their legs touched. A spicy, woodsy scent drifted into her nostrils.

Johnny DeDecker.

Strangely, he'd sat down awfully close to her. Audrey couldn't lower her arm without her elbow grazing some part of him. She tucked both arms close to her body and chewed methodically, trying to calm herself, aware that all the girls in the cafeteria would have their eyes plastered on him—and also, therefore, her.

"Heya, Audrey." Johnny forked several pieces of apple pie and shoveled them into his mouth, simultaneously waving at a tall, popular basketball player lumbering by.

She bobbed her head in silent acknowledgment then stole a look at him through her bangs. Johnny's full, reddish lips reminded her of ripe cherries. He must've felt her eyes surveying him, because he looked at her and smiled, crumbs clinging to his lips. Audrey blushed and bit into her peach.

"Say, sis, I never properly apologized for that one time, you know." He nudged her leg with his knee, and she shot him a skeptical look. Johnny thrust his chin in Cliff's direction. "Cliff over there is just a Neanderthal. But I'm sorry for my part."

Audrey couldn't tell if he was being sincere, but she flashed him a smile.

"Freddie here is like the morality police, you know—keeps us all in line. Hey, look." He paused to chew a heaping forkful of macaroni and cheese. "We all know you've had it rough. I mean, we don't know for sure, just have had that impression since we were kids."

His comment about her circumstances, pointing out how they differentiated her from the rest of Freddie's friends, made her face grow hot.

"Look on the bright side. You're one of the prettiest girls in school now." He brightened as though he'd said something clever. "So you got that going for you, right? Took Freddie here to get us to notice you. Why do you hide under all those...? I mean, such weird..." He clamped his mouth closed and paused. "It's just that, hey, I bet you got a dynamite figure under there. Are you dating yet? We're both sophomores. I'm already sixteen and a pretty good-looking guy if I do say so." He chuckled at his self-flattery. "Maybe we can go out sometime."

At that moment, Freddie looped an arm over Audrey's shoulder and drew her toward him while his laughter rang loudly in her ear. He said, "Eat up, Aud. We've only got five more minutes. I'll be right back. Growing boy here."

Then Freddie was off, speeding to the cafeteria counter as if his life depended on another helping of whatever he craved. No amount of food ever filled that boy up.

Johnny started rubbing his leg against hers. From the corner of her eye, Audrey watched as he downed a turkey sandwich, the last item on his tray, like nothing at all was happening under the table.

"Wait, Freddie, wait," she exclaimed, chucking scraps into her brown sack. Eyes around the table followed her as she clumsily yanked her pocketbook off her chair.

Johnny flashed her that wide white grin of his, which most girls at school seemed to find irresistible. "You don't have to run away. Just get back to me," he said.

Audrey hustled after Freddie. If she thought honestly about their friendship, he treated her more like a protective big brother than a boyfriend. But as one of Freddie's best buddies, Johnny had no business asking her for a date.

Something was off about the guy. Audrey could feel it deep inside her bones.

CHAPTER 10

Audrey

On Valentine's Day, couples routinely ducked behind classroom and locker doors to steal smooches. But Audrey and Freddie had only shared a warm embrace in the morning before classes. He'd fondly kissed her cheek and patted her back, saying, "You know I love ya, kiddo." Other than stirring her heart with his persistent, engaging grin, Freddie had done nothing else special.

Weeks passed, and Audrey still found herself pondering the possibility they might become an actual couple. Freddie's attentiveness toward her continued unabated, and they were together between classes whenever possible. She was inexplicably drawn to him like a child to her favorite security blanket or teddy bear.

On a sunny and cool spring day, Audrey arrived home to find a note on the kitchen table. Mother was working at the church all afternoon. She was thankful that someone was earning a little money for the family again. Daddy was napping, and Harry had sequestered himself in the parlor to listen to one of his after-school radio programs.

She would not be watched.

When Audrey raced out of the house, she was clutching a red Folgers coffee can to her chest like a prized trophy, which it was. The ground had been constantly muddied by steady March rains, but after days of warm temperatures and steady sunshine, the soil would be dry and pliable, exactly right for digging.

Soon, her treasures would be safe.

Running was impossible in her skirt, stylishly narrow at the knees—a gift from Mrs. Littleton. Audrey resorted to walking in short, brisk steps toward the Ritters' garage. It sloped like the Tower of Pisa, in danger of one day collapsing. Audrey's own home was falling down around them as well. Her history teacher had said people in large cities were experiencing a postwar boom since they had jobs and plenty of money to spend. But most families like hers living in small rural towns continued their struggle to survive, let alone prosper.

She skittered by Mr. Ritter's pigeon coop, which radiated the sour smell of bird poop, then ducked out of sight behind his garage. Audrey pretended she was a spy like Ingrid Bergman in *Notorious*, someone who needed to hide her many secrets and could never be sure whom to trust.

She found a thick, straight stick and started to scrape the ground near the foundation. Digging a hole in Illinois's rich, black dirt in the springtime was easy, unlike during the summer when the earth would be cracked and baked. She completed the task, lowered the can into the hole, then brushed dirt over it. After patting the mound, she twisted her stick there to mark the spot, just like she had for all the other cans buried nearby.

Each had been stuffed with pages from her diaries. Audrey thought of them as her secret garden of words.

While rubbing her hands to brush away the dirt, she started down the gravel driveway toward the Ritters' house, where she would turn to head back to her own yard. A door slammed, and Mr. Ritter emerged onto his back stoop, eyes focused on Audrey through round wire-framed glasses, no doubt wondering what she was doing there.

She'd buried a whole row of cans without once being detected, but Mr. or Mrs. Ritter might have seen her that time.

"Hello, young lady," he said.

Audrey was fond of Mr. Ritter, and she liked his funny accent. Mother had made it clear she did not. Then again, she hadn't acknowledged that the war was over, or that Germans were no longer their enemies. To think of the Ritters that way seemed ridiculous to Audrey. Mr. and Mrs. Ritter had been American citizens for some fifty years.

The old man's fluff of gray hair was sticking straight out—foreign to a good combing—and he sported wrinkled tan trousers that were belted and hiked far above his waist. His thin lips stretched into a grin, and Audrey smiled back, relieved.

When she'd been much younger, Audrey had spent many lazy, scorching summer Saturdays with Mr. Ritter. Usually, she'd been hiding from Mother, and he'd jokingly assured her that he needed to stay out of his wife's way. Whenever Mother was gone or too busy to notice Audrey's absence, she'd lain on the soft, warm grass in the Ritters' front yard while he lounged in his green metal rocker. Together, they would find animal shapes in the clouds or count the cars on trains that rolled by on the other side of the highway.

"Hello, Mr. Ritter. It's nice to see you," she said with forced cheer.

Amusement twinkled in his eyes. "Out seeing the pigeons this morning?"

"Yes, sir. I just wanted to take a little walk around our yards. Such a nice morning." Audrey wrung her hands. She was getting good at lying to Mother, but it still didn't come naturally and was even harder with someone she respected.

"We haven't seen you in so long. You're in high school now, right? What subject do you like the most?"

She nodded. "English, I guess. I love to write. I want to be an author, maybe a reporter like Lois Lane." Citing a fictional character from the radio probably sounded pathetic to the old man, but for too long, she'd wanted to tell someone that. When she was growing up, Mr. Ritter had been an adult friend to her until Mother put a stop to it. He wasn't necessarily a confidant but someone she'd relied on for a kind smile or hug.

"Audrey, what are you doing over there?"

Audrey nearly jumped out of her shoes. Mr. Ritter's eyes flicked to where Mother was standing, and she shifted her gaze as well, just enough to see the woman standing with her legs apart, hands on her hips, near their porch. *Shit, shit, shit.* She couldn't let Mother see the dirt stains on her hands and knees as she would be in enough trouble for just visiting with Mr. Ritter.

"I-I'm sorry, Mr. Ritter. I need to get on home."

She took a step, but Mr. Ritter's bony fingers gripped her arm. Audrey could feel Mother's glare boring a small hole into her back. She was a human bull's-eye.

"Your mother wasn't always like this. I know that's hard to believe, but things happen to people. They happened to your mother. Makes 'em change."

"I don't know what you mean." Audrey easily extracted her arm from his frail grip. She didn't want to know, either, and sped away toward her house.

Audrey made a wide circle around her glaring mother, who was huffing and puffing, before hopping up the steps. Mother was quick and shoved her. She tripped and fell against the porch railing, immediately embarrassed to think Mr. Ritter might have seen the attack.

When Audrey looked out, the old man was shaking his head. He slowly turned away. She couldn't even imagine what he'd witnessed over the years, living next to her grandparents and then her parents.

The fact that he seemed to have a soft spot for her mother was odd. She brushed herself off and went into the house.

Her cans were safely hidden, and that was all that mattered.

CHAPTER 11

Edith

Before leaving the house to meet with Howard DeDecker, Edith needed to tend to Red, who'd been complaining constantly that he didn't feel well. She buttered some toast and dropped two pieces into her husband's hand, but her gesture was met by his disappointed, lackluster eyes. Frustrated by his lack of appreciation, she marched into their bedroom to get dressed.

Years had passed since she'd spoken with Howard about their deal, and Edith was eager to get reassurance from the town's wealthiest businessman that everything was arranged as they'd agreed.

The vibrant green-and-blue pattern of her dress, a donation from one of the do-gooding women at First Baptist, turned her eyes into emeralds. Edith could do nothing about the fat rolls bulging through the polyester fabric. She was almost forty, after all. Satisfied, she nestled a hat on her head and angled it to one side the way the do-gooder ladies did.

Half an hour later, Edith was swaying along Main Street, enjoying the swishing sound her nylon stockings made when her thighs rubbed against each other. Howard would see she had class. The DeDecker family had made a fortune in farm implements and supplies and were a big name in the whole county. Somehow, they'd managed to thrive or at least maintain their status during the Depression. Howard was the patriarch, known for his churchgoing and altruistic giving, which Edith found highly amusing.

While Edith walked, she practiced in her head the conversation they were about to have. She'd arrived at the critical juncture, at last. In a few months, Audrey would be sixteen, and by the time she was seventeen, Edith wanted the engagement to Howard's son to be announced. Then, when Audrey was eighteen, the two would be married.

She picked up her pace, practically salivating. When Edith ventured over a cross street, she glanced sideways, down the few blocks to Whiskey Row, where bright awnings and tavern signs could be seen. She snorted at the sight and looked away, arms pumping at her sides while she progressed.

Finally, she waltzed up to the offices of Willowdale Farm Implements. Edith stopped to adjust her bra and hat, then she clopped through the entrance, waiting a moment for her eyes to adjust to the lobby's dim light. She removed her gloves and stuffed them into her pocketbook then gave her friendliest smile to the bright-eyed young man approaching her.

"I'd like to see the owner, please," she said.

"Do you have an appointment, ma'am?"

Edith rolled her eyes. "Tell him Mrs. Scott is here."

The man tipped his head politely then maneuvered around tables and leather sofas before pausing at a corner office enclosed by glass windows. Edith could hear the low rumbling of their voices, could see Howard ensconced behind a massive oak desk, his head settled against the back of a black leather chair. The striped tie he wore arced over a rotund belly and disappeared under the desk. She watched as he toyed with his bushy mustache. His head turned, and he peered through the glass at her.

Edith waggled her fingers in silent greeting.

The man summoned his large girth and rose to his feet then motioned Edith to join him. Clutching her pocketbook to her stomach,

Edith marched into his office, shoulders back and head high. She smiled. Like her, Howard was much fatter now.

"Good morning, Mrs. Scott." Howard pushed up round, black-framed spectacles and looked at her with curiosity. "I'm afraid I don't recall an appointment with you. How may I help you today?"

His tone was formal and, while not exactly unfriendly, stuffier than Edith had anticipated. Keeping her standing was not polite, so Edith returned his rudeness by closing his office door without permission and sitting down in one of the two chairs facing his desk.

"It's been a long time, Howard."

He raised his eyebrows, which made his glasses slide to the tip of his nose. "Excuse me?" he said, dropping into his chair, the leather groaning.

"I'm here about my daughter and your son," she said, eyeing the family photos displayed on the credenza behind him, one of them of his two children—a boy and a younger girl—and his priggish wife. Thankfully, the boy was good-looking, like Howard had been once.

"Who exactly is your daughter, ma'am? Is she going out with Johnny? Is there a problem here?" His voice was tinged with alarm.

Edith crossed her legs then uncrossed them, bewildered by his questions. They'd made a deal when their children were in first grade, and he'd practically signed it in blood back then—his, not hers. *He'd better not be trying to pull something.*

"There's no problem, nothin' like what I believe you're thinking. And no, they're not going out, not that I know of. That's why I'm here. It's time to get these two together."

"I have no idea what you're talking about," he said, shuffling papers on his desk.

"Oh, I think you do." Edith leaned forward and put both of her palms flat on his desk. "Audrey and your son will be married, and you're going to make that happen. I want an engagement within a year."

Howard's face screwed up, and he gaped at her like she had three heads propped on her shoulders.

"Mrs. Scott"—he spat her name—"that's the most ridiculous thing I've ever heard. Now, if you don't mind, I'm actually quite busy."

"You can pretend all you want. Got your reasons, I'm sure. But that don't mean you can back out of our deal." She puffed herself up. "You keep your word, and I'll keep mine."

At those words, his mustached lips puckered like a hairy, dried prune. "My dear woman, what you're saying is fictitious. We don't have a deal of any kind."

"Oh, but we do."

"I haven't seen you in years, Edith." He dropped the ruse with the use of her first name.

"Does the name Poodles ring a bell?" she asked, batting her eyelashes.

Howard's eyes flashed with recognition for just a split second, but Edith saw it.

Howard averted his eyes and cleared his throat. "No."

"I'll be damned. You're such a fool, Howard," Edith said, rising. "You can say that now, but I bet your memory will return. We'll talk again soon. Best thing for you—and I'm sure you know what I mean—is to get those kids together."

She snatched her pocketbook and leveled it in the crook of her arm before strutting into the lobby.

As she walked out the door, Howard shouted, "Goddammit!"

She breezed into the sunshine with a wide grin on her face, basking in the confidence that soon, she'd have the whole world at her feet.

CHAPTER 12

Edith

Kneeling in a row marked Potatoes, Edith dropped several seeds into black soil and swept rich earth over them. She didn't like gardening but had learned young that a poor family might starve if they didn't plan ahead for bleak winter days. Thanks to Edith's canning skills, they always had just enough food to get by—not that any one of them would thank her for it.

She grunted and glanced toward the Ritters' once-beautiful garden. The large rectangle patch was overgrown, filled with thistles, grass, and tall, oppressive weeds. What a pity that Mrs. Ritter's green thumb was decaying inside a casket, lowered into the ground, appropriately enough, on April Fool's Day. Fighting some kind of cancer, the woman had lived like a hermit for the last few months then died a few weeks back. Edith hadn't spoken to her for years, so she saw no reason to pretend sadness of any kind. She hadn't even bothered to pay her respects to the woman, who'd been her own mother's dearest friend. The children had wanted to go to the graveside service, but Edith refused to let them, and Red wisely hadn't interfered. He knew better.

Admittedly, when Edith was a child, she'd been fond of Mrs. Ritter. The woman had often shared her freshly baked sugar cookies with her, and sometimes, she'd slipped pennies into Edith's small palm so that she could buy licorice at the five-and-dime. But once Edith was older, she resented Mrs. Ritter's self-proclaimed role as a tattletale, and the last straw was when she overheard the woman call her an old maid when Edith had just turned twenty.

Of course, if Mrs. Hamilton had been around, she would've insisted Edith attend the funeral, and they would've had an intense argument about it, just like they'd had about everything. Her mother had left the family five years before, and not a single day passed when Edith missed her.

She stretched her stiff neck, catching a glimpse of her son, who was sporting a St. Louis Cardinals baseball cap and a red T-shirt while he mowed the grass, his regular Sunday chore. He was such a good boy, obedient and respectful. Closing in on his twelfth birthday, Harry was skinny and the shortest boy in his sixth-grade class. At a mere five foot nine himself, Red was clearly responsible for her son's stunted growth, but at least in looks, Harry resembled Edith's handsome father, who'd had blond waves, a distinctive cleft chin, and hazel-brown eyes. Thankfully, her son had not inherited Red's shock of reddish hair and ruddy complexion.

She rolled her neck to each side and wiped her brow, sweating even though the day was temperate. From the corner of her eye, Edith spotted Mr. Ritter shuffling toward a patio chair, shoulders hunched. He appeared ancient, much thinner, weaker, and pale too. Without his garden, he would have little to eat come wintertime, but Edith shrugged the thought away.

Nothing about him had ever been her problem.

Red's figure loomed into her peripheral vision, and she slid her eyes to stare at her husband, who was standing on the porch with a death grip on his Pabst—midmorning being Red's usual clock-in time. The tails of his unbuttoned short-sleeved shirt hung loosely off his hips, and his gut protruded over the waist of high-water pants. Red was waving both arms and calling to Edith, but his words were garbled by the clickety-clack of metal blades spinning as Harry labored to push the heavy mower across the lawn.

Edith grunted and pulled herself up, brushing dirt from her knees and the hem of her dress. Audrey joined her father on the porch, wearing a light-pink jumper Edith had never seen before. She squinted to give her daughter a once-over. Several blouses and skirts had been magically appearing in that girl's closet, Audrey claiming a new friend at her school had outgrown them.

She watched her daughter with interest. Audrey seemed to be growing more beautiful every day, blossoming naturally like a wildflower. Imagining her in a wedding gown, the picture-perfect bride worthy of a DeDecker, was becoming easier. Edith's lips curved into a sly smile until Audrey wrapped her arms around Red's waist from behind and hugged him. Then her mouth turned down into a straight line. They were laughing—not just chuckling but guffawing. Audrey moved to stand next to her father, and Red casually laced an arm over his daughter's shoulder, chatting away. After a minute, Audrey bounded down the steps and shouted a greeting to Mr. Ritter before rounding the corner of the house, gone.

Edith marched toward Red with her fists clenched. Red lowered the beer can to his side.

"Mind tellin' me what that was about?" she asked, her hands on both hips.

"Just talkin' with the girl."

"Tell me right now what you two was saying. Making fun of me, maybe? And where the hell is she off to?"

"Nothin' to tell." He slurped from his can of beer. "But you need to leave her the hell alone. She don't deserve how you treat her."

"You're an idiot."

"That girl is scared o' you and for good reason. Why you always being so mean, downright nasty to her? Audrey ain't never been nothin' but well-behaved. Fact is..." He paused. "She despises you, and I don't blame her."

Edith moved up a step just as he exhaled a mixture of tobacco and beer breath into her face.

"Proud of yourself?" She waited for him to respond, to see how brave he had become.

Red looked down at his bare feet rather than at her.

She spat, "You don't deserve respect from anyone, especially not me or that girl."

Red's head popped up. He looked at her squarely, his expression harder than she'd ever seen before. Their eyes locked until her husband shook his head. He broke the staring contest and plodded back into the house.

Edith stared after him, brow furrowed. *Can it be?* After all this time, her husband might have grown a most problematic backbone.

CHAPTER 13

Audrey

Freddie's whole gang was going to the Sunday matinee of *I Was a Male War Bride*, and he was paying Audrey's way. She wasn't sure if it was a date or if Freddie had simply assumed she didn't have any money to join in the fun. As Audrey hurried into town, she realized she'd never felt happier. Daddy had been home, and she sought his permission to go rather than sneaking away, which she gladly would have done to avoid contact with her mother. He put his arm around her and squeezed her shoulder then told her in a conspiratorial tone to "scoot on out of here."

Mother would be furious.

Freddie let out a long whistle when he spotted Audrey, and the heads of people in the ticket line turned. He didn't mind that she was wearing his mom's old clothes, and not in a million years would he let on to the others, enjoying their little secret.

"You look like a million bucks," he said into her ear while greeting her with an affectionate hug.

But when Freddie pulled back, his expression was serious. "Are those bruises on the back of your arms?"

Audrey hesitated. "Does it matter? I'm here now, thanks to you." She beamed and patted his cheek. "Don't worry, I have everything under control. Let's go."

CHAPTER 14

Audrey

Without any explanation, Daddy had begun staying at home with the family most nights. Audrey liked to think her Christmas wish had come true even though she really didn't believe in magic.

Still, it was like a miracle.

At the supper table, she and Harry were exchanging wide-eyed glances while Daddy chowed down on a turkey leg and a mountain of steamed carrots. Sober and affable, he was oblivious to Mother's loud sighs and angry, snappy retorts to whatever he said.

Once Harry licked his plate clean, he asked to be excused and bounded into the parlor to tune the RCA to his favorite Tuesday-night program, *Adventures of Superman*. Daddy finished soon after Harry and belched, which made her brother giggle from the other room. He winked at Audrey, patted his big belly, and grabbed a beer from the icebox. He left the women to clear the dirty dishes in uncomfortable silence. While they washed and dried, laughter floated in from the parlor.

After drying the last pan, Audrey tossed the damp flour sack onto the table and strode into the parlor with a faint smile and an air of confidence.

She'd come up with an idea, and Mother was in for a major surprise.

CHAPTER 15

Edith

Flipping the plastic washbasin of dishwater upside down, Edith watched the liquid drain before smacking it against the sink. She arched her eyebrows, surreptitiously eyeing Audrey's backside as the girl sashayed into the parlor.

After weeks of behaving herself, including holding back her sassy tongue, Audrey was giving every indication she was nothing but a sweet, obedient daughter.

But Edith didn't buy it. Something about her daughter was different.

Audrey's voice carried into the kitchen. "Hey, little brother, is *Superman* on tonight?"

"Will you listen with us, Audrey, please?" Harry answered, sounding hopeful.

Judging by the round of giggles and repeated cries of "Stop!" that followed from Harry, his sister was tickling him. When they quieted down, Edith heard Red's and Audrey's murmuring voices. More than likely, the two of them were talking about her. She fumed. Despite her efforts to keep Red's influence on Audrey at bay, their relationship seemed stronger than ever.

The realization irked her, and Edith bit down hard on her lip, drawing a tiny droplet of blood. She had no intention of joining their family time. Instead, she grabbed her mother's ice pick from the utensil drawer and tugged open the freezer section of their icebox. Edith began to chip, chip, chip at the hard layers of frost, stabbing the ice with practiced strokes. She was the very picture of her mother—same freezer, same ice pick.

As a child, Edith had stared down the sharp end of that pick whenever Mrs. Hamilton used it to threaten her.

The sound of Harry squealing pulled Edith from her thoughts, and she slammed the freezer door and threw the pick into the sink. She untied her apron and decided to get off her aching feet. She was always the only one working.

One step into the parlor, Edith stopped abruptly.

Perfect little Audrey had had the temerity to sit in her mother's armchair, adjacent to where Red had settled in his rocking chair.

Her husband was relaxing with an after-dinner beer, and a pack of Marlboros peeked from his shirt pocket. His expression was one of delight as he watched Harry, who was clapping with excitement in front of the radio's speaker.

Audrey turned to Red and spoke in a childlike voice. "Daddy?"

"Can't you be quiet until the shows are over?" Harry whined.

"Where's your whistle, Harry?" her daughter teased.

Harry's eyes bulged before he raced up the stairs then quickly returned with a proud smile and something clenched in one fist. For some reason, the boy considered the whistle, which a teacher had given him, to be a good-luck charm. He unveiled it to Audrey and plopped down cross-legged next to the speaker again, only to jump up when the *Superman* music played.

Edith made her way to the couch. During the two fifteen-minute episodes, Harry performed for them, stretching his arms in front of his lithe body and running loops through their house, pretending to fly. Nobody spoke until, at last, the programs were over and Audrey broke the silence.

"Can I talk now, Harry?" she asked, flipping her wavy bangs. "Daddy, how do you feel about women working? You know, like Lois Lane making a living as a reporter?" She was cooing like one of Mr.

Ritter's pigeons, and Red was falling for her act. "Women have careers these days, you know? It's exciting to think about writing for a living."

The muscles in Edith's jaw tightened. She'd ordered Audrey to forget any such notions. Edith shot her a warning look, but she had focused her adoring eyes on her father.

"Audrey," Edith barked like a guard dog.

But Audrey ignored her. "It's an admirable thing, Daddy. Women worked all kinds of jobs during the war. And I don't mean just selling Tupperware. Doing important stuff."

When Red finally looked at Audrey, he smiled like the dimwit he was and rubbed his scruffy chin. "Well, honey, you know my head ain't right."

Audrey nodded, encouraging him to say more.

"It's hard for me to keep a job, you know, that's why your mama works. Nothing wrong in that—just the way it is. But I'd guess lots o' ladies earn a respectable livin' nowadays."

"I want to be a writer, you know, like in St. Louis or Chicago. Maybe Des Moines. Not too far away, Daddy, I can absolutely swear."

The tips of Edith's ears grew hot, and a flush spread up her neck to her plump cheeks. Audrey had been trying to fool her up until then, and she was playing with fire.

Edith jumped to her feet.

Audrey sprang from her mother's chair and gently tapped her daddy's shoulder, leaning close to his ear. "I know how Mother feels about it, Daddy, but I wondered what you thought. Doesn't that matter? I mean, I'm your girl too."

The walls felt like they were closing in, confining Edith to a jail cell. She was vaguely aware of Harry running by her, shouting, "Up, up, and away!" She riveted her gaze on Red just as he lit a cigarette and blew smoke out the window.

"Well, Audrey, your mother doesn't like the idea of you writin'," he drawled.

That was better, exactly in line with her thinking, what Red had known all along he'd better say. After another puff and a long exhale of smoke, he turned away from the window and looked right into Edith's eyes.

"But guess I don't see the harm in it. It's your life, Audrey. Never hurts anybody to have a dream." Red was brandishing defiance like it was his shiny new armor.

Edith flew at him. "Encourage her to move away and get a job? So she can support some bum like you? Now, there's a dream." She was breathing heavily. "I spend years gettin' that foolish idea out of her head, and now, you go puttin' it right back in there."

Red flicked his cigarette butt out the window and stood with effort, staring her down. When he spoke, his voice was frighteningly calm. "You been going on and on for years how this girl's goin' to redeem this family. Like some goddamn messiah. Just what is this plan you got for Audrey? You sure enough ain't shared it with me."

Audrey stepped away from them. Befuddled, Harry sought shelter in his sister's arms, his former glee forgotten. She cleared her throat. "Daddy, she wants me to—"

"You shut up. He's got no business knowing my business," Edith snarled. "Lost that right a long time ago. You keep what I told you to yourself."

"And if I don't?"

The room was silent, tension blanketing them under a suffocating cape.

Edith moved toward her daughter. The girl's eyes widened, and she shrank back, tightening her arms around Harry. That was a ridiculous thing, Audrey believing she held trump cards in her deck when the hand was definitely Edith's.

"Go upstairs. Now," she commanded.

Harry looked distressed, and Audrey still pretended to be brave, but they moved quickly away from her and up the stairs. Red followed them but turned for the bedroom.

Bumping into him, Edith grabbed a corner of his shirt.

"I want you to leave this house." *Go get drunk. Or better yet, walk in front of a speeding car.*

He whirled around. "What the hell did you mean, that Audrey's life ain't none of my business?"

"Because you get no opinion in this house. You're no husband or father. I do everything."

"You're like a damn horse clomping around with blinders on. You're not gonna get that girl to do anything she don't want to." Red's mouth curved into a smirk. "Know what I think?"

"No. I don't care. I know what's best for Audrey."

"You don't give a damn about that girl. Or Harry, for that matter." He wrapped his fingers around Edith's forearm and squeezed until she yelped. "It's all about you and only you."

Edith examined his cold eyes.

The man was a newly worthy opponent.

"I can mess up your so-called plan. Don't even care what it is," Red said. "Perhaps we should have a good long talk 'bout your mother."

Edith jerked her arm, and his grip loosened and released. She said, "Got no idea what you mean."

He walked into their bedroom, speaking over a shoulder. "I'll get on out of here. But I'll be back. You can count on that. Those kids need me."

Red snatched a coat and hat then pushed by her. He threw open the front door and blasted down the steps. Soon, his figure melted into the twilight and vanished.

Edith slammed the door and glared at it, her chest rapidly rising and falling. Outraged by Red's sheer audacity, she skulked into the bedroom and angrily undressed, flinging pieces of her clothing across the room. She tugged her nightgown over her head and shoved her feet into slippers. Then Edith stormed into the kitchen while listening for sounds from the floor above. The children would've heard the door slam, but from years of experience, they would know better than to trudge downstairs and ask her questions.

Edith searched the cupboard for tea and, finding none, folded with disappointment into a chair. She clicked her nails on the wooden tabletop and focused on the opposite wall, seeing nothing but signs of coming trouble in each chip and crack.

Red had said he could mess up her plans. She wasn't sure what he thought he knew, but it was possible he could.

Even more likely that he would.

She removed the hairpins keeping her bun in place and tossed them onto the table, scratching her scalp and loosening the strands. Edith stretched out her legs. Within half an hour, long shadows crept across the kitchen's walls and swallowed all the remaining light, shrouding her in inky darkness. Still, Edith didn't move.

Like the rats scurrying around in her basement, she remained invisible, twitching and gnashing her teeth in the dark, quietly calculating her important next move.

CHAPTER 16

Edith

Edith dug her toes into the warm grass as she plucked breeze-dried shirts and pants from the clothesline, their spring freshness filling her nostrils. The scent was a change of pace from the sickly smell sticking to the walls inside her house. She pitched the clothes into a basket and dropped clothespins into a bucket, moving down the line and repeating the process with practiced precision.

Chores were a relief from Red's incessant whining, and having escaped it, Edith would take her sweet time outdoors. Either the flu bug had bitten him hard, or her husband's lifetime of smoking and drinking had caught up with him. He was nauseated and weak, too ill to pester her any longer about Audrey, too busy throwing up or complaining how shitty he felt. He kept insisting that she wait on him. Edith's biggest problem had become how to get him to shut the hell up.

Finished gathering their laundry, Edith looked up to see her daughter scurrying up the driveway, books clutched to her chest. She was late coming home again—the fourth time in two weeks. Audrey kept insisting she was getting homework help at school and taking the late bus, which dropped her off near Lucky's, but Edith suspected the girl was lying. Without a telephone, finding out if she was telling the truth was impossible, and Edith would never set foot inside that high school anyway, even if she had a car. She'd avoided Sauk River High since graduating and saw no reason to dredge up memories from her days there. Besides, those teachers couldn't be trusted and would lie to her on Audrey's behalf.

Her daughter's skirt was swaying effortlessly with the alluring motion of her hips. Her previously stick-thin legs had become a young woman's shapely, toned calves. Her naturally curly hair, once frizzy and unmanageable, now lay coiled in soft waves that washed over her shoulders, so dark that it flashed tones of deep blue. Under the books she carried, Audrey wore a long-sleeved light-yellow poplin blouse that, once again, Edith did not recognize as one of the church do-gooders' donations.

Audrey had grown into a real beauty, just like Edith had hoped. Elizabeth Taylor had nothing on her daughter.

The fact wasn't lost on Edith that any red-blooded American boy would find her daughter's hourglass figure, sweet triangular face, and crystal-blue eyes attractive. But only one boy mattered and would ever matter.

She puckered her lips and snatched the laundry basket, considering when she should visit Howard again to get things rolling. *The sooner, the better.*

Edith's eyes tracked Audrey as she scampered up the back porch steps without as much as a how-do-you-do then let the screen door bang behind her.

She sighed. That girl would be the death of her yet.

Audrey

Audrey charged up the stairs to avoid her mother and closed her bedroom door softly. She'd seen the questioning look in the woman's eyes. She hastily changed into denim pants and a short-sleeved pink T-shirt, hanging the yellow blouse in the back of her closet. Safely burrowed inside her bedroom, Audrey tried to catch her breath, but her eyes continuously darted to the door.

To her surprise, her commandant had not followed her to pepper her with questions.

When a listless breeze wafted through her room, carrying the perfume of lilac bushes below, Audrey sidled over to her open window. She shut her eyes and filled her nostrils. To her, the sweet scent equated to springtime, to nature's proof of a promised renewal. When the screen door below her room slammed, Audrey's eyes snapped open, and she observed her brother speeding toward the field.

Even though he was almost a teenager himself, Harry still seemed like a child to her, especially since he enjoyed playing games of pretend. Superman was his favorite. Audrey assumed he needed an escape from their parents like she did, and fantasy was his solution.

As she watched him run with such energy and abandon, Audrey's heart ached. She missed her little brother. For many years, she'd adopted the role of an Indian chief to Harry's cowboy, and they would end imaginary confrontations by smoking a peace pipe together, a long stick he would carefully select. She grinned at the memory while watching Harry lope on through the field, a spirited gazelle seeking shelter within yonder trees.

Audrey suspected that, like her, Harry had few friends. Then again, she really didn't know anymore. She'd spent little time with him since school began. Freddie occupied her thoughts, and clandestine writing took up the time she spent in her bedroom. Even if Audrey wanted to explain herself to her brother, the possibility that he would innocently reveal one of her secrets to Mother was too much of a gamble. Harry was just a kid who wouldn't understand the wrath he could bring down on her.

As she watched, he ambled through the field's underbrush, no doubt headed for the fort he'd been building deep in the woods. That was Harry's secret. He hadn't confided in her about it, but she'd easily figured it out a year earlier. The field was sparkling with sunny veins of crimson and gold, and she soon lost him in the hazy hues. The sun was dipping lower in the sky, and the treetops in the distance were already drenched in shadows.

Audrey worried that her brother might not make it home before sundown. But then again, Mother wouldn't care if her favorite child was late. Audrey sighed and crossed her arms on the sill. Luckily for Harry, Mother had never whipped him, and Audrey believed she never would.

With Harry out of sight, Audrey wandered over to her dresser and picked up her hand mirror to examine her face.

She'd never considered herself pretty, but Freddie and Johnny had both told her as much. Plenty of boys at school stared at her while they whispered to each other. But they didn't gawk at her because she was "weird Audrey Scott," the pitied outcast. She was Audrey Scott, caterpillar turned butterfly, or as Freddie had called her, "the bee's knees." She wasn't invisible anymore, thanks to the stylish, flattering clothing Mrs. Littleton continued to give her.

Staring at her image, Audrey wondered which boy Mother believed she could force her to marry. More than likely, he would be some wealthy snob at Sauk River High or a nearby high school. Eventually, Audrey would learn his name, but once she knew, she intended to stay as far away from that boy as possible.

Freddie was the one who mattered to her.

He'd ushered her into his wide circle of friends and insisted that she belonged as much as anyone else. While Freddie had never been physical with her or asked for a private date, she could tell he was fond of her. School had become less stressful because of him, more fun even. He always made her laugh, especially when he cussed, which was pretty much all the time, and he walked with her between classes. Freddie understood her better than she understood herself. He would announce what she was thinking or feeling before she had figured it out for herself. Audrey had heard about couples who did that, like Humphrey Bogart and Lauren Bacall in *The Big Sleep*—not that she'd personally seen the movie.

Is that love?

But trying to get comfortable around his friends was another matter altogether. If Freddie wasn't in the mix, they acted indifferent and aloof sometimes, as though being poor was a disease they might catch if they got too close to her. And her feelings about Johnny, Freddie's closest and oldest friend, were especially confounding. One moment, she would be enthralled by how handsome he was, and her heart would leap from her chest whenever he paid attention to her. He was as good-looking as a movie star. But other times, he gave Audrey the heebie-jeebies for reasons she couldn't explain. Beautiful girls at school, especially the cheerleaders, fawned over Johnny, apparently not minding how crass or disgusting his comments could be and not giving a hoot about the ugly rumors that surrounded him.

Audrey set the mirror down and riffled through the various blouses in her closet, fingering soft fabrics and admiring delicately sewn stitching. Being with Freddie had another benefit, too—his mom. Mrs. Littleton was the kindest woman Audrey had ever met, and earlier, after school, she'd barely been able to squeak out a thank-you for the yellow blouse.

"I'm sure I have more things that are just your size," Mrs. Littleton had said, reaching out to pour glasses of fresh lemonade for her and Freddie.

After they gobbled up some chocolate chip cookies, Mrs. Littleton led Audrey up their curved staircase, her stockinged feet cushioned by a plush teal-blue runner smattered with tiny yellow-and-white flowers. Audrey obediently followed the woman into a guest bedroom. She was reluctant, even embarrassed, to accept another item from Freddie's mom, but Mrs. Littleton had coaxed her into it.

"It doesn't fit me that well," she'd said with a mischievous smile.

If Mother had noticed her new wardrobe items, she hadn't said anything. As confident as Audrey was in her ruse, she was extremely careful not to go too far. After all, everything unrecognizable to Mother had come from Mrs. Littleton, her perceived enemy. But Mother didn't like anyone, really.

The sound of footsteps pounding up the stairs sent Audrey scrambling. They could belong only to her mother.

She began to straighten her quilt, hoping to exude an air of nonchalance even though her heart threatened to burst from her chest. She heard Mother's fast breathing in the doorway and turned her head with a false smile, which instantly evaporated at the sight of papers gripped in her mother's fist. The muscles in Audrey's legs went weak. She reached for the iron post at the foot of her bed.

"Are there more?" Mother's voice cracked like thunder.

"Those are so old, Mother. Goodness, I thought I'd thrown them all away. I did that, you know, like you said to." The lie fell easily. Audrey had no idea what those pages said or where Mother had found them.

"I knew it. I just knew it," Mother said, about to blow.

Audrey crossed to her dresser and threw her voice over her shoulder. "C'mon, Mother, I don't keep a diary. I've told you that. I swear. I mean, I know better."

"I found these hidden in the basement, behind an old paint can. You stashed them there. Don't you lie to me, Audrey Mae. I'm goin' to whip the devil right out of you."

Audrey swung around. Mother's eyes were bugged out. No longer hazel, they'd darkened to a rich coffee brown. She would never let Mother whip her again, but the woman might kick her out of the house or come up with some other way to hurt her. She lowered her eyelids and glared back at her, suddenly tired of acting the weakling.

"Have you forgotten I can tell Daddy about your ridiculous plan?" she asked.

She'd been saving her best card to play.

Mother's hand struck Audrey's cheek with such force that her head twisted to one side. She stumbled against her dresser and slid to the floor, stunned. Mother stood over her. She tore the papers into bits and sprinkled them over Audrey's sprawled frame. The handprint burned on her cheek, and she rubbed it, more infuriated by the slap than hurt.

"Are you stupid, girl? Think you can threaten me? Your daddy doesn't give a crap about you. He never has."

Audrey didn't believe that even for a second, but with Mother towering over her, she had to go along. "I'm sorry I said that. I truly am. I would never tell him. I-I was just lashing out because you didn't believe me. I'm telling you the truth, and I'll do whatever you want. You want me to marry someone, and I'll do it. Okay?" She rolled her eyes up to Mother's face with the most earnest expression she could muster.

Silence.

After a long moment, Mother put her hands on her hips. "That's more like it. One day, you'll thank me."

"I'm sure I will." Audrey stayed down on the floor and smiled up reassuringly.

Appeased, Mother turned to leave.

Audrey pushed up onto her elbows and raised her eyebrows sharply. "Mother? I think I deserve to know now. Who is this boy you want me to marry?"

CHAPTER 17

Edith

The children were in school, and Red was asleep in his rocker in the parlor with a blanket tucked under his chin despite the warm, stuffy household.

Edith overturned the pickle jar she kept hidden in her middle dresser drawer and counted out a dollar and seventy-five cents in change. She would have to ask the pastor for work, seeing how money was so damn low. Because Friday was the preferred do-gooder volunteer day at First Baptist Church, she could also bring home handouts of food and clothing.

Unfortunately, that meant spending time around those nauseating women.

Edith had never thanked the ladies of Willowdale for their charity and never would. The thought made her want to spit on each and every one of them.

She dressed in brown slacks and a green polka-dot blouse that didn't match well, but most of her wardrobe was dirty. She stuffed her feet into worn-out mules that were dreadful looking but well-suited for long walks.

Earlier, Red had asked her—begged her, frankly—to fetch him a doctor. To stop his fussing, she told him she would, knowing full well they couldn't afford one. With the little money Edith would earn, she needed to buy household supplies, put some toward the electric bill, and, until the garden produced, also purchase food—depending, of course, on what the do-gooders provided. Unfortunately for

Red, his beer and cigarettes were the first items she'd scratched off her shopping list. He seemed too sick to tolerate either vice anyway.

No, the doctor, too, would have to wait.

After settling a pillbox hat on her head, Edith stretched its dark netting across her eyes. She liked hats with netting. The fabric allowed her to watch people without them knowing it. As she ambled to the back door, she glimpsed Red slumped in his chair, pale as a ghost and thinner than he had been in years. Along with his appetite, her husband's paunch had been steadily eroding.

She closed the door softly behind herself and trudged down the hill, rounding by Lucky's and thinking how strange it was that Red wasn't in the place, getting sauced. Edith took a right onto Fourth Street and, several long blocks later, turned left to plod the final eight blocks to First Baptist. By then, she'd pasted a stoic look on her face to show the do-gooders she was neither pleased nor offended by them.

They simply didn't matter to her.

At the church's side entrance door, Edith paused and listened to the squawking cacophony on the other side. The ladies were hard at work—gabbing being what they did best—in the church hall. She stepped inside, refreshed by the cool air that always lingered in the basement's great hall, and breathed in the aroma of sweets baking in the kitchen at the back.

She started to push through their ranks, refusing to look at any one person.

The rich hens had no way of knowing that soon they would be kowtowing to her as a new member of the wealthy and respected DeDecker clan. They would have no choice. The thought was more delicious than any cookie, tart, or pie ever made for one of the do-gooders' bake sales.

The do-gooders, who wore expensive pearls and teased their locks into magazine-worthy hairdos, took pride in their purchases from upscale stores in other towns. That was where they bought immodest skirts and scandalous peep-toe shoes with high heels that showed off their legs.

As much as the women disgusted her, Edith would join their ranks. But she would never be like them. She would soak up the power and status that came with money but be a positive moral influence. Their volunteer work was only a fashion show they put on for one another under the guise of helping others.

She continued to walk, focused on reaching the kitchen.

Dodging tables loaded with piles of sorted clothing, toys, and household goods, Edith kept her eyes out for Pastor Dressler. She could feel the ladies' eyes following her and perceive their cautiously exchanged glances. That was how these snobby women communicated with one another—silently. Not one of them spoke to Edith or nodded at her even though they all knew her.

Perhaps they believed she required their pity, but never their friendship.

A smile pulled on the edges of her mouth. She was so much better than the do-gooders.

Edith searched over the flock of bobbing heads to find the pastor. How he managed to endure those chatterboxes was beyond her. In the kitchen, a dozen women were scurrying around and bumping into each other like confused ants. Then Edith saw her.

"Dammit," she muttered and stopped, her eyes transfixed by the flowing hair and beaming smile. Then she heard that high-pitched laugh rise over the others. Edith shuddered involuntarily.

Even though the sight of Mrs. Somebody was always jarring, Edith had learned how to remain calm, to skulk around the corners of the room to avoid being seen by her. Usually, she managed to steer clear of any encounter, which was important because Edith wasn't sure if she could mask her hostility. She stared at her.

Always the main attraction in the do-gooder crowd, Mrs. Somebody was talking with more animation than Bugs Bunny himself. The self-proclaimed queen of Willowdale society attracted women to herself as if she were warm shit and they were hungry flies.

Mrs. Somebody's sheer pastel-green blouse was tucked neatly into a perfectly pleated linen skirt. The waist-high serving counter hid her hemline, but Edith was certain it would be too short. Her pointy breasts jutted out like two enormous mountain peaks calling out to be climbed. Only a whore would purposely draw attention to a place meant for children to suckle, and Edith was suddenly embarrassed. She looked away.

"Mrs. Scott?"

Edith's palm covered her throat as she turned toward the caller.

Dear God. Mrs. Somebody had exited the kitchen and was making a beeline for her. Hiding was impossible. She tugged the netting farther down, her vision slicing the woman's face into hundreds of miniature diamonds, an intriguing effect she liked.

"I'm looking for the pastor," Edith said when the woman was close. With the spotlight on her, she had to feign cordiality.

"I'm happy to see you, Mrs. Scott," Mrs. Somebody gushed. "Pastor Dressler isn't here today, but I've spoken with him, and he thought you might show up today. There's plenty to do—mostly upstairs in the sanctuary and offices, I mean. He asked that I help get you started."

Peering at the woman through her netting, Edith mentally ticked through delicious possibilities. She could gouge her eyes out or wallop her haughty puss with her pocketbook. More reasonably, though, she should simply nod and go along so that she could work and get paid.

Before she could respond, someone in the kitchen called out, "Annette? We need your help over here!"

Mrs. Somebody waved an arm behind her back as if dismissing the plea, still beaming at Edith with the sweetest of smiles. "Dusting and scouring today? You know where the supplies are, right?" She snapped her fingers as if she had just recalled something important. "Oh, and the pastor said I should pay you when you're done. Is that okay?"

Edith let her eyes skim the woman's flawless complexion. If only she could spit into that perfectly made-up face and watch Mrs. Somebody's horrified reaction as she wiped Edith's phlegm from her cheeks. That was a pleasant thought that made her smile. Edith nodded, turned, and headed for the stairwell.

"Oh! Can you wait a second? I wanted to talk to you about something else."

Edith glanced over her shoulder, wondering what more the woman could possibly want. She recognized the look, that polite, patronizing expression wealthy people wore when they were pretending poor people were their equals. She stiffened.

"You know how my Freddie and your Audrey are friends?" Mrs. Somebody spoke in a breathy voice, a veritable Lauren Bacall.

Edith gawked at her without responding. That Audrey was friends with Mrs. Somebody's kid was news to her. The boy was a year behind Audrey in school, and over the years, she'd occasionally seen him in town with his mother. He was certainly nothing to brag about in the looks department, which Edith found highly humorous.

"She's a sweet girl, your Audrey," Mrs. Somebody continued. "She's been coming home with Freddie quite often after school. He's fond of her, always saying how smart she is. I think so too." She smiled.

Complimenting Audrey had to be the woman's good deed for the day. Then her words soaked in. *Audrey is going to that woman's home after school and lying about it.* Edith narrowed her eyes to quivering cracks.

"I wanted to, you know, talk to you and Mr. Scott about her. I think she's got great potential, and, well, I was wondering if I might assist in her social lessons?"

The loud jabbering nearby in the kitchen subsided.

"Mrs. Scott?" The woman's blue eyes twinkled with anticipation.

Edith fumbled with the latch of her pocketbook, pretending she needed something from inside, but her hands were trembling.

The two of them stared at each other while the large room's din steadily dwindled into hushed silence. The do-gooders seemed to sense an imminent dustup.

When Mrs. Somebody parted her lips to respond, Edith pointed a finger at her and hissed, "We don't need you or your pity. Who do you think you are, interfering with my girl?"

A hurt look crossed Mrs. Somebody's face but swiftly changed to one of confusion. She batted her eyes and stepped back.

"And another thing. That boy o' yours, Freddie? Keep him away from my girl. I won't allow any more consortin' between those two."

"But I only wanted to—"

"Take over raisin' my child? Keep that ugly kid of yours away. Or else." Edith punched the air with her last two words, a boxer fit for more rounds.

Around her, ladies gasped in unison.

Their do-gooder queen was out of her fucking mind if she thought Edith would jump at the chance for her to teach Audrey manners and etiquette. *How can she not know I hate her guts?*

Just then, a slim woman with short brown hair and small-rimmed glasses veered over to Mrs. Somebody and touched her elbow. Edith blanched, recognizing the woman as Mrs. Howard DeDecker.

"I'll be back after a while to get paid," Edith said, putting an end to the scene. She pivoted and headed for the stairwell, outraged that her first opportunity to talk with Mrs. DeDecker had been spoiled.

Edith pulled herself up step by step, glad that she'd rightfully put Mrs. Somebody in her place. Any woman of breeding would reject such an offer, an insult to Edith's abilities to groom her own daughter.

By the time Edith reached the main sanctuary level, she was hopping mad and ready to throttle Audrey for lying to her. The girl's bullshit writing was one thing, but fraternizing with that Freddie boy was another, something Edith would never, ever tolerate.

What a damn mess Audrey had made of everything.

CHAPTER 18

Harry

Harry ambled off the school bus in front of Lucky's and trudged up the hill, swinging his tin lunch bucket and banging it against his leg. His tummy growled, a reminder of the chintzy cheese sandwich on stale bread and the small red apple Mama had packed him.

Even though he didn't like school all that much, Harry didn't necessarily like being home either. Since that was Friday, he had two whole days of stretched-out boredom ahead. Recently, he'd taken to spending most of his time in the woods. Audrey had done the same when she was younger, before Mama had forbidden it. Mama didn't pay him much mind recently, and even though the rule was still in place, she hadn't said a word, what with Daddy being sick and her constantly fretting about Audrey.

Being alone wasn't so bad—much better than listening to his folks argue, although that had simmered down. Daddy seemed too weak to take Mama on, so he mostly heard catfights between his sister and Mama. Audrey always backed down, making Harry wonder why she even bothered.

Audrey didn't give him the time of day anymore either, and he missed her. But Harry didn't blame his sister. She was a real teenager, and he was just a kid who liked to play in a fort and run around barefoot, catching bugs or being a superhero. Besides, for his whole life, Mama had favored him over Audrey, and his sister probably resented him for it.

When the heel of his left shoe began to flap, Harry stopped and looked down where the rubber had separated. He groaned. As it was, his big toe was busting through the remaining thin threads on his other shoe, so they were racing to see which one fell apart first. Those shoes might make it through the end of the school year but not a minute longer. In another month, summer recess would start, and he could go barefoot all the time. By the time Labor Day rolled around, he would hopefully fit into the larger charity ones Mama had stored in his closet.

Drawing closer to home, Harry heard loud voices. He bowed his head and shook it slightly, knowing right away who was making all the fuss. Bits of gravel crunched under his shoes, and he thought it funny to have a driveway when they'd never owned a car. He flapped up to his house then paused, leery of going inside.

Instead, Harry crept to the parlor window, set his books on the ground, then knelt just under the ledge to listen to their argument.

"What did you call me?"

Audrey's voice was too loud. Shouting at Mama wasn't smart.

"You think because I'm friends with Freddie Littleton that we're doing something... something immoral?"

Harry regarded his peeping toe. He'd never heard of a Freddie and wasn't certain what "immoral" meant.

"You staying late for homework? You're a damn liar, Audrey Mae."

"You make me lie about Freddie, and—"

"And what? Don't blame your sins on me. This crap with that Freddie stops now. It's Johnny that you—"

"What? What did you say? Johnny who?" A long pause was followed by "Johnny DeDecker?"

The howl that followed was so haunting that Harry winced. He wasn't sure if his sister was laughing or if Mother had belted her.

"Is that him? When I asked you before, you refused to tell me." Audrey's voice was low and even. "The boy you insist I marry is Johnny DeDecker?"

Curiosity boosted Harry onto his tiptoes to peek. Mama did not cotton to snooping unless she was the one doing it. He could see her planted next to her chair with a puckered expression that resembled a wrinkled old tomato. Audrey, who had her back to him, stood closer to the window next to Daddy's rocker, her back rigid.

"You agreed. Or have you forgotten? It's settled. I've—"

"You've what? Gone off your rocker? Seriously, Mother. I should have figured it would be the richest kid in the whole county."

"He's a good-lookin' boy. Rich and handsome. What's your problem?"

Harry had never understood what Mama's plan was for Audrey, but he'd overheard enough to understand that wild horses could not force his sister to marry someone.

"No, what's *your* problem? You've always hated Mrs. Littleton. Why, Mother? A stupid grudge? Or could it be you hate her even more now for liking me?"

Harry held his breath.

"She's been more of a mother to me than you've ever been. Ever will be."

Harry dropped to his knees. Surely, Daddy could hear their argument, not that he'd ever been one to interfere. Even if he wanted to, his father could barely crawl out of bed lately. Harry had lost track of how long Daddy had been laid up, but it seemed like weeks.

The room was too quiet, and when he stretched up and looked again, Mama's eyes were so huge they reminded Harry of a close-up picture of a fly he'd seen in a science book.

"Mighty big talker you are," Mother said.

He gulped, half expecting the two of them to begin circling each other like rabid wolves. He wanted to look away but couldn't.

To Harry's surprise, his sister hadn't flinched, hadn't backed up one inch. She was standing ramrod straight. After what seemed like an eternity, Mother turned on her heels, shooting a look at Audrey so menacing that the hair on his neck itched and stood straight out.

After Mother was gone, Audrey fell heavily into their daddy's rocking chair, and a loud sigh whooshed out of her. Harry squatted down as quickly as he could and held his breath.

"Harry?"

At the sound of his name, Harry froze then slid up the wall and sought his sister's eyes. Audrey's gaze was unfocused, as if she were looking through him rather than at him.

"Audrey?" Harry bit his lower lip.

Wordlessly, she covered Harry's hand with hers and held his fingers captive on the sill. He looked at her hand, at the chipped paint and dead flies scattered around their grasp, then up to his sister's face.

"Mother has never hurt you, right?" Her voice had an insistent quality, strangely urgent.

He shook his head no. That was true enough, but he'd become more and more spooked by Mama's behavior, fearful that one day, she would. Sometimes Mama's eyes seemed wild, which frightened him.

"Okay." Audrey looked preoccupied, as though she'd drifted away. She slid the tip of her tongue across her lower lip before seeking his eyes again. "In case you haven't noticed, things between me and Mother are getting bad—real bad."

As Audrey squeezed his hand, her eyes darted to the kitchen doorway. Harry understood because he, too, was concerned Mama might reappear.

"If you get between us, she might hurt you. Do you understand me?"

"I do. But she wouldn't." Harry's toes were cramping, and he felt silly that his sister was holding his hand. He wanted their impromptu talk over with.

"Don't ever let her know you overheard a thing we said today."

He nodded again, understanding that advice much more.

"I've been thinking," she said then.

He saw a change. A familiar twinkle had popped into her eyes.

"I know you have a secret place in the woods. I do too."

She winked at him, and he smiled back, not denying it. This was the Audrey he knew well.

"Don't tell Mother about your fort, no matter what she says or how nice she acts," she said, the words rushing out. "She doesn't know the woods like we do. If you ever need to, go there and hide. You'll be safe."

Safe? The tinny sound of alarm bells rang in his ears. Audrey was right. He could go to his fort for a while to let Mama cool off if something bad happened.

"Okay, I will," he said, hoping to reassure her.

When she released his hand, Audrey's smile washed away, and she looked into the distance, no longer interested in him or his presence. Even though she was the prettiest girl he knew, Harry was struck that her features had hardened into something darker, sullen, and uninviting.

Harry dropped down and fetched his schoolbooks, more worried than ever about what he'd witnessed. His sister had been brave, and Mama had surprisingly walked away from a fight. He'd never seen either before. It was too weird to even comprehend. He was certain of one thing, though. His sister and mama were headed for a massive confrontation, the kind of battle that might lead to an all-out war.

Whether or not Harry understood the reason did not matter.

He only knew that one day, maybe soon, he'd be forced to choose a side.

Edith

The argument with Audrey was over, but Edith was steamed up like a boiling pot, nervous energy propelling her like never before. She dusted furniture, chipped the icebox, and swept the floor until she worked up streams of sweat that rolled down her neck. Of course, her house still looked like hillbillies lived there, but the effort served to cool her temper.

After that, Edith began pressing hamburger into a meat loaf. When the butcher had offered her several pounds of close-to-expired hamburger, she was indignant at first but took it anyway. Right then, her stomach was growling with an appreciation she would never express to the butcher. She hated pity even when it fed her family.

After she patted the meat loaf into a pan and sliced up some potatoes, Edith slammed the oven door shut with her hip and set the timer. With a *whump*, she plopped into her chair in the parlor. Red was in bed, and she would have to fight to make him eat—yet another battle.

Briefly, Edith wondered where Harry was, then she pressed her back firmly against the chair, not really caring that much. As for Audrey, she'd confined herself to her bedroom, obviously to stay out of Edith's way. Edith closed her eyes. She needed to do something so bold that her daughter would be shocked into permanent submission.

Audrey refused to answer her call for supper, and Red was sound asleep, so only Harry joined Edith at the table to eat. He was quiet, which was fine by her. None of his incessant chitter-chatter would interrupt her thinking. Normally, Harry gobbled up anything in front of him, but he picked at his food, overly focused on shuffling bites of meat loaf around his plate.

Cleaning their two plates at the sink, Edith grumbled to herself, dreading the coming encounter with Red where she would have to listen to him whine about his head, his stomach—soon, his pinkie toe would be hurting too. Taking care of him was becoming a full-time job.

Once he'd finished eating, Harry visited the outhouse and went to bed early. Edith pulled on her nightgown, grabbed her pillow and sheets, and made up the couch, her new place to sleep as of three nights before. Red had shat himself and their bed. Edith had to clean it up, gagging and cussing at him the whole time while he simply lay there, looking green and pale but not apologizing.

As Edith tucked a sheet under the sofa cushions, a flush of optimism surged through her. A handsome boy like Johnny would snag her daughter's affections easily. And Audrey was prettier than any other girl at the high school, which meant Johnny would notice her, would want to woo her. An order to do so was just added incentive.

She had to see Howard again and take care of all this business once and for all.

Edith padded toward Red's rocker, sat down, and turned on the lamp. She stuck her head out the window to inhale the refreshing night air then lengthened her aching neck, cracking it. Something shimmered below her window, just under the ledge. Curious, she scanned the rocks and zeroed in on the spot. Something small—not a coin, though.

A flash of red, Harry's Superman whistle.

He would be frantic that it was missing.

Edith poked the soft tissue of her cheek with her tongue, unable to think of a reason Harry would play under the window. Because her eyelids were growing heavy, she decided to let the mystery go until later. She could fetch the whistle the next day.

Edith crawled between the sheets she'd placed on the couch and yawned.

Tomorrow will be a big day.

CHAPTER 19

Edith

The next morning, Edith was dressing for the day while her husband slept. She paused to study Red's face—the ashen skin color and sunken complexion—and her eyes rolled over his body, lying on his side under a blanket, bones poking out like sharp tent poles.

She was about to leave when he groaned.

"Please get a doctor," he said, croaking like a toad. "Please, Edith."

"Let me fetch you some water." Edith traipsed into the kitchen and returned with a full glass. Red downed it all in thirsty gulps then caught her sleeve with outstretched fingers.

"I'm not gettin' better. I need a doc."

She looked into his dull, imploring eyes and at the mop of greasy hair matted down by sweat. Edith nodded her agreement and walked out of the room, ignoring his pitiful outstretched hand.

After securing her pocketbook under her arm, she went out the back door and locked it behind her. Edith momentarily wondered why she even bothered when nothing of value was inside.

Mr. Ritter, the fool, was already tending to his pigeons, the top half of his lanky body tucked inside the coop to scoop out feathers, seed, and bird shit.

Edith rolled her eyes, annoyed by the sight of the filthy pooping machines and the person tending them. Mr. Ritter considered the feathered beasts his pets and the hobby a noble one. Every so often, he would set a few pigeons free then pace around the yard, eagerly awaiting their return for hours on end, just to ooh and ahh when they soared and circled before setting down.

When she was about ten, Mr. Ritter had told her that homing pigeons were a breed of doves that could carry messages for long distances and that they'd been used as couriers during wartime. He found them fascinating and had tried to convey his passion to Edith, but even as a child, she'd found it all mystifying.

Turning away, she bounded down the steps. Mr. Ritter would see her, of course, but she had no stomach to exchange pleasantries. Once upon a time, she'd liked the old coot, but after Mrs. Ritter died, he sealed Edith's disdain by appointing himself the official nosy neighbor.

She scurried down the driveway and followed the worn path to town. Her destination, Mrs. Somebody's house, was an easy three-mile trek on a breezy morning under a cloudless sky. The walk would be pleasant enough except for the billowing aroma of flowers, which made Edith's nose itch. Mother Nature was like a tiresome old lady who doused herself with too much perfume.

As she strolled, Edith considered the conversation she intended to have with Freddie. The Littleton family would be following their regular Saturday routine. Mr. Somebody would be bossing employees around at his bank, and Mrs. Somebody would be shopping for groceries or meeting with friends in downtown stores to gossip or buy pretty things.

If the pattern was normal, Freddie, an only child, would be home alone.

Once she turned onto Victorian Row, Edith walked along the manicured street as though she belonged there, head high, slowing when she saw a cheerful two-story yellow framed house, the brightest spot on an already vibrant block of colorful exteriors, latticework, and iron railings.

She marched up the sidewalk between rows of pink and yellow tulips and stopped in front of a door painted forest green. After adjusting her blouse, Edith lifted the brass knocker—a cockamamie lion's head—and tapped it several times. She shifted her weight from leg to leg, impatient, then rapped much harder.

Though Edith had seen Freddie only a few times—and even then, the sightings had been from a distance—she recognized him as soon as the door slid open. When he saw her, his eyes doubled in size, and his mouth dropped open. Reddish-brown freckles liberally speckled Freddie's face, and his hair was orange like a clown's wig. Too bad for him, the boy shared none of his father's handsome features.

"Mrs. Scott?" It took several seconds for him to find his tongue. "Uh, I'm sorry, but my parents aren't home right now."

Excellent. That was exactly what Edith wanted to hear. If they'd been home, she would've made up a question about church donations, bemoaning the fact that she didn't have a telephone and stating some urgent request.

"You're Freddie," she said matter-of-factly. "That's fine. I'm here to see you."

The boy frowned and reached under his pajama top to scratch his stomach. He yawned.

"Young man, it's not polite to keep someone standing outside on your doorstep. Where are your manners?"

Obediently, Freddie moved aside, and Edith pushed by him into a large, open foyer, greeted by the aroma of freshly baked bread. She glanced into the parlor on her left and gaped at the floor-to-ceiling brick fireplace that commanded the majority of the wall. Its ornately carved mantel held a dozen framed photos, each featuring family members beaming with broad white smiles. She scanned the glossy pictures depicting the Littletons at Christmastime and Easter. Several depicted the happy couple clinking glasses during celebrations, and one showed a proud Freddie dangling a large bass fish.

The room was immaculate, tastefully decorated with two facing couches, one beige and the other a velvety chestnut brown, and several wing chairs, all with matching pillows. A creamy oval rug accented by swirls of blue, green, and lavender stretched across the floor, mimicking a colorful garden. The effect was feminine and tasteful, like a picture Edith had seen on the cover of a magazine. She eyeballed a shiny grand piano holding court by the front windows, draped with blue curtains that pooled onto the wood floor.

She pirouetted to scrutinize the dining room, her eyes landing on a walnut table with high-back, blue-fabric-covered chairs that dominated the room. A tall hutch, bursting with glinting glassware, stood against the wall behind the table.

Edith turned her gaze to Freddie, who'd been watching her with sleepy eyes.

"We need to talk. I'm here about Audrey," she said.

As she spoke, Freddie wrapped his arms around his shoulders like a shy child, and Edith understood her advantage. The silly boy would be as malleable as clay, Silly Putty in her hands. She stepped up to him.

"Listen. You stay away from Audrey. At school. At home. Anywhere. If you don't, I'll get the sheriff involved," she said. "It don't matter who your daddy is."

He stared at her cockeyed.

"I don't want you around her, see? Parents got a right to protect their children, and that's what I'm doin'. I'm giving you fair warning."

Freddie dropped his arms to his sides and curled his lips into a smirk. "You're giving me a warning?" he asked, scoffing. "That's rich."

Edith's eyelids fluttered.

"No disrespect intended, ma'am, but you got it all wrong. Audrey and I are just friends." Freddie leaned toward her. "Let me repeat that. Friends. We like the same things, but we're not dating or any-thing. It's not like that, if that's what you're worried about."

Just friends? "My God, you're a liar, just like your old man. I don't believe you for a second."

Freddie met her cold stare, and a smile began to twitch on his lips. He seemed more interested in Edith than he had been on her arrival and, now, totally at ease. He hadn't backed away from her or cringed at her insult.

"Your parents may let you run around wild, but I run a respectful home. I forbid her to come here or be with you anywhere." She paused. "I can have you arrested."

Freddie's smile waned, and a wave of uncertainty washed over his face. She'd gotten through to him.

When he responded, his voice was full of disdain. "A respectful home? Pardon me again, ma'am, but I don't think so. And you can't tell me to stop being Audrey's friend. It's a free country." Freddie's voice softened. "It's like this. Audrey's got nobody but me. You act like you care about her, but I don't think you do."

Edith bristled at his impertinence. "That girl lies. She—"

He put up a hand to hush her. "Sh-she's sweet, you know? Used to be afraid to speak her mind, but she's getting much better. Did you know she has dreams, can make—"

"Who do you think you are?" Edith interrupted, spittle flying from her lips. "You Littletons. Always thinking you know better than everyone else. You'll stay away from her because I'm telling you to."

Freddie shrugged.

"Those are words I'm pretty sure work on Audrey," he said. "But not me. I can be friends with whomever I want. And, just to be clear, my folks don't let me run around wild. I'm not like that." Freddie's eyes shone. "Sorry if you think I'm brash, Mrs. Scott."

Edith couldn't believe her ears. She leaned her head far back, stretched out her neck like an ostrich, and closed her eyes. She struggled to catch her breath until an idea came to her, so fine and perfect it was like the sharply cut crystal in Mrs. Somebody's elaborate hutch.

Edith lowered her head and leered at the boy, who thought he was so fucking smart.

"You think you can do whatever you want?" She ran her tongue over her lips, a lion salivating over fresh prey. "So, how 'bout this? You go right ahead. Keep seeing my Audrey. Yes, you do that, and here's what will happen. I'll take it out on her in ways you can't even imagine."

Freddie's eyebrows shot up.

"You won't be able to stop me either. You got no say-so. I'm her mother. Nobody's business what I do. Is that what you want, to see her get punished?"

Edith watched Freddie recoil like she'd slapped his silly pale face. He appeared dumbfounded. Every freckle on his nose had condensed into one big red blob.

"You would do that?" he asked.

She sniffed. He must have cared about Audrey to be so stricken, which meant Edith had been right about the two of them. Freddie had changed into a feckless mouth breather with slumped shoulders, all his former bluster gone. Satisfaction was a delicious, hearty meal.

"I see we have a deal," she said. The scent of victory was better than the lingering aroma of Mrs. Somebody's bread.

Edith's eye caught movement behind her. She pivoted in time to see a swinging door, which likely led from the dining room into the kitchen, swaying as it settled back into place.

Freddie had said they were alone, but Edith just caught a glimpse of color through the opening. Somebody was behind the door. She'd seen olive skin, a flash of dark hair, and thin burgundy stripes from what was surely a man's tie.

She shook her head, muttered, "Coward," under her breath, then turned back to Freddie, who looked as though she'd just killed his dog. "I expect you will see to this, Wallace," she said loudly, tossing out the words like scraps. "Or you know I will."

With a victorious air, she made her way to the door. "Ta-ta, now."

After leaving Freddie, Edith steered her way to First Baptist to meet with Pastor Dressler as he was her only means of contacting a doctor. Edith had never had a physician to the house before because the ability to pay had always been a problem. But Audrey and Harry had been pestering her for some time to contact someone, and Red wouldn't shut up about it.

Edith entered through wide double doors and strolled onto the red carpeting of the lobby, called the narthex. She turned and tromped down a well-lit hallway, passing several small offices cramped by desks and gray filing cabinets. Upon reaching the last one on the left side, which featured a wooden plaque that read Pastor, she knocked.

Five minutes later, Edith emerged with Pastor Dressler's assurance that Dr. Greenhagen would visit the very next day to examine Red. To relieve her worries, he'd told her not to give a second thought about the doctor's fee, saying the church would cover the expense. The offer had been somewhat of a relief even though Edith had never intended to pay him anyway.

Edith clopped down the hall and out the door, tilting her face upward when she emerged into the sunshine. She had one more important thing to do before returning home, then her errands for the day would be complete.

The First Baptist steeple was several blocks behind her when Edith turned onto Maple Street, headed toward the heart of downtown Willowdale. For years, she'd stood in line for handouts of government-issued blocks of cheese. Disgusting and tasteless though it was, the cheese was free and had always been a staple in their house, like potatoes or dried beans. As Edith neared the block where the familiar green truck always parked, she spied a handful of people already milling around. Most folks needing the handout were colored, but some whites like her were just as hard up—some more embarrassed than others about being poor—and none willingly missed the monthly giveaway.

She merged into a small group of whites gathered around a red fire hydrant, their faces downcast to avoid looking at each other. They seemed to belong together, as though everyone had dressed for a family portrait in the same drab clothing that matched their dour faces.

While waiting, Edith strained her neck to scan the intersection, hopeful that a certain man would be along soon to join the lineup for cheese. If he didn't show, her plan would be delayed or possibly ruined. Her pulse quickened, and her mouth went dry as she searched for him. When the truck roared up and parked, the throng formed a quiet line, but Edith held back from joining it, aware she could slip ahead of the coloreds at any time. They were always relegated to the back of the queue, regardless of what time they'd arrived. That was an unspoken rule nobody had ever challenged.

Given how unusually tall Ed Trent was, he would be easy to spot. Though Edith rarely gave anyone the time of day, she liked him. Ed was a friendly sort who'd worked in the coal mine with Red in their earliest days. Having stood with her in the cheese line many, many times, he spoke kindly to her. She'd learned that Mr. Trent—Edith called him Ed—was compassionate about Red's mental condition and understood how his family suffered because of it. He was polite to her, too, always tipping the brim of his cowboy hat like a gentleman whenever he bade her goodbye.

At last, Edith spotted him crossing the cobblestone street, clad in a black cowboy hat and high black boots, a six-and-a-half-foot figure outfitted in navy-blue striped overalls cut so wide that Ed looked like a gliding rectangle. With his long stride, he reached Edith in no time, and together they edged ahead of the Shantytown coloreds, who wordlessly stepped aside. She snorted after seeing several of them roll their eyes as though they were being put out.

After exchanging pleasantries, Edith tapped Ed's arm. She looked up into his face and offered him a genuine smile.

"Ed, we've known each other quite a while," she said. "And you know it's not like me to go about askin' anyone for help." She lowered her eyes for a moment then found his again. "But I find myself in a bit of a pickle, and well, I recall hearin' that you're in one too."

Ed leaned down, and his tanned face wrinkled with a look of concern. He puckered his lips until they practically disappeared behind his handlebar mustache.

"I'm thinking we can help each other," Edith said.

Ed's head bobbled in agreement, and his eyes lit up with curiosity.

Edith considered where to begin, knowing that baiting her hook carefully was critical. Once Ed swallowed her tale hook, line, and sinker, Edith would easily reel him in.

She took a deep breath and began.

CHAPTER 20

Audrey

Late on a hot Sunday afternoon, Dr. Greenhagen arrived, a roundish man with dark-brown hair that stuck out below his fedora hat. He was grasping a black medical bag. After a hushed conference with Mother in the hallway, he strode into the bedroom to see Daddy, with Mother tagging along at his heels.

Audrey stopped at the threshold, deterred by the sickly smell that seeped into the hallway, but she wanted to be close to hear what Dr. Greenhagen said. Harry leaned on her as he peered over her shoulder, his heart thumping in rapid beats against her back.

When Daddy lifted a weary arm to shake the doctor's hand, Audrey saw the bleakness, the worry in his upturned eyes, how sallow they'd become. The contrast between him and the doctor, who she figured was about the same age, was stark, like the difference between a burgeoning leafy tree and one that was barren and withering away.

Her eyes glanced back to Daddy and flitted over his gaunt skin and the graying strands of hair sticking out every which way from his head. A stubbly beard grizzled his face. Audrey couldn't recall the last time he'd bathed. Even with his body under a blanket, she knew he'd gotten thin, eating only what Mother forced into him until he would adamantly refuse any more. Daddy had become a shadowy remnant of his former self.

Dr. Greenhagen placed his hat on the bed, and right away, her stony-faced mother snatched it and placed it on the dresser, aggravated because strangers' hats put on beds brought bad luck. He shot a puzzled look at her mother then turned to Daddy and opened his medical bag, rummaging around inside. He located a pair of gold eyeglasses and folded them over his ears.

Audrey couldn't help but watch his every move, the way his long fingers carefully unpacked the bag. Next, out came a square white cloth followed by strange-looking instruments that he nestled upon it.

"How long have you been ill, Mr. Scott?" The doctor's eyes roamed Daddy's face like he was searching for clues. He placed his fingertips on his patient's throat.

"Couple of months is all, Doc," Mother answered. "Back in early March, I s'pose." She walked to the opposite side of the bed and folded her arms across her bosom.

While the doctor examined Daddy, Audrey scanned the bedroom. Discarded clothes were strewn across the floor, and half-empty water glasses lined the dresser top. At least Mother had tried to ease Daddy's queasiness, indicated by several empty bottles previously filled with gooey dark Coca-Cola syrup. But when Audrey's eyes landed on the chamber pot under the window, nearly overflowing with Daddy's urine, she winced. Her mother couldn't even be bothered to tidy up the room.

Only a week before, when Audrey begged Mother to get a doctor for her father, she'd been soundly rebuffed.

"It's not my fault he's sick," Mother said, waving her away.

It wasn't Daddy's fault either, Audrey reasoned silently. His deep cough and constant nausea were so upsetting that, days later, she insisted on fetching a doctor herself, but Mother had only lost her temper and slammed a cooking pot against the counter.

Audrey leaned back against her brother's chest for support. Praying might help Daddy get well, but Audrey had no idea how a person did that or what words one would use. She considered whether people prayed aloud or just in their heads, if one way was better than the other. Freddie had been adamant that God was real. He regularly attended the church where Mother sometimes worked. She trusted him more than her own mother, who'd told her God was a fantasy like Santa Claus.

"Would you children—and Mrs. Scott—please excuse me while I conduct a more thorough examination?" Dr. Greenhagen's tone was rich with authority, and although his words were polite, Audrey sensed he wasn't actually asking.

"I'm staying, if you don't mind. Me and Red, we got no—" her mother began.

"Sorry, madam. I'm sure Clarence here will be more comfortable with a private exam, and I know I would." He removed his specs and employed his tie to clean his lenses.

Mother made a face the doctor didn't see, but Audrey recognized the emotion behind it. She was pissed off but powerless to ignore the doctor's feigned request. It would've been amusing if Audrey weren't so worried.

After glaring at the doctor, who paid her no mind, Mother shot an indignant look at her husband, but Daddy was intently studying his blanket. With a frustrated scowl, she hurried from the room in a huff, shoving Audrey and Harry aside before stomping into the kitchen. They wandered into the parlor.

To pass the time, Audrey suggested she and Harry play a game called I Spy with My Little Eye, where they took turns guessing a visible object that the other had selected, giving only its color as a clue. But Audrey's stomach was doing flip-flops. The possibility of living with Mother as the only parent was too much to bear. She pushed the thought away, tickling Harry until he begged her to stop, the sound of his squeals out of place at that moment. After thirty minutes, the bedroom door creaked open, and Harry and Audrey exchanged nervous looks.

"Mrs. Scott?" Dr. Greenhagen called out.

Mother flew past the parlor doorway.

"Stay put," Audrey whispered to Harry, who was sitting cross-legged on the floor by Daddy's rocker. Clenching her toes, she clambered onto the couch and balanced herself on the cushions, then she flattened an ear to the wall to listen through it.

Their voices were faint but distinguishable. When Audrey heard the doctor say, "It may be cancer," her heart skipped out of rhythm and began to beat wildly. She collapsed against the wall with a low thud, still listening. Mother was mumbling something about Daddy's work in the mines, that he was probably sick from all that poisonous gas or dust. Then Dr. Greenhagen's voice was clearer, saying something about tests he could run.

After a long pause, Mother mumbled about having no money for such things.

"Without tests, there's no way to be certain what's going on," the doctor said much more loudly. "There's nothing else I can do from here."

Audrey's knees buckled. She dropped in a heap on the couch and leveled anxious eyes on Harry, alerting him something was very wrong. His already pale face turned ghostly white. Then she leaped to her feet and barreled into the hallway, where she stretched her arms wide to bar the front door.

"You have to make him better. You have to," Audrey implored. "I heard you. You can do tests."

The doctor put a finger to his lips as he reached back to click Daddy's bedroom door closed.

Harry crept up to Audrey, his eyes glued to the physician. "What's wrong? Audrey, why are you crying? Is Daddy going to be okay?"

Standing behind Dr. Greenhagen, Mother was glowering, her lower lip jutted out like a pouting child's. She could make all the faces she wanted. Audrey didn't care, nor would she heed any of her mother's warning looks. She fixated on Dr. Greenhagen, whose own earnest face had softened, his kind eyes gliding between her and Harry. Hat in hand, the doctor set his physician's bag on the floor.

"I know you're frightened," he said. "I'm sure your mother will explain about your father's illness, but…" Dr. Greenhagen coughed once. "It's possible he could get better. That's not a promise, mind you, but a possibility. I can't be sure what's ailing him, and, well, finding that out would be quite costly, I'm afraid."

Audrey nodded to show she understood, then she draped an arm around Harry's shoulders. They were poor. No tests would be done. But Daddy might recover. The doctor had said so, and she would choose to believe that was true. Freddie always insisted that anything was possible.

Pulling Harry closer, Audrey asked, "What can we do?"

After glancing over his shoulder at Mother, Dr. Greenhagen settled his hat atop his head and lifted his bag. He came to Audrey and cupped her chin. Touched by his display of compassion, Audrey's cheeks flushed pink. He turned to Harry and playfully tapped the end of her brother's nose before clasping the boy's shoulder and squeezing it.

"Your father has led a rough life, a tough one. It's difficult work in those mines," he said, speaking slowly. "And you know smoking, sniffing tobacco, drinking too much alcohol… Well, all those things do damage to a body. That kind of living catches up with folks."

She and Harry began to weep.

"But wait, now." The doctor held a palm turned out toward them. "Let's not give up on him yet. You both can help by making him comfortable. Assist your mother with his diet. Soft foods only, like soup, mashed-up fruits or potatoes. Small amounts, though. And lots of water."

"Thank you. We'll do our best, Doctor." Audrey looked at him with gratitude.

"If his fever spikes, get to Pastor Dressler, and he'll call me. I'll come right over. I promise." He made an about-face. "Is this agreeable with you, Mrs. Scott?"

She motioned for her children to leave the hallway. Harry sprinted up the stairs, but Audrey dallied, roaming into the parlor and lingering near the doorway to eavesdrop. Dr. Greenhagen's voice had become subdued. Absent was the tenderness he'd shown her and Harry. His voice was monotone as he spouted orders for Mother to follow, which she would not like at all—things like "Keep his room clean" and "Only serve fresh, soft foods." They needed to buy more cola syrup for his nausea. And if Daddy started to experience a lot of pain, they were to let the doctor know, and he would prescribe codeine drops or methadone, but they would have to work out a payment arrangement.

Audrey eased into Daddy's rocker, pressing her hands against her upset stomach.

She should've helped before, done more, but she would make it up to Daddy. She could cook his meals from then on, attend to his needs whenever she wasn't in school, do whatever he wanted or needed. Nothing would be too great or too minor. If he was in pain, she would figure out how to pay for medications if Mother would not. If Daddy was going to get better, she needed to take charge and fight with her mother tooth and nail if that was what it took.

After all, they were already engaged in a war, albeit a mostly silent one. But this particular battle could mean life or death.

Edith

After saying a curt goodbye to Dr. Greenhagen and refusing to let the words "thank you" fall from her mouth, Edith slunk onto the back porch and bent over the railing. She spurned the frightened looks on her children's faces, accusing ones, to her mind, feeling no empathy whatsoever.

That doctor had dared to imply that Red's condition was all her fault.

Edith stared at Mr. Ritter's overgrown yard, scowling. Dr. Greenhagen could take that little black bag of his and shove it up his ass.

Dr. Greenhagen had said to let him know if Red's fever came back or if his condition worsened, but she could never permit a second visit. The first one might've been free, but a return trip would surely cost money they didn't have.

Her eyes rolled to Mr. Ritter's pigeon coop, and Edith straightened. She'd never loved someone or something as much as Mr. Ritter loved those damn birds. If she had, it wouldn't matter anyway. That's what always happened to love. Fleeting and undependable, love never lasted, just like her marriage to Red.

Edith determined she wouldn't waste any money on doctors for Red. The money was hers, after all. No doctor, especially one who looked down his nose at her like that Dr. Greenhagen, was setting foot inside her house again.

CHAPTER 21

Audrey

After the doctor left, Audrey got busy in her father's room, removing dirty dishes, sweeping, and dusting, even emptying his chamber pot. She scrubbed every piece of dirty clothing against the washboard and hung them to dry on the clothesline. Lastly, she wiped down his bedroom furniture with disinfectant until the only smelly thing in the room was Daddy. Harry helped in his own way by reading to their father while she bustled around them.

Daddy smiled at her weakly, while Mother kept her distance. Audrey felt invigorated.

At dinnertime, she and Harry took turns spoon-feeding her father mashed apples and cooked carrots and got him to drink as much water as he could hold. After he emptied his bladder, Audrey tossed the pee from the chamber pot into the backyard and pledged to make that her regular morning and evening chore.

When evening fell, she curled up on the floor next to her father's bed and read a few chapters out loud from a Nancy Drew book. When he whispered to Audrey that he loved her, she blinked hard to stave off stinging tears and steeled herself. It wouldn't do for him to see her cry.

At last, when she heard his soft snores, Audrey pulled up the sheet and tucked it under Daddy's chin. Harry was already preparing for bedtime upstairs, and Mother was settling onto the couch to sleep there once again.

Talking with Mother was the very last thing Audrey wanted to do, so she crept up the stairs.

After she donned a nightgown and crawled into bed, Audrey lay unmoving and drained, listening.

Nighttime in the Scott household was lonely. They were each confined to their room, separated because of Daddy's illness, but frankly by their dubious—secretive, in her case—and disparate lives. Audrey blamed her mother for that.

She rolled onto her side, thankful she was nothing like that woman and never would be. If she had her way, Daddy would get well soon, back to his old self, and her mother would be the one who got sick and died. She sighed, knowing to think that way was wrong, yet she was comforted by the very idea.

Because then everything would be all right.

On Monday, Freddie didn't meet Audrey at her locker before school.

She was tardy for her first class, forced to slink into the room while thirty pairs of eyes gawked at her.

Walking in the hallway between her second and third classes, Audrey spotted him through the library's large windows, sitting at a round table with three students she recognized but didn't know. Relieved, she stopped and furiously waved to get his attention, but when he looked up and saw her, an expressionless Freddie returned a half-hearted flip of his hand.

The hallway cleared, but Audrey remained, staring through the glass, willing him to rush to her and explain himself. As long as Audrey had known Freddie, he'd never been rude or excluded her. She thought about their last conversation after school on Friday. Freddie had cheerfully said, "See ya later, Toots. Now, don't do nothing I wouldn't do," then blown her a goofy kiss.

Long after the bell rang, Audrey entered her biology class, enduring disapproving stares and a stern reprimand from the teacher, Mr. Newton. After that was her lunch period, and Audrey bustled down the hall toward the cafeteria. Freddie would have a good explanation for his behavior, and he would be saving her seat next to him at the gang's table. She pushed her way through a huddled queue of hungry students.

Audrey sat down next to Freddie's empty chair. Ten minutes into lunch, she gave up looking for him, feigning interest in her peanut butter and jelly sandwich between sips of milk. Enthusiastic bursts of laughter and mottled conversations punctuated the air around her, and once again, she felt entirely alone. She was invisible, just an insignificant girl who'd been allowed at that particular table only because of Freddie.

Where is he? Audrey swallowed, and the peanut butter stuck in her throat. His friends might have known what was going on and were keeping secrets from her. So far, aside from their first polite hellos, the gaggle had left her alone, and with each bite, Audrey's urge to flee grew stronger.

Then, out of nowhere, Johnny plopped down in Freddie's chair, clipping his tray on the table edge. A heaping plate of crinkled fries skittered down and almost toppled onto Audrey's lap. The others laughed at his clumsiness, one guy shouting, "Great catch, Johnny boy!"

Audrey looked away and reached for her carton of milk, sucking on the straw while she purposefully angled her body away from him. Other chairs were open at the table. At first, Audrey suspected Johnny was taking pity on her because Freddie wasn't around. Then again, Johnny wasn't that nice.

Maybe Audrey had found him appealing before, but Mother had ruined any feelings like that with her revelation. The fact that Mother thought Johnny was some sort of prince and Audrey was obligated to fulfill a prearranged marriage with him was bad enough. Letting herself be attracted to him was out of the question.

Besides, Johnny was something of a prick.

Next to her, he was shoving fries into his mouth, chomping noisily. Audrey could feel the heat from his body and pulled her elbows to her sides, shrinking. But she snuck a peek at him.

Not for the first time, she wondered what her mother had on Johnny's father to make him agree to such nonsense—if he'd even done so. Johnny couldn't know about the so-called arrangement, because he would've teased her about it and certainly would never have agreed to it either.

Audrey stuffed her trash into her brown lunch bag, and as she rolled the top down, something pressed down on her thigh and squeezed. She stilled, realizing Johnny's hand was caressing her leg. After a beat, Audrey slapped it away.

"Where's your boyfriend, sis?" he asked, teasing.

She glared back, furious that he'd touched her but liking how he had called Freddie her boyfriend. The acknowledgment was like salve soothing a painful wound. Audrey pushed back her chair and scuttled away.

Once outside her next class, Audrey plunked down on the floor to wait, settling her books in her lap. She fingered the fabric of her blouse, a prized gift from Mrs. Littleton.

She dared to look around, hoping that Freddie would come racing down the hall at any second, winded and apologetic, his pinkish lips spread in a foolish grin.

Where could he be? The question clapped through her mind with a rhythmic clickety-clack: *Where is Freddie? Where is Freddie?*—like the freight trains that rolled through town after midnight, their simple cadence able to lull her back to sleep. But this refrain was loud and overwhelming, drowning out her other thoughts.

For three more hours and as many classes, Audrey forced herself to focus on her teachers' lessons even though she wanted to hide in a closet, put away like a broom. When the last bell rang, she hurried to her locker, clinging to the hope that Freddie would come and explain himself. His freckles would squash together while he grinned, and he would say something like "It's really simple, Toots. Had a toothache then a dentist appointment. What's got your dander up?"

She waited.

No flustered Freddie plowed through the shifting maze of students escaping to buses or cars. Audrey scrutinized every red-haired person that walked by until the clatter had ceased, the last locker door had slammed, and the swarm had dispersed to a few meandering students.

Audrey rested her forehead against the cold metal locker before dialing the numbers on her lock to open the door and grab her diary. She walked quickly to catch her bus, head bowed and with watery eyes. She'd wanted so badly to tell Freddie about Daddy being ill, how a doctor had made a house call, and how she'd stood up to Mother yet again despite her fears. Freddie had been helping her to find courage, and he would've been proud of her.

Audrey was new to the whole friendship thing. She didn't know if one strange day meant anything at all.

Maybe there was only one thing to do—and that was simply to trust him.

CHAPTER 22

Audrey

Trust was for suckers.

Freddie dodged her every day for the rest of the week, nodding in her direction either to be polite or acknowledge her existence, but then he promptly looked away. Audrey figured he couldn't handle her scorching gazes.

On Wednesday, she ate lunch by herself at an unoccupied table, just like she had in pre-Freddie days, determined to learn if he would join his friends if she weren't there. He did indeed. By the time Friday arrived, Audrey was slouching from class to class in a daze.

In the months since he'd forced Cliff and Johnny to apologize to her, Freddie had regularly escorted her to classes, eaten lunch with her, and brought her home from school. Mrs. Littleton had always greeted Audrey like a favored, long-lost child, cheering with delight whenever she followed Freddie through the back door into their kitchen. The woman had never hesitated to wrap her in a welcoming embrace. Audrey had become accustomed to that closeness, to how Freddie's mother smelled like Dove soap and Aqua Net aerosol.

But that was over.

Audrey sat on the floor with her body crammed between her bed and the wall, a willowy pretzel slouching against her mattress, knees bent to secure her notebook, bare feet pressed below the windowsill.

Mother was out doing whatever she did on Saturdays, and Harry was mowing yards in nearby neighborhoods, earning money. Anytime Audrey had suggested she find a job to help out as well, Mother had rejected the idea outright. The situation was different for young boys, she'd said, who had to learn to be providers, but working was not appropriate for girls.

Audrey was sick of that whole refrain.

The notebook on her lap was open, and her pencil hung limply between her fingers. She'd practically spilled blood on every page since Monday, pouring out her heart, taking great risks that her nosy mother might nab her in the villainous act of keeping a diary. She chewed on the end of her pencil, digging her teeth into the metal cylinder connecting the eraser tip. Doing so was strangely satisfying. Finally, she started to write in neat, cursive letters.

I know I'm obsessing about this, but I just can't figure out why Freddie dropped me. Is that what happens when a guy breaks up with you? Or was I just his friend? Doesn't he owe me an explanation? I guess not, if this was all just an elaborate joke and I'm the big butt of it. If that's the case, Freddie and his friends are all cruel and hateful, and I don't want any part of them. Do they still believe they are better than me? And Freddie now, too? If so, I was better off keeping to myself. I should have kept to myself. Losing friends is worse than having none.

Audrey wiggled her toes on the wall. A light, scented breeze drifted through the window without lifting her mood.

She'd told Freddie so many things, especially stories about her home life that she'd never told another soul before. Thinking about how she'd trusted him was mortifying.

She wrote more.

What if he's told kids at school my deepest secrets? Totally betrayed me? Oh my God, like the awful things my mother has done to me. Like all the times she switched my bare legs or my arms or sometimes my back, leaving all the scars I have to hide.

Audrey tapped the pencil on her front teeth. Freddie had once made a comment about that, making her laugh. She put the pencil to work again.

I remember Freddie's serious expression when I told him about getting red welts that stung for days, how I'd always have to dress to hide them. He was upset and angry. But then he took my hand and put it over his own heart and, with a straight face, said, "C'mon, Audrey. From now on, don't let the witch use the switch." I laughed so hard after that. Freddie knew how to make me feel better. Laughing about it, about her, made me feel like someone understood, that someone might help me.

Audrey stared at her words.

Her heart felt lighter after spilling her thoughts onto paper. It usually did after a frenzied writing spree. She had dozens of diaries buried where Mother would never find them, full of stories she could draw on one day for a memoir or even a scary novel. And her writing was flowing more easily and was improving.

A realization struck Audrey, and she gulped. She could have revealed her mother's plans to Freddie, but she hadn't. If that news had spread around school, she would be worse off than just being pitied. She would be a laughingstock.

Lesson. Learned.

In giant letters, Audrey wrote, "Never trust a boy."

After an hour or more of journaling, Audrey's wrist was stiff and achy. She looked forward to the day she would own a typewriter, a Smith Corona or maybe a Royal, and she would be able to type her stories. She shook her sore hand, clasping and unclasping her fingers.

Then she heard something.

Her head snapped to attention, and her eyes locked in place, all her senses on high alert.

The back door was opening, its old springs creaking and moaning in protest.

Mother was home. Audrey cocked her head then slid her feet down the wall, pencil still dangling from her mouth like a cigarette. She heard footsteps moving up the stairs.

"Fuck," she whispered. Thanks to Freddie, she'd learned to curse and was surprised by how much she liked it.

Audrey lobbed her notebook and pencil under the bed and squirmed out of the tight space. She scrambled across the mattress, and the springs erupted in a loud chorus that would broadcast her presence. Her eyes darted to the door. The footsteps were coming closer, moving faster.

She jumped to the floor and pulled her quilt down until the hem kissed the floor, hiding her notebook from Mother's prying eyes. Grabbing her biology book from the top of her dresser, Audrey plopped onto her bed.

I was studying science, Mother, she would say.

Her mother was lingering just outside her room. Audrey's heart thundered in her chest. Her palms were clammy. She scolded herself for letting Mother frighten her as though she was still a child. Audrey summoned her courage and forced herself to read a paragraph describing the science of naming plants. "Nomenclature." She mouthed the word.

A shadow crossed the threshold, and Audrey looked up, prepared to smile.

But Mother was not standing there.

The person focused on her wasn't even a woman.

A tall man she didn't recognize entered her room in two elongated strides. Audrey's mouth fell open, and she tried to scream, but no sound came out. She jumped off the bed and ran to her dresser, flattening her back against it. The knobs dug into her flesh.

He stepped closer, a giant in her eyes. Terrified, Audrey scanned the room for any kind of weapon. Seeing nothing she could use, she felt her heart sink to the pit of her stomach. When Audrey again tried to scream, the result was more of a mouse squeak than a bellowing cry for help. She wondered if Daddy was strong enough to come to her rescue even if he did hear her.

For the first time in her life, Audrey wished Mother had come home.

Rigid like a giant sequoia, the man was silently appraising her. His dark, bushy eyebrows and full mustache partially concealed a leathery complexion. Brown eyes studied her from under a black cowboy hat. A patch on the man's work shirt read Bell & Zoller, the name of the mine where Daddy had gotten hurt before she was born. Seeing that, her mind whirled with a tornado of questions and possibilities.

If he was there to see Daddy, he should just say so. He had no business being in her room and frightening her so badly.

No, this was about something else, a gut feeling told her. She had to act.

Audrey fled to the window. Since it had no screen, she could jump right through the opening, and if she broke both legs on the ground, so be it.

She didn't know that hulk of a man. He could hurt her.

Before Audrey could get a knee across the sill, the man's two large hands encircled her waist, and he tossed her like a rag doll onto the bed. Gasping for breath, she scrambled across the quilt to reach the door.

If she could beat him down those stairs, she could fetch a knife and cut him then run, or she could grab a cast-iron skillet and swing it at his head. Daddy's gun was in his bedroom. Mother's smaller gun was hidden somewhere too. She'd been taught to use both. But searching would take too much time.

"Whoa there, Audrey!" the man shouted at her, blocking her way. He grasped her shoulders and pushed her onto the bed then loomed over her. "I didn't mean to scare you." He put his hands up. "Stay put, and lemme explain."

She gasped. The man knew her name.

"Your mama said it was best you didn't know I was coming."

Audrey was startled at the mention of her mother. She'd immediately recognized his southern Illinois drawl, common among the hicks and farmers, clearly making him a man from these parts.

"I'll explain while we pack you up," the stranger said.

Audrey batted her eyelids, momentarily more puzzled than scared, and sat up straighter on her bed. "I'm not going anywhere, mister. I don't know you."

"No, you don't, but I know all about you. Your mama is Edith Scott. Known her and your daddy for years, the poor son of a bitch," he said, shaking his head. "Worked with your daddy in the mines. I see your mama now and again on cheese days." He bent over to meet Audrey's eyes. "Hard life, that mama o' yours has."

She shook her head, unconvinced. "My daddy is downstairs. I'll scream, and he'll come running."

"C'mon, girl, I know your daddy is ailin'. Gettin' better, I hear, but your mama said he's always sleeping. Best to leave a sickly man be so's he can get better."

Audrey lowered her gaze to his cowboy boots and asked, "Who are you?"

"Ed Trent. I farm 'bout thirty miles from here, near Wantaka. Small town, bigger than Willowdale, mind you—nice people, all the same. My wife took a bad fall, and she's been recuperating. Needs help. You're coming with me to work for the summer. Hard, honest labor that'll do you good."

Audrey eyed the door as he walked to her dresser, wondering if she could beat him out of the room. When Mr. Trent opened the top drawer and began to fling her underthings onto the bed, her face reddened.

"What are you doing? I... I have another month of school. I need to finish. It's important. And Daddy would never approve of me leaving." If she sounded desperate, she was. "Stop it! Those are my things."

He grunted and turned his weathered face back to her, brows furrowed. "Your mama told me about you, how you won't follow rules. Ornery. Disobeyin' her and givin' her a hard time. Your mama don't need that kind of sass, let me tell you." He adjusted his hat. "Don't mind sayin' that bothers me. The wife and I don't have children—couldn't have 'em. But I know how children should behave. I was raised right. So your mama and me? We decided we could help each other."

Audrey's shoulders sagged as she began to understand.

Mother was sending her away.

Harry. Daddy. A lump formed in her throat, and she swallowed hard to force it down.

"Mr. Trent? Just tell her I wouldn't go, that I promised to do whatever she says from now on."

He had returned to emptying her drawers.

"She lies, Mr. Trent. I'm not what she's told you. You don't know what she's like. Can't you just leave? Find someone else to help your wife?"

The contents of four drawers lay in a pile on her bed, and he'd turned his attention to her closet. "Your mama's the one in charge, right?" he said. "Hell, I 'spect even over your daddy. She knows what's best, deserves respect. Besides, we made a deal, and I ain't 'bout to go back on it and disappoint my wife. Or your mama."

Thinking of making a run for it, Audrey's eyes swiveled to the doorway.

Maybe he was telling the truth, maybe not. Trent could be a made-up name, and the man in her room could be a random psychotic cowboy who kidnapped girls. He must have sensed her rising panic because he was beside her in seconds.

"I shoulda shown you this right off," he said. "You trying to jump from the window threw me off." He pulled a folded piece of paper from his shirt pocket and handed it to Audrey. "Read that. It's proof 'bout what I'm saying."

She unfolded it. The handwriting was her mother's.

After reading it, Audrey stuffed the note into the pocket of her dungarees. She would not cry. She would not give this man or her mother that satisfaction.

"Clear enough now? Let's get going."

He scooped up an armful of her belongings, and she gathered the remainder.

When they walked downstairs together, then into the kitchen and out the back door, Audrey did not bother to shout to Daddy.

Audrey obediently plodded behind Mr. Trent to his pickup truck, her feet slow and heavy like an elephant's. He'd parked along the side of the highway in front of Mr. Ritter's house—clever of him not to park in her driveway.

Audrey's eyes breezed over the yard to the picture window of the old man's house. If Mr. Ritter were watching, he might grab his cane, scurry outside, and indignantly ask what was going on. Then he might make a demand like "Stop! Unhand her!" But that happened in fairy tales, not in front of old houses belonging to Germans in a small town like Willowdale.

When told to, Audrey tossed her clothing into the dirty truck bed. Mr. Trent opened the passenger door, and Audrey climbed in. The stranger she was off to live with jumped into the driver's side, turned the key, and revved the motor as though the trip were an everyday thing.

Audrey was being hauled away like trash.

They pulled away. Through the car window that separated her new world from her old one, Audrey's eyes sought out Mr. Ritter's Ford. He never parked the car inside his ramshackle garage, having told her once that he worried the lopsided structure might collapse on it. What was more, he never drove anywhere in town on Saturdays because "too many people were out and about," even in their small town.

Mr. Ritter's car was nowhere in sight.

As they gained speed on the deserted highway, Audrey watched her home and the Ritters' shrink in size in the side mirror, eventually disappearing from view. She pressed a knuckle to her lips and stared at the road ahead.

Mr. Ritter's car had been gone.

Clearly, he hadn't been home, but Audrey couldn't understand why.

Then Audrey's mouth slackened, and her hand dropped onto her lap. She closed her eyes and squeezed them shut, blocking out the light to wallow in the deep gulfs of her soul.

Her mother had thought of everything.

CHAPTER 23

Edith

Edith returned home around lunchtime, ducking inside the kitchen just as ominous, swirling clouds broke open and a torrential rain smacked the earth. She tossed her pocketbook aside and looked around. The floor was speckled with dry mud, and Audrey's jacket, which had been on a hook near the basement door, was gone.

She grinned from ear to ear.

Because Harry was mowing and Red would be asleep, the house was hushed—only the icebox was humming, and the wall clock was ticking off seconds. She entered the parlor, which was tidy and vacant, then went to her bedroom, taken aback to find Red sitting on the edge of their bed with his feet on the floor, head hung low, swaying like he was dizzy.

"Lie back down, Red. It's lunchtime. I'll be right back with food," Edith said.

He dropped backward on the bed. Edith helped settle his head onto a pillow, just like the old days when he passed out drunk.

She pulled up the sheet. "Stay put."

After closing the bedroom door, Edith climbed the stairs, her anticipation building.

In Audrey's room, the floor was covered with dusty shoeprints and crumbles of dirt like those in the kitchen—a sign that Ed Trent had indeed been there. Edith clasped her hands together with the glee of a toddler. The bed was made. The closet was empty except for skirts and dresses, useless on a farm, and when she opened the chest drawers, Edith found only hairpins and ribbons.

She closed the girl's window and, from the corner of her eye, caught sight of a Jif peanut butter jar in the corner, filled with purple and white lilac blossoms. Their fresh petals were perky and vibrant. Edith lifted the container to her nose and sniffed their fragrance, letting her thoughts drift to a former time, if only momentarily.

"Get those lilacs out of here," Mrs. Hamilton had barked to a nine-year-old Edith when she presented a fistful to her mother, a peace offering of sorts, for whatever she'd recently done wrong. "You got nothing better to do?"

But little Edith had held fast to them, adoring the sweet, delicate fragrance. "I want to put them in water. I'll keep them in my room."

Her mother had plucked the blossoms away from her and thrown them into the trash pail, discarding them as though they were potato peels. Edith found herself out the back door moments after that, stunned by her mother's reaction then her words: "Useless. That's what you are, useless."

Edith had repeatedly punched her fist into the screen, making it cave inward while she screamed, "You're horrible! And mean! Those were mine, and I want them back!"

When Mrs. Hamilton turned from the sink to come after her, Edith had run into the yard, her short legs capable of great speed whenever she needed to avoid the switch.

Edith scowled at Audrey's jar of flowers and put it back onto the floor. In September, when Audrey returned, they would be dried up, dead.

She fluffed her daughter's pillow and propped it against the headboard just so. The girl's biology book was on the floor, which reminded her to let Audrey's teachers know Audrey would miss the remainder of the school year because of a family emergency. She'd have to use the telephone at Lucky's.

Everything had gone exactly the way Edith had hoped. Audrey would no longer be able to see or talk to Mrs. Somebody's ugly son, Freddie—or anyone from Willowdale, for that matter—for the next four months. That was more than enough time to break a habit—and Audrey's spirit as well. After all, the job was punishment, not public employment as a working girl, which would obviously ruin her chances of becoming a society lady.

Even better, Ed had agreed to mail Audrey's weekly pay to Edith. He insisted on paying a fair wage for her hard work. In return, Edith promised the money would be put into savings for Audrey.

Too bad her claim hadn't been the truth.

As far as Edith was concerned, the girl would never know wages had been paid and never see a single dime. The money was rightfully Edith's, for all the trouble she'd gone to with that girl. She would have money in her pocket without being the one slaving away at church, and Audrey would be the miserable one, breaking her back on a farm.

Edith squealed and clapped her hands. The situation was a win-win.

CHAPTER 24

Harry

Harry crept up the stairs, knowing that if Mama heard him, she might take all the money he'd earned mowing lawns. The morning had been full of back-breaking work, and he wanted to keep some of what he'd earned for himself, maybe fifty cents. He didn't mind giving Mama some of the money to help out the family, but taking all of it was unfair. His sister had told him as much and had encouraged Harry to secretly hold some back. He'd chewed on her suggestion for a while then decided a boy of twelve had a right to pocket his own earnings without feeling bad.

Safe at the top, Harry lifted an arm to sniff his armpit. He stank of dried sweat and grass. Bath night was later, thankfully, and he would be able to scrub off layers of grime. Unlike when he'd been younger, Harry welcomed a soak in the silver tub that Mama dragged into the kitchen and filled with pot after pot of water she'd heated up on the stove. As the youngest, he always had the last turn. The water was never hot enough or clear enough, suitable only in that he could get wet and wash his body.

He rapped on Audrey's bedroom door then barged in before she could respond. As Harry's eyes combed her room, his mischievous grin faded away. Her bed was neatly made, and a pillow was propped against her headboard rather than tossed at the foot. He could even see the floor. It wasn't cluttered with Audrey's usual mess of shoes, books, hair ribbons, or hastily tossed-off clothes, and her nightgown and underthings were not strewn like confetti over the back of her chair.

Mama must've forced her to clean her room, and he was glad not to have been around for that exchange.

The room was unusually stuffy too. Harry checked out the window, which was closed, and his eyes grew large. That was odd. Audrey never closed her window except during wintertime, and even then, he occasionally found her curled up under covers sprinkled with snow. He padded to her closet and, after hesitating, threw the curtain aside.

Most of Audrey's things were gone.

He checked her drawers. All were empty. As Harry's eyes flashed around every corner of her room, his heart rate skyrocketed into a full-blown panic. Panting for air, he ran to the window, threw it open, and sucked in oxygen like a drowning man breaking through the water's surface.

Audrey would not run away. She would not do that without telling him.

He stood shaking between her bed and the window, the place Audrey liked to think and write, something he would never tell Mama. He spied the jar of flowers and knelt. Audrey loved lilacs. He cupped the jar like a priceless thing, sniffing the blossoms over and over, thinking of her face, her smile. He peeked under her bed, and there, nestled among an army of dust bunnies, was one of Audrey's notebooks and a pencil.

Harry lay flat on the floor, knowing what it was: a diary of Audrey's private thoughts, the ones Mama had forbidden her to record. He reached out an arm to touch the notebook. Audrey had warned him about getting caught between her and Mama because if he did, she had implied, Mama might hurt him.

Harry hadn't believed that at the time—still didn't—but the hidden notebook seemed like a bomb that could blow up their world if Mama found it.

An hour later, when Harry came into the kitchen, Mama shifted cool, appraising eyes his way then returned to peeling long narrow strips from a carrot.

"You smell like it's been a good morning's work," she said. "Bath tonight after supper, after your daddy and me." She motioned for him to sit.

He slid into a chair.

Mama began chopping the carrots into bite-size pieces, the jowls of her cheeks jiggling with each whack. "Where's the money you made?"

When Harry was silent, she turned to gape at him.

He took a quick breath and spilled out, "Where's Audrey, Mama? Everything in her room is gone."

"What?" She rolled her eyes, annoyed, like he'd asked her if the moon really was made of cheese. "Your sister's staying with a distant cousin of mine for a spell, helping her out. Ain't that nice? It'll bring in money we surely need."

"But Mama, you don't have a distant—"

Harry stopped and pushed back against his chair, his heart in his throat. In an instant, Mama had bolted to his side and was scrutinizing his face, her eyes wild and suspicious, with too much white circling her pupils.

She spoke without her lips moving. "What's that? Are you questioning me, boy?"

He didn't know what to say, what to do. Mama had never talked to him so sternly before.

"I... I just meant that can't be right. You—"

She got so close that her pillowy bosom pressed Harry's ear. He looked down at the paring knife still in her hands and noticed her fingers twitching. His ears roared like a powerful, deafening waterfall. In his whole life, Mama had never threatened him.

When the small blade moved close to his face, Harry shrieked and jerked his chair to the side. He toppled over but wrangled himself free and hustled to his feet, breathing hard and staring at her in disbelief. His mama gave him a small smile.

"Best to keep what you're thinkin' to yourself, Harry. Audrey will be back in a few months."

Harry nodded vigorously, and his eyes darted to the hallway, to Daddy's room. Mama eased away from him and resumed chopping.

"You scared of me, Harry?" she asked and swiveled her head to look him in the eyes.

He didn't return her gaze but instead focused on the floor.

Mama was testing him, just like she had Audrey. He could feel the intense heat of her stare, baking him like bread, looking to get a rise out of him. She was checking for signs that he had somehow changed, all because he'd questioned her about where Audrey was.

"Long as you never lie to me, you got no worries," she said in a cheerful voice that made Harry's skin crawl. "You've always been such a good boy."

Mama went back to her chore, but Harry did not move, unsure if he'd been dismissed. Then she made a sucking sound as though she'd suddenly remembered something.

"Oh, and one more thing, Harry. Don't you go telling Daddy where Audrey is. Ain't your place. I'll be telling him in my own time. Understand?"

"Yes, ma'am," Harry said, nodding, because he was not brave at all and because he'd almost peed his pants.

CHAPTER 25

Edith

Edith had gleefully cashed two of Ed Trent's checks, which had arrived right on time each week through the post. The money went directly into her pickle jar, but she'd changed its location just in case Red got any greedy ideas or Harry developed sticky fingers.

One rainy school day, gloomy and chilly, Edith found herself in Harry's room to tidy up a bit and maybe take a good look around. The boy had been awfully quiet since his sister left, often leaving the house for hours on end to go God only knew where, or he chose to spend his time with Red—never with her.

Edith ran a dust rag across his bed frame and dresser while eyeing two books Harry had left teetering on the top of the radiator. One was *The Little Prince*—she rolled her eyes at the title—and the other was *Stuart Little*, which appeared to be about a mouse family. His wobbly bookshelf was overflowing. Harry was an excellent reader. Edith stacked the two library books on top of several others, feeling pleased.

While she'd never enjoyed reading herself, the hobby was a good one for a boy. If Harry did it well, that was a sure sign of intelligence, which would attract a high-quality wife. Once they were related to the DeDeckers, he would be a magnet for gorgeous, well-bred girls anyway. She moved on to Harry's closet, shaking his extra pair of shoes and running her fingers through his pants and shirt pockets.

After that, Edith hoisted one side of his mattress to check underneath. Satisfied, she ran her palms between his sheets and smoothed them out, tucking the corners under as Mrs. Hamilton had always insisted upon. In his chest drawers, Edith found a four-leaf clover wrapped in paper, a discovery since the last time she'd looked. The boy's superstitious nature irked her, like the Superman whistle her son believed to be a good-luck charm.

Yes, there was that business with the whistle.

For a full year, her boy had carried that whistle everywhere he went, yet he hadn't said a word to her about losing it. He'd lost things before, and she'd done nothing other than scold him. But it was odd that the whistle had been lost so close to the house, just below the window. Then again, Harry played imaginary games with pretend friends all the time. He could have crouched in that place while hiding like some jailbird.

She thought back.

Edith had discovered the whistle the very same day she and Audrey argued about that ugly boy, Freddie—and about Johnny. Harry might have overheard. Then Audrey could have corrupted him in some way, involving him in her misdeeds.

She put a thumb to her lips, lightly tapping the lower one, recalling how Harry had tried to question her about having a distant cousin. He knew that neither she nor Mrs. Hamilton had siblings, but speaking up to her wasn't like him. Something else was going on in that head of his.

The following week, Harry remained strangely aloof although he continued to be polite. Nevertheless, Edith kept a close eye on him. Finally, when she felt certain her son was just sad from missing his sister, she relaxed and stopped her constant spying. Edith had nothing to worry about when it came to Harry.

She also went shopping.

After that, fine, soft linens caressed Edith's body when she slept on the couch. In the mornings, she could choose hot tea from an assortment of Lipton flavors or enjoy Folgers coffee, which she perked in a brand-new WearEver percolator.

She visited the beauty parlor, too, for a cut, color, and permanent wave, resulting in a short, curly do that was a rich brown. Edith couldn't help but run her fingers through the soft coils. What fun it had been to see the stunned looks on Willowdale's finest female faces when she sauntered in and demanded the services.

Oh, just you wait, she'd thought then. *This is only the beginning. This ain't nothing.*

True to form, Red had failed to notice her new hairdo or how much younger she looked, but it was better he didn't ask where she'd obtained the money anyway. Edith's good mood had seemed to buoy him, though, as he had been saying "please" more often and smiling at her. Feeling better and much more alert recently, he'd finally inquired about Audrey's whereabouts.

When Edith explained that their daughter was away helping a distant relative, he closed his eyes and went quiet for a spell. She braced for his reproach, ready to squelch any of his opinions or objections, but none came. He'd only whispered, "It's good the girl can help."

Red's cheeks were rosy, and he was sitting up on his own with a pillow propped behind him. Busy in the kitchen, Edith had even heard him laugh at something Harry must have said or done. She planned to prepare a special supper to celebrate his improving health. As she bustled around the kitchen, snatching the supplies she needed to make her husband's favorite meal, her spirits were upbeat.

More than an hour later, Edith was attempting to clean up parts of the kitchen. She'd always been a messy cook, but at least Mrs. Hamilton wasn't around to chide her about it. And she was making a commendable effort for Red. Edith set a spatula on the counter then untied her apron, slung it over the back of a chair, and headed out-side.

Their outhouse was the original one she'd used growing up, and not even a two-holer like the modern ones. As she trudged toward it, Edith thought about the indoor bathroom she was going to have. Not in that house, of course, but in a beautiful home on Victorian Row, or maybe in one of those new homes people had built on the other side of town. A linen closet would store fluffy towels, new sheet sets and quilts, and a large variety of after-bath powders. She would have a fancy pull-cord toilet and real toilet paper, not pages torn from a magazine to wipe her ass, and a deep claw-footed tub scrubbed sparkling clean by a maid. Hot running water would splash down from a golden spout until it covered her naked body up to her breasts, and Edith would lie back to relish the warmth before cleansing her hair with the finest shampoo.

Quite possibly, she would live with Audrey and Johnny. But if her luck held, the DeDeckers would buy her a grand home. The thought gave her a pleasant shiver as she walked.

Edith was a few steps from the shitter when she heard a squeal. She stopped and looked back. Her son, who had been reading to his daddy, was with Mr. Ritter on the old man's patio, his back toward Edith, gesturing wildly with his arms. The old geezer, who seemed to be listening intently, had a large shopping bag looped over one hand. She couldn't read the letters emblazoned on it, but the blue markings looked familiar.

Edith cupped her hands to yell at Harry but changed her mind and lowered them to her sides, squinting to read the bag. It was from a prominent ladies' store in Penshaw and looked like the one a do-gooder had filled with clothes and given to her. Edith had intended to throw it away. The bag looked like the very same one. She focused on Harry's backside and headed straight for the two of them.

The old man looked up and, after spotting her, leaned his mouth close to Harry's ear. Edith walked more quickly. Then Mr. Ritter hurried away with a toddler-like gait, the bag swinging from the crook of his elbow, cane clacking on the patio bricks with each step. Within seconds, Mr. Ritter had hobbled up the steps and disappeared through his back door.

Harry spun around with a bright smile.

"What you doing talking to him, Harry?" she asked when they were face-to-face.

He shrugged his shoulders. "Just visiting."

"Was that my bag?" Edith studied his expression.

He nodded yes then said, "I was coming from the outhouse, and he waved at me, asked if we had a big bag he could use. I didn't think you'd mind, so I found that one. Are you mad, Mama?" Harry looked up at her and tilted his head to one side, the picture of innocence.

"So why did he run away like a guilty thief? Not that he can run, that is." Edith thrust fists onto her hips. "Something was in the bag. What was it?"

Harry recoiled almost imperceptibly, but Edith had seen it. She waited while his eyes skimmed the ground, then they flitted upward to find his answer in the clear sky.

"Um, I don't know. Guess I wasn't paying attention, Mama." Harry's big, barefoot toe was making a small hole in the dirt.

Edith pasted her eyes to her son and reached into her apron pocket.

"Look at me when I'm talking to you," she snapped. "Ain't you been missing something?" As she uncoiled her fingers to reveal his whistle, Harry shriveled, his lanky arms and legs collapsing into each other like a spider dancing on a hot plate.

"I... Well, I knew I lost it. Just didn't know where. Been looking for it."

"Did you try under the parlor window?"

Her son's eyes widened, and a brief glimmer of understanding shot through them.

"Be very, very careful, Harry," she said.

Edith dropped the good-luck charm back inside her pocket, patted the fabric, and turned toward the outhouse, leaving her son with his mouth hanging open as she strolled away.

CHAPTER 26

Harry

After his encounter with Mama, Harry ran into his house and perched at his father's side, seeking refuge from what he feared was an oncoming storm. Thankfully, Daddy was looking better than he had in a long while. His complexion was still sunken but pinkish, and he greeted his son with a pat on the head and a reassuring smile.

Up close, his father smelled something awful.

Daddy brought up his favorite topic, radio shows. As Harry listened, he thought about Audrey and wished she was home to see the change in him. The whole summer would pass before she came back, and he had no way of contacting her. But once home, she would be thrilled and relieved.

He grinned at his father, who was talking about a comedian named George Burns and sharing how much he looked forward to listening to his radio show from his rocker. Then he said something about wanting a television. Harry nodded with gusto because he wanted a television, too, as long as a channel carried a Superman program.

Mama stuck her head into the bedroom and said supper would be ready in an hour and she was making Daddy's favorites, like bread, potatoes, roast beef with gravy, and cooked carrots. They needed to celebrate, she said, because Daddy had finally developed a good appetite and was getting out of the woods. Daddy's face lit up, and he patted Harry's leg, oblivious to the squinty-eyed, questioning look Mama had cast on Harry before leaving.

His body shivered. Mama was giving him the creeps, a confusing turn of events he didn't know how to handle. She'd told him to be "careful," intentionally trying to scare him. She must've assumed that he'd eavesdropped under the parlor window that one day and that he knew what Mama was forcing Audrey to do. He wanted his whistle back, but not if that meant telling Mama he'd done exactly that.

And he would never spill his guts to her about taking Audrey's diary from under her bed. If she wouldn't tell him where his sister was, he wouldn't share any information with her either. Mama nearly catching him handing off a shopping bag to Mr. Ritter—with that very same notebook inside—had been a close call Harry did not care to repeat.

Daddy jostled his shoulder. "We'll be gettin' a real good supper tonight. Your mama sure is workin' hard at it. Been takin' good care of me, son."

"I can tell you're better, Daddy," Harry said with enthusiasm, avoiding any comments about his mother's nursing skills. "Water?" When his father grinned, he hopped off the bed and poured a glass.

The room smelled sour and sickly, but the stinky air didn't seem to bother Daddy. Harry wondered if he could smell himself. In the past, unless he'd been drunk—which had been most of the time—Daddy had always reacted poorly to disgusting aromas that most people could tolerate, like the stench from the outhouse on a blistering day. Anything gross that came from inside a person or animal's body revolted him, and sometimes he would gag uncontrollably. Other times, he would even throw up.

Years ago, when Harry asked his father why he had puked after a mere whiff of someone else's puke, he'd replied, "That's just the way I'm made, son."

Harry had thought about that for a long time, how people could be so different, not boy-girl different—he knew all about that—but the strange ways people reacted to different things.

Harry put Daddy's empty glass on the table. "I'm going to wipe down your room real fast, Daddy. Then we can get you up for supper. Be right back."

He delighted at the spark in his father's eyes, his own suddenly misty. He'd missed him so much. Daddy wasn't a perfect father, not by a long shot, but that didn't matter.

When Daddy leaned back and closed his eyes, Harry headed for the kitchen to gather cleaning supplies. Mama would also be pleased if he tidied up the bedroom. He would wipe everything down with disinfectant. He hoped to earn a few desperately needed brownie points from her for his efforts.

Harry peeked around the corner into the kitchen, hoping Mama wouldn't bite his head off. A few feet in front of him, Mama was on her knees, rummaging around inside a cabinet. She lifted out a tin canister, set it up on the counter next to a steaming bowl of potatoes and a carton of milk, then stood, slamming the door with her foot. She either didn't see him or simply paid Harry no mind. He could already taste the milky, buttery potatoes.

Mama was making a special meal, which meant everything was truly going to be all right.

He stepped forward as Mama shook flour from the canister into the potatoes.

"Why is the flour down there with the cleaning supplies?" he asked.

Mama's hand jerked up, pitching a billowy white plume into the air that hung aloft before descending in a fog. White stuff coated her arms, the counter, and the floor. Harry gasped and jumped back. The mess was his fault. Mama would be furious.

"So's it's close to my work here." Her teeth clenched, jaw muscles pumping, while she wiped the mess up with a damp dish towel. "It's handy. Who are you? Mr. Nosy Boogers? Look what you made me do."

She threw the dirty towel into the sink.

"I'm makin' a fancy potato dish your father likes, all cheesy, and you gotta bake it." Mama's eyes snapped to him, and she scowled. "Why you sneaking up on me like that? Go on, get out."

"But I want to get—"

"Don't care. Go keep Daddy company till I get supper on the table."

His head hanging low, Harry did as he was told. A half-hour later, he helped his father wash his face and hands in the water basin and change out of his pajama top into a clean shirt. When Mama hollered that everything was ready, he led Daddy into the kitchen, shuffling in small steps alongside him.

Grinning like a jester, Harry pulled a chair out for his father. "Sit, Daddy," he said excitedly. Having Daddy out of bed after so many months, sitting upright at the table and happy to eat, was like a miracle. And Mama preparing a nice, hot meal of his father's favorites was perhaps the bigger miracle. He could picture Audrey's delighted face when he got the chance to tell her.

They never prayed like other families, so each of them jumped right into their portions, smacking their lips and slurping water between bites. Mama helped Daddy cut his meat, jab carrots with his fork, and scoop up additional potatoes when he asked for more. Harry tore off pieces of her homemade bread and stuffed them into his mouth, greedily eyeing the potatoes, of which she'd forbidden him to have even a spoonful.

"Those are just for your daddy," she'd said at the start of the meal, much to Harry's disappointment.

The aroma of bubbling cheese, onions, and garlic was enticing, and Daddy ate several helpings of potatoes with gusto. He smiled at his wife. Harry dug into as much roast beef as possible.

"Thank you, Edith," Daddy said, lowering his fork.

"Me too, Mama," Harry added, still seated although he'd cleaned his plate some time before.

Mama bobbed her head, looking pleased, even somewhat pretty with her new hairdo. Daddy wiped his mouth with his arm and rubbed his shrunken belly while Harry beamed at them both.

Maybe his father coming down sick hadn't been the worst thing for their family after all.

"Eatin' this meal has me tuckered out. Worth it, though." Daddy winked at his son. "Now, don't you go worrying about me anymore, you hear?"

After his father settled back into bed to rest, Harry returned to the kitchen to help Mama clean up the dishes. As he worked, Harry pondered whether he should keep worrying about his daddy.

For the first time in far too long, Harry decided he would not.

Later that night, Harry undressed down to his boxers, slipped between cool bedsheets, and lay flat on his back. Most nights, he would gaze out the window until his eyelids became heavy, but he was restless. After an hour, sleep was still eluding him.

Harry was relieved beyond words that Daddy was getting better, but he was bothered that his sister had no idea. She'd been very worried about their father, and letting her go on doing that wasn't fair. Harry was certain Mama wouldn't let her know, which meant it was up to him.

Harry fluffed his pillow. He'd overheard Mama and Audrey arguing about that boy named Freddie that one day, and he seemed to be a good friend of his sister's. He took a long breath, hoping that Freddie could tell him where his sister was living.

Harry sat up and hugged his knees. If he couldn't sleep, then he could check on Daddy to see if he needed fresh water or the chamber pot—or just to straighten his covers if he was asleep. Harry put a

T-shirt on and traipsed into the hallway in his underwear. A stealthy cat, he slunk to the stairway and down them, pushing his palms flat against the walls and swinging his body to avoid stepping on boards that creaked. He didn't wish to wake his mama.

When the unnerving howl of an injured animal pierced the silence, Harry hovered above a step. He listened in the darkness. Another scream skewered the air, and Harry's heart began to pump with wild abandon. He swung over the last several steps, landed hard, threw the stairway door open, and followed the sounds coming from Daddy's bedroom.

He stopped short of entering the room and gaped wide-eyed at his father, who was on his hands and knees next to the bed, spewing vomit, missing the pot right under his nose. He hadn't seen Daddy throw up like that for weeks, and never before had he known it to be so violent. Harry fell against the doorjamb. He clapped a hand over his mouth and looked at Mama, who was standing behind Daddy with her back to him. His father's vomiting subsided, but he continued to heave in a long, gut-wrenching spasm where he seemed incapable of inhaling. When that ended, Daddy gasped for air and rolled himself into a tight ball, groaning. His hair was soaking wet, and his pajamas looked like they'd been splattered with globs of oatmeal.

Harry whimpered. Mama, aware of his presence, shot an icy look his way but stayed where she was. Daddy's moans grew loud again as he clutched his abdomen.

As much as Harry wanted to go to him, his feet did the opposite thing, retreating until his back was pressed against the hallway wall. "What's happening? Mama. Mama! What should we do? How do I get the doctor?"

"Go upstairs now. That's what you should do."

But he wasn't about to obey. Harry wanted to call someone for help. Mr. Ritter didn't have a phone. Harry's eyes darted frantically around as he tried to clear his head, wishing he could block out the terrifying sounds. Then just like a bat swooping down out of nowhere, Mother was right in front of him.

"Harry. Look at me." She shook him by his shoulders. "We don't need a doctor, you hear me? There's nothin' here I ain't seen before. Your daddy's just sick again. He ate too much. It'll pass."

"But he was better, Mama," Harry said, wiping his nose with the back of his hand. He muffled another sob.

Mama bent to her son's eye level, and he was compelled to meet her eyes, which flitted over his, her breathing heavy and sour in his face. A little voice inside Harry's head was telling him to run to Lucky's, to neighbors to knock on doors to find a phone. Daddy needed help.

He pushed his mama roughly aside and lunged for the bedroom door, determined to see if Daddy could talk, to find out what his father wanted him to do. But she was faster and ducked inside, slamming the door in his face. The lock turned. He pounded once on the door—twice. Harry stared at the door. On the other side, his father was coughing, but at least he'd stopped shrieking and groaning.

Harry slumped on the bottom step with his head cradled in his hands. The house grew quiet. Only the shuffling of feet could be heard from inside the bedroom, along with an occasional moan.

After several minutes, Harry trudged up the stairs and melted like warmed butter into his bed. Daddy had stopped puking. He'd be okay.

And Harry couldn't be mad at himself. After all, he was only twelve, just a twelve-year-old boy.

Only twelve, dammit.

CHAPTER 27

Harry

When Harry awoke, his stomach was rumbling. He yawned and listened to a chorus of birds singing merrily, welcoming their morning. He pried his eyes open and glanced at the clock. He'd already missed the school bus. Mama hadn't come to fetch him, either.

He threw a clean three-quarter-sleeve T-shirt over his head, pulled up loose denim pants, and belted them so that they wouldn't fall down. He would probably have to stay home all day, given that he didn't have a ride to school. But the teacher wouldn't be doing anything important or new anyway. That week was Harry's last in sixth grade.

Long summer days stretched ahead after that, the unbearably hot, sticky ones when there was little to do for fun except work on his fort. He could cut people's lawns to earn money, and if Daddy was still on the mend, he could spend time with him and keep his room fresh and clean. Before he fell asleep, Harry had promised himself he would do better about that, and he would. But without Audrey around, the boredom would be worse than ever.

He hurried out of his bedroom, eager to see how Daddy was doing and spend the day with him.

Harry jogged down the steps. The house was quiet, and he figured Mama and Daddy were both sleeping after such a long, horrible night. When Harry peeked into the parlor, he was perplexed by her absence. No way had she slept in the bedroom with Daddy, so she'd more likely departed to get something—maybe more cola syrup for Daddy's nausea.

His stomach growled. Harry headed to the kitchen to forage for something but was stopped short by a stab of guilt. Looking in on his father was much more important.

He did an about-turn and softly knocked on the bedroom door before creaking it open. A pungent odor sent him reeling. He'd tasted it on his tongue too. Mama was there, sitting on the end of the bed, looking out the window, her shoulders slumped. Harry's eyes darted to the floor, where the crumpled figure of his father sprawled on its side, facing the wall. He swallowed air, stunned to see him sleeping there.

Mama should have woken him up last night to help her settle Daddy into bed. Harry's fury was stoked by the pitiful sight of his father, and he glared darkly at Mama. She should've known better than to serve such a big meal, should've known Daddy couldn't keep it all down. She must have felt his laser-like stare because she wheeled around and looked at him.

Mama's face showed no emotion, but her eyes were sunken and bleary as if she hadn't slept, and the flesh below them was dark and cavernous, a strong contrast to her pasty skin. The effect was Halloweenish, and she looked as scary as any witch Harry had seen before.

"Good. You're dressed." She raised a finger to point at Daddy. "Run downtown to First Baptist and ask for the pastor. Tell him that your daddy is dead. He'll know what to do after that."

Harry's jaw dropped. He rushed toward his father, falling to his knees and bursting into tears. Mother leaned over and grabbed his forearm. She pulled.

"No, no, it's not true!" he howled and threw off her grasp. Harry wanted to nudge Daddy awake, to get him back into his bed. But deep down in his gut, he sensed an agonizing truth. Daddy wasn't moving at all, and he looked funny. Harry was afraid to touch him, terrified of clammy, cold flesh or—if he rolled him over—of eyes that might be open and fixed. His sobs turned into hysterical hiccups.

"No point in crying about it. Nothing you can do," Mama said.

He heard infuriating condemnation in her voice and looked up at her with accusing eyes.

"You feel sorry for him, Harry?" She crossed her arms. "He was a drunk, you know that. You're looking at what hard livin' does to a body, just like the doctor said. Gave him the cancer, you can be sure of that. Now, go on. Or do you just wanna leave the man lyin' here?"

CHAPTER 28

Harry

Besides Harry and his mother, only a handful of Red's buddies—mostly his fellow town drunkards—came to pay their respects at Daddy's graveside. Daddy's folks had passed on years before, and Mother had said he had a brother out west somewhere, but nobody knew where.

Standing next to her in shorts and a collared button-down shirt, Harry couldn't take his eyes off the long mound of dirt. He tried to comprehend that Daddy was in the pine box buried just beneath. The scruffy part of the cemetery was designated for paupers, people like them who couldn't pay for a decent burial, Mother had said. She'd grumbled that it was a "fittin' end" for his father.

The graves surrounding Daddy's had no headstones, no markers except for the few makeshift crosses people had crafted from sticks and strings. He knitted his brow, worried that Daddy's gravesite would eventually disappear under unkempt grass and weeds. Harry was concerned he wouldn't be able to locate Daddy's grave again. He wanted to show Audrey. He glanced around, seeking landmarks he could remember. After that, he snuck a look at his mother's passive face, certain that in her black dress and lacy veil, she was only pretending to be a grieving widow.

Mother had not shed a single tear, at least none he had seen.

She'd planned no service, spoken no final words over Daddy's final resting place, and when Pastor Dressler showed up at their doorstep the day he died, Mother had stiffly turned down any assistance for a proper burial.

His father's death was too much for Harry to grasp. Daddy had been getting much, much better. He'd even wanted to locate Audrey somehow, to let her know the good news, but everything had changed overnight. Mother had fixed a nice meal, full of Daddy's favorites. He ate a lot. Got sleepy. Became violently ill. Died.

Is that how cancer works?

Harry blinked back tears. Aching for Audrey was almost as painful as standing next to his mother without her. He knew Mother—the name "Mama" was a thing of the past—had not bothered to let Audrey know their father had died because wild horses and grizzlies couldn't have kept his sister away from Willowdale, from this. Calling her Mother helped Harry feel closer to Audrey and also distanced him from that woman. Audrey would be pleased they had that in common, not that Mother had noticed the change.

The small group of mourners was meandering toward him and Mother. They filed up, and each man in turn tipped his hat, nodded solemnly, and shook their hands limply. Their hands were jittery, just like how Daddy's had gotten when he'd been without booze for a few days. Each one mumbled what a great guy Red had been or spoke brief remembrances, and several patted Harry on the head. Mother seemed to relish the attention, tilting her head as though paying attention to their kind words, even smiling politely.

When the backs of the few mourners were far away, she barked, "Let's go," and extended a hand for Harry to take, but he walked off without doing so. As they ambled in silence across the grass, Harry looked over his shoulder for a parting glance at Daddy's grave. The largest, oldest oak tree in the area stood near it, a landmark he could remember, and he counted his steps to the main sidewalk. Mother, in her low black heels, clumped along behind him and complained for the hundredth time that Willowdale needed a bus.

Harry looked back one last time. He saw a figure emerge from a small cluster of shade trees, heading in the direction of Daddy's grave. A woman, a tall one at that, was carrying long-stemmed flowers, and Harry instantly knew they were carnations. He smiled for the first time since his daddy had died.

Daddy had loved carnations.

"What on earth are you looking at?" Mother slowed, turning her head too. Then she stopped walking altogether.

Harry snuck a glance at her. Veins around Mother's temples had popped out, her lips were tightly puckered, and her whole body was rigid. The weather wasn't really hot, but Mother's plump cheeks glowed cherry red.

His gaze shifted back to the figure. She was strolling closer to Daddy's grave. Once upon it, the lady knelt and gave the sign of the cross on her shoulders and head then laid the bouquet on the mound of dirt. She bowed her head as though praying.

The scene was a curious one for Harry, but Mother looked furious, so Harry pointed at the woman, blonde and wearing a black hat. "What's wrong, Mother? Do you know that lady or something?"

CHAPTER 29

Edith

The bedroom where Red had died still reeked a week after his burial. Other than washing sheets and making up the bed to sleep in, Edith had maintained the room as it had been. The stench saturated the hall, parlor, and kitchen. Harry had been opening windows and complaining about the sickly smell, but the truth—which Edith would never admit to her son—was that she enjoyed being surrounded by the odor of her husband's death.

It smelled like freedom.

Wearing a new red nightgown, Edith was lounging at the kitchen table with a glass of iced tea while she sorted through the morning mail. Before long, sweat was rolling into her eyes and down between her breasts. Edith silently cursed another steamy June day, but the refreshing brew provided some relief.

Grunting noisily, she hiked her nightie up to her groin and opened her knees wide to let her lady parts breathe, appreciative of her new kitchen fan's power. By ten in the morning, Edith's house was already heating up faster than her oven. She was tossing useless advertisements onto the floor when her eyes landed on the small, steady scrawl that belonged to Ed Trent. Edith ripped the envelope open and pulled out her weekly check. She kissed it with a flourish.

Not one bone in her body regretted sending Audrey away. That was for her daughter's own good, after all. Edith had every right to benefit from such a stroke of genius.

At first, she'd wanted to save up for a car, but she decided the effort would take far too long. By the time she had enough dough, Audrey's betrothed family would be providing her with one anyway. She was excited to think that, soon, she would learn to drive, something Red had never done.

Edith drummed her fingertips on the tabletop while her thoughts wandered.

Since the burial, she'd tried to stop thinking about that woman. *Why did she visit Red's grave?*

She'd pondered that question a hundred times or more, always piqued when any sensible answer failed her. No way in hell could Mrs. Somebody have known Red. That infuriating woman associated only with her kind, the snobby social set. Never in a million years would Edith have expected to see her visiting a pauper's grave, especially one interning a dreaded Scott.

Yet she'd been there, and with carnations no less. *Carnations.*

Even from a distance, Edith had known what they were. The delicate pink blossoms had been special to Red because of his mother, probably the only woman in his miserable life that he'd truly adored. He would have crawled across a hot desert for her on his hands and knees.

Alice Scott had gardened beautiful carnations around their rundown shack of a home, where Red and his brother had been raised. She had filled their tiny rooms with a variety of colorful blossoms, but the pink ones were special. Red had shared with Edith how, after his mining accident and throughout his convalescence, his mother had filled his hospital room, then his small bedroom, with vases or cans—whatever she could find—of pink carnations. He said his mother believed they symbolized gratitude, and she wanted Red to know how grateful she was that he'd survived. She'd wanted him to be grateful too.

Edith thought the whole notion of flowers symbolizing anything was ridiculous, but she'd kept her opinion to herself since they were newlyweds when he shared the memory. Red had also told her that, when Alice died three years after his accident, he'd cut enough pink carnations from Willowdale yards to cloak her grave, hoping she'd see how grateful he was for her.

Edith set the glass next to the sink and headed for the bedroom to dress. She was planning to go shopping downtown, but first, she intended to corner Pastor Dressler and ask him what he knew about those damn flowers. Perhaps he'd sent Mrs. Somebody as a representative of the church.

But if not, she would pave hell over to learn just how that woman had known Red.

CHAPTER 30

Harry

Harry raced through the kitchen on his way to the outhouse for an urgent first-morning pee, clad only in his boxers. His mother's pocketbook was gone, which meant she was out running errands. He doubted she'd gone to the church. Mother hadn't worked there for some time, yet they always seemed to have money to spend.

He didn't want to question her.

After relieving himself, Harry rooted through the cupboards and settled on a fresh apple. He opened the window next to Daddy's chair then tried to nudge two more parlor windows up, but their sashes stuck, making his attempts futile.

Once he settled in Daddy's chair, Harry bit into the apple's tart flesh, chewing loudly, just the way his daddy had. When the house was quiet—which was most of the time—he missed his father's sense of humor the most. With him gone, Harry felt like Mother had banned laughter the same as she had done going into the woods, although she hadn't specifically given an order. The house was somber. Laughter did not fit in.

He stopped chewing and wished he could dig a hole down, down, down until he ended up in China, which was what Daddy had said would happen. He wondered if Audrey was happy to be away—maybe not in China but away from their mother. In that way, he felt a twinge of envy.

He was glad Mother had gone somewhere, weary of walking on eggshells in her presence. As much as he didn't want her around, Harry yearned to feel closer to his father, pretty much every minute of every day. He stopped rocking and sat up straight. After tossing his apple core out the window, Harry hopped off the chair and headed for his parents' bedroom.

He opened the door. The room smelled like an animal had died there.

Harry held his nostrils closed and walked through the room, disgusted by what he saw and realizing that Mother was actually sleeping within the filth. He made a snap decision. Harry stacked up moldy plates and dirty glasses from the nightstand, balancing them like a circus performer on a tightrope, and he walked carefully into the kitchen. He scrubbed the plates and glasses and rinsed them all, putting each aside to dry. A smile crossed his face. Doing something worthwhile for a change felt good, which Daddy would have appreciated.

Harry scooped up his father's clothes after that and threw the whole smelly pile onto the back porch. Later, he could haul the washtub out of the basement and scrub the whole bunch. He just needed to find the washboard and soap. But before doing that longer, more tedious chore, he decided to wipe down the bedroom with ammonia, not just to erase Daddy's lingering smell, but to honor his father's loathing of gross odors. Audrey would be proud of him.

In the kitchen, Harry rummaged through the cleaning supplies, figuring his mother had stolen most of them from the church because the cupboard was chock-full. He threw a dry sponge over his shoulder, pushed baking soda, bottles of vinegar, and bleach out of his way, and grinned when he found the box of Rinso laundry soap. He just needed ammonia.

He spied a bottle of Clearex and smirked, wondering when his mother had ever cleaned a window. He hunted for the ammonia bottle way in the back. Mother's apron was folded across several canisters, so he lifted the bundle out and onto his lap. Harry recognized one of them, the shiny tin Mother had put into Daddy's special potatoes on the night before his father had died. He turned it over in his hands, and his eyes fixed on the label. His jaw dropped as a gasp caught in his throat. He couldn't breathe.

Harry glanced at the door. Mother could walk in at any moment and find him sitting there.

Heart racing and with trembling hands, he put everything back in the cupboard before scrambling to his bare feet.

Then he ran.

Harry pounded on Mr. Ritter's back door, his heart hammering against his chest like machine-gun bullets. When at last the old man appeared at the screen door, Harry hesitated, suddenly afraid of him, of everything. He jumped off the stoop and paced in a tight circle, shaking his hands high in the air like a monkey in a zoo.

"Tell me what's wrong," Mr. Ritter said, sounding alarmed, practically tumbling through the door to reach Harry, who'd started to bawl.

The old man hobbled toward Harry and wrapped his arms around him until the boy's sobs quieted. He guided him to the side of the house, and Harry understood right away that Mr. Ritter was removing him from Mother's view.

"Shush now," Mr. Ritter said, patting Harry's head. "It's going to be okay."

They stood together under the eave, cooled by its shadow. Harry forced himself to take several deep breaths.

"It... it's not okay," he said. "It's... it's my daddy. He didn't die from cancer, Mr. Ritter. He'd been so sick, always throwing up. He threw up real bad before he died because Mother made him a big meal." He fidgeted with his hands.

The muscles in Mr. Ritter's face twitched. His eyes were tender as he bobbed his head, encouraging Harry to continue.

"That's... that's how she did it." Harry looked up into Mr. Ritter's squinting, bespectacled eyes, wondering if the old man would believe him. He'd helped him out once before, after all.

"Did what, Harry? What are you talking about?" Mr. Ritter was wheezing through his nose the way old people did sometimes, but his eyes had locked onto Harry's.

"Daddy had been getting better—I swear. Then Mother made him a big meal, and he got even sicker, and that night, he died." Harry became still. "She didn't use flour in the potatoes, Daddy's special potatoes, like she said, Mr. Ritter. I just saw what she put in there. It was rat poison."

Harry buried his face in the old man's shoulder and sobbed without holding back. Mr. Ritter held him so tightly that Harry disappeared inside his warm, reassuring embrace, a fatherly tenderness he'd desperately needed. He let himself melt into that safe place for what seemed like a long time, unwilling to let go or be let loose.

"What's going on here?"

Harry's eyes shot open, and his knees gave way as Mr. Ritter attempted to hold him upright. The man's grasp fumbled, and Harry slid to the ground in a heap. Clad only in his boxers, Harry felt exposed as though she'd found him naked. He forced himself to stand. Without a glance at either grown-up, he moved between them.

"Um, nothing, Mama," he said, returning to his childish moniker for her. "I was helping out in the house—cleaning, I mean. And I just got to thinking about Daddy, that's all, missing him, and... well, you weren't home. I saw Mr. Ritter outside and came over."

Harry covered his face with the palm of one hand and watched her between his fingers. Mother was studying him with half-closed eyes and a skeptical expression, the tip of her chin raised. She was wearing makeup, the kind that turns women's cheeks pink.

He was praying that Mr. Ritter would somehow get Mother away from him. Nevertheless, he was surprised when the man's hand clasped his shoulder.

"Harry, how 'bout you go home so your mother and I can talk?"

He had not expected that. "Mr. Ritter, please—"

"Yes, Harry." Mother swept her arm in the air with dramatic flair. "I don't want to hear any more about your daddy. If you want to cry about it, do it inside the house. In your room."

Harry hated it whenever she said that, but at least Mother had believed his story. He dared not look at Mr. Ritter, so he started home, dread squeezing his throat with giant, fat fingers. Maybe he'd just made a terrible mistake.

What if Mr. Ritter tells Mother what I believe?

CHAPTER 31

Edith

Watching Harry amble away, Edith shook her head and moaned under her breath, galled that her son had been sobbing like a little girl. At least he'd only made a fool of himself in front of Mr. Ritter, whose opinion did not matter much, if at all.

"Mrs. Scott." Mr. Ritter cleared the frog in his throat.

Edith despised his accent. He'd been in America long enough that he should speak English like an American. "What do you want, Mr. Ritter?" she asked, folding her arms.

"I'm not going to beat around the bush, Edith."

She bristled at the use of her first name. No longer a child, she deserved respect, especially from a German.

"I been living next to you most of your life, since you were little. Seen a lot back then I'd like to forget, maybe even more with you and your children. Let a lot go for your sake." Mr. Ritter wet his lips, and when he swallowed, his Adam's apple bobbled. He glanced away briefly and shook his head in dismay. "Guessing now I've been wrong to do that."

Edith waddled up to him and leaned in to sniff his clothing, seesawing her nose over his shirt and neck like a dog checking out another mutt's butt. The old man took it.

"Mothballs," she said, stepping back. "Old and smelly, just like you."

Her laughter subsided when she saw he was regarding her with sympathetic eyes, something she couldn't tolerate from the likes of him.

"All right, Adolf—oops, I mean Alfred. What the hell are you talking about?"

"I've been putting things together, things that bother me."

Edith lowered her eyelids and curled her top lip, curious about an old man's amateur sleuthing.

"Audrey's gone away, and I hear you're saying she's helping out a distant cousin. Seeing how neither you nor your mama had any siblings, that can't be true."

The nerve.

"How is what I tell people any of your business? You better—"

"And before Red passed on, Harry told me he was throwing up blood, but you didn't call on a doctor."

"You think a twelve-year-old knows anything about anything? Is that it?"

"Your boy saw you use rat poison. Believes you put it in Red's supper."

Edith held his brazen gaze. The boy had seen nothing, knew nothing. "Listen to me, you dried-up prune. Are you so bored you got to stir up trouble for a poor widow and her son? People around these parts don't take well to that kind of thing."

He flinched.

"You think you know my family? I got second and third cousins on my father's side. And when Audrey comes home after the summer, she'll tell you that."

He shut his eyes for a long moment like someone fighting off a headache. "What about the rat poison, Edith?"

She looked away briefly and blew a raspberry through her lips. "That's ridiculous. You think I use poison to season my suppers? The kid's got a wild imagination, can't deal with his father gettin' sick of his own accord. And you're fool enough to believe him."

Edith's heart was beating like the wings of a hummingbird. "Listen, Alfred. Everyone in Willowdale knows Red died because of how he lived. Plain and simple. Even the doctor said so."

When Mr. Ritter did not respond, Edith turned her back to him, eager to deal with Harry. "Now that that's settled, it's time I—"

"You know, Edith," he interrupted, speaking slowly. "I still can't help but believe that boy."

She didn't turn around.

As if on cue, the ground beneath them began to quiver with the initial vibrations of a freight train rolling their way. In the distance, a locomotive horn blew twice—one short toot followed by one long whistle—the warning that it was nearing Willowdale street crossings.

"Believe what you want," Edith said. She turned on her heels and stalked away.

Once she reached her house, Edith sat down on a high step with a huff, her bottom teeth jutting out, as angry and irritated as a fire-breathing dragon.

That boy was up to something, daring to tell Mr. Ritter such a tall tale. Harry had changed since Audrey left home, and not for the better. He'd become even more out of sorts with Red's passing.

Edith glanced behind herself at the screen door then changed her mind about giving the boy a strict talking-to. The time for conversation had passed. Clearly, she couldn't trust her sweet boy anymore. A strong lesson was called for.

She slapped her knee, stood, and headed for the woodpile to find just the right switch for her son.

CHAPTER 32

Harry

When Mother trudged into the parlor, Harry was sitting in Daddy's rocker, staring out the window, his lips tucked into a sad pout. Seeing her hard expression, he gripped the chair's wooden arm and willed himself to make eye contact with her. He wouldn't let her see that he was afraid.

Both of her hands were behind her back.

"You told Mr. Ritter I put poison in your daddy's food." Mother's voice was too calm—flat and, Harry sensed, threatening.

Harry breathed hard, his chest pumping rapidly. "I'm sorry, Mama. I don't know why I said that. I mean, I know you'd never hurt Daddy. You took such good care of him." The lie fell from his mouth. He offered her a reassuring smile followed by a few persuasive nods then said, "I won't say stuff like that again. Promise. It was stupid, I—I just got confused, I guess."

Mother inspected him from head to toe. She was looking for signs of deception just as he'd seen her do with Audrey, studying his posture, facial expression, and nervous gestures. He needed to convince her he was sincere, then he would be off the hook for a while. His armpits grew damp.

"You will stay away from Mr. Ritter. You hear me?" Mother's arms were still hidden behind her back.

Harry was glued to his chair. He nodded with such vigor his neck cracked.

Mother's steely posture softened, and Harry thought about soldiers standing at ease. He exhaled a stream of air but kept his eyes on her. She was holding a switch behind her back—Harry could just see the tip peeking above her shoulder.

Mother had been planning to whip him like she'd done to Audrey so many times.

At suppertime, Harry could only pick at his food. His appetite had vanished, along with the whip. Mother served him a hearty portion of meat loaf, collard greens, and applesauce, but when she was not looking, he spat every mouthful into a paper towel on his lap. Dismissing the one nagging question in his head was impossible.

Harry was scared to eat the food his mother had prepared.

While Mother cleaned up the kitchen, Harry sat on the back porch steps, hugging his knees until long after the sun set. In the dusky twilight, Mr. Ritter emerged from his house and shuffled through the yard toward his pigeon cage. Harry watched him, trying to decide if he felt guilty for involving the man or mad that it hadn't helped. He'd wanted Mr. Ritter to do something, say something, but the result had just created big trouble.

After darkness fell, Mother shouted at Harry to use the outhouse then come inside, suggesting they listen to the radio together while she darned a few socks. If she wanted to pretend everything was normal, that they were a normal family doing normal things, he didn't want to play along.

Because they were not.

As politely as possible, Harry made the excuse that his stomach ached and he wanted to go to sleep early. But he thanked her for the suggestion and grinned. "My front tooth is coming in," he told her.

Mother seemed to like that, but the smile she returned did not erase the suspicion in her eyes.

Once upstairs, he pattered around like a prowling burglar, tiptoeing and listening intently, his ears attuned to Mother's movements below. He might have been just a dumb kid, but Harry was not stupid enough to think Mother would forget what he'd said to Mr. Ritter or that he might truly suspect she'd murdered his father.

He crawled into bed. A breeze flitted through his room like clockwork, first blowing the fringe of his curtains so that they waved at him then withdrawing, sucking the curtains halfway out the window. Maybe he hadn't lied after all about his stomach hurting, for it ached as he thought about Daddy, missing him something fierce. Harry's thoughts turned to Audrey, and he agonized over her too.

If his sister were by his side, she would know what to do. Audrey would want to fetch that canister Mother had used and check it out. The label had spelled Hot Foot Rat Killer in huge letters, set above an image of a skull and crossbones. There had also been a cartoon drawing of a rat gone belly-up. With his own eyes, Harry had witnessed Mother removing that very silver canister from the cupboard. When he startled her, she threw the powder everywhere, and some must have sprinkled into Daddy's potatoes. She might have added even more.

Poisoning Daddy might have been her plan all along.

Then again, the white stuff could've been flour, as Mother claimed.

Harry swallowed hard and crossed his arms behind his head, uncertainty making his skin itch.

With his mind mulling over the same questions, a revolving merry-go-round he couldn't climb off, Harry found sleeping impossible. Around ten o'clock, he heard Mother's footsteps moving around downstairs, and when he heard nothing more for ten minutes, he was certain she'd gone to bed. To be safe, he waited another hour before heading down, eyeing his clock with growing impatience. He'd already thought about what to say if she caught him, something about needing to use the outhouse because his stomach hurt so much. Or if she caught him looking in that cupboard, he would say he was hunting for the cola syrup and hadn't wanted to bother her. He could play the stupid kid.

Downstairs, Harry saw the door to her room was ajar. He held his breath, hearing Mother's deep breathing and the whistling through her nose whenever she exhaled. He slunk into the dark kitchen and crouched, opening the cupboard. As quietly as possible, he removed bottles and tins, placing each one gently on the floor. When his fingers touched Mother's apron, he pulled it out then felt around far in the back, where the canister had been.

Finding nothing of that size, his mouth dragged down to one side. Harry stuck his head into the dark cupboard to look, hoping his eyes would quickly adjust. He scanned the remainder of the contents.

No canister. No rat poison. No flour.

Harry pulled back and hastily returned each item before closing the cupboard with deft fingers. He had to get back upstairs.

When the overhead light flipped on, Harry winced at the instant, blinding brightness. He didn't twitch, move, or breathe. Thirty seconds passed, which felt like an eternity, before he risked looking up at his mother like a small mouse cornered by an alley cat.

I was looking for the syrup, right? For my stomachache.

Wait. He could say he needed ammonia because he'd thrown up and needed to clean. *No.* Mother would go upstairs to check out his story.

Maybe he could make it to the door, unlock it, and run.

Standing over him, Mother coughed. Harry bolted on hands and knees for the door, which seemed like a thousand miles away.

CHAPTER 33

Edith

Edith poured a cup of java from her percolator and inhaled the rich, delicious aroma. After a few slurps, she sauntered to the kitchen window and looked outside, hoping the day would not be unbearably sultry. Right away, her eyes spotted Mr. Ritter on his slow way to feed his precious pigeons.

As far as Edith knew, Harry had stayed away from the trouble-making Kraut, which had solved the problem of the pair's friendship. She'd handled the other problem, too, beginning the night she'd found her son snooping in her kitchen cupboard. Several thrashings with a stick and multiple nights sleeping on the hard basement floor had done Harry good. The boy would never again share the lie that she'd poisoned Red.

A week before, she'd stood next to Harry as he apologized to the old man for making up a story, promising he would never tell a lie like that again. He'd become meek once again, more like the child she had raised.

Honestly, Edith had just wanted her innocent little boy back. She hadn't wanted to hurt him. But Harry hadn't given her a choice. Far too much was at stake. Since the whole matter was handled quite well, she'd turned her attention to dealing with Mr. Ritter. His interference, along with his aggravating audacity and boldness, had required an entirely different solution.

After another sip, she blew across the liquid to cool it and examined her reflection in the window. It was distorted somewhat, but

Edith could tell she looked better than ever. The new red nightgown was not only bold and colorful, but the color brought out the greenish-yellow flecks in her hazel eyes. And for weeks, she'd been applying whipped cold cream to her face at night, so the lines on her forehead and deep crow's feet had already softened, becoming less pronounced.

She continued to follow Mr. Ritter's progress, convinced that if he walked any slower, the man would be moving backward. A question occurred to her. *If Mr. Ritter is German, were his pigeons also dirty Krauts?* They certainly were dirty. Maybe the birds even cooed in German. Edith's lips curled up into an amused smirk, delighted with her own sharp sense of humor.

When he was close to the coop, Edith strolled out to the porch in her nightie, mug in hand.

That stupid coop with its tiny birdie shelters and system of perches was a source of great pride for Mr. Ritter. Edith had watched him construct it when she was a small child. Now, the wooden stilts were rotting, and the whole thing was leaning to one side. The only stable part seemed to be a sturdy, tall pole with a bright yard light at the top.

His faint, chattering voice floated across the yard, babbling baby talk as though those stupid birds understood the words he said. He leaned his cane against one of the stilts. Edith leaned over the porch railing and contentedly sipped her Folgers, which was smooth, hot, and earthy. Her tongue played with the liquid, swishing it into her cheeks before she swallowed, just to prolong her enjoyment.

She wasn't even startled when he shrieked, a wail that ripped the stillness apart like an unexpected clap of thunder.

Then she heard, "Oh my God! Oh my God!"

Leaning over, Edith rested her elbows on the rail, lifted her mug, and sipped. She narrowed her eyes at the old fool, who was fumbling with the coop's lock, trying to pry the mesh door open. Mr. Ritter's arms went inside the coop, then his head, seemingly without a care that he was deep in pigeon shit as he scooped up the stiff bodies of two pigeons. His head swiveled back and forth, his mouth agape, taking in all the dead birds.

Mr. Ritter pushed back and stumbled, almost losing his balance, which would have been amusing, had it not been so pathetic. The man looked like a crippled sot. Edith watched as he clawed at his chest. She could hear his full-throated sobs. As though he could feel her staring at him, the old man raised his head and turned.

Their eyes met over the expanse of the two yards.

Mr. Ritter took less than a minute to figure it out. She knew when his crumpled expression smoothed and his eyes widened. Hatred shone behind his long, silent stare. Then the old man's face collapsed into itself again, grief wracking his broken-down body. He reached for his cane and leaned against it.

"Good morning, Mr. Ritter," Edith called out to him. "Is something wrong?"

He ignored her. She finished her coffee.

Another five minutes went by before Mr. Ritter took his first unsteady step back home. Only then did he glance Edith's way, a bent-over, beaten man. Edith lifted her empty mug high and pretended to clink an imaginary one of his, toasting their mutual agreement.

So far, she'd taken care of anyone who'd posed a problem for her: Red, Harry, Audrey, the boy Freddie, and of course, now poor Mr. Ritter. The biggest task remaining was to ensure Howard DeDecker came through on their deal, which meant writing a letter to his wife. If he kept his word—which Edith would know on her next visit—she would burn it. If he didn't, she would make good on her threats.

In the kitchen again, humming under her breath, Edith poured another cup of coffee and found a sheet of paper and a pen.

Edith licked the ink tip and started to write.

Part II

CHAPTER 34

Audrey

Audrey lifted the last cast-iron pot from the dishwater and scrubbed it, then stacked it atop the other dishes while simultaneously reaching for a flour-sack towel. The bright red-orange-and-yellow rooster embroidered on its white fabric made her smile, and she fingered the short, perfect stitches. Mrs. Trent had dedicated herself to the kitchen's farm-animal décor. The cookie jar was painted to resemble a rooster, with a lid in the shape of a red comb, and three black-and-white-checkered canisters displayed smiling cows with round pink udders. Mrs. Trent's favorite tablecloth was canary yellow and covered with colorful farm animals in motion.

Before coming to the Trents', Audrey hadn't known that rooms even had themes. The farming decor wasn't really to her liking, but the style had grown on her. It seemed friendly, welcoming, and warm, like Mrs. Trent.

Audrey had baked two dozen oatmeal muffins and several loaves of wheat bread, which were cooling on racks. The kitchen was stifling, and she blotted her brow with the end of her apron. Just one month into her stay at the farm, Audrey was already becoming skilled at cooking and baking. Under Gladys's direction, she'd created tasty chicken and beef dishes and cooked perfectly textured fresh vegetables. She had mastered the art of baking soft bread, with crust that came out an even, golden brown, not hard and crusty like Mother's.

When a breath of air drifted through the window above the sink, she turned, closed her eyes, and let the breeze caress her face for the brief moment it lasted. Audrey looked beyond the barn toward the expansive field, then she gazed at the small, fenced-in backyard. Being with the Trents wasn't so bad, at least not in the way Mother had intended it to be.

Mrs. Trent—who'd insisted Audrey start calling her by her first name, Gladys—was more like a tutor of sorts. She liked to sit on a high stool while Audrey worked, her crutches always close at hand, and she would prattle away, interrupting herself to give Audrey instructions like "A little more garlic, dear" or "If you use that knife there, it'll go much faster."

Gladys was older than Audrey's mother, maybe in her midforties. Her skin was deeply tanned, not as weathered as her husband's, and her hair was cropped short, "Easy and fast to take care of," she'd explained to Audrey. Although the light ashy color was uninspired, the pixie cut framed Gladys's face and accented her blue eyes, which were clear and bright and sparkled whenever she laughed, which she did a lot when her leg wasn't hurting. Rounds of daily farm chores had kept her body lean.

Even though Audrey considered herself a hostage, she'd grown fond of Gladys and was grateful for the kindness she'd shown since her strange arrival. Audrey knew she was there to fill the woman's shoes as best she could, and Gladys instructed Audrey patiently, like she was her student or maybe like how a mom might instruct her daughter. Her engaging smile and fast wit reminded Audrey of Freddie, but she always pushed the feeling aside. That hurt to think about.

Mr. Trent was another matter altogether. As far as Audrey could see, his only redeeming value was how much he seemed to adore his wife. He obviously thought poorly of Audrey, but she couldn't blame him for that, considering the lies Mother had told him. Around Audrey, he was dismissive and gruff, always gawking at her from under his cowboy hat as though he expected she might steal something.

Even so, Audrey had come to admire the farming couple and the way they lived. The Depression and its aftermath had been hard on everyone, including them, yet they'd somehow kept their farm going and eventually prospered, thanks to Mr. Trent's decision to concentrate on growing soybeans. Gladys had told her that farmers' wives worked harder than most women because they were in an economic partnership with their husbands. They shared the land, the work, the risks, and the rewards.

In their home, Audrey had eaten and slept better than at any other time in her life.

"It's pretty much dawn to dusk around here," Gladys had said the day she moved in, which made Audrey feel oddly worried and invigorated at the same time.

Every night afterward, she dropped onto her sheets exhausted but strangely fulfilled, glad that fatigue always lured her away from sad thoughts and into a dreamless sleep.

Gladys was a force, even with her leg in a cast. She'd told Audrey about her accident, how she was running to fetch her husband from the field, tripped, and snagged her shoe under a tree root and tumbled forward, hearing the awful snap of bones. Before her accident, she'd done all the cooking and cleaning, but she'd also pitched hay, driven the tractor, tended the garden, and even cleaned the stalls for Suzie and Dander, their two horses. At twice Audrey's age, the woman seemed to have double her energy too.

A few days before, when the two of them were side by side, dicing tomatoes and cucumbers for salads, Gladys had answered one of Audrey's questions with a wry smile. "When Ed needs my help, I drop what I'm doing in the house. We have to get those crops to market, so I jump as high as he needs, no matter what I still got to get done."

"But you make all the meals, shop, and clean," Audrey said, feeling resentment on the woman's behalf. "He doesn't help you at all with those things."

"Crops bring in the money, dear. Besides, hard work is good for a soul—a body too. Never hurt no one." Gladys's eyes skimmed to the thick plaster cast binding her leg. "Except maybe me."

They both giggled.

At times like that, Audrey wished she could confide in her and admit what her life had been like at home. If Gladys heard about Mother's plan to force her to marry someone, to coerce her in any way necessary—including sending her to the farm as a punishment—she would be infuriated. Gladys would understand how worried she was about her father and how much she missed her little brother. Audrey also thought Gladys would believe her mother had lied to Mr. Trent. But she'd been warned not to "lie her way out of things" by the husband whom Gladys adored.

On the ninety-minute drive from Audrey's home to the farm that day, they'd been silent most of the way. Miserable and frightened, she stared blankly out the open window, letting the wind whip her hair as cornfields and clapboard farmhouses whizzed by. She wouldn't travel the same road again until late summer when her exile ended. By then, the straight rows of short cornstalks would be sky-high.

"You'll call me Mr. Trent or sir," he said after an hour. "The wife and I are hard workers. If you're not, you soon will be. There'll be rules. Strict discipline."

He tapped on the steering wheel, apparently keeping time to a catchy tune playing inside his head. After that, Mr. Trent reached across her knees and popped open the glove box, from which he grabbed a crinkled red-and-white bag of chewing tobacco, rolled down from previous use. With one hand, he steered the truck at forty-five miles per hour while his other pinched the snuff inside his lower lip.

Audrey managed a few sideways glances, wrinkling her nose whenever he spat out the window. She'd never liked Daddy's chaw either and couldn't figure out why men put such repulsive, smelly shreds into their mouths and got pleasure from it. Even as he sucked on the tobacco, Mr. Trent's neutral expression did not fluctuate—it was neither soft nor hard. She knitted her brow, wondering what he'd meant by "strict discipline."

Then he said, "One other thing."

His voice was authoritative and loud, ensuring she could hear him over the wind rushing through their windows.

"Don't bother telling me or the wife how bad you've had it. Lots of folks got it bad. And your mama tells me you'll deny everything you've done. I don't tolerate lying. So don't be sharing your nonsense with Mrs. Trent, or you'll pay hell for it. Understand?"

After they arrived, his wife's welcoming nature was a relief. But she hadn't asked Audrey a thing about her family, probably assuming she knew enough already. During the first week of her confinement, Audrey plotted different ways to escape. Some ideas were better than others, more realistic, but still, she never exactly put any of them into action. The Trents had a telephone, but she didn't know anyone's phone number, and a phone directory was nowhere in sight. Hitchhiking was too dangerous, and even if she made it home safely, Mother might trick someone else into kidnapping her again. Her situation could get much, much worse than her current one.

Audrey came to understand how much the Trents needed her help, and even though Mother saw her time with them as punishment, she'd been wrong in picking Mr. Trent. She made a point of following Gladys's instructions thoroughly, asking questions to show that she wanted to please. At night, her calves often barked when she settled onto her mattress, and her fingers would burn from burgeoning blisters.

Still, she was homesick at times.

She'd written letters to Freddie, hoping his attitude toward her during the last week of school had been a fluke, and also to Harry and her father. No response came from anyone. Of course, Mother was intercepting Audrey's letters to Daddy or Harry, but Freddie's silence was painful. She had to accept that if he was receiving her letters, he was choosing not to write back. Audrey had written her letters filled with hope, but he'd apparently written her off.

"Audrey?" Gladys's sweet voice pulled her gaze away from the window.

She folded the dish towel and tucked it through the oven's handle. "Coming," she answered, glancing at the calendar tacked to the wall as she walked by.

Audrey had been crossing out each date, eager for the day she would see Harry and Daddy again. The laugh would be on Mother then, because Audrey's so-called prison time hadn't broken her. Frankly, living with the Trents was only serving to make her stronger.

CHAPTER 35

Audrey

Two weeks later, Audrey was sitting at the small desk in her bedroom, which was on the first floor in the back of the Trents' two-story farmhouse. Her room also had a teensy closet, a dresser, and a twin bed. Scribbling away and deep in thought, she didn't hear Gladys's crutches thumping across the hallway's squeaky peg-and-plank floorboards.

"It's time for morning chores," the woman said in a singsong tone. She shoved Audrey's door wide open.

Audrey jerked her head around with alarmed eyes, her cheeks flushing crimson.

"What on earth?" Gladys said. "Do I look that bad? I didn't mean to frighten you."

Audrey twirled a lock of hair around her finger and stammered, "I-It's just that you surprised me."

Gladys shot her a quizzical look. "You've seen me every morning for almost two months. Today you jump like you saw a ghost?"

Fessing up would be hard, given that Gladys believed she was a liar, a thief, and a difficult, disobedient teen. But she'd been caught red-handed. The evidence was on the tabletop in front of her. Honesty was her only option, so Audrey turned to face Gladys and drew in an uneasy breath.

"It's just that I, well, I took a notebook from Mr. Trent's desk. I'm sorry. I should have asked permission. I know he'll be angry."

Gladys continued to focus on her but said nothing, letting the moment between them settle.

"I see," she said at last, listing against her crutches. "Well then, next time, just ask for one. Now, stop frettin' like you got caught with your hand in the cookie jar. We have plenty of notebooks. And between you and me, Ed's more talk than action." She winked. "While you're with us, just ask for whatever you need. I mean that." When Audrey's face sparked with relief, Gladys leaned over her shoulder. "What you doing here?" she asked.

Audrey slapped her hand over the page without thinking.

"Oh, it's personal?" Gladys's tone percolated with amusement. She made her way to Audrey's bed and sank onto the patterned quilt she'd stitched a few years back, for which she'd won a red ribbon at the county fair. She tilted her crutches against the mattress. "A diary, I suspect? You know that when I was a teenager, I had one, real important to me. I used to hide it from my folks."

Her eyes slipped to the opposite wall. A framed photo hung there, of a drab two-story house with a wide, welcoming brick porch flanked by a circular pattern of fir trees. Audrey turned to look at it too.

"I'm glad I kept that photo. When I look at it, I go right back to that time when I was growing up on the farm, 'bout ten miles from here. I can hear my parents laughing while they cooked dinner, usually fried chicken crackling on the stove."

"That house is where you grew up?"

Gladys nodded, and her eyes went to a faraway place. She pulled them back to look at Audrey.

"Why did you keep a diary? I mean, was it for personal reasons?" Audrey hesitated. "Or did you want to be a writer?" She lowered her eyes and stared at her feet.

"Well, for me, it served as an outlet. Growing up on a farm was real tough. I had little time for friends, so I poured my feelings into a diary my mother gave me. Just turned into a habit, I guess. Kept it going for years."

"Your mother knew you wrote down personal things?"

"Sure. And as far as I know, she never tried to read it." Gladys chuckled. "Suppose she understood, being a girl herself, that we need to have our secrets. Right?"

The muscles in Audrey's jaw tightened. Mother had burned one of her notebooks, taken others, whipped her for keeping them. She clenched her teeth, hot anger quickly returning.

"Audrey." Gladys stood and hopped on her good foot the few steps to reach her. She bent down and, with one finger, lifted Audrey's chin. "Ed's told me that you've been in all sorts of trouble. Got a poor relationship with the truth. I must say that rather surprises me since getting to know you."

"My mother lies," she said, her voice overflowing with loathing. "She told your husband that I'm bad, that I lie, but it's her. And I haven't been in trouble, either—not the way you think, anyway. But I'm..." She paused, her eyes darting around the floor. "It's just, well, I'm not supposed to tell you anything."

"Oh? Who told you that?"

She was about to respond when Gladys hushed her with a raised finger and whipped her head around to face the door. Hallway floorboards were groaning under Mr. Trent's heavy footsteps, coming closer. He appeared in her doorway, clothed in workaday overalls, and, with a commanding air, proceeded inside. Instantly, her bedroom felt cramped. His body swallowed up the space like a full-grown Saint Bernard stuck in a puppy pen. The area suddenly smelled like him, too, a sweet mixture of dried sweat and hay.

"Hello, dear," Gladys said, offering her cheek for him to kiss.

After he brushed his lips against her face, Mr. Trent rolled his long sleeves up to his elbows, forming wide cuffs. When they were outdoors, he chose to cover his arms completely, regardless of how steamy the day was. She'd never seen him protect his face from the sun, though, which explained his dark, leathery complexion.

He snorted. "Breakfast's been over for an hour. You got chores lined up for her, Gladys? If not, I got two stalls that need cleaning, and there's work in the garden, and then some."

"Oh, stop being such a taskmaster." Gladys frowned. She secured her crutches under her armpits and looked up at her husband, who was a good head taller. "Got plenty of laundry, Ed, some apples and pears to put up. Just mind your own. We got plenty to do inside before you go pushin' her out into the heat."

Mr. Trent managed a slow nod then patted her shoulder as if she'd been a good girl. "Go on now, I need to talk to Audrey."

"I don't see what—"

"Got my reasons. Please, Gladys."

His stern tone did not sit well with her. Gladys straightened, and the muscles in her slight frame tightened until she looked as unbreakable as the plaster cast encasing her leg. Evidently, Mr. Trent recognized the reaction because he sighed and placed his large hands on her shoulders.

"Sorry, dear. I just need a quick word with Audrey. We'll be out in a minute."

Gladys smiled, stole a glance at Audrey, then cleared the doorway. When the sound of her crutches clip-clopping on wooden boards faded, Mr. Trent reached behind Audrey and picked up her notebook.

"Did you have permission to take this? Cuz I know I didn't give it." He shook a finger at her, and Audrey grimaced. "Your mama said you write things not fittin' for a girl your age. Or a good Christian. Said she don't allow it at home, but you go sneaking around, doing it anyway. I won't allow filth in this house."

To prove his point, Mr. Trent flipped through several pages then began to read her words aloud in his deep nasal twang:

"Today, I worked with Gladys canning peaches and cherry preserves until almost sundown. But I guess it was more fun than it was work, spending time with her and learning. I like helping her. She's kind and funny and smells good too. It's so much better here than at home. I have several meals a day! And I'm pretty sure neither Gladys nor Mr. Trent would ever whip me."

Audrey folded her hands in her lap, watching his reaction. He looked taken aback. His eyes scanned the rest of the page, then he flipped to the next. He began to read again, this time in a softer voice, one she'd never heard before:

"My outdoor chores are super hard, like backbreaking hard. Gladys is more than twice my age, but she did the very same hard things before she broke her leg, so I'm trying to prove I can do them too. Like washing down the stalls, pitching hay, and even scooping up horse crap into tall piles. That's in addition to all her housework! I hope to always remember how good it feels to sweat while doing chores, and the great sense of satisfaction that fills me up. I am proud of myself when my back is sore and my legs ache. One of the best parts of being here—Diary, don't ever tell Mother this—is that I get to take baths in a real bathtub with hot running water and soap. Being clean helps me sleep better, too, when it's so hot."

He turned another page and continued in a more somber voice:

"Mostly, I like staying busy because I know Gladys appreciates it. But it also keeps me from thinking about Daddy. He was so sick when I left, and I don't know if he even knows where I am. I miss him. I miss Harry. It makes my heart hurt so much sometimes that I can hardly breathe."

Audrey looked out the window, wishing he would just get her punishment over with. The silence stretched on until she realized he was still reading, but only to himself. She remembered what she'd written next, something about how unpredictable Mother's temper was, about hiding her scars, and how fortunate she was to know someone like Gladys.

To be living with the Trents.

Mr. Trent smacked his lips and lowered the diary, offering it back to Audrey, who'd been busy picking at a cuticle. She was surprised when he nudged her with the notebook then stunned when she glimpsed his sorrowful expression. She accepted it. He rarely looked at her directly, mostly when he was barking an order, but he caught her eyes and held them.

"I'm not one to stick my nose in other people's business," he said.

Audrey shifted her gaze back to the window. The small brown sparrows were playing out there, chirping and jumping from branch to branch in their simple pursuits.

"Listen. I believed the things your mama told me. Had no reason not to. But after reading this..." His voice trailed off, only to come back even stronger. "Seems to me a person tells the truth in a diary. Can't see any sense in lying to yourself. Unless you was hoping I'd come across it, convince me to feel bad for you?"

Audrey's shoulders slumped. She did not reply.

Mr. Trent's callused hand cupped the top of her head, so briefly that Audrey wondered if she'd imagined such a simple, affectionate touch. "My wife likes you, Audrey. She's got good sense 'bout people, knows a good one when she sees one. Far as I know, she ain't been wrong yet."

"I like her too," she said in a small voice.

"Seems to me there are two sides to this coin. Maybe I need to look into that."

Audrey wanted to thank him for believing her, but he'd already started toward her door. The words "Thank you" stuck in her mouth. Instead, she said, "Be out in a jiffy."

Farther down the hall, his voice boomed. "Don't think I'm not watching you, though. Now, let's all get to work."

CHAPTER 36

Audrey

A week later, after supper, Gladys was teaching Audrey to knit while they relaxed in cozy rockers in the living room, a large window fan blowing warm air into their faces. The scent carried a hint of welcome refreshing summer rain, which the Trents had been steadily praying for. They turned their needles in companionable silence, Gladys with practiced hands and Audrey's twisting in slower, less certain loops. If she got the hang of it, Audrey hoped the result would be a nice hat for her little brother.

"How does it feel to have that plaster cast off?" Audrey asked, making a miniature circle and mouthing "purl two" to herself.

Gladys, whose calf was wrapped in stiff white gauze and elevated on a hassock, wiggled her toes. "Can't wait to ditch those awful crutches," she said. "My armpits are darn sore. Doc says it's going to be a full month till I can put weight on it."

Mr. Trent was engrossed in the *Penshaw News* Sunday paper, having just eaten three warm oatmeal cookies, now an Audrey specialty. He'd tried to sneak them into the living room but dropped a trail of crumbs from the kitchen to the couch, where he plunked down and munched on them while hiding behind his paper.

From the corner of her eye, Audrey saw Gladys glance at her several times, no doubt checking on her progress. But she seemed uncomfortable, twitchy, and apprehensive, which was not like her. After half an hour, Gladys inhaled deeply, and Audrey figured whatever was on her mind was finally going to come out.

"Honey, you've said very little the past few days. I'm... Well, I'm worried about you. It has to be difficult being away from your family, your home. I want you to know how much I appreciate all that you do. But are you okay?" Her hands stopped moving, and she looked at Audrey.

Audrey looked back at her then returned her focus to knitting while she sought the words to respond. The sincere look of concern on Gladys's face had caught her by surprise. The very idea of someone truly worrying about her was new, at least since Freddie had become her friend then not her friend.

After a long silence, Audrey set the needlework on her lap.

"There's a boy, yes?" Gladys sounded hopeful.

"Sort of. I mean yes, there is a boy, but we're just really good friends, I think." Audrey had given up writing to Freddie. But if Mr. Trent had mailed her letters, he knew about Freddie and had probably told his wife.

Gladys peered at her husband, her face flushed like she was about to cry. Audrey was puzzled by her reaction and looked over at Mr. Trent too. He was peeping over the top of his newspaper.

"Well, you'll be going home just shy of two months now. A true friend will stick around," Gladys said.

She resumed knitting, more furiously, whirling her needles in precise, measured strokes. Audrey worked the yarn again too, following her lead. She heard Gladys swallow hard, feeling the giant lump move as if it were in her own throat. Instinctively, she knew that whatever Gladys was feeling or had wanted to say had just been pushed down, far down.

"It's a boy named Freddie," Audrey piped up. "To be honest, I'm quite fond of his mother too, Mrs. Littleton. This past school year, they were kind to me. Up until right before I left, anyway." Her tone was wistful.

"What about your family, er, your mother?"

Audrey forgot which stitch came next in her overly simple pattern. "I don't really have a mother, not the way other kids do."

Audrey squirmed in her chair, sensing more questions coming her way, then she caught the couple's exchanged glances, the shared looks that Audrey didn't understand but was confident they did.

She'd trusted them—more correctly, had learned to trust them—but her stomach roiled with uncertainty.

Some nights, falling asleep was hard, or staying asleep, even for people like Audrey, who were used to sultry southern Illinois summers, where even at midnight the temperature might not dip below ninety degrees. And that night, she tossed about, yearning for a breeze through her window.

In addition to suffering from the heat, Audrey had been letting her mind conjure up worst-case scenarios concerning her stay. A gut feeling told her something was about to change. The Trents had been acting aloof, shooting looks at each other when they believed she wasn't able to notice. If Mother had gotten to them, she would've lied again, erasing any positive opinions they'd developed of her. Then again, Gladys hadn't seemed angry or judgmental. Mostly, she'd seemed distracted and sad. Audrey was confused because she'd embraced the farm life, readily accepted both the good and the bad. And she had willingly worked her tail off.

Seven days a week, the horses needed tending, the garden required weeding, along with watering during the dry spells, and piles of clothes had to be washed or mended. She worked with Gladys to prepare three meals a day. Dinner at noon was the biggest and most important. And through it all, she had sweated bucketfuls for her efforts.

Many times after supper, Mr. Trent would invite Audrey to go riding through the horse pasture and on winding dirt roads. She'd learned to saddle and bridle Dander, his gentle sorrel quarter horse mare, and to ride her with confidence. Audrey knew how to hold Dander's reins in her left hand, how to stop moving by pulling both reins slowly into her abdomen, and how to tell Dander to walk by kicking her heels against the horse's ribs. When the mare trotted unexpectedly the first time, Audrey bounced wildly until she got the rhythm Mr. Trent demonstrated and thrust her bottom forward to match Dander's gait.

On Dander, she felt free, in control. And Mr. Trent had been nice enough to treat her to the experience, to let her enjoy those moments of freedom.

Audrey bounced onto her back and crossed her arms, gently rubbing her fingertips on her clammy skin. She was not homesick anymore, having decided that Daddy and Harry were just fine without her. But returning home meant facing Mother and taking her on with all the guts and determination she could round up. That wouldn't be easy, but she felt different somehow—stronger, more confident. Audrey hadn't learned or accepted the "no questions asked" obedience her mother had apparently expected her to learn.

No. Those days of her childhood were over.

CHAPTER 37

Edith

Edith had slept poorly through another sweltering night. In the late morning, she crawled out of bed and shuffled into the kitchen to turn on the box fan she'd bought from McClain's. Soon, her nightgown was rippling like waves across a wind-swept lake. Dry-mouthed and weary, she scooped coffee into the percolator.

Saturday was her favorite day. Like clockwork, Ed Trent's checks arrived regularly each week, just as he'd promised. And with Audrey working for him and his missus for five more weeks, Edith could keep right on riding the money train without punching her own ticket.

After finding a pencil and a pad of paper, she poured her first cup and plopped into a chair to write her shopping list. Harry's clothes could come from the do-gooders—how her son looked hardly mattered—but Audrey's fall wardrobe would require some nice things like a couple of pretty dresses, a sweater, and maybe a pair of high-heeled shoes. Edith might have to spring for bows and a new haircut for her daughter. Audrey would have to look like a debutante to assume the role of one, which meant saving money in the pickle jar rather than spending it all like she had been.

For herself, Edith wrote down *new dress and matching hat*, which was small potatoes compared to what she deserved, but she had to be smart and start looking ahead. As for food, she wrote down *pork chops* and *whole chicken*. She added laundry soap and milk to the list and set it aside, gulped the remainder of her cup of hot coffee, then hovered by the front door's mail slot. The mailman was late. Deciding that a watched pot never boils, she returned to the kitchen and poured another cup. She began to pace. When she heard the whoosh of envelopes slide through the slot to the floor, Edith rushed down the hallway and gathered the flyers and envelopes, eagerly sorting them.

Finding nothing from Ed, she snorted and pulled a sour face. *Where is my check?* Edith lobbed the whole lot of junk mail onto the table.

Close to lunchtime, someone knocked on the front door. Harry had yet to emerge downstairs. Edith raced out of her bedroom, cheered that the mailman had returned with her missing envelope. When she peeked through the front door's curtain—a lady could never be too careful—Ed Trent was looming large on her stoop. Her jaw dropped. Edith patted her curly hair into place and threw open the door with a smile.

"Ed, what an unexpected surprise. I'm delighted to see you." She ushered him in like a gentle woman of breeding would know to do. The effort was likely wasted on a simple farmer, but she needed to practice her manners.

He followed her down the hallway but, with a shake of his head, politely refused to step into the kitchen, which was fine with Edith. His boots would leave a dirty mess everywhere. Ed removed his black cowboy hat and held the brim to his chest, the grip so firm that his fingers blanched white. Tension oozed from his pores, bracing the straight stance he'd assumed, and engulfed the room. The hair on Edith's nape prickled.

"Something bring you by, Ed?" Edith asked in a small voice. A knot formed in the pit of her stomach. "Did that girl do something to upset you or your missus?"

Ed's bushy eyebrows arched into two triangles. He cleared his throat and ran a hand through slicked-back hair. "Got a couple things to say—won't take long. I heard in town the other day that you lost Red." His eyes held Edith's briefly. "My condolences to you and yours."

Edith shrugged one shoulder, thinking how dim-witted Ed was to have gone out of his way for a condolence call. Then her expression brightened. *Of course.* He'd decided to personally deliver the check. She made an effort to look sad but succeeded only in producing a lopsided frown. "Well, that's super nice of you, Ed. Red was a sick man. You knew that better than most people in town."

She shifted her weight from one hip to the other and waited.

"Why didn't you get someone to bring you out to the farm, to tell us? Or write a letter? Seems to me you'd make an effort to let Audrey know something like her father's passing, no matter what."

A peasant farmer with no children thinks he knows how to parent. Edith smirked but tried to disguise her annoyed reaction with a fast, agreeable nod. "I plan to tell her when she gets home in a month—it's best that way. You want her bawling about it and not getting work done? Making excuses because of it? That's what she'd do—mark my words."

Ed's mustache quivered. Edith didn't care whether he agreed with her decision or not. He'd overstayed his welcome already.

"Speaking of work, Ed, your check wasn't in the mail today. Every week, you been sendin' it like regular, and I do appreciate that. I suppose you have it with you?" She cocked her head.

Lips puckered, Ed narrowed his eyes, his expression transforming from irritation to downright anger. "I need to know the truth," he said. "Do you whip that girl?"

Blood rushed to Edith's face, and it flamed hot. "What? No. Why you askin' me something like that?" Edith stepped up to him.

"Oh, I see," she said, drawing out the *s* sound. "The girl told you that. Have you forgotten that our Audrey lies?"

"Lies? That girl's done nothing but work hard and be a right nice young'un to my wife. I think you played me for a fool, Edith. That's exactly what I think. And here I been sending you her wages. Does she even know I'm paying for her labor?"

"Maybe it's Audrey been playing you for a fool. That girl..." Edith paused then said, "Hush," just as Harry emerged from the stairwell in shorts and a T-shirt, clutching a frayed toothbrush in one hand. He eyed the sink behind Edith then took in the two of them as though they were interlopers.

"Say hello to Mr. Trent, Harry," Edith said. "Don't be rude."

Her boy was filthy, and she wondered when he'd last bathed. When Edith motioned for Harry to stand next to her, he complied, but she made the mistake of patting his back. He flinched from her touch and lunged toward the back door, where he stopped to scowl at her. The screen door banged shut behind him.

"The boy sure loves to be outside—most of the time, really. Just hates to take baths. You know boys." Edith released a small cough.

"I don't," Ed said.

She rolled her eyes. "What about my check, Ed?"

Without a response, he turned on his heel and walked out the back door so abruptly that Edith was stupefied. Recovering quickly, she followed him.

"You owe me a week's wages!" she shouted, running across the length of the porch. Ed's truck was parked in the driveway, and he was aiming for it.

He opened the passenger door and stretched inside the cab. Edith could see Ed through the truck's oval rear window, frowning while watching him open the glove box and remove a stack of rubber-banded envelopes. He yanked one out and put the others back before slamming it shut. He walked to the tail of the truck and stopped.

Edith bounded down the steps. Before she reached him, Ed dropped the envelope onto the gravel and hoofed it toward the driver's side. She swooped down and snatched it at the same time his door jerked open with a squeal. Ed hoisted one leg inside the truck before whirling around to face her.

"That'll be your last payment," he said. "We had a deal. Deal's done now."

Ed nosedived into the cab and slammed the door.

"What? That ain't right." Edith bounded toward him and pounded on his window. Ignoring her, he revved the truck's motor and backed down to the highway. Edith stared at the road long after his truck had disappeared, wishing she'd spit on him. After all their years of friendship, he'd just shown her no courtesy. Ed was nothing more than a baboon in overalls, an ape of a man who should've minded his own business and kept his opinions to himself.

But at least she had another check.

CHAPTER 38

Audrey

To escape the heat, Audrey had taken shelter in the shade of a giant bur oak tree, leaning against the Trents' white picket fence, which desperately needed painting. Mr. Trent had built it himself, he'd said, but too long before to remember exactly when. It made their farm seem picturesque, like something on a postcard. The fence enclosed the house and the tall trees in the front and wound along the driveway to encompass the barn, garden, and equipment shed in one large, protective rectangle.

Early in the morning, the air was already steamy and heavy, hampering Audrey's movements until they were sluggish. She'd risen with the rooster's crow. Since then, she'd collected chicken eggs, swept the barn, and fed Suzie and Dander and a stray cat named Tipsy, who was supposed to be the Trent farm mouser. She was giving herself a little breather before checking a long stretch of the pasture fence for splits, bound to be her most time-consuming and tedious chore for the day.

Like Mr. Trent, Audrey had taken to wearing long-sleeved shirts to protect her skin from burns, but she preferred to wear shorts rather than long jeans. She stretched her long, tan legs, which were far more muscular than when she'd arrived, and yawned. After nearly three months with the Trents, she hadn't attempted to leave. Her forced confinement had turned out to be much like going to finishing school. Audrey had learned to cook and bake, quilt, knit, darn, and clean like a proper housewife. Mr. Trent had given her full responsibility for the care of both of the horses, too, as well as that dumb cat.

Nobody had ever trusted her like that before.

It gnawed at Audrey's insides that her daddy, a grown man who could stand up to his wife if he just tried, hadn't made an effort to find her. When she did go home at the end of summer, war would certainly break out between her and Mother, and she had to be prepared, mentally and physically. As much as she wanted to stand up to her, the thought gave her goosebumps.

Audrey shivered in the heat.

Mother would be furious when Audrey told her that Gladys had allowed her to keep a diary—and gleefully tell her, she absolutely would. She'd written whatever she pleased, including her thoughts, dreams, and memories. Audrey no longer had intentions of keeping stories about Mother to herself, either. The best part of going home would be throwing that tiny tidbit in her face. The notion of getting even with her had kept Audrey sane, especially when old terrors sabotaged her thoughts. Imagining victory was like tasting one of Gladys's rhubarb pies, with mouth-puckering fruit, tart and sweet at the same time. One day, Gladys had confided that tiny "red hots," cinnamon candies, were her secret ingredient. She would sprinkle them into the sugar, and after the pie baked, the splashes of red in the filling also made the pie curiously festive.

Audrey wiped her brow and heaved herself forward to head for the pasture, ready to get her chore over with, a small notebook and pen in hand to jot down the locations of broken wire. After she trudged about a quarter mile, she spied dust kicking up and swirling along the road far ahead, moving toward the Trents' farm. With a hand shielding her eyes, Audrey squinted at the vehicle causing the miniature tornadoes. She turned to glance back at the Trent house just as the figure of Mr. Trent appeared on the covered porch. He padded down the steps, swerving his head in every direction. He must have spotted her, because he waved.

"Audrey, come back now," Mr. Trent called out, his hands cupped around his mouth.

She didn't want to disobey him, but Audrey's feet had a mind of their own. She hightailed it in the opposite direction, all the while scanning the pasture fence for drooping or broken barbed wire. When at last Audrey found a gaping hole, she pushed through it. The barbed wire grazed her shoulder, and she winced as it cut through her shirt and into the flesh beneath. Panting, she rushed the distance to the pasture's far side and found a short span where the top fence wire was missing. She pushed the lower wires down and gingerly stepped across on tiptoes. She climbed over the pickets after that. Audrey raced to the barn, wind rushing in her ears and blood pounding in her head.

The heavy barn door rolled aside with some effort, and she bounded in, yanking it closed behind herself as soundlessly as possible. The barn was stuffy yet cooler than the outdoors, bearable because of the sweet smell of straw and hay and the lingering leather scent of the horses' saddles.

Bent over with her hands cupping her knees, Audrey wheezed, trying to catch her breath.

Why did I run like that? She'd bolted without really thinking. A car had been headed to their house. Mr. Trent had been waving her in.

Instinct.

Suddenly, Audrey felt ashamed, cowardly.

Dander welcomed her with a low, welcoming nicker, and she went toward the stall. While stroking the horse's muzzle, Audrey's heart rate gradually slowed to normal. The mare nosed her shoulder for a treat, and Audrey laughed, surprising herself, and gave her an apple from among those scattered upon a nearby shelf, courtesy of

Gladys. She watched with pleasure as her beastly friend crunched the treat.

The barn door began to slide open, and Audrey gasped and whirled around, blinded by the sunlight flooding the dark barn. The stream revealed millions of dust particles dancing in the air between her and a figure standing in silhouette.

"Audrey? You in here?"

She waited for a beat, stunned by the voice. It couldn't be.

"Freddie!" She burst from the shadows and into his outstretched arms.

He held her tight, and she let him.

"Hey, kiddo. We're here to take you home." Freddie released her and playfully knuckled her chin.

"I can't believe you're here," she said. "But, what? You said *we*?"

"You think I got a license yet? My mom drove. She's been looking for you since, since..." Freddie's voice ebbed away. He reached for her hand. "After you left, my mom saw your mom and asked where you were, just curious because I'd told her you had left school. Your mom said you were in St. Louis helping out a cousin all summer."

Audrey blinked twice and stared at him. So that was the story Mother had told people, the one she would expect her to stick with when she was back home.

"So how did you find me?"

"My mom had let it go—none of her business, you know. But then some other things happened, and—"

"Other things? Like what?"

Freddie swallowed hard, his Adam's apple sliding slowly down and back up. Audrey stepped away from him.

"Well, we found out where you really were when we got a visit from Mr. Trent."

"What? Mr. Trent came to see you?"

"Yeah, I guess he thought it was time you went home." Freddie glanced at the ground, but not before she saw a strange look in his eyes.

She dropped his hand, frowning. He was acting funny, not like Freddie at all. Then again, he had been awful to her that last week at school.

As if he could read Audrey's mind, Freddie reached for her hand again and placed her palm on his chest.

"You should be mad at me, I know. I'm sorry for how I acted, you know, that last week you were in school. I've been a chickenshit, a big chump. I'll explain later, I promise, but I want you to know that I'm sorry. That it won't happen again. I swear."

His eyes were warm, and his hand squeezed hers. The apology seemed heartfelt, too, and a rush of affection swept through Audrey's body. She still wanted to know why he'd humiliated and hurt her, but that would have to wait.

"You look amazing," he said. "Beautiful, even. For Christ's sake, why are we still standing here? Mrs. Trent has packed up your stuff."

"What? The Trents knew about this? That you were coming?" She was stunned. They still needed her.

"Yes. Oh, and wait, there's one other thing." Freddie grinned at her. "I want you to know I finally got your letters, and I've read them all. Came personal delivery, courtesy of Mr. Trent. He'd been keeping them, I guess—didn't say why but changed his mind about it. Seemed to feel bad he'd done it."

Together, they stepped into the blinding brightness.

Freddie waved at his mother, who was half sitting on, half leaning against the car's hood, gabbing with Mr. and Mrs. Trent. When Audrey saw the cheerful yellow hat and the woman's long, slender legs, she started to cry.

CHAPTER 39

Edith

When Edith heard a motor rumbling, she peeked through the back-door curtains and scowled at the sleek black car driving up to her shed. It stopped, and as she watched, the driver's door opened and long, lanky legs wearing black heels swept out. Those nyloned legs, she knew too well. The passenger doors opened after that, and Mrs. Somebody's ugly son and her own gorgeous Audrey stepped out of the vehicle. The three of them then lifted multiple bags from the trunk.

The curtain fluttered back into place as Edith stumbled backward, bumping into the table and grasping for a chair to right herself.

That goddamned woman and her kid, whom Edith had gone to great lengths to keep away from Audrey, were here—together. Edith staggered to the counter to snatch her ice pick. She held it tight in one fist and waited for the knock to come.

She heard rustling on the porch then the light rap of knuckles against her door, a clear breach of etiquette. Polite people always called at the front entrance. Cradling the pick, Edith inched the door open and peered through the screen separating them. They stared at each other until Edith could not bear the indignity of the intrusion any longer.

She said, "Yes?"

"Good afternoon, Mrs. Scott. So sorry about coming here without an invitation. May I speak with you briefly, please?"

Edith breezed through the screen door in a swift, fluid motion, making Mrs. Somebody jump back. "What do you want?" She rubbed her nose and bestowed a scornful sniff upon her unwelcome visitor.

Unfazed, Mrs. Somebody stared back at her. "I don't like to get involved, Mrs. Scott, but a man named Mr. Trent came to my house yesterday. He told me that Audrey has been working for him and his wife this summer under some possibly misconstrued circumstances."

Such big, fancy words. Edith lifted her empty fist and bit into a knuckle. "I'm sure I don't know what you mean," she said.

"It's just that you'd told me, and others apparently, that Audrey was in St. Louis. Of course, it's your business what you tell people about your daughter's whereabouts. But Mr. Trent was upset and said as well that Mrs. Trent has been positively distraught, that it's likely Audrey is unaware of her father's passing."

"He's pulled you into my family's affairs? And then, you think it's fittin' to fetch my daughter and bring her home without my permission?"

Edith's eyes darted across the yard. Audrey and Freddie were nowhere in sight.

Mrs. Somebody raised her chin and pursed her painted red lips. "Mrs. Scott, I'd never met the man before he came to my house. He wanted to deliver letters that Audrey had written to Freddie at the beginning of her stay. I gather he'd kept them then felt bad about that decision."

Edith couldn't wait to get her hands on that girl.

"He said Audrey should come home, that he wouldn't feel right having her stay any longer, given the circumstances," she said. "But he did not wish to speak to or, I dare say, see you again. So I offered to bring her home." She squared her shoulders. "Mrs. Scott, you absolutely need to tell Audrey her father has passed. She deserves to know."

The woman was delusional, thinking she could tell Edith what to do. But she kept on yapping anyway.

"What's more, Mr. Trent made it clear—and wishes for you to know—that he believes Audrey isn't what you made her out to be. He defended her character most adamantly."

From the corner of her eye, Edith saw the missing pair emerge from behind the shed, and they were holding hands, swinging them playfully as they walked. Audrey looked up and, seeing her mother for the first time in months, stopped cold, a bunny in the sights of a hungry wolf. Edith eyeballed her, riveted. Her daughter was tan. Her hair was smooth, silky. The shorts she was wearing exposed long, muscular legs.

She was stunning.

Edith turned her attention back to Mrs. Somebody, eyes flashing. "You think you know so much? That you're better than me?" She toyed with the ice pick, considering how easy it would be. "Audrey is my daughter, not yours. You don't know shit about my business."

When the woman took a step back, Edith moved into her space, close enough to absorb the palpable nervousness tinged with fear.

"I've done what I can." Mrs. Somebody turned abruptly and pranced down the steps toward her car.

Once there, she motioned to her son, who released Audrey's hand and made his way to the car and quickly got inside. Then Freddie waved at Audrey, who had not budged, as their car rolled backward and out of sight. The girl turned to stare at her mother with a blank expression, but her stiff stance seemed more defiant than compliant.

"Come inside, dear," Edith cooed, motioning. "Mother has much to tell you."

Audrey

After Audrey carried her four bags into the house, Mother shooed her up to her room rather than allowing her to see Daddy. Since she didn't want to begin an argument within minutes of coming home, Audrey complied, but her mother would soon know she had no intentions of taking her orders or her punishments.

Audrey was eager to get resettled anyway and even more anxious to see her father, so she began unpacking. She wanted to hug him and tell him everything about her adventure, including what Mother had tried to do. While Audrey worked, she also got excited about seeing Harry, half expecting her brother to burst into her room at any moment.

The reason she'd been brought home weeks before school would restart was a mystery. Neither Freddie nor his mom had explained their arrival other than claiming they'd been worried about her, and the Trents thought it best she return home. Their goodbyes had been too rushed for Audrey to get a better explanation, but Gladys had struggled to hold back tears, trembling with emotion, and Mr. Trent had wet eyes and a worn, tender expression. She would miss them terribly.

But the time had to come.

Her room was stuffy after being closed off. Mother had tried to erase her existence with the simple click of a door. After opening the window, she spied the jar of dried-up lilacs and reached down to scoop them up. Audrey paused, thinking, then knelt to check under the bed, spying balls of dust but no notebook. Of course, Mother would have found it and definitely would've read every word. She stood and shrugged, no longer giving a damn. She'd boldly brought several diaries home with her, chock full.

Audrey folded clothing and organized her wardrobe in drawers and her closet, marveling at the generosity shown to her by the Trents. The task completed, she stood in the center of her bedroom, concerned that the nightmares of her childhood were burrowed deep into the walls, prepared to creep out at night and terrify her despite her fortitude. Then she thought of the colorful quilt Gladys had made just for her and pulled it from a bag set near the door. After spreading it over her sheets, Audrey smoothed it to perfection.

Her brother hadn't swooped down on her yet, so she padded into his room and was surprised to see it orderly. Harry's bed had been made, the books shelved, and the floor decluttered. He'd gone off somewhere and would soon tell her all about his summer and taking care of Daddy. Audrey was eager to see if Harry had grown a few inches taller or filled out some.

A sense of urgency overwhelmed her then. Audrey inhaled sharply.

She flew down the stairs, suddenly desperate to see her father. She jumped the last step, where Mother intercepted her.

"He's not here," she said.

"Is he at Lucky's?" Audrey's heart, and her hopes, plummeted. *Daddy is drinking again.*

"No. He's dead."

Audrey shook her head, certain she'd heard her mother incorrectly. She blinked a few times and reached for the counter to steady herself. Mother was studying her, amusement lighting up her eyes.

"It's time for supper, and I expect you to help. Garden's going crazy, thanks to my plantin' early." She waltzed away and bent over to pluck onions out of a bin Audrey had never seen. Then Mother began to chop, chop, chop with vigor, her back to Audrey.

Audrey sprinted to her parents' bedroom, where a new flowery quilt adorned the bed. Daddy's hat—always perched on a hook on the washstand—and his washcloth, shaving brush, and razor were gone. She frantically tore open drawers and rifled through them then looked in the closet. Only a few things belonged to Daddy.

Died? That was impossible. Someone would've told her.

She arched her neck back and closed her eyes, stretching her arms high and spinning in tight circles until she was woozy. She keeled over and shrank to the floor. Sobs erupted from somewhere deep inside Audrey's belly, grief and pain desperate to explode from her mouth. She felt sick to her stomach and thought she might hurl.

Clutching her abdomen, Audrey cried, wailing uncontrollably, screaming, "No, no, no!" until she was exhausted.

"Do you believe me now?" Mother stood behind her in the doorway, but her voice was a fleeting, faraway echo.

The rage in Audrey's chest burned like a wildfire, painfully hot, and threatening to blaze out of control, a destructive force seeking its target.

She hated her mother's voice, her words, her very being.

Audrey looked up, hair tangled and twisted around her neck, and set thunderous eyes on her. "Why? Why didn't you let me know? Daddy dies, and you don't write me? Come get me?"

Her mother's expression had been impassive, lips squeezed into a straight line, but they turned up into a smirk. She disappeared from view, leaving her crumpled on the floor with a knifelike wound in her chest.

Audrey understood then she'd been brought home to learn that her daddy was gone. Dead. She struggled to her feet, wiping her eyes and nose on her bare arm.

Harry.

She followed her mother into the kitchen.

"Where is Harry? I want to see Harry." Audrey's voice was so hoarse she could hardly eke out the words.

Her eyes followed Mother's every move. The woman reached nonchalantly into a bin and retrieved two potatoes. Dropped them into the sink. Turned on the faucet. Selected a paring knife from a drawer.

"Did you notice I had my hair colored and cut? Had it done at the beauty parlor. Look younger, don't you think?"

Audrey's body slid down the lower cabinet's facade until she collapsed into a lump, head hung low, hair strands strewn over her face. "I... I need to see Harry," she whispered. "Please. Where is he?"

After she trimmed and sliced the potatoes, Mother scraped them into a frying pan along with the onions. She clicked the burner on. The stove was new, similar to the Trents'.

"I don't know where he is."

"What do you mean?"

"I mean what I mean. Sometimes, he comes home. Sometimes, he doesn't."

The vegetables sizzled as Mother stirred them.

Audrey covered her ears. She could hear Mother speaking to her, but Audrey was underwater, close to drowning, and glad the voice was coming from another world far, far away.

Three days later, Audrey had still seen no sign of Harry.

She'd endured her mother's prattling on about Johnny DeDecker even though she secretly gnashed her teeth and fisted her hands, pretending to accept the idea of marriage to buy herself time. Often, she wept alone in her bedroom until she was hoarse. Audrey longed for one more whiff of Daddy's cigarettes even though she'd hated the smell, was hungry for the sound of his voice to soothe whatever was left of her shattered spirit.

Dressed, with nowhere to go, Audrey had been wandering around the parlor like a lost lamb, finding nothing to comfort her, no one to guide her, and riddled with guilt that made her mouth taste sour and her heart ache in constant spasms. Audrey had been away at the farm, even happy, when Daddy had needed her most—Harry too.

Finally, she fell into Daddy's rocker and closed her eyes, inhaling deeply to detect whatever scent of him still remained embedded in the fabric.

He had died. Mother would not talk about it at all. She'd provided no details and given Audrey nothing to hold onto other than to say the sickness got him. She couldn't know anything about the potential of her mother's hand in his death, but Audrey was certain she hadn't taken good enough care of him. Had she been home, Daddy might've lived. Mother had kept the gut-wrenching news of his death from her, just to ensure she kept working on the farm.

She also worried about her brother, sweet Harry, who'd always been the favorite. *What kind of mother has no clue where her child is?*

CHAPTER 40

Audrey

Early the next morning, Audrey arose with a renewed sense of purpose.

She splashed cool water from her washbasin over her face, brushed her teeth, then dressed in long shorts and a pink T-shirt. She tied her hair into a neat ponytail.

To find Harry, she had to start somewhere, and Mr. Ritter would be as good a place as any, especially since he'd likely been watching the comings and goings at their house.

Walking over, she noticed his garden was barren and had become overgrown. Healthy weeds had sprouted between the patio bricks, camouflaging most of what was left of them. The lawn was in desperate need of mowing too.

The old man was surprised to see her and greeted her with a huge grin before limping down and off his back stoop to wrap his arms around her. He looked older, as weathered as an old barn.

Audrey made a silent vow that after she found Harry, they would help Mr. Ritter with chores.

"Did you know I've been gone? That Mother sent me away?" Audrey asked, gently releasing his hands.

Mr. Ritter clasped his age-spotted hands to his chest, wobbling somewhat without his cane, and nodded solemnly.

"My father died, and nobody told me."

The old man's lips trembled, either because he was struggling for a response or attempting to control his emotions. "I'm sorry about your papa," he said, sneaking a quick glance at her house. He cleared his throat. "Should you be over here, Audrey?"

She ignored his question, wanting only to talk about Harry. "Mr. Ritter, Harry is missing. I've been back four days, and he hasn't been home once. I'm worried," she said.

Behind his spectacles, a glint flashed through his tired eyes. "I don't know where he is, Audrey. Sorry to say."

"But Harry wouldn't just run away. Have you seen him at all? Mother says he comes home sometimes. I thought maybe you'd spoken with him or you might know of any friend he's made."

The old man rubbed a thumb over his lips. "I've seen him around some."

"You have? Have you talked with him?"

He raised his gray eyebrows but shook his head no. Audrey detected sadness in the gesture, the grim face, and his slumped back.

"Glad you're back home safely, Audrey. It's good to see you." He patted her shoulder and hobbled toward the stoop.

"Wait. I don't understand." The abrupt dismissal shocked Audrey, and she jumped in his way, putting the palm of one hand on his shoulder. "Please," she said. "Do you know anything?" Audrey stared at him, willing the man to tell her something, anything that might be helpful.

He eyed his stockinged feet and began to mumble.

"I can't hear you, Mr. Ritter."

"When you find him, you both have to leave," he said.

"What did you say? Leave?"

He looked up then, seeking her eyes. "Yes. But before you do—leave, I mean—you must come to see me first. Do not forget."

Audrey went home, pushed Mr. Ritter's strange comments from her mind, and changed into nicer clothes for her next errand.

The cotton shift Gladys had purchased for her was a deep blue that she'd said offset Audrey's pretty eyes and complexion. It subtly framed her curves too. After she undid her ponytail, her hair fell in soft waves to the middle of her back. She dabbed on a bit of rouge—another gift from Gladys since Audrey was "becoming a young woman who should accent her beauty."

Downstairs, she clipped toward the back door in low black heels comfortable enough for walking. Without warning, Mother came from behind her and grasped Audrey's arm with such force that she nearly lost her balance.

Audrey ripped her arm away, turned, and smiled cheekily, a change from her behavior of the past several days.

"Wipe that smile off your face. You're not going anywhere."

Undeterred, Audrey thrust her nose right into Mother's face. "I'm not? I went away to live on a farm, didn't I?" She squinted and set her jaw. "Where did all the new things come from, Mother? The stove? Your quilt? The bins? The fan? Do you think I'm so stupid I wouldn't figure it out?"

Not waiting for a response, Audrey smacked the screen door open and was proceeding through it when Mother shoved her, sending her stumbling down the porch steps and falling to the ground. When she looked up, Mother was on the porch with arms crossed over her chest, looking down upon her.

Just like the old days.

Slowly, Audrey got to her feet, taking her time to build up her backbone and tamp down her fears. She swiped at her dress, which was stained with streaks of dirt and grass, and straightened it before rolling her eyes in an exaggerated gesture. She sighed.

"Nice try, Mother," she said.

Mother's face clouded over, and her arms dropped to her sides. Audrey wanted to remember that surprised look of defeat. Even the tiniest victory should be savored. She strolled away with her head high, acting more confident than she felt, barely brave enough to keep her feet moving. When she reached the path along the highway leading to town, Audrey heard her mother shrieking her name, and she smiled.

Edith

Edith spat obscenities as she circled the kitchen like an agitated tiger at the zoo. She'd sent Audrey away to get her under control, and Ed had failed her miserably. She balled up a fist and pounded it on the table. The upper hand was still hers. *Dammit!* She had to do something before her daughter spoiled everything. The future—all Edith had ever wanted—was at stake.

Audrey could not win this round or any other. And she had to make damn sure that *they* wouldn't win.

Gripping the edge of the sink, Edith sought to steady herself. Her bugged-out eyes scanned the room in herky-jerky fashion, unwilling to let a thing slip by, and seeing nothing, she perked up her ears to listen for them.

But she was alone.

Moving to the back door, Edith pushed her ear against the screen and again listened intently. Then she opened it and walked out.

She marched into the grass, passing the old coot's empty pigeon coop and the rambling shed Red had never fixed up, to beyond the woodpile. When Edith reached the edge of the field, she stopped and stared toward the horizon, where the brown-and-green palette of the woods collided with the blue sky. She stood there, as rigid and still as the towering trees. A breeze flapped the folds of her dress and cooled her upturned, flushed face.

"Goddamn you!" Her voice skewered the air. Several nearby robins took flight, leaving their worms behind. She raised a fist and bellowed, "You will not stop me!"

Edith's oath spewed forth like smoke belching from a chimney. As the words shot high into the air, she shut her eyes and silently commanded the wind to carry them into the woods, drop them in the clearing.

There, and only there, would her words be heard, and heeded. They would not be ignored.

The breeze fell away.

She opened her eyes and focused on the wood line with an expectant expression, lips parted, chest heaving. A minute passed before the wind shifted direction, returning a message to her. The breeze toyed with Edith's dress and tickled her exposed flesh.

Cocking her head, she listened.

Then Edith tossed her head back and laughed.

CHAPTER 41

Audrey

The Littletons' sunflower-yellow house stood out like a bright beacon calling out to lost sailors.

Just as Audrey reached for the knocker, the door swung open. Surprised, she jumped back. A tall man with dark hair and deep-set blue eyes gave her the once-over, his long, dark eyelashes gliding up and down. Embarrassed by the scrutiny, Audrey plucked a tiny leaf from her bangs and fidgeted, her fingers wiggling by her sides.

"I-I'd like to see Freddie, please. My name is Audrey Scott. W-We're friends," she said. "Oh, maybe Mrs. Littleton is here?"

The man in gray slacks and a collared white shirt had to be Freddie's father, so she gave him her prettiest smile, but he didn't return the friendly greeting.

Instead, Mr. Littleton stepped through to the outside, closing the door behind himself. His cologne, which reminded her of vanilla, instantly filled the air. "I know who you are, young lady," he said, casting his gaze on her. "I'm surprised to see you here, but actually, I'm glad."

She took several steps backward, putting space between them. "I just need to see Freddie, please."

"Now, I'm happy you said that. This gives me the chance to speak with you."

Audrey looked down at her shoes to avoid his penetrating stare, wondering if he was really as kind as Freddie had indicated. He certainly didn't seem to be, given his commanding presence and serious expression.

"I'm sure you're a sweet girl, but I don't want you hanging out with Freddie. I believe your mother has also made that quite clear to him."

Hearing Mother had spoken to Freddie, Audrey's head snapped up. "But Mrs. Littleton said—"

"Please don't involve my wife. It was wrong of her to interfere in your family's business the way she did." He bent over until his eyes were level with hers. "I've seen to it that Mrs. Littleton won't do anything like that again."

"But that's not necessary, uh, sir." Audrey gulped, her pulse picking up. "You see, my father died, and I didn't know it. Mrs. Littleton, she only—"

"Yes, yes, her intentions were kind. But she had no reason to get involved in your private matters. I've ordered Freddie and Mrs. Littleton to keep their distance from you, from your family. I don't want trouble with your mother. And I daresay she needs your full attention, not this distraction of yours with my son."

Audrey's lips opened, but she did not speak. She saw herself in that moment through his judgmental eyes. The pitiful daughter of a woman everyone in town shunned had just shown up on his doorstep in a filthy dress, presumably for a handout from his son or wife. She was a problematic, cancerous tumor needing to be excised.

But she'd come about Harry. Audrey straightened up, wet her lips, and cleared her throat, undeterred.

"Sir, it's just that I came about my brother—"

He pointed a long finger directly at her face. Her eyes darted around the yard, hoping Freddie would come loping around the house to stand up for her.

"This discussion is over," he said. "Go home. Take care of your mother. It's obvious to anyone she needs you."

With a curt nod, Mr. Littleton turned on his heel and disappeared inside the house before Audrey could manage a retort. She stared at the closed door, dumbfounded, and for several heartbeats imagined the collective hot stares of the Littletons' neighbors attempting to melt her into the sidewalk.

Audrey forced one foot in front of the other and began the walk home. Freddie might be under the thumb of his father, but if she found him, he would help her find Harry. *Wouldn't he?*

She heaved a heavy sigh. Freddie might not be able to defy the man he idolized. And that went double for Mrs. Littleton.

CHAPTER 42

Edith

Edith was enjoying her daughter's new submissive attitude, reveling in the next steps about to come. She was certain the silly girl had marched over to see Freddie and his mother and they'd handily turned her away. That was no big surprise to her, but Audrey seemed to be taking the rejection hard. No way in hell would Mrs. Somebody, her husband, or her son risk sticking their noses into her business again.

And, of course, Edith had been right to think her daughter would seek them out. She had nobody else. Audrey had returned home dejected and demure and had been respectful to her for a good week. Her quiet behavior was even better than what Edith had hoped to achieve by sending her off to work on the Trent farm. Thrilled at the change in Audrey, she considered sending Mrs. Somebody a basket of muffins as a thank you. Unfortunately, she was out of money to buy the ingredients to bake them.

With things settled, her plan was, at last, ready to be put into motion.

Edith was on her way to see Howard, cheered that everything was going her way.

She glided through the entrance of Willowdale Farm Implements and loudly demanded to see Mr. DeDecker. A cocky salesman tipped his hat to her. Annoyed, Edith judged the man for wearing a hat indoors, and in a lady's presence, no less. He scooted through the lobby toward the boss's office.

Within minutes, she was escorted into his office. Edith had worn her most stylish hat—the one with the two peacock eye feathers—and a striped dress that she had smartly belted at the waist. She had overheard a chubby woman in McClain's say that belts made a person look slimmer, not heavier, so she'd purchased two.

"What can I do for you today, ma'am?" Howard pulled his bulky frame up from the chair but once again failed to invite Edith to take a seat.

"I'll get right to it," Edith said, flopping down. Cradling her pocketbook, she leaned in conspiratorially. "It's time now, you understand? Audrey's been away for the summer, helping a relative. That's the kind of girl she is, you know. But she's back now, and school's gonna be startin' up. You need to get the ball rollin' on puttin' these kids together, as we agreed. Instruct your boy." She listed against the armrest and batted her eyes.

The leather chair creaked when Howard sat down, adjusting his glasses higher on his nose and puckering his lips. He eyed Edith with full disdain, as though she were a hoodlum who'd just scratched his new Ford.

"Oh, don't give me that look," Edith snapped then rapped her knuckles once on his desk before tilting her body away.

Howard covered his eyes with a hand and lowered his head.

"Headache?" she asked.

When he looked at her again, his face had hardened into something more impassive—a businessman's move, she suspected, to hold his cards close. No way would she fall for it.

"Audrey is ripe for the pickin', a real beauty," she went on. "Your Johnny is a lucky boy. They can marry young, Howard. Lots of the kids do while they are still in school. Perfectly normal and respectable, as you know. No need to wait."

He spun his chair slowly around to gaze at the row of family photos on his credenza. When he ran his thumb around a framed photo of Johnny, Edith rolled her eyes.

"Touching," she said.

"You crazy-ass woman," he muttered, swerving back to meet her eyes. "Don't come back again. You will not be welcomed here." He stood abruptly, a signal she should leave.

The corners of Edith's mouth twitched and curved into a sly smile.

Snapping her pocketbook open, knowing his angry eyeballs were set on her, she retrieved a folded sheet of paper and pushed it across his desk. He looked down.

"Do you want your wife to have this instead?" she asked. "C'mon, Howard. Let's get this thing done."

CHAPTER 43

Audrey

Whenever she could, Audrey holed up in her room to avoid conversing with Mother, but when that was impossible, she gritted her teeth, forced herself to be polite, and did what she was told without argument. The only thing Audrey truly wanted to talk about was her brother, but Mother refused to engage. To say they were getting along would be going too far, but Audrey was making an effort to ease the tension between them. If Mother began to trust her, she might open up about what had happened to Daddy and give her clues as to Harry's whereabouts.

Sitting on her bed, Audrey was waiting until she heard the back door slam. She jumped up and ran down the stairs and outdoors to the shed, ducking inside. After that, she hustled toward Mr. Ritter's garage, carrying a spade and hugging two coffee cans she'd retrieved. She doubted she would run into Mr. Ritter because he rarely appeared outdoors anymore, but if she did, he would probably run inside as he had the past few times. When Audrey previously prodded him for information, for his help, he'd been reluctant to say a word about Harry. Now, he seemed to be avoiding her.

The mid-August day was steamy, and Audrey was instantly coated in sticky sweat. The rain shower during the night had raised the humidity to an insufferable level, but at least the ground would be soft and easy to dig into. Earlier, while drinking her hot tea, Mother had said she would be away for quite a while, off to visit someone she had called "really important." Audrey had stared at her with faraway eyes, not caring about whatever fantasy the woman was currently playing out in her head, especially if it had to do with Johnny DeDecker.

When she reached her secret garden, Audrey found it overgrown with thistles and pokeweed plants nearly the size of small trees. That was all good cover, so she didn't mind and began to dig a hole. Once the task was completed, she dropped in a can, covered it, and inserted a fat stick in the dirt to mark the spot. She then counted the other sticks, half visible in rows that extended the length of the garage.

If Audrey was remembering correctly, twenty-two sticks should've been standing guard amid the weeds, but some were missing. Before burying the second can, Audrey dug under the very first twig she'd ever put in the garden, expecting to tap a lid about six inches down. Nothing was there. She dug deeper then moved on and pulled up several more sticks, scraping in the dirt below them. Puzzled and becoming frantic, she flung dirt and weeds around, working to the end of the row. Audrey sat back on her haunches with tears brimming in her eyes, heart caught in her throat.

They were all gone.

Some sticks had been replanted, which was just the type of depraved thing her mother would do. Somehow, she'd known to look in this very place for her diaries.

Audrey smothered her face with mud-stained hands, whimpering but refusing to let herself lose control, to blubber like Mother would want her to. The loss was too big for her to comprehend, let alone readily accept, and she bobbled her head as disbelief grew into anger. Mother was more diabolical—if that were possible—than she'd ever fathomed. She'd removed them while Audrey was far away but had known her handiwork would be eventually discovered. She would have delighted in that fact.

Audrey tossed the spade onto the helter-skelter mess of foliage and ragged holes she'd created, the unspoken arbiters of her defeat, then got to her feet.

The stories were still in her mind, and while she could not recreate everything she'd written in those diaries, Audrey decided she'd begin anew. Mother's actions would not deter her, stop her, or bring her to her knees, no matter how much it hurt. Mother had yet to learn of her intentions to tell the world, even if it was just the small world of Willowdale, about their lives. Audrey looked forward to that day.

But first, she had to find Harry.

Later in the day, Audrey was perched on the couch, cutting tiny slits into the armrest with a paring knife. She felt eyes on her and sensed a presence, figuring and even hoping it was her mother. Audrey turned her head and looked up.

"Oh my God, Harry!" she yelped.

She jumped to her feet and raced over to throw her arms around his shoulders. Harry rested his forehead against her, but his arms hung limply, as if they were too heavy to return her embrace. He'd grown taller but was gangly, with long, unruly hair that smelled like oil and dried sweat.

"Where have you been?" Audrey whispered. "Did you know I was back?" She released him gently and examined her brother's blank face. His eyelids were droopy, like he badly needed sleep, and his lips were badly chapped. Harry returned Audrey's gaze with a haunted, faraway look she didn't recognize.

Clutching Harry's hands, she slipped to her knees before him and threw her arms around his waist. She pulled him to her and rubbed his lower back. "What's happened to you? Harry, I'm here now."

He didn't respond. Then she felt something under her fingertips and raised her eyebrows in alarm.

Audrey stood and, without hesitation, pulled up his shirt while issuing a crisp "Turn around, Harry."

Welts. Long pink lines. Scars. She recognized them immediately. *Lashes. The stick.*

Mother had used the fucking stick on her brother.

Harry pulled his shirt down and turned to casually walk into the kitchen. He grabbed the sole apple from a bowl on the table, rubbed it against his shirt, and hungrily bit into it. Audrey followed him numbly, wringing her hands. Several times, Harry's eyes darted to the back door. She knew why.

"Harry, oh my God, talk to me," Audrey said, her hushed voice cracking. "Why did she do that to you? What happened?"

The boy glanced at the clock then at the door before motioning for her to follow him.

"Talk to me, Harry," Audrey begged as she fell in behind him.

He opened the basement door and started down the dark steps. Audrey flicked a light bulb on to dimly light their way. "Why are we going down here?" she asked.

The coal-fired furnace room was on the left at the bottom of the stairs. The opposite, larger storage room stretched off to the right. Harry made a beeline to the bigger room, rushing up to a tall but narrow set of shelves their grandfather had supposedly built years before. When she reached the basement floor, Audrey snapped on a hanging light bulb, which managed to cast a thin yellowish veil around them.

"Harry, why are we down here? Harry, why won't you talk?" She was instinctively whispering.

Her brother was staring at something on the shelf, and she followed his gaze to a lineup of bottles, tins, paint cans, and an old black iron.

"What? What is it? This is stupid, Harry." Audrey's patience was waning. She was tired of playing one of Harry's games when she needed to know where he'd been and what had happened to him.

When he tapped one of the tin cans, Audrey squinted and looked closer.

"Dah-ee." His voice was scratchy, nearly inaudible, not at all like Harry's.

Then he jerked his head toward the stairway and froze.

She murmured, "Harry, what—" But Harry was gone, tearing back up the stairs like he'd heard a ghost, leaving Audrey gawking at his spinning legs. "Harry. What did you say? Wait, don't—" Then she heard heavy shuffling and slapped her hand over her mouth.

"Why were you down there? What were you doing?" Mother's voice sailed down to her ears, a sinister growl more terrifying than her angry screams. Audrey cringed when the screen door slammed, and Mother yelled, "You come back here right now!"

She kept her wide eyes glued to the stairway, willing her mother to go outside or into the bedroom so that she could get out of the basement unseen. Mother's dark, serpentine shadow was wavering on the landing wall as though she was unable to make a decision. Audrey's own thoughts waffled between being brave enough to engage in a long-overdue confrontation and being terrified. Crouching low, she swept into the furnace room and squeezed behind the large coal contraption near the far wall, scooping lumps of the black stuff around herself before tucking herself into a tight ball.

Mother was humming. The sound was growing louder, eerily closer with each heavy footstep. Ears buzzing, Audrey strained to hear her next movements. The humming stopped when her feet thudded onto the concrete floor. To Audrey's relief, Mother headed into the other room. She was scouting for something amid the broken chairs, rusted tools, buckets, and pots, the hodgepodge of junk her grandparents had long ago relegated to the gloomy basement.

Breathing only sips of air, Audrey stared wide-eyed at the black metal an inch from her eyes, blinded except for the bulb's barest, dull light. When it went out, Audrey was consumed by blackness. Still, she didn't flinch. Mother huffed her way back up the stairs, mumbling incoherently. Audrey waited, praying her mother would not accidentally lock her in. The landing light clicked off. The door slammed.

After several minutes, she scrambled to her feet and, with arms outstretched, cautiously slunk into the other room. Fragments of daylight from a deep window well glazed the walls just enough to calm her nerves.

Stooping before the shelves, Audrey found the same square tin that Harry had pointed at and picked it up. She stared at the label as her eyes adjusted. Gradually, she made out a skull and crossbones and a cartoon rendering of a dead rat, belly-up. *Rat poison. Arsenic.*

Audrey's hand flew to her mouth.

What on earth was Harry trying to tell me? That we have rats in the house?

Her brother had insisted she follow him into the basement but hadn't answered a single question even though Audrey had begged him. Harry could be playing one of his silly games—refusing to speak—but his scars had been very real. And their daddy was very dead.

CHAPTER 44

Edith

Edith had begun to prefer Red's rocker to her own chair, so she dropped into his cushion with a long sigh and tipped herself back and forth with her toes. Eventually, she dropped her head on the cushion and closed her eyes.

It had been some day—a good day. She'd convinced Howard to come through, and her day would finally come.

Blackmail always worked in stories. It had worked for her too.

Too bad she hadn't caught Harry, though. The boy had slipped right through her grasp. Edith would've liked to lock him in the basement again for a few days. The boy's behavior was mystifying. Something had changed him from a sweet, obedient child into a delinquent, a sneaky, untrustworthy scamp no longer worthy of joining the DeDecker family. The few times he'd bothered to come home, he'd refused to speak to her. The very proper Mrs. DeDecker would not think well of such poor manners. She shuddered.

Wherever her son was regularly getting off to, he was bound to come home again, especially if he figured out Audrey had returned. Then Edith would deal with his behavior and straighten him out.

"Hello, Mother."

Annoyed by the intrusion into her thoughts and period of repose, Edith slowly lowered her head and opened her eyes, preparing the words to scold Audrey. She did a double take.

Standing with her feet apart, her eyes flashing deep blue, Audrey was holding aloft a willowy but sturdy whipping stick—one of

Edith's favorites she'd stored under the porch—as if brandishing Miss Liberty's torch. The sight tickled Edith, and she chuckled.

"What are you doing with that? Put it back," she said.

"Is this the one you used on Harry?"

With a long groan, Edith leaned forward, planted her feet, and stood. She studied her daughter. Audrey's legs and arms were smudged by coal dust, and her clothes had been soiled everywhere by the smelly black powder. Washing it out completely would be nearly impossible.

"I gather you saw Harry?" she said, raising her eyes to meet her daughter's. "In the basement, I see, judging by your clothes? What were you two doing down there?"

"I've seen the welts, Mother. Felt them. They are just like mine, only not all healed over. Why did you whip him? Your precious little Harry?"

Edith fluttered her eyelids. "I didn't do nothing that boy didn't deserve. This ain't none of your business anyway. Now stop botherin' me, and go put that back."

"It is my business, Mother. What did he do?" Audrey sidled closer to Edith. Her hands were trembling. "I couldn't understand why Harry wasn't here, at home. Now I do. How could you? You're nothing but a vicious, cruel—"

"How dare you raise your voice to me like that. I have every right—"

The wiry limb came down fast.

It cracked across Edith's shoulder and grazed her neck. She wanted to rub the skin where the whip had struck but held herself back from showing any sign of weakness. Instead, she drilled Audrey with her rabid eyes. The color in Audrey's cheeks had flamed high, and she was practically foaming at the mouth, spittle outlining her lower lip as her hands squeezed the weapon tightly.

"Where are my diaries?"

Edith tilted her head to the side like an innocent puppy. "I don't have any of your damn diaries. If you still had any, that makes you a damn stinkin' liar."

With a fierce cry, Audrey struck her again with her makeshift whip, lashing her mother's cheek. A streak of blood rose to the surface, and this time, Edith touched the gash and stared at the bright-red glob on her fingertip.

"Admit it," Audrey said. "You dug them up. They're all gone."

"You were hiding diaries, then? So I was right all along." Edith took a single step forward, eyes glued to the stick. "What are you goin' to do, Audrey? Nothing, that's what. No Littletons to help poor little you anymore. Throw that thing down now, dammit, or you damn sure will regret it."

Audrey's chest was heaving. "You stole the money I made working for the Trents."

Edith shrugged her shoulders. "It's my money. That's not stealin'."

"You stole. We both know it. And you really hurt Harry. You destroyed my diaries. So what if I lied? My God, Mother, you're a monster. You had no right to do those things." Audrey jutted out her chin. "But I have a great memory. Destroying my diaries doesn't mean a thing."

Edith scowled and took another step forward, determined to snatch the whip. Audrey held her ground and snapped the tip in the air, forcing her mother to bend backward.

"What did you do to Daddy?"

Edith recoiled, rolled her neck around, thinking.

"Did you poison him, Mother?"

"Why the hell are you asking me something like that? Harry put that idea into your head?"

Audrey thrust her arm back and brought the whip down harder than before, then again. Edith ducked and put up her arms to cover herself. Losing herself in a frenzied rage, the girl thrashed her mother's hands and arms, shoulders, and face. When at last the whipping stick slackened and broke, Edith snatched it from Audrey's hands and hurled it out the window. Audrey raced into the kitchen, and she charged after her, pausing at the counter when she saw Audrey standing on the threshold of the open back door. Edith's fingers traced the stinging, bloody cuts.

Audrey was holding the door open, half bent over to catch her breath, her eyes filled with a shining mixture of anger and anguish, but not regret.

"You're nothing but a bastard child."

Audrey blinked at her mother's insult as though it hadn't registered, then replied with one of her own. "You are nothing but the white trash Grandmother Hamilton said you were."

Edith's eyes narrowed to slits, and she growled in her throat.

"I will never marry someone just to please you. You're done, Mother. I will never, ever live here again."

Still unfazed, Edith replied with a snort. "You have nowhere to go."

"You've never gotten it. I'd rather be anywhere than with you. I will never—and I mean never—be what you want. Do what you want. In fact…" She paused, pushing the door open wide. "If I was your only hope to get rich, you're through. You lose."

CHAPTER 45

Audrey

Audrey ran as fast as she could down the hill, stopping only when she reached Lucky's and was out of breath. Strangely, she wanted to laugh hysterically. She'd hated her mother for sending her to the Trents' farm, but that was the only decent thing the woman had ever done for her, although unknowingly.

And with the swing of a stick, she'd just set herself free.

Audrey didn't feel bad about it. Actually, she felt good—really good—until she lumbered by the tavern and glanced its way. Her shoulders sagged, and her eyes welled up with tears. So often, Daddy had parked himself on a stool in there, just beyond that blue door in a room thick with smoke. She would give anything to rush in and throw her arms around him. Before Mother sent her away, something had changed about her father, and he'd been paying more attention to her and Harry.

Maybe he'd finally become her ally.

She scurried by Lucky's, shaking the useless thought from her head. What a sight she had to be to people in passing cars. Audrey considered her predicament, panic rising inside her chest. She had no money or clothing, no place to stay, no job experience, and no friends to speak of—not the kind where she could just announce herself at their doorsteps and ask to be put up. The Littletons might help her, given her new situation, but neither Freddie nor Mrs. Littleton had checked in on her since dropping her off at home.

A few blocks before Audrey intended to turn onto Victorian Row, the sharp blare of a car horn so startled her that she jumped sideways into the grass. She glanced quickly behind her to see a sleek, dark-blue convertible with wooden side panels was pulling up and would soon be alongside. Audrey picked up her pace and kept her eyes focused straight ahead.

"Hey, sister, wanna ride in the Super Deluxe?"

The horn tooted again as the car rolled beside her.

"Audrey, stop, damn it all. Let me help you."

She slowed up and turned. Johnny was waving at her, his smile radiant against darkly tanned skin, fringes of his sun-streaked hair wisping over one eye. Audrey stopped and bowed her head, peering at him from under her eyelids. He turned off the ignition and slid off a red leather seat to hop over the driver's door, looking every bit the fashion icon with cuffed jeans, penny loafers, and a crisp white T-shirt. He was taller than the last time she'd seen him, months before at school.

"Leave me alone, Johnny," Audrey said, her cheeks burning with embarrassment. "I-I don't need your help."

When he reached her, Johnny put a hand under her elbow.

"I think you do. I mean, look at you. This look's bad, even for you, and I've seen you wear some weird shit. Whadja do, crawl through a mine shaft? Is that what you do for fun?"

He laughed at his own joke, but when Johnny scanned her face, he dropped the smile. "Sorry, sis. You been through something, huh? How about you come home with me? You can have a bath and change clothes. You'll feel better—promise. And you can tell me what's going on."

Audrey couldn't tell if Johnny was being sincere because he was a practical jokester, after all, and flirted with every female. He'd also put an unwelcome hand on her thigh at school and squeezed it. She checked out his expensive car and doubted she would be welcome in his home.

"And your parents?" she asked.

"By the looks of you, your mom's probably gone batshit crazy again. Am I right?" He served up the same goofy grin other girls went gaga for. "They'll be cool, I'm sure."

Audrey wasn't sure if Johnny was being kind or humiliating her for fun. She knitted her brow, unable to make a decision.

"Sis... I bet I know what's bugging you—I mean, in addition to whatever caused this train wreck." He pointed at her. "It's about Freddie, right? He wouldn't care. I mean, the two of you are over, right?"

Shaken by his comment, Audrey pressed a thumb into one eyebrow and shut her eyes, swaying slightly.

"Audrey. C'mon, man. Get in." Johnny poked her playfully in the ribs. She nodded shyly, finally agreeing. Staying with Johnny would give her time to develop a plan.

He jogged to the car's passenger side and opened the door for her while grinning broadly, pleased with himself. They left with a squeal of rubber and headed straight for Johnny's home, located outside the town's limits. Johnny hummed and tapped his fingers on the steering wheel, oblivious to Audrey's growing anxiety, while she gazed at the blurry rows of cornstalks whizzing by, eager to avoid conversation. Drawing near a woodsy area, Johnny turned left and eased his car through an entrance topped by a decorative wooden arch. The road zigzagged below lush poplar tree canopies until Audrey spied a large home emerging in the distance. Soon, she was admiring manicured bushes and colorful petunias that edged a large covered porch, filled with various pieces of welcoming white wicker furniture.

The DeDecker home was unlike anything Audrey had ever seen, let alone set foot inside of as a guest—an invited one, no less. Although Freddie's home was charming, Johnny's house was a brick-

and-mortar symbol of grandeur, a gentleman's country house she'd seen only in magazines.

They parked in front of a three-car garage painted to match the white house. Johnny jumped over his door, but Audrey hesitated before cautiously opening the convertible door. Her eyes roamed to the top of the house, to the dormer windows on the third floor, then to the second-floor windows perfectly aligned below. All were adorned by crisp green-and-white-striped awnings that mimicked the natural beauty around them.

Johnny motioned for her to follow him, but Audrey dragged her feet until he ushered her through a back door, and they took off their shoes in something called a mudroom. They ambled by a small indoor bathroom, which he called a powder room, and entered a large, bright kitchen.

The room was a celebration of pink. Shiny pink aluminum cabinets filled the gentle curve of the opposite wall, their perfect symmetry broken by a window, a white refrigerator, and a stove. The countertops were minty green with silver edging that matched every glossy handle and knob in the room. Wallpaper covered the walls, printed with vivid irises, roses, and mums. For a moment Audrey thought that if she tried hard, she might just smell their exotic scents.

In all her life, Audrey had never seen a room so cheerful or colorful.

"Well, who do we have here?"

Audrey turned toward the voice and saw a tall, thin woman wearing oval eyeglasses, flashing a smile that seemed genuine. Unlike Johnny's blond locks, his mom had short brown hair, teased inches above her head. She was wearing an ivory dress, black pumps, and a short string of pearls.

"Hello, Mrs. DeDecker," she said uneasily and looked over at Johnny for help.

At the same moment, Johnny pulled his head out of the humming refrigerator and said, "Mom, there's no beer in here. I need a cold one."

He offered her a teasing smile, but she crossed her arms and furrowed her brow in displeasure. Johnny winked at Audrey, wandered to a glass jar with Cookies printed across it, and grabbed two sugar cookies then handed one to Audrey. "Okay, okay. This is Audrey, Mom. I told her she could clean up here, maybe stay the night if that's cool with you. Look at her. She's a mess."

At first, Mrs. DeDecker's expression was puzzled, but she recovered quickly, saying, "That's not very nice, Johnny."

"C'mon, Mom. Audrey Scott? You know, the daughter of that crazy woman you and Dad always talk about?"

His mom's cheeks turned Pepto-Bismol pink. She looked at Audrey, who reacted by hunching over, wishing she could shrink out of sight. When no one spoke, she looked up shyly through her eyelashes to find Mrs. DeDecker holding out a hand to her.

"Never mind him," she said, folding her fingers around Audrey's wrist and coaxing her out of the kitchen. "I'm pleased to meet you. You're in Johnny's class, right? I'm looking forward to him being back at school next week. He and his little sister have been driving me bonkers. You two are friends, then?"

Mrs. DeDecker led her across the dining room's polished floors, bypassing a formal parlor filled with overstuffed furniture, and toward a wide, winding staircase with dark walnut banisters. She let Audrey's hand go as they walked to the top of the stairs. Mrs. DeDecker turned right and entered the first room along the hallway, which she called the "guest quarters."

Johnny's mother fetched a robe from her own bedroom, and while she straightened the bedspread and plumped pillows, Audrey shyly undressed, hearing explanations about where to find the guest bathroom and every sort of toiletry she might require.

"I'll gather some clothes and pajamas for you," Mrs. DeDecker said. "I have quite a few things you might want to keep that don't fit me anymore. Too much pasta." She winked at Audrey, looking just like Johnny at that moment, and patted her stomach with a grin.

Audrey smiled back, grateful for her attempts to help her feel more at ease. Wrapped in the large bathrobe, she tied it at her waist and slipped into the satiny slippers Mrs. DeDecker had placed in front of her. When she looked at her hostess, the woman's eyes were clouded over, her lips parted to speak.

"Honey, I'm aware you lost your father and that things haven't been easy for you, well, for a very long time. Small town, you hear these things."

Audrey swallowed and started to mumble, "Thank you," but the words didn't come out.

Mrs. DeDecker turned away and scooped up Audrey's dirty clothing from the floor. "You come from a troubled family, Audrey," she said. "Most people in town don't like trouble, don't want to get involved in matters that aren't their family's business. Things can get complicated. Bad feelings all around. Do you understand what I'm saying, dear?"

That was just like what Audrey had heard from Mr. Littleton. People made excuses for letting bad things happen to other people: *"It's not proper to interfere,"* or *"A family's business is their own."*

"It's nice to have you here, sincerely. But what I'm saying is, if your mother comes looking for you, there's not much I can do. It's best we make your stay for just one night." She brightened. "But we're happy to help you, dear."

Of course, Mother would never think to look for her at the DeDecker home, but Audrey realized Mrs. DeDecker was alarmed by the prospect of becoming involved in Scott affairs, Mother's reputation being what it was. She smiled politely and nodded her understanding. Relief washed over the woman's face. At least she was kind enough to be honest and to help her for a night.

"Thank you, Mrs. DeDecker," Audrey said and meant it.

The woman left and clicked the door closed, leaving Audrey to take a good look around the room. She stifled the sudden urge to giggle, despite her predicament. The irony was too rich.

She'd been welcomed into the DeDecker home without pulling a single trick and was standing in a glorious bedroom.

After peering out the door to be certain she was alone, Audrey made her way down the hallway adorned by swirls of gold wallpaper. She paused at a walnut console to scrutinize a large photo of the DeDeckers' extended family wearing smiles and extravagant clothes, looking the very picture of success, captured in a portrait of happiness she'd never known.

Once in the bathroom, Audrey turned the *H* and *C* faucets on simultaneously, and water cascaded into the deep claw-foot tub until it was half full. After disrobing, she settled into the warmth, which felt pleasing on her skin despite the heat of the day. She washed her hair then scrubbed herself until her flesh was pink. Satisfied, Audrey sighed deeply and lay back against the porcelain.

Maybe she'd misjudged Johnny after all.

He was cocky, all right, but behind that big mouth and underneath all those muscles was a kind boy, a generous person, someone willing to help her. And the DeDecker home—what she'd seen of it so far, anyway—was tasteful and poshly decorated, as though Elizabeth Taylor lived there. The kitchen had the latest gadgets and an upbeat, bright decor, and they had indoor bathrooms and several cars. The DeDecker family could likely buy anything a person might dream of having.

Audrey inhaled the gardenia-scented soap she'd found and began rubbing it over her arms again. She slowed, her eyes circling the small room, then dropped the soap into the water.

This was the life of pampering and social status Mother craved for herself, so much so that she would sacrifice her own daughter. Nothing else in the world seemed to matter. Her fantasy had always seemed illogical and absurd.

But Johnny wasn't so bad after all.

Audrey slipped farther into the water, letting the water cover her mouth and lap against her earlobes. She let Mother's ideas flutter around her head, as bright and fresh as newly hatched butterflies.

CHAPTER 46

Edith

Standing outside her bedroom door with her hands on her hips, Edith surveyed the meager furnishings. For the first time since Red died, she'd been thinking about him for more than a few seconds—not because she missed him, but because he was back.

Red was probably angry that she'd given away most of his things. For once, Edith had been the proud do-gooder and not the recipient, a sign of what was to come. She'd kept Red's shaving kit to give to Harry, although strangely, it no longer sat on the dresser where she'd left it.

Edith walked in and sank onto her bed to pout, livid at her daughter and worried for the first time that she'd lost control of her. Audrey had left the previous day after behaving like a wild animal. The curtains rippled lightly from a gentle breeze, and she turned toward the window. Edith wiped her brow with a forearm then stilled herself to listen, blocking out chirping birds and the distant *tap, tap* of someone's hammer. After a long minute, she screwed up her lips and shook her head as though disgusted.

"Get out of here," she said aloud, pushing a palm outward. Edith had no desire to deal with Red right then, having bigger fish to fry. He was carrying a snootful as usual, speaking nonsense and guffawing, as though he had a right to make fun of her. Of course he was too afraid—ever the coward—to show himself.

Edith stood and walked to the window. She slammed the pane down then wheeled around when his guffaws grew louder inside her bedroom.

"You always were so fucking dumb, Red. Couldn't get it through that thick skull that nobody wanted you. I didn't want you. Yet here you are, come back again."

Edith flipped her middle finger to the room, and while she stood there in staunch defiance, an idea occurred to her, something brilliant.

She scurried from the room.

Red was still good for nothing, but she needed a new plan, and listening to her dead husband had given her exactly that.

CHAPTER 47

Audrey

Audrey stirred in her sleep, floating to consciousness like a slow, meandering bubble. She'd been dreaming that someone was knocking on her bedroom door, and she was running and running toward it, certain it was Daddy, but the door kept drifting away, always just out of reach.

She opened her eyes, momentarily unsure of her surroundings. Audrey squeezed her eyes closed and popped them open again. Fan blades whirred softly just beyond her bed, and a canopy hung over her head. The sheets were wonderfully soft and smooth.

She was in the DeDecker guest room. Like in her dream, she heard the urgent rapping of knuckles and bolted upright, clutching her sheet to her neck.

When Audrey shimmied to the floor, the satin nightgown she wore fell from her shoulders and threatened to slide off her body. She gathered the fabric and held a fistful between her breasts. "Hello?" she whispered at the door.

"It's me, open up."

Audrey unlocked the door and cracked it.

"Hey, sis." Johnny was all lips and teeth in the murky opening. "Can I come in? Been thinking about you all night." His breath reeked of beer. As Audrey stepped back, he pushed his way in, grinning, then pressed a wobbly finger to his lips. He closed the door and moved toward her.

"Shhh. We have to be quiet." His words were slurred. Johnny reached for Audrey's hand.

She veered toward the bed to escape his advance. "You can't stay in here. What's going on? Do you need to talk?"

Johnny clumsily removed his T-shirt and dropped it on the floor. With elongated steps, he reached Audrey and pulled her into a bare-chested embrace. In the darkness, she reveled in the comfort, the strange feeling of another person's warm flesh against hers, but the moment passed quickly. The connection was unfamiliar, too intimate, and she pushed him away.

Johnny leaned down and kissed her anyway, pushing hard on her lips, working to open her mouth with his tongue. Her first kiss tasted like cigarette ashes and booze. Audrey struggled to get away, but his hand wrapped firmly around the back of her head. In the darkness, his hair had taken on a black sheen. With both hands, Audrey shoved him away as hard as she could, and he stumbled against her bed and fell backward to sit on it, where he swayed in a way that reminded her of Daddy.

"You're drunk," she said in a jittery voice. "What made you think you could do that? Get out of my room."

Johnny tucked his chin down and belched softly but did not move. His chest was rising and falling rapidly. "Get out of here? Out of my own house? Keep your voice down. My mom would be pissed if she knew I was in here."

Audrey clutched her nightgown to keep it in place, suddenly aware of how naked she was underneath. "Leave now," she said with a confidence she did not feel, "or I will scream and wake your mother myself."

Before she knew what was happening, Johnny grabbed her and put a hand over her mouth, throwing her onto the bed. Audrey wrestled against him until Johnny gripped her wrists and held them together over her head, and she winced with pain, then the weight of his body crushed her. She wanted to scream, but Johnny's mouth covered hers, pressing so hard that her head sank into the mattress. She did not return his kiss, not wanting to, or even knowing how. His closeness was suddenly too familiar, too horrifying. Fractured memories spun through her mind in dizzying patterns—images of Mother tying her to her bedposts and leaving her helpless and unable to move freely.

With one hand holding both her wrists, Johnny fumbled with Audrey's nightgown with his other and slid it up. Somehow, his shorts had come off, and she felt the heat of his groin against her bare skin. Her mouth was vibrating from his moans, and she rolled her head from side to side, repulsed by his lips. Audrey kicked her legs and bounced her hips on the mattress to throw him off, but nothing worked. Johnny was strong.

Audrey felt pressure as he pushed himself inside her, his hips digging sharply into hers, then a searing pain, as though her vagina were too small, refusing him, ripping. The ceiling whirled as she separated from herself and floated above the bed, watching Johnny's back and smooth white butt and the squirming figure under him. When the boy released her lips and lifted his head, his entire body shuddered, and he groaned.

She was aware when Johnny rolled off the bed, one foot landing on the floor. Audrey felt an awful wetness spreading between her legs, and she tugged her nightgown down to cover herself. He was dancing into his discarded shorts then working clumsy fingers to poke his head through his tee. At her door, Johnny turned to Audrey and smiled glibly as his hand twisted the doorknob.

"Be quiet when I open the door, okay?" he said. A ray of pale moonlight gave his face a ghostly glow. "And hey, sis, next time, get into it a little more. You know, I mean, don't just lie there like a rug. You'll have more fun."

Audrey said nothing. She'd gone numb from head to toe, inside and out, as if her body belonged to someone else.

Once he was gone and the room was silent, Audrey curled up on her side. She hugged her pillow and cried softly, unable to comprehend what had just happened to her. The only explanation was that Johnny must love her. That had to be it. It explained so much. And maybe now, she would be welcomed by his family.

Johnny would want her to stay.

Early in the morning, Audrey's room flooded with sunlight, awakening her from a dull, troubled sleep. She drew herself out of bed with difficulty, surprised that her joints were stiff, sore and achy like an old charwoman's. Both wrists had turned purplish blue overnight, and she rubbed them, growing concerned about the sharp pains jabbing her abdomen, as well.

Sleepily, Audrey lifted a button-down dress off a hanger, one from a small selection that Mrs. DeDecker had given her after supper the night before. They'd eaten meat loaf, mashed potatoes, green beans, and rolls and had even enjoyed cherry cobbler for dessert. During the meal, Johnny's thirteen-year-old sister Julia had chattered on like Harry used to. Mr. DeDecker was working late, and Mrs. DeDecker had seemed upset about it when Johnny questioned his father's whereabouts, slapping potatoes with ferocity onto their plates.

Audrey dressed then snuck down the hall to the bathroom, walking with her legs apart like she'd ridden a bucking bull. After she brushed her teeth, Audrey used the toilet, gingerly dabbing her private area and throwing the tissue into the bowl. Her eyes flew open. Blood was on the tissue and in the toilet.

Audrey's period wasn't due—that much, she knew—and bleeding explained the stabbing pain. Johnny could have damaged an organ. *Does bleeding mean I'm going to die?* Fear seized Audrey's throat, and her heart thundered in her chest.

To see a doctor about their premarital sex would be humiliating.

Audrey pulled the cord to flush, stuffed toilet paper in her underwear, and scrambled back down the hall. She neatly packed everything Mrs. DeDecker had given her inside a brown leather suitcase that the woman had called "my lovely old Louis Vuitton" and told Audrey to keep. She'd been welcomed to spend the one night and would comply by preparing to leave. But Johnny needed to drive her to a doctor right away. They could talk.

After descending the stairs with her suitcase in hand, Audrey walked swiftly by Mrs. DeDecker, who was pouring batter into a waffle iron, to set it down by the patio door. With Johnny nowhere in sight, she didn't know what to do next.

"Sit down, I'm making plenty," Mrs. DeDecker said, pointing at a chair.

Audrey inhaled the delicious aroma and did as she was told. Soon, she was digging into three thick waffles smothered in maple syrup.

"Leaving us already?" Mrs. DeDecker asked, nodding toward the suitcase while pouring more batter onto the hot iron.

Audrey couldn't help but notice phony disappointment in her voice. After all, she'd given her the instruction.

"I, uh, have something I need to do. But I need to talk to Johnny. Is he... I mean, is he up?" Her stomach cramped on cue.

"Not yet," Mrs. DeDecker said crisply. "Did you decide it's best to get back home?"

Audrey stared at the back of her head.

"Morning, Ma."

Audrey's eyes swept toward Johnny, who was shuffling into the kitchen in shorts and a rumpled T-shirt. His hair was matted, and he stank from last night's booze. Mrs. DeDecker either pretended not to notice or didn't mind. She simply dropped several fluffy waffles onto a plate as he plunked into a chair.

"Hi, Johnny." Audrey hated that her voice sounded meek, but she needed his attention, to get him alone.

Rather than answering her, Johnny chewed loudly, mouth open, and asked, "Mom, did you remember that Nancy and I are going on a picnic today? Can you make up some fried chicken and other stuff for a basket? I think her mom's out of town or something."

Smiling, Mrs. DeDecker reached to pat his head. "I'd be happy to. She's such a nice girl, that Nancy. Such a good family, too. Your father and I hope you two get serious by the time you graduate, if not sooner."

Audrey audibly gasped, and Mrs. DeDecker shot her a curious look, eyes wide and questioning behind her glasses.

Johnny's mom must have meant Nancy Matheson, the snooty head cheerleader at school.

"Yes, Mom," Johnny said, annoyed. "That's my plan. Can you drop it for now?" He winced and vigorously rubbed his temples.

Johnny eyeballed Audrey then, who was wearing a bewildered expression. "Hey, is Audrey going to stay with us for a while?" He winked at her.

She heard the sound of footsteps approaching, and a large man swaggered into the kitchen with glasses perched low on his nose, wearing a gray pin-striped suit. He carried a folded newspaper in one hand and a red bow tie in the other.

"Coffee and toast, Donna. No waffles." He dropped heavily into a chair and snapped open his paper.

"Howard, this is Audrey—Audrey, um, Scott," Mrs. DeDecker said, reluctantly including her last name.

Mr. DeDecker lowered the broadsheet and raked his eyes over Audrey's face, then he glanced at his wife's old suitcase on the floor.

He made a *harrumph* sound, folded the *St. Louis Post-Dispatch*'s morning edition, and put it on the side of his plate.

"I know your mother," he said, his voice dripping with disdain.

"I-I'm sorry," Audrey mumbled.

"I assume you have a good reason for being here?" When Mrs. DeDecker tried to interject, he waved her off. "Or is it that you're in cahoots with your mother?"

Johnny looked up from his plate, his bloodshot eyes bouncing between Audrey and his father, the word "cahoots" apparently having garnered his attention.

Mr. DeDecker bent sideways and patted his son's shoulder fondly. Apparently catching his foul aroma, he made a face of disgust. "Nothing to concern yourself about, Johnny. I can handle Edith Scott. Been doing it for years." He looked at Audrey. "Was it your idea to come here, young lady? I should say you're likely as nuts as she is, then." He sighed, having seen a look of appeal in his wife's eyes. "Look, I'm sorry for your circumstances, I truly am. It's just that your mother is loony tunes—always has been. And now, I find *you* here. What else should I think but this is one of her crazy schemes to get to me?"

Three pairs of eyes landed on Audrey, the latest attraction in their amusement park, and she shrank back as though he'd slapped her. They believed she was as nuts as her mother, capable of participating in her ridiculous scheme, the daughter judged guilty of the sins of her mother.

She was not.

She sat up straight and returned each of their stares, consuming the family in three bitter bites. Johnny, an indulged little prince, was pale and disoriented. Mrs. DeDecker, a neglected wife, looked confused, perhaps angry or worried. And Mr. DeDecker, whose overbearing stature had been meant to intimidate her, had not succeeded. He was a condescending ass.

Johnny finally piped up. "Dad, I brought Audrey here. It was my idea. I don't know what's going on, but you don't need to insult her."

He might have defended her, but Johnny was far from her hero. Audrey's abdomen was still throbbing. When she started to push back her chair, Mr. DeDecker tapped her wrist, either ignoring her bruises or wishing to remain ignorant of their cause.

"I don't care how you got here. It's best for everyone that you get back home," he barked. "And be sure to tell your mama that none of her shenanigans will work. Period."

At the griddle, where she was prying off a smoking, burnt waffle, Mrs. DeDecker sucked in a hollow breath. "What are you talking about, Howard? What is her mother trying to do? What shenanigans?"

A chair scraped against the floor when Johnny roughly pushed it back. "Remember the picnic basket, Ma," he said. "See ya, Audrey. I got to find some aspirin."

Audrey felt blood rush to her cheeks as he waltzed away into the dining room, not looking back—not once.

"Thank you for taking me in last night and for the suitcase... everything," she said, wanting to get out of there immediately. She slid off her chair.

Mrs. DeDecker, who seemed unaware Audrey had spoken, dropped her spatula and walked to the table. She glued accusing eyes on her husband.

If only in that moment, Audrey pitied her, a woman being kept in the dark with just enough light to see something scary coming her way. Mother had the goods on Mr. DeDecker—Audrey was certain of it. But he, too, had apparently refused to go along with blackmail that meant a shotgun wedding for his son.

That realization provided a moment's pleasure. Mother had lost all around.

Audrey opened the screen door and set the suitcase outside before turning to speak to the couple. They were both gaping at her. Mr. DeDecker was still waiting for her answer, and his wife was impatiently waiting for his.

"My mother might be crazy, but I'm not here because of her... what you called shenanigans. I knew about her plan for me and Johnny, but I swear not until recently." Audrey swallowed, holding back tears she would rather die than let them see. She'd actually considered how wonderful becoming part of their family would be. "But the idea was hers alone. I'm not like that. I'm not like her, and I don't care if you believe me or not. Yesterday was a coincidence, is all. Johnny offered me a place to stay for the night, and your wife was kind enough to let me."

The urge to go on was strong, to tell them about their son going into her room the previous night and how he—*But how would I explain it?* A small voice inside her head said, *"Yes, tell them,"* but another shouted at her to shut up, that those people would never believe her anyway. Johnny would lie. An accusation of any sort would only make things worse, confirming Mr. DeDecker's suspicions about her.

"What plans for her and Johnny?" Mrs. DeDecker's face had gone pale.

The couple had turned toward each other. Audrey left them.

She ran across the yard like a hunted deer, suitcase banging against her thigh, springing over the lush lawn until she reached the winding drive. Holding her expensive suitcase, Audrey seemed like an important traveler going somewhere special.

But she was not.

Audrey moped along under the encompassing shade of tall oaks and broad sycamore trees lining both sides of the unpaved road. The morning was warm, not yet stifling as every August day became by noon. Mrs. DeDecker's dress was too big on her frame, loose and baggy, helping her body to stay cool. After walking half a mile, Audrey sat on her suitcase to rest, bending to hug her knees, then dropping her face into her palms. Tears flowed from her in wave after wave of anguish. She was alone, unwanted.

Gradually, when she'd worn herself out, the sobs subsided, and Audrey sat listening to the birds, the rustling of leaves around her. She stared at the road ahead.

She had been raped.

Audrey knew nothing about sex or love, but she'd mixed them together somehow, thinking one couldn't exist without the other. For a passing moment, she wondered if what had happened was her fault. She certainly hadn't tried to attract Johnny in any way. He'd picked her up in his car, appearing to be kind and compassionate. But drunk, Johnny had used her, hurt her, and perhaps torn up her insides.

A squirrel crawled close to her, chipping away at a nut. She'd been so still and quiet that it hadn't detected her presence.

Audrey hung her head, feeling like a fool. In their house, she'd let herself picture, even for the briefest of moments, what a life with Johnny and the DeDeckers would be like. She'd never wanted it before. Yet in just one day on her own, she'd been enticed into thinking about it. Those people were the in-laws Mother had coveted for years. They'd welcomed her, fed and clothed her—liked her—then they summarily dismissed her.

But Mother was the one they couldn't stand.

A future with Johnny might have been possible if Audrey had ever truly wanted that for herself—and she had not—but Mr. DeDecker despised her mother. Ironically, her mother had ruined her very own plan, not Audrey. One day, she would toss that revelation into Mother's face like a scalding pot of water.

CHAPTER 48

Harry

After Mother walked down the hill and was out of sight, Harry inserted Daddy's key into the back door lock and went inside their house.

The key had been a useful addition to his growing collection, allowing him to take whatever he wanted. A week or so earlier, when Mother discovered canned goods and utensils missing, she'd paced on the porch and yelled obscenities at his father, calling him a thief. Although her behavior spooked him, it gave Harry an idea.

If Mother lost all her marbles—the few he suspected she had left—she might just up and leave. To go where, he did not know or care. Better yet, if someone in town had her hauled off to a nuthouse like the one in Penshaw, they would never let her out again. Either way, with Mother gone, he and Audrey could live in their house, go to school, and take care of each other.

Harry checked the cupboards and the icebox for food. He collected a handful of carrots, two oranges, one tomato, and three cans of applesauce, dropping them into the fold of his shirt. Unfortunately, Mother's cupboards were practically bare. He pitched his findings under the porch, planning to retrieve them later under cover of darkness. Once, Mother had arrived home unexpectedly, and Harry had hidden in his own closet for hours, unmoving and barely breathing, worried Mother might hear him and shoot him. She had a .22-caliber Brownie, a small gun meant for a lady.

Harry had learned how to use his mother's gun, as had Audrey. Daddy also showed them how to load and shoot his heftier .45 Colt, which he'd kept hidden in the bottom drawer of his dresser. Both were hand-me-downs from Daddy's side of the family.

He intended to find one of those guns when he had more time.

In his bedroom, Harry grabbed another pair of pants, socks, and what remained of his underwear, doubtful his mother would notice anything missing. He tossed them under the porch with the food then scurried to Mother's bedroom. He snatched her winter boots, which were too big to wear but would keep his toes toasty when frigid nights came. If he was still in his fort then, he would have to be prepared.

Harry scanned the room, wanting to find something to steal that would infuriate his mother. His eyes landed on her chamber pot—which was empty, thankfully—peeking out from under Mother's bed. Filled with mischievous glee, he snatched it and ran outdoors, locked the door behind himself, and gripping his prize, headed for the woods.

After darkness fell, Harry made two round trips from his fort to the house, pretending he was a soldier on dangerous nighttime missions. He knew the way through the woods by heart, but the bright moonlight helped, and within half an hour, he was safe and sound in his fort, dividing his possessions into various sections. He was using Daddy's flashlight, which he'd stolen weeks earlier. He was not proud of being a thief, but Daddy would've understood why.

Leaning back against a tree stump, Harry swept the light around the perimeter, stopping when the spotlight landed on Daddy's shaving brush and razor. He set the flashlight on the stump and crawled to them, thumbing the bristles thoughtfully as an ache filled his chest. Often, Daddy had asked Harry to rub his smooth face after a shave, always saying the same thing. "Smooth like a baby's butt, hey, Harry?"

He kneaded Daddy's belt between his fingers after that, then examined Daddy's shoes, the brown ones with the worn toe, wondering if Daddy had been buried in his bare feet. Touching Daddy's things was becoming a nightly ritual, and not an especially helpful one, so he turned the flashlight off and ducked out of the fort into the hot night.

Except for the wildlife, Harry was alone in the woods. He could even scream if he wanted to. He found a sharp stick and wielded it, ready to embark on another dangerous military assignment. He jogged around the dark trees, ducking under low branches and slipping through the narrowest gaps to escape his enemies. Barging into the field, Harry headed toward the shed for cover. The night was cloudy, and the glow from Mr. Ritter's yard light helped guide him to the woodpile where, panting and dripping with sweat, he listened to the katydids and tree crickets making their usual racket.

He spied on his enemy target and, after seeing no movement, made a beeline for the porch. Once there, he hit the ground and slithered on his belly until he was under the parlor window, elbows and knees scraped by the gravel. He could hear her inside.

Carefully, Harry raised himself to peer through the window. Mother's back was to the window, so he stretched higher. She was much thinner than he'd seen before, and her frizzy hair fell below her shoulders, not pinned up in her customary bun. She was talking, flapping her arms, and bobbing her head like a bird about to take flight. He couldn't hear what she was saying, but Mother's voice was high-pitched and animated. When she moved closer to the couch, he looked around the rest of the room, puzzled.

Mother was by herself.

"Get the fuck out of my house. Leave me alone!" she screamed.

Mother shook her head and raised a fist in the air, but when she let out a prolonged bloodcurdling scream, Harry was so shocked that he fell back from the window and tumbled onto the gravel. The hair on the back of his neck stood on end, and he had no desire to see what she would do next. He ran, afraid she might've heard him, pumping his arms and legs with all his might.

Mother was off her nut.

And if she really was going crazy, he would have to be very careful.

CHAPTER 49

Audrey

Audrey opened her eyes under the boughs of thick holly shrubs, too dazed and sleepy to be sure where she was. She sat up and rubbed her stiff neck, achy from using her suitcase like a pillow, and swept prickly branches aside to observe her surroundings through the hedge. That early in the morning, the park's swings and slides were lifeless, undisturbed by the throngs of children who would later come to play. Picnic tables were empty, and the kiddie pool sparkled with a blue reflection from the sky. Somewhere far off, a dog barked.

Willowdale City Park.

Mother had brought her to play at the park only twice that Audrey could remember, when she was quite small, and she'd always thought it was the best place on earth. Now, she was sleeping in the bushes like a vagabond, afraid for her safety and needing shelter. She rubbed her eyes and thought back, conjuring what she could recall from the previous day.

By the time Audrey reached downtown Willowdale on foot, the pain in her abdomen had decreased to occasional dull throbbing, so she'd put away the notion of finding a doctor. Without Johnny, the discussion, along with an exam, would've been too embarrassing. Besides, she had no money.

Audrey cleaned up inside a Sinclair gas station's tiny bathroom, grateful to find that she was no longer bleeding. She doused her hair with water and curled strands around her finger to set them that way. As she brushed her teeth with the toothpaste and brush Mrs. DeDecker had provided, Audrey made up her mind to find a job.

Afterward, she slogged up and down both sides of Main Street, applying for jobs at McClain's Mercantile, Willowdale's two small grocery stores, the lone drugstore in town, the two cafés—waitressing had the added advantage of tips—then at nearly every small shop she walked by. Even the manager at the movie theater—where a person could work as an usher or a concession girl with no experience—had turned up his nose at her.

After sunset, the town's sidewalks had all but rolled up except for the busy theater, so she ended up in the deserted City Park, arms aching from carrying her suitcase. Strangely, not a single person had questioned her about lugging it around. Instead, all she'd heard was "We aren't hiring" or the kinder "Thanks for applying. We'll get back to you."

Tucked inside rows of green hollies, Audrey yawned, and her stomach grumbled. When a robin hopped close to the hedge, searching for worms, her eyes followed its jerky movements and how it plucked the ground for its meal. She could fill her stomach in a similar way by picking fruit like apples, blackberries, and elderberries. That wasn't like stealing from a store. Audrey needed something to tide her over until she figured out her next move. Tugging her suitcase into the open, Audrey retrieved her toothbrush and paste then hid the luggage back under the bushes. She padded to the water fountain, wondering if anybody was watching.

While brushing her teeth, Audrey considered who might help her.

Not Mr. Ritter, who seemed terrified of Mother. Audrey couldn't possibly ask that sweet old man to take her in. He lived too close to home, anyway. She thought about Freddie or Mrs. Littleton. Audrey swished water in her mouth and spat on the ground. Mr. Littleton was a man-sized problem she didn't know how to get around. Maybe his wife and son didn't know either.

Her mind locked on the Trents as a possibility. Audrey had grown fond of them both, and they'd been kind to her, but with Gladys on the mend, they didn't need permanent help. And she certainly had to consider Harry. She doubted anyone would want to take in and raise a teenager and a young boy.

The only other people Audrey could think of were her former teachers, but all of them had ignored or pretended not to see her plight during every grade in school. She'd kept her head down largely to remain invisible, a habit she still employed. But she was sure they'd seen her bruises, the hungry desire in her eyes for a friend, for someone to take an interest in her life. All of them had looked away—until Mrs. Patton.

Mrs. Patton had many students, and Audrey had been just one of them, no more important, no less so. Her teacher had taken pity on her—that was all. Her current predicament was all Mrs. Patton's fault, though. She was to blame for Audrey's diaries. Mrs. Patton might feel terrible if she learned what had happened to Audrey, but it was one thing to supply a student with notebooks and a whole other thing to invite a teenager home to live.

When Audrey's stomach gurgled again, she returned to her nest and got her suitcase. The park's modernized restroom offered a clean, private place to change into another outfit. She had a whole day ahead of her to apply for jobs, and being tidy would increase her odds. Only a few businesses remained as options.

Audrey slid into the restroom facility with heavy shoulders. While she would never, ever beg for money, she would definitely have to beg for a job.

She tugged her blouse over her head then paused and stared at her image in the bathroom mirror. Despite her resolve, Audrey's eyes betrayed her fears, dulled by the painful awareness that she didn't belong anywhere, and likely never would.

She raised her chin, her thoughts churning, because she did know of a place.

In just that moment, Audrey knew where she had to go.

Harry

Lying under his blankets, Harry reached a hand over his head to retrieve a carrot then lazily munched on it inside his makeshift bed. He had a pretty good supply of food between what he'd taken from Mother's cupboard and the box he'd found inside Mr. Ritter's garage. The old man had left him several cans of peas and peaches, even a few ripe bananas.

Thank you, Mr. Ritter, he thought once again, grateful for all the apples, slices of bread, walnuts, and occasional jugs of cold milk or juice. A week before, his silent conspirator had draped a heavy afghan over the handles of his lawn cutter with a note attached that read, "For Harry."

Somehow, Mr. Ritter had guessed that Harry was living nearby, but the man had no way of knowing his young friend had holed up in the woods. Still, he was doing what he could. Harry would've preferred to be sheltered indoors, hidden away like some Jews had been during the war. But because he was frail and terrified of Mother, Mr. Ritter would never take such a risk. Harry couldn't blame him. Mother had poisoned the man's beloved pigeons, all right. Harry had observed her messing around at the coop the night before they were found dead. Not once in his short life could he recall Mother going near that coop—until then.

Daddy had died. The pigeons had died.

Mother was responsible for both.

After he confided in Mr. Ritter what he had suspected his mother had done to Daddy, she'd been outraged. Harry had acted repentant, and to his relief, she let it go. But the second time he went against Mother—when she discovered him searching for the poison—she beat him on and off for days and locked him in the damp basement. He was overwhelmed and terrified, trapped in her lair with limited supplies of food and water. The stuffy air and confinement made Harry feel suffocated and fearful, like a prisoner of war, but instead of learning his so-called lesson, he became angry. He spent hours daydreaming about getting out and getting her back.

Unfortunately, that was when his voice vanished, perhaps wanting to hide out for a while. Harry guessed it was his body's way of forcing him to shut up and remain that way for his own good.

When Mother let him loose, Harry was mute, which she mistook at first for submission and shame. He started staying in his fort most of the time, going home only now and then, enjoying the fact that Mother had no idea where he went. He felt safe there. The fort was insulated with leaves, old clothes, newspapers, and piles of brush, and it was strong. Even a slashing rainstorm didn't destroy the tightly woven sticks, reeds, and limbs he'd tethered with long, thin reeds found here and there. After all, his sister had told him—long before, it seemed—to run to his fort and stay if he ever had big trouble with Mother.

Then Audrey returned, and he was filled with hope.

Harry was shocked to find her at home that day, weeks before the time Mother had told him she would come back. His sister was furious when she saw his scars, marks gifted to him by their mother. But he wanted her to understand about Daddy and tried his best, despite being unable to speak. When Harry came back days later, Audrey had disappeared again, except her things were still in her room, untouched. Now, he had to wait for her return all over again.

Harry yawned and stretched.

If the day was nice, he would work on the narrow aboveground tunnels he'd been creating between bushes and short trees in various parts of the woods. Being small, Harry could easily crawl through them on his hands and knees.

Winter was coming.

Maybe he would go to town. There, he could steal a nice pair of heavy socks, and a new wool sweater would be terrific. Unfortunately, the Willowdale shopkeepers had come to eye him with suspicion, as did lady shoppers who couldn't mind their own business. Once, a nosy woman approached and asked his name. Harry had run away, not wishing to be caught and sent to some orphanage.

He always told himself the same thing. *Audrey will come back.*

Until then, he would have to figure out how to make it on his own.

CHAPTER 50

Edith

Edith wasn't sure how much time had passed since she'd seen either of her children, but the trees were mostly bare, and a frigid nip had settled into the air. She suspected the date was late October—maybe November.

Sitting cross-legged on the rug in the parlor, the hem of her nightgown tucked into her lap, Edith was studying the strange slits she'd found all over her couch. Exasperated, she clasped her hands behind her head and curled down into a ball.

Of course they'd done this. And they were watching her, laughing at her—taunting her.

They'd started earlier than usual, when Edith had been barely awake. She'd simply wanted to make hot water to drink when Red hissed at her like the radiator pipes, urging her, *"Come find me."* Red would only speak, never show himself to her—a cruel irony because Edith wanted to kill him all over again.

She covered her ears and screamed.

Those two were ganging up on her.

After several minutes, Edith got up and headed for the back door. She strolled out to the porch, clad only in her slippers and nightgown, far too sheer for a frosty morning. *Fuck you both*, Edith thought, silently daring them to join her outdoors. She angrily kicked at crinkled brown leaves to scatter them. The dreary weather had cast a gray pall over everything. She sucked in the icy morning air until her lungs burned, and she hugged herself when the wind battered her like a thousand sharp blades. Edith stared wide-eyed at the frost-tipped grass, captivated by the sparkling blanket of diamonds.

Beyond, the stark trees in the woods arced like broken appendages, and for the first time in a long time, she thought about Harry. He'd always liked playing in the woods. By then, he'd probably been taken in by another family and was living high on the hog somewhere. Edith's snort sent wisps of white vapor into the air. Shivering uncontrollably, she went back inside.

After boiling water in her electric coffeepot, Edith poured herself a cup and flopped into a chair, letting the steam moisten her face. She shut her eyes and, imagining the flavor of coffee beans on her tongue, sipped the tasteless brew to warm her body. Her eyes gradually drifted toward the basement door. After a minute, Edith tilted her head to the side and squinted, trying to concentrate, to drown out their annoying, critical voices.

They were right, though. She'd given up far too easily, just as they'd predicted. Edith believed she could always find a new way to get what she wanted, yet she'd been moping around her godforsaken house, lamely accepting her fate. She was penniless and near starvation because the garden had fizzled out. Perhaps she should've tended to it better, like watering the plants during the summer drought and picking the few vegetables the garden produced before they'd shriveled away. But she'd had better things to do. Edith eyed her cupboards, aware of how little was stored inside.

She'd simply lost her focus after Audrey left. That girl had been a waste of her time and effort for years. Then Harry had turned on her, and—much worse—Howard had reneged on their deal. Of course, she'd seen to it that he would pay for that fateful decision. Nevertheless, their desertions had resulted in a triple whammy that spoiled her plans.

Edith studied the wall, angry that Red had distracted her from acting on an idea she'd thought of because of him. Hungry and fed up, she resolved to stop her pity party and shuffled into her bed-room to get what she needed. The bedroom smelled like stale piss, but Edith didn't mind. Peeing into an old cooking pot was a small price to pay to avoid the outhouse on frigid nights, and the stinky brew kept Red away. Her chamber pot had vanished—clearly one of Red's tricks—and she'd instantly known how to get even with him. Hers was the last laugh.

She knelt and probed through the clothing scattered across her closet floor, searching for her boots. She tossed socks and shirts aside, growing frantic as she pawed through the piles like a stray mutt desperate to find its bone. Edith sat back on her haunches, huffing.

The boots were gone, along with the letter she'd hidden inside one of them.

In the past, Edith would never have been able to use his words against him—and he'd known that. Her reputation, such as it was, would have been permanently damaged by any sort of claim. He'd told her he would deny their affair, deny the letter was in his hand. He hadn't wanted her—and while they'd been together, she'd been too stupid to see it.

With the passage of time, her original fears were no longer rel-evant. He would pay for her continued silence. Her new plan wouldn't net Howard's level of wealth, but she would be rich enough and get even at the same time.

Edith pushed a fingertip into a pulsating eyebrow to ease the growing pain.

"What the hell have you done?" her mother had said that drizzly autumn day, one hand straddling her hip and the other shaking a bat-ter whip at Edith. "You been sneaking around with that rich boy, thinking he's going to marry you?"

Edith left the closet and threw herself down on her bed. She grabbed a pillow and stuffed her face into it, gripping the edges when

Mrs. Hamilton's face swam in front of her eyes, her small mouth and tongue moving in slow motion.

The nitwit Clarence Scott had been her only solution.

"He's idiot enough to believe your baby could be born prematurely," her mother had said, eyes snapping with reproach.

Finding someone else to marry was what the baby's father had suggested Edith do, and her mother had forced her hand. Seeing no way to escape her fate, Edith had seduced Red, slept with him, then married him, claiming he'd gotten her pregnant. Everything that had happened to her since then—her shitty life, her repugnant husband—was Mrs. Hamilton's fault. Edith pinched her eyes more tightly together, hating her as much as she ever had.

And now Red was stalking her, stealing things from her bedroom to toy with her. But taking that precious letter was the very last straw. She would slosh every drop of her piss in their bedroom to ensure he stayed out, the perfect garlic to ward off her personal vampire.

Edith raised her head from the pillow. The laughter and the low guffaws were growing closer. Clearly, the tittering was not Red's. They were high-pitched cackles, more like a witch's—more like her own mother's laugh.

She sat up quickly and swung her legs to the floor. "Damn you," Edith said tersely, sensing Mrs. Hamilton was nearby, getting her kicks again. "It was you. You think it's funny, taking my boots? My letter?"

Then Edith snapped her fingers. *Of course.*

She knew where Mrs. Hamilton would have hidden the letter, doubting Edith would have the gall to return there. She roared with laughter that bounced off the walls, because as had always been the case, her mother did not know her at all.

CHAPTER 51

Harry

The night before, Harry had let himself cry for hours like a baby. He was tired of being alone and hopeless, scrounging for food, and being a known criminal in town. Worse, he was terrified of freezing to death. Temperatures had been dropping, and for days, the skies had been threatening with low, plump clouds that would soon burst open with snow. He worried whether the fort would hold up and if building a fire inside was safe.

When he opened his eyes after a fitful night's sleep, they were swollen and dry, so he kept them closed for a bit longer, thankful for the warmth his body had created inside his cocoon. Harry poked an arm out of the covers and snatched a block of cheese then a handful of grapes from the stash next to him.

One day, Harry would do something special for Mr. Ritter to let him know how much he appreciated his kindness.

When Harry was many years younger, he'd witnessed hoodlums harassing the Ritters outside their own home, battering their house with eggs or writing bad words with soap on their windows. Mother said it happened because they were Krauts, and she seemed to enjoy the couple's troubles, while Harry was confused and sad, feeling sorry for them. He'd hated how two regular people could be preyed upon and frightened out of their wits by their neighbors.

Harry continued to gnaw on the cheese, unsure how his stomach might react to it, and revolted by his own foul breath. He needed to brush his teeth with the paste he'd taken from Mother's dresser. Often, he worried his teeth might rot and fall out like an old man's. He was worrying constantly about everything, with survival at the top of the list.

Stealing from Mother was easy, but nabbing items from town was a greater challenge. A few weeks before, Harry had stolen a woolen scarf and matching gloves without a morsel of guilt because he was, after all, like Robin Hood. He'd already fled a store when a woman shouted his name. Being recognized had terrified him. He was certain that, if caught, Harry Scott, thief, scoundrel, and fugitive, would go to jail for the rest of his life.

He popped two grapes in his mouth and chewed, purposely letting juice drip down his chin like an uncivilized Neanderthal man. Harry would've started seventh grade in September. At school, they served stuff like meat loaf, chicken noodle soup, and hot dogs, sometimes even pizza. He stared at his few remaining grapes.

His life was not fair, not by a long shot.

Harry had gone to the woods like Audrey had told him to do, and she should've come for him by then.

After throwing off his hodgepodge of covers, Harry hastily dressed in more layers and topped them with his coat. He slicked his long hair behind his ears and shoved a lambswool cap with earflaps over his head. He slipped gloves on then pulled up two more pairs of thick socks. Mother's boots would be too big for his feet, but the fur would keep them warm. While he worked in his tunnels, his feet would remain dry.

As he pushed his left foot inside that boot, Harry's toes scrunched something at the toe. He took the boot off and peered into it then shoved his hand inside to pull out a piece of paper. Scrunching his face, he unfolded what seemed like fancy stationery with faded cursive handwriting. Weirdly, Mother had a letter hidden in her boot. Curious to read it, Harry perched on the lone stump and flattened it against his leg. The letter was dated October 29, 1932, and addressed to his mother:

My dearest Edith,

I apologize for how I reacted a few days ago, not responding to your news how you wished me to, being quite a brute by leaving you alone and crying in the woods, in the one place that is so special to you. I can only say that my surprise and trepidation took over my sensibilities, and I needed time to think, which I have since done. This letter is nearly impossible to write, let alone trying to imagine you reading it.

Harry's eyebrows dipped inward. Mother hated the woods, so that part of the letter could not be real. He continued to read.

What I'm about to say now may be unforgivable, my dear Edith, but I cannot marry you.

Our time together has been special, but I never intended for it to be permanent. For many months now, I've been seeing another—a woman of whom my parents approve—and for my family and our position in this town, I am planning to marry her as I have also fallen in love with her. I had intended to tell you this before you shared your news with me. I hope you believe me.

I know this is difficult, but you must understand that my family would brand you as an inadequate match and would never accept you, given a pregnancy out of wedlock. That is not a life I wish for you.

Doing what we did, Edith, was wrong, I see that now. We are both at fault. But you, I am afraid, are the one who will bear the consequences. I urge you to marry quickly to salvage your reputation and secure your future.

Harry's eyes bulged.

As much as it pains me, I must warn you. If you should endeavor to tell anyone that I am the father, I will strenuously deny such an accusation. Without proof, I'm afraid you would be mocked, dismissed, even ridiculed. It is far better that your child belongs to your new husband, not regarded as a bastard.

I regret that I cannot offer you the life you've dreamed about, but I wish you well and am confident you will find your way.

The letter was unsigned.

That pregnancy had to have been Audrey. Harry knew little about sex other than two people got naked and touched each other, and that it wasn't permitted until after people were married. His mother had broken that rule then had been jilted, and by someone who seemed to be important. Maybe her being dumped was the reason Mother had always been so cruel to his sister. He gulped. *Had Daddy known this secret?*

Mother had kept the letter for years and years. Surely it mattered to her, a lot, and if he could locate Audrey and show it to her, they could use it against Mother, even if he didn't know quite how.

But his sister would.

He stuffed the letter deep inside his coat pocket, vowing to never let it out of his sight until it was safely in Audrey's hands.

CHAPTER 52

Audrey

Audrey liked wearing a uniform on the job—the red apron tied at her back kept her black skirt clean, and the white blouse fit her nicely. But the garter belt holding up her sheer nylons was an uncomfortable nuisance she had yet to grow accustomed to.

"Hey, doll, bring us a few beers, will ya?" A bearded man snapped his fingers at her and winked.

Audrey waved at him with a smile pasted to her face, thinking that the scraggly old men at his table had downed one too many beers already. At sixteen, she could've been one of their daughters, yet they flirted and took turns smacking her behind whenever she walked away. Bessie had said she should indulge them within reason—better tips that way—so she did, and sometimes hiked her skirt just above her knees—accidentally, of course.

She saw no harm in it, and sure enough, more money had flowed her way. In just a few months, Audrey had earned enough from tips and her meager paycheck to buy new clothes and snacks to stash in her room. Like Bessie, she hid leftover cash inside her pillowcase rather than depositing it in a bank.

Audrey slung a few more beers, keeping her eye on the entrance of the Wooden Shoe Tavern, as always. If she was seriously lucky, her mother would walk in one day and insist on dragging her home. Willowdale was such a small town that word would get around, and Audrey was counting on that. The idea of her daughter working on

Whiskey Row would send Mother into a tizzy, further enraging her because she'd lost the battle to control Audrey's life.

Bessie signaled from across the room that she was taking a break, pointing toward the door to the back room where she and Audrey each had a bunk. The manager of their bar, the liveliest dive on Whiskey Row on weekend nights, let his two full-time waitresses live rent-free in what used to be the owner's quarters. Thanks to Bessie, who basically ran the joint, Audrey hadn't only been hired but given a room and full use of the bar's indoor toilet and shower. Her new coworker was about thirty, making her nearly twice Audrey's age, with the blackest skin Audrey had ever seen. Bessie had a little boy named Artie, who lived with Bessie's mother somewhere on the edge of Shantytown, and she spent every Sunday with them.

"What can I do for you, girlie?" Bessie had asked Audrey the morning when she first walked into the bar. "We ain't open yet."

Audrey was tongue-tied.

Bessie slapped a rag onto a table and strutted her way. "This ain't no place for a young girl, anyway. Just look at you with that fancy suitcase, a real gentle woman of breeding. You down on your luck or something?"

Audrey had rarely conversed with a colored person because the darkies at her school always kept to themselves. They seemed to view the white students with skepticism and sometimes contempt and smartly—she'd determined—allowed their tight clique to protect them like a fortress wall. But while gazing at Bessie, Audrey realized the thin woman's deep-brown eyes were sparkling with humor, so she gathered her courage. "I'm looking for a job. I mean I need a job. Pretty badly."

"Do you know where you are, sweetie?" Bessie answered, gesturing to the tables around them as though Audrey had no clue. "This ain't the North Pole, where elves do all the work."

When Audrey hesitated then nodded, Bessie's smile faded away, and she scratched her scalp through curls the color of coal, cut short like a boy's. Moving behind the bar for a moment, she poured Coca-Cola syrup and soda water into a glass, added iced cubes, and offered the drink to Audrey.

"Just so happens we got an opening," she had said.

Now, as Audrey balanced four glasses of whiskey on a tray, she dipped her head at Bessie and winked. The place was slow for a Friday afternoon, but business would pick up in the evening, and then they would both make a killing in tips. The tavern was small, and the regulars packed the place.

After she delivered the whiskeys, the entrance door creaked open, and a blast of frigid air blew inside. Audrey looked sideways, and her mouth dropped. Wearing a long coat and a hat dusted by snowflakes, Mrs. Patton was closing the door behind herself. Her former teacher was holding an armful of books and, after stomping her boots, searched the room with bright eyes. Mrs. Patton seemed perfectly at ease, which was surprising, given she was in a seedy dive bar that decent people avoided.

Her eyes landed on Audrey, and she grinned.

Audrey rushed toward her, ignoring a customer's guttural "Need a whiskey over here."

"Um, hello, Mrs. Patton," she said, approaching her. "What are you doing here? Want a drink? Maybe some nuts?"

"It's nice to see you too, Audrey," her teacher replied drolly, dropping her load onto the counter. She tugged on the fingertips of her gloves with her teeth, pulling them off. "I have a few things here for you."

"It's... great to see you," Audrey mumbled, quickly rubbing the wetness from her eyes.

"I heard you had a job." Mrs. Patton paused, and when Audrey did not interject, she went on. "I think it's commendable that you're making a living. Very independent of you, very grown-up. Even though I hope this is just a temporary solution to your situation."

Audrey didn't know how to respond, so she stood mute, unwilling to reveal any details. Too many people had let her down. Then she frowned.

"And what if it's not temporary?"

"What I meant, Audrey, is that I hope you finish high school. I can help you find a way to do that." She pointed at the counter. "These are for you."

A loud voice called out, "Waitress, you work here or what?"

"I'll be there in a minute," Audrey replied over her shoulder, her eyes fixed on a thick green science textbook. Beneath it lay a mathematics book then a small English grammar book and several spiral notebooks, all topped by a box of pencils.

"This will get you started if you're interested," Mrs. Patton said. "Your teachers—who would have been your junior-year ones—will give you assignments and grade your work. The first ones are in here. I'll be your liaison, meeting here or wherever you want every week." She tapped the spirals with a pretty, red-polished fingernail. "Audrey, there is a bright future for you. As I recall, you've got quite a gift for words."

Too stunned to respond, Audrey ran a finger over the science book. At first, she was moved by the gesture and the teacher's faith in her. But then she realized how ridiculous Mrs. Patton's idea was, no matter how kind. She wanted to say, *You're wrong. I can't do this. I'm not that person anymore.*

"You have a phone here, right?" Mrs. Patton, ever the bulldozer, wrote her number on the inside page of a notebook. "Call me, and let me know where you want to meet or if you need any help." Mrs. Patton smiled at Audrey then turned on her chunky black heels and clicked smartly over the uneven floor slats.

"Mrs. Patton?" Audrey called after her while waving off two customers pounding on their table to get her attention. "How... How did you know where I was, that I was here?"

The woman pressed her lips together, gliding delicate fingers into her smooth leather gloves, considering the question. After she opened the door, an icy gust rushed in that set off a groan of revolt from the tavern's few customers.

"Oh, everyone knows, dear," she said. "We all know."

When the busy Friday night shift ended, Audrey settled into her bunk. Bessie was lying in the one above her, sucking on a Camel cigarette with great relish.

Audrey was flipping through the English textbook Mrs. Patton had provided, her brow knitted as she strained to read in the dim light. When Bessie hung her head upside down off the bed, she laughed and turned her eyes on her friend.

"So, you gonna do it? Go back to school with that lady's help?" Bessie seemed more excited than Audrey herself. "Nobody'd do that for a colored, tell you what."

Without saying so, Audrey agreed with her. But she also thought it pretty odd that somebody wanted to help her. "It's pretty amazing for me too. I'm just a dropout. Do you think I should do it?"

"Fool if you don't." Bessie pulled herself up and settled back onto her squeaky mattress, her words drifting through the air with her last plume of smoke. "You know, I never finished high school either. If someone gave me a way to do that, I'd jump on it."

Neither spoke for a while. Drips plopped rhythmically from their leaky faucet on the far side of the room.

While scanning a page, Audrey scratched her leg, and her fingers absently ran over multiple raised scars. Harry had some now too. She shook her head to fling the thought of her brother far away.

She couldn't think about him, about what had happened to him. As Mother's favorite, that had most surely been a fluke, a one-time thing. He was much better off staying with her and going to school. Besides, she couldn't take care of a child while living in a tavern. That would not be allowed.

Audrey dropped the book onto the floor and rolled off her bunk to snap the light bulb off. In the dark, she eased back under her blankets.

Above her, Bessie sighed heavily. "I'm gonna make sure my little boy gets an education so he can make something of hisself. Everythin' I do, including workin' in this dump, is for him."

The wistful comment hung aloft, and Audrey smiled. She and Bessie had quite a lot in common. They had both grown up poor and would be considered low-class citizens, although for Audrey, the reason had always been her family, not her skin color. Most respectable places in Willowdale would not hire a colored, but Whiskey Row was color-blind, thankfully. The way some white men treated Bessie bothered Audrey, though. Some called her awful names or tried to grab her breasts, and when she would slap them away, they would roar with laughter. A few had refused to let her serve them. Frankly, Audrey hadn't figured out why those men frequented the bar if they felt that way.

Bessie's soft, regular breathing indicated she was asleep, and Audrey felt a pang of gratitude for her friendship and how it had helped open her heart. She'd come to admire Bessie's strong work ethic and character, how she always put her family's needs ahead of her own.

Audrey rolled onto her side contentedly.

Just like Bessie, she was doing the right thing for everyone.

CHAPTER 53

Harry

While Harry worked for days to reinforce his tunnels, rolling debates consumed his thoughts. He wanted to wait for Audrey to find him, but he also wanted to go look for her. He wanted to show her the letter but worried she would be too upset by it.

Even though Harry was mad at his sister for deserting him, he finally decided to think of their past and how they'd supported each other. He had to take a chance on her. Audrey was practically a grown-up and would handle the news in the letter better than he ever could have. She would know what to do with it too.

But his biggest reasons were that the weather was getting too cold to hold off any longer, and he was lonely.

On a chilly November morning, before bundling himself up, Harry practiced speaking aloud, but something akin to mouse squeaks came out. He scribbled a message on notebook paper that he'd swiped from the house.

Hello. I'm Harry Scott. Do you know where my sister, Audrey, is?

He threw on layers of clothing, a coat, and a hat, and protected his feet with four pairs of his daddy's socks before sliding them into Mother's boots.

As he scooted through the fort's opening, Harry patted the coat pocket containing the note. He set out through the woods toward a back road that would take him to a neighborhood near downtown.

Trudging along the street known as Victorian Row, Harry scanned the mailboxes in search of the Littleton name. That was the first and best idea that had come to him, knowing Audrey had been good friends with Freddie. If anyone knew where she was, it would be him. At the least, it was a good place to start.

After several long blocks, Harry drew close to a yellow house with the name Wallace Littleton splayed across a black mailbox. He sucked in a mouthful of the warm air trapped in his scarf and gaped at the property. The place was big, but it looked welcoming, friendly even. Harry's heart skipped a beat before he turned onto their front walk.

Audrey could be inside.

He ambled up to the door, which was a shade of blue he'd never seen. He could barely reach the lion knocker, but he smacked it against the door and waited, then he knocked again, harder. When the big wooden door opened, Harry was looking up at one of the prettiest women he'd ever seen. Her hair was long and golden like wheat, and her white teeth sparkled between perfectly shaped red lips.

At first, the woman's face registered surprise, then she exclaimed, "Harry, my gosh, is that you under there? I'm so glad to see you."

He stepped back from the doorway and stared at her.

"You're Audrey's brother, right? I'm Mrs. Littleton, but I guess you know that, since you're here." She smiled. "Will you come inside?"

Harry was breathless with anticipation to see his sister but could not bring himself to go in.

"I've seen you in town a few times. Are you okay?" Mrs. Littleton said, lowering her head, her eyes roaming over him. "Son, a friend of mine said you've been in town, stealing. Is that true? I-I called after you the other day downtown, but you ran away. I'm sorry if I frightened you."

Harry fumbled in his pocket to retrieve the note, which was difficult with his gloves and stiffened fingers.

"I can't keep this door open, Harry, it's too cold. Won't you come inside and warm up?"

He latched onto the paper, nervous because she was eyeing him so closely.

"Harry, why are you here? Is your mother all right? I haven't seen her in months. She hasn't been by the church, and I... well, I—" She stopped. "Oh, Harry, I should have checked on your family. It's complicated why I haven't—grown-up stuff you wouldn't understand."

He pulled the note out, rubbed it between his gloves to flatten it, then stepped closer to her.

"Oh, my, that's no excuse, though. I know your mother isn't well and you're just a little boy. I imagine if you're stealing, it's for a good reason. For heaven's sake, Harry, it's freezing out here. Do come inside."

Harry ignored her prattling and held up his note, stretching his arm to give it to her. He peered around her, hoping to see his sister. She took it from him with a confused expression then scanned his few words before turning her eyes back to him. Her facial features softened, as if something had occurred to her, and she leaned halfway out the door, bending over to his eye level. A sharp wind swept across her face and whipped her hair back.

"Why aren't you talking to me, sweetheart, instead of giving me this note?"

Harry glared at her and pointed at the note hanging from her fingers.

"Do you think Audrey is here?" she asked, motioning behind her.

At last, she got it. He nodded eagerly.

Mrs. Littleton straightened and pushed the door wide, visibly shivering. "Let me help you. C'mon, please step in and warm up."

If he went into that house, Harry would be trapped there. She'd mentioned that he was a known thief and might call the sheriff.

"I'll tell you where she is if you come in."

He shook his head no, repeatedly jabbing his finger toward the note.

Mrs. Littleton's sigh produced a white cloud. "She's not here, son, and I haven't seen her in some time. But I heard that she's—she's working downtown." Her eyes darted to the left then back to him. "Would you like me to get word to Audrey to come home?"

He bit his lip to stop himself from crying and nodded earnestly. Mother's letter was expanding in his pocket with a life of its own, ready to jump right into Mrs. Littleton's hands. His fingers twitched, aching to give it to her, to have someone help him figure everything out. But not her.

That could only be Audrey. And he had to start waiting all over again.

CHAPTER 54

Audrey

"I just found out where you've been all this time." Freddie leaned forward on a stool, searching Audrey's face as she worked behind the bar, topping off a foamy beer for a customer, one of only three in a late-afternoon lull.

"Get out of here, Freddie. Why are you here, anyway? Slumming?"

In the tavern's subdued light, Freddie's orange hair seemed duller, rustier, and his freckles were deep pink from exposure to the cold. Only five minutes before, he'd breezed through the door as if he owned the joint, and when Audrey caught sight of him, she drew in a sharp breath. At first, she forgot herself and grinned broadly, happy to see him, then turned her back suddenly, remembering that Freddie was loyal only to his father, not to her. He was not her friend anymore and hadn't even tried to see her after she returned home from the Trents'.

And most hurtfully, according to Johnny, he'd also unceremoniously dumped her for some other girl. Maybe she shouldn't have believed anything Johnny ever said, but she had.

"Don't say that kind of thing. I'm here to find out what's going on with you. Why you're not in school and working here, of all goddamn places."

"You know you have to be eighteen to be in here. Guess you need to go," Audrey said, mustering an air of authority. She glanced over to Bessie, who was wiping off tables on the far side of the room but was

272

clearly scrutinizing the freckled boy in the expensive, heavy trench coat.

"Well, I hate to point out, Miss High and Mighty, that *you're* working here. Want me to tell the owner you're still sixteen?"

Audrey rolled her eyes. "Stop it, all right? Who told you I was working here?"

"My mom."

Her eyebrows bobbed up, anxious about what Mrs. Littleton probably thought of her. She smacked a wash rag angrily against the edge of the counter, and water drops showered the surface.

"Audrey, I'm fucking serious. What happened? Where are you living?"

Audrey jutted her chin in the direction of the back room. "I got a warm bed in there and a bathroom over there. All for free. Better than at home, and without the drama." She looked over at Bessie. "See her, over there? That's my friend and roommate, Bessie. We have bunk beds and share the room."

Freddie removed his stocking hat and caught Bessie's eyes before whisking it across his body, a knight greeting a lady. "How do you do? I'm Freddie," he shouted.

Bessie made a face, but Audrey saw a smile tugging at the edges of her friend's lips.

A familiar warm feeling of affection spread through Audrey's body. The boy had always readily accepted everyone.

"So why did you leave home? Ditch the old witch?"

Before she could answer, Freddie put up a hand to hush her.

"Wait. I'm sorry. That wasn't funny. I shouldn't have called your mother a witch. It's probably been hard on her since your dad died. And on you." For the first time since Audrey had been friends with Freddie, he looked uncertain. "Look, I owe you a big apology. Yes, I know. Again. I-I should have been checking on you instead of being afraid of my old man. He told me you came to our house one day, looking for me, that he sent you away. I was furious." He reached over and grabbed her hand. "I mean it, I'm a dumbass with no balls. When school started up and you were nowhere, I was frantic."

"Does your mom know you're here now?"

"Yes. When she told me where you were, I said nothing would keep me from seeing you. Nothing. Not even my father." Freddie's hand folded into a fist. "I was pissed because my mom knew where you'd gone, some time ago. I guess she figured it wasn't any of her business, let alone mine."

"Of course. Why should she check on me when I'm probably a whore now?"

"Jesus, just listen. Mom said you were okay and doing what you wanted, that we had no business being involved. It had nothing to do with thinking you're a whore. That's just stupid."

"Why do you even care? You've seen me, so you can go. I've got stuff to do." *Like deliver a beer to an irritated customer.*

"You're such a lamebrain. When school started and you weren't there, I spied on your house for a few days, and I only ever saw your mother. I was going loopy, not knowing if she'd shipped you off somewhere again." Freddie took a deep breath and put up a hand to stop Audrey from interrupting him. "Then Johnny told me you'd spent a night at his house just before school started. He said you were a dirty mess, that you'd run away." He shook his head. "I figured, well, *Audrey wants to be on her own. If she wants to talk to me, see me, she will eventually.* I knew you were probably upset about my dad. And me. I don't blame you."

She held her breath, not even worried whether Freddie actually had a girlfriend like Johnny had said. *Did he tell Freddie about that night?* If the kids at school knew, she would be considered a slut, some poor runaway girl who'd eagerly traded her body for a night's lodging. Freddie was talking again, and she tuned back in to catch the last of it.

"That Mrs. DeDecker is one good lady. I'm glad you landed there even if it was brief." He wiped his mouth. "My mom is, too, you know. But she's all about obeying my dad, always being the perfect *Good Housekeeping* wife." He shrugged. "I'll never understand his beef with your family. He's such a fucking snob."

Audrey let the air out of her lungs. Johnny hadn't told him.

She said, "I'm good here, really. Your mom is sort of right—I'm not your problem to solve. But I do appreciate you coming clean about everything. I guess we're still friends, then. Maybe."

Freddie's face collapsed with relief, and he smiled at her in his goofy way. After a long pause, his expression became serious. "Your little brother came to our house this morning, looking for you."

"Your house? What did he say?"

"That's just it. He didn't speak. He handed my mom a note that asked if she knew where you were."

A small pebble wedged itself in her throat. "He wasn't talking?"

"Listen. My mom said he smelled super bad, even standing out-side in the cold. And he wouldn't come into our house, was acting all weird like he was afraid. She said he was wearing layers of clothes un-der his coat, real bulky, and his boots looked too big."

Audrey pulled her eyes off Freddie then shuffled right past him. She scooped up a few nickels from a table she had served earlier, aware of his eyes on her back. "Okay, so what? It's no secret we're poor," she said, pocketing the change. "Thanks for pointing it out."

"What the hell, Audrey? He's your brother."

"Yes, my brother, not yours." She strolled to the sink.

"He's stealing, Audrey. My mom thinks either your mother is putting him up to it or he's out all on his own. What is he, twelve? Thirteen?" He sounded indignant.

"I need to get back to work, Freddie. Thanks for telling me." Au-drey picked up a mug and began to rinse it.

Freddie's lips puckered like he'd eaten a lemon, and he leaned over the bar top. "That's it? Thanks, Freddie? It's fine for you to leave school. You're sixteen. You can make that choice. But Harry isn't even enrolled in school, and that's not so fine. My mom checked up on it."

Audrey's nostrils flared. "Your mom? Do you mean the lady who's been keeping my whereabouts a secret from you? Doing only what your father orders her to do? That sweet mama? The one who took me away from the farm where I was finally happy? Just to come back and find—"

She stopped midsentence, and he jumped in loudly.

"Yeah, that mom. The one who welcomed you into our home and shared her clothes with you. Car rides. Food. And who brought you home because Mr. Trent thought you should know about your father."

From the corner of her eye, Audrey glimpsed Bessie scurrying toward them, wearing a frown as wide as her hips.

"Shush up, you two," Bessie whispered when she reached them. "Don't be yelling like that in here. You want one of these customers to complain?" Her eyes scoured the room, then she poked Freddie in the ribs with a finger. "Why you in here upsetting this girl? Ain't you been taught manners?" She snapped the bottom of her apron at him. "Hit the road, junior."

Freddie glanced back and forth between them, opening and closing his mouth like a fish struggling to breathe out of the water. He shook his head. "I'm sorry about that, ma'am." He sucked in his cheeks and nodded toward Audrey. "I wasn't trying to upset Audrey or cause a scene. I just wanted her to know what was happening to Harry, even though she's being obstinate and refusing to listen. There's something wrong with that kid not talking and all."

"Who's Harry?" Bessie asked, her eyes widening.

"Her *little brother*. Maybe you can talk sense into her." He smacked a hand on the counter as a parting gesture, snatched his hat, and rushed out the door, slamming it so hard after himself that glassware rattled and every eye in the bar turned to see what the fuss was all about.

After their shifts were over, Audrey and Bessie retreated to their room, and as was their ritual, they quickly hid their tips. Audrey scrubbed her face clean with a thinning bar of Palmolive soap while Bessie lit a Camel and paced around the room, occasionally flipping ashes into a tray next to their bunks. Whenever Bessie paced, she had something big on her mind.

Audrey pulled a flannel nightgown from her drawer, observing Bessie's movements from the corner of her eye, hoping to gauge how upset her friend was. *That damn Freddie*, she fumed, *sticking his nose in my business when I have everything under control.*

At last, Bessie came up to her and exhaled smoke in her face. "You got yourself a little brother?"

Wriggling into her nightgown, Audrey nodded, hoping her assent would be the end of it.

"But he's at home, alone. With your mama." She drew on her cigarette.

Audrey waved the smoke away. "Let it go, Bessie. In the first place, he's not little. He's twelve."

"Twelve is a child," Bessie interjected, bopping her head around. "Why are you here if he's there? You said your mama was crazy, that she beat you, and he—"

"No. She's not like that with him. Just me. I'm the one who had to get away. She—"

"Might have killed your father. That's what you said." Bessie grabbed her nightgown from a drawer and slammed it shut. "You leave your kid brother with a killer?"

"Okay, I said that," Audrey admitted. "But the truth is I honestly don't know for sure. Harry showed me a can of rat poison in our basement and was being all weird about it. I confronted Mother, asking if she'd poisoned my father, and she didn't deny it. I think I just jumped to a ridiculous conclusion."

Bessie tossed her blouse and skirt onto their only chair and pulled the nightgown over her head, after which she lit another cigarette with the cherry of her just-smoked one.

"What did your brother say about the poison?"

Audrey's tongue dawdled on her lips, moistening them, while she considered how much she wanted to reveal. "Nothing, actually. One day, he appeared out of nowhere and had me follow him to our basement."

"Appeared? What is he? A ghost?"

Audrey turned her back to Bessie and unwrapped her ponytail. "I'd been back a few weeks. You know, I told you about the farm, but I hadn't seen Harry anywhere. That particular day was the first time he... I don't know, he just showed up."

From behind her, Bessie gasped. "So your brother was missing? Weren't you worried your mama had sent him away like she done you?"

She wanted to say yes—yes, she had been—but an admission would only encourage Bessie. Instead, she retorted, "Bessie, I'd just learned my daddy had died, and I wasn't thinking straight, okay? I just figured Harry was staying with someone, that he'd come back when he wanted to. Mother said he'd been doing that all summer. And he did come back." She folded her arms squarely across her chest. "I'm tired. Let's get to bed."

Before she could climb in, Bessie eased herself onto Audrey's bottom bunk, scooting to lean against the shadowy wall. "Okay. I'm just trying to make sense of it," she said. "What made Harry think your mama had poisoned your father?"

Audrey sat on the edge of her bed and curled one leg under the other, resenting the cross-examination. "Well, he... he didn't actually say anything. I got the sense that he couldn't talk or something. I just figured it was a game. Harry always plays silly games. It wasn't something to take seriously."

"But if that boy Freddie said your brother didn't speak to his mom, doesn't that bother you? Like maybe he couldn't? That it's something serious?" In the dark, Bessie's eyes were gooey like dark, melted chocolate. "I think your mama did something to scare the voice right outta that boy. That's why he didn't talk to you that day or since. He can't."

Apparently, Bessie thought she was a doctor. Audrey didn't want to hear any more.

"Why don't you get off my bed and get in your own?" She stood so that Bessie could crawl out. "I know you mean well, but I know what's best for Harry, and that's being at home. Just because you're a mother doesn't mean you know more than I do."

Audrey knew she was coming off as defensive, even angry. Bessie inched her way off the bed, her previously concerned expression crestfallen. Briefly, they stood side by side, so close that their arms touched, but an invisible rift was separating them for the first time. Unexpectedly, Bessie took Audrey's hand in hers, and they looked at each other.

"I git that you have an awful mama," she said, "that all you want right now is to show her she can't control you no more."

Audrey stared at Bessie's pink oval fingernails. She could never admit to her—or anyone, for that matter—that being free of Mother's control was just half of it, that she wished with every fiber of her being that her mother had been the one to die, not her father.

"Seems to me you got the best of her. You're out. You're free." Bessie raised her chin and spoke softly. "But what about your little brother?"

Audrey's head snapped up as she let Bessie's hand drop. "You got all the answers, then? You think he can live here with us in this tiny place? I'm the one who has to be here. I'm the one sacrificing to make a living." Audrey clenched her fists at her sides. "When I have enough money, I'm going to take him. I'll figure it out then."

Trembling, Audrey stooped to climb under her covers as Bessie snapped off the light bulb. Darkness enveloped them like a dense fog. Without saying good night, Bessie climbed the creaky ladder and crawled onto her mattress.

The weight of Bessie's condemnation bore down on Audrey's chest, crushing her lungs. She would undoubtedly scream if Bessie piped up about anything else, so Audrey breathed in a loud, regular rhythm, pretending she was asleep until she heard the other girl's snoring from above.

Bessie had no right to judge her. Her words had made Audrey seem selfish, as though she were thinking only of herself and not her brother's welfare. Audrey was so infuriated that she wanted to kick the springs under Bessie's sleeping body and bounce her onto the floor. She'd told Bessie early on about Mother, how she'd never cared about what Audrey wanted or needed and thought only of herself. Even if she'd meant well, Bessie had insinuated she was like that too.

Audrey rolled onto her side and shoved her palms under her pillow to prop up her head. Know-it-all Bessie could think that way all she wanted and for as long as she wanted.

She did not care.

CHAPTER 55

Harry

For days, Harry had been keeping an eye out for Audrey, watching his house from inside Mr. Ritter's garage, craning his neck at a sharp angle to peer out a window. Maybe the old man had seen him come and go, but he never came outdoors.

Harry watched as Mother appeared on the porch, dressed in a warm coat and hat, and locked the door, leaving for what Harry assumed was a walk into town. Finally, he had a chance to go inside.

When Harry was certain the coast was clear, he unlocked the door and ran straight up to Audrey's room. He ran his fingertips over her pretty afghan and lifted it to inhale her aroma, his chest hurting from how much he missed her. He could picture her brushing her hair and humming, turning to frown at him whenever he would rush in uninvited. Harry blinked quickly. Only a little kid would cry.

The room was as frigid as his fort. Mother was probably rationing whatever coal she had remaining and had cut off heat to the upstairs.

Last night, snuggled under his heavy, nearly suffocating covers, Harry had remembered his sister's blue ribbons, the ones she used in her hair. He threw open her drawers and rifled through her clothes, finally sliding a handful of them into his coat pocket, certain his sister would recognize them. The way he figured it, Audrey would visit her tree after she came back.

Harry raced down the stairs. Before leaving, he threw open the kitchen window, and an icy wind immediately blustered through the room. Then he ran out, laughing for the first time in weeks.

Edith

Did I forget to lock the door? Edith traipsed into her kitchen, expecting a semblance of warmth to embrace her. She was chilled to the bone after walking home from the church, only to find the room as cold as her icebox. The do-gooders had come through as she'd hoped. She dropped two overflowing bags onto the table then slammed the windowpane down with a bang.

"Stop fooling around in my house," Edith said while tossing her gloves onto the table. Rubbing her hands together, she swayed into the parlor and switched the radio on, turning up the volume until music reverberated off the walls.

"I can drown you fuckers out," she said. "Don't think I can't."

She clapped to applaud herself and returned to the kitchen, keeping her coat wrapped around herself. Edith emptied the bags and soon after was anxiously waiting for her percolator to perk. *Coffee at last. Real coffee.* Her trek to the church had been a humiliating excursion for sure, but she'd had no choice.

A nearby floorboard moaned, emitting a long creaking sound as though someone was stepping on it. "Mrs. Hamilton?" she whispered, her eyes sweeping the room. The woman never showed herself. "You idiot woman. Go ahead. Open the windows. Unlock my door. Steal my stuff. I don't give a shit what you do."

Edith paced around the room until the coffee was ready then sat and warmed her throat, her stomach, then her body with the soothing drink. She tilted her head, listening, because they were walking around her now. "You know," she said, with a touch of sarcasm, "I'll be out of this place soon, living high on the hog. You two will be here for eternity. So, I was thinking you'd better learn to live with it, me outwitting you. Oh, wait, you can't live with it. You're both dead, dead, dead."

CHAPTER 56

Audrey

Since having called Mrs. Patton, Audrey had met her twice at City Park to exchange her completed assignments for new ones. She was thrilled to be learning again, reading and devouring her lessons, and devoted most of her downtime to her studies. Discussing her work with her former teacher was time Audrey treasured.

Mrs. Patton had invited Audrey to the Sunday smorgasbord at the Tipsy Pig, and they'd just scooched into opposite sides of a booth with cracked red plastic cushions. The scent of smoky barbecue was so enticing that Audrey inhaled deeply, a drowning person guzzling oxygen with deep gratification. While they sipped sodas, Audrey passed her homework across the red-and-white-checkered tablecloth, and Mrs. Patton stuffed the papers into her satchel.

They ate delicious sandwiches after that, discussing Audrey's previous assignments and what the other teachers had said about the quality of her work. To Audrey's relief, Mrs. Patton never asked her personal questions. However, as she had during their first get-together, her teacher encouraged her to write free-flowing prose, suggesting she start up a diary again. Audrey couldn't bring herself to admit the trouble such an effort had created for her and only nodded as though she would consider the suggestion.

After their meeting, she shyly thanked Mrs. Patton, and they agreed to meet in City Park the following weekend. Audrey walked alongside the woman to her car before heading back to the tavern, her new assignments tucked inside her notebook.

Whiskey Row was quiet and deserted, the previous night's revelers likely sleeping off their overindulgences in gutters elsewhere. The early afternoon was breezy and warm for mid-November, and Audrey unzipped her coat, tipping her face upward to let the sun's rays kiss her cheeks. When the Wooden Shoe's awning loomed into view, Audrey's pace slowed, and her pulse quickened. Maybe she would go to the park and enjoy a few hours of reading on a nice winter day—anything to avoid Bessie for a bit longer, with her recriminating stares and silent treatment.

Freddie's visit had changed everything between them.

Bessie was constantly laying sorrowful eyes on Audrey, wordlessly judging her, which she couldn't stand. Every look seemed to be a reproach. Their relationship had become awkward, and they rarely talked about anything.

Just a few days before, during a busy night with rowdy drinkers, Bessie had dragged a tall, bearded man away from Audrey after he made a pass at her, scolding him and threatening to kick him out. Livid because of Bessie's interference, Audrey stormed into the bathroom to gain control of her anger away from the customers.

She bristled when Bessie came in to check on her. "You just cost me big tips from that table. I don't need you protecting me."

Bessie had looked hurt then disgusted before walking away.

Audrey shook off the memory and walked briskly toward the Shoe's entrance, recalling that Bessie was gone all day because she spent Sundays with her son and mama. She pushed through the unlocked tavern door wearing a chip on her shoulder and an attitude the size of Illinois. Blinded until her eyes adjusted to the murkier light inside, Audrey dropped her things onto a nearby table and jumped, startled, when she glimpsed the outline of a person sitting on a stool at the bar.

Her heart beating wildly, she edged toward the entrance. The form swiveled to face her, and Audrey saw the legs, the hat.

Mrs. Littleton.

"It's good to see you, Audrey," Mrs. Littleton said, tipping a mustard-yellow hat.

Audrey gawked at her. Then her eyes roamed the hazy room to be sure they were alone. The bathroom door was open, and the door to her and Bessie's room was closed. She raced behind the bar and switched on several lights.

"What are you doing here?" Unintentionally, Audrey's tone was rude. "I mean, who let you in here? We're closed."

Mrs. Littleton swung her stockinged legs to the floor and stood, immaculately dressed in a pressed dark-gray skirt and a colorfully speckled sweater. Her coat had been folded and placed on the counter as though she'd been waiting for some time. Audrey flushed pink at the very idea of Freddie's mom sitting in a Whiskey Row bar. The mixed odors of barf and stale beer clung to the walls, an assault on the noses of those not used to it. Mrs. Littleton did not belong. No doubt, she was just as appalled as Audrey was embarrassed.

"Your friend let me inside to wait for you," Mrs. Littleton said, advancing on Audrey, her hands clasped over her heart.

Of course. Bessie would've found out who this woman was and let her inside just to spite Audrey.

Audrey skirted out from behind the counter and stood directly in front of her unexpected caller. "Mrs. Littleton, this isn't the kind of place for a woman like you. Does Mr. Littleton know that you're here?"

"Even if he did, don't you think it's time I start to be brave, Audrey? Like you?"

The question caught Audrey off guard. "What do you mean?"

"Just that many things have gone so far wrong, Audrey, so off track. And Freddie pointed out that I..." Mrs. Littleton stepped up to her. "That I've let you down. I've been too uncertain, more worried,

I'd say, about standing up to my husband, telling him that helping you, getting involved, is the right thing to do."

Even if that was an apology, Audrey did not want it.

"Audrey." Mrs. Littleton inhaled and held her breath. Air rushed from her mouth. "This will surprise you, but I knew your father quite well. A long time ago, I helped care for him. It was after his accident when he was in the convalescent home in Penshaw. I was young, just a helper there. My mother was a nurse."

Audrey let that sink in. "Your mother worked? But you're rich."

"I grew up in Willowdale, and my folks were respectable but certainly not rich. Enough, I guess, that Wally looked twice at me. One thing my mother did care about was a good match." The muscles in her jaw tensed. "But my mom worked because she loved nursing and people. She saw goodness in others. Most people do not. It's funny, you know. Freddie is just like her."

Mrs. Littleton stared into the middle distance beyond Audrey, a mixture of pride and sadness crossing her face like a passing mist.

Audrey looked at her sideways. If Mrs. Littleton had befriended her father a long time before, that could explain why Mother hated her so much. She bristled, not wanting to hear any more about their supposed relationship. "Who cares if you knew my daddy? Why are you telling me any of this? I just want to know why you're here."

"Because for years I knew he needed help, that your family needed support, and I wasn't sure what to do. I'd married Wally, and he'd married your mother. Wally was against interfering with your family, social mores and all. But I've always had a soft spot for your daddy. He was a good man, Audrey. Kind. He didn't deserve what happened to him, not the accident, and not—"

The bedroom door creaked open, and Mrs. Littleton stopped cold, looking sideways. The door closed with a whisper of a thud. *Bessie.*

"Not what? He didn't deserve his accident and what else?"

"Your mother, Audrey, I'm sorry to say. Red barely knew her when they got married. He had dreams of making a good life despite his head injury. And now he's gone." She held Audrey's eyes. "I know you miss him, and I'm so sorry. I shouldn't have let convention stop me from doing more for your family."

Audrey didn't know what to say or how to feel. Her emotions were jumbled like scattered puzzle pieces—pity and sadness for her father alongside hatred and anger for Mother.

Suddenly, she wanted the woman to leave.

"Look, you brought me home from the Trents', and I'm thankful for that. That was nice of you," she said. "But I've got a job now, I've put the past behind me, so you can stop beating yourself up. I survived, as you can see. I'm even going to school."

"Yes, and I'm proud of you for taking care of yourself." She waited a beat then said, "But we need to find out what's going on with your brother." Below her defined eyebrows, Mrs. Littleton's blue eyes had sharpened.

A current of anger surged through Audrey. Everyone was worried about Harry when she was the one working in a seedy dive. "Harry is—"

Mrs. Littleton hushed her. "I understand from Freddie that you refuse to go home, and I don't blame you. Really, I don't. Right now, you're too young to handle all of this, this..." Mrs. Littleton hesitated. "This mess. You have to take care of yourself. That's the best way you'll end up helping Harry. But somebody has to check on him."

"Harry has always been fine with Mother. Even if he wasn't in school when you checked, he will be soon, I'm sure."

"Please, hear me out." Mrs. Littleton's tone was soft but insistent. "Your mother's not right in the head. It's different from how your daddy was, you know that. But she's worse than I've ever seen her. When she came to the church for supplies, she was talking gibberish, lashing out at everyone. Even talking when nobody was near her."

Audrey's eyes widened. She crossed her arms.

"I'm done doing what my husband says, even if he gets angry at me. Times are changing. And Red would want me to do this, to check on your brother."

Audrey's eyes flitted over Mrs. Littleton's willowy frame. She was no match for Mother, who hated her guts and was unpredictable. She uncrossed her arms and said, "I think it should be me. I'll go out there. You have no idea what Mother—"

"I can handle it," Mrs. Littleton said decisively.

Audrey paced around one table then circled another, head bowed, a finger pressed to her lips. She stopped and looked directly into Mrs. Littleton's steady gaze. "If... If Harry's not okay, and you take him away from her, what happens then?"

"We'll go to the sheriff, follow the law," she said. "We'll figure something out, I promise you."

An unanticipated flood of relief coursed through Audrey's veins. She walked into Mrs. Littleton's open arms, a mollified child, and closed her eyes, wrapped in the woman's reassuring embrace.

As the older woman stroked Audrey's hair, the bunk room door creaked open, and she stole a glance, catching Bessie's smile beaming in the wide crack. She'd been listening. When the door opened all the way, Audrey reached out an arm toward her friend and motioned for her to join them.

CHAPTER 57

Harry

Clouds had been gathering all day, low and dense and so puffy that Harry expected snow to burst from them at any moment. Dusk hadn't fallen yet, but the sky was already the color of a sleek dolphin. So far, he'd been able to keep a small fire going in the middle of the fort, but staying awake to stoke it had been impossible. If a heavy snow came, his little home would surely be destroyed. Where he would go was a question Harry would have to answer, and soon. Even jail sounded good, a place where he would receive food and water.

He was hurrying through the woods to the clearing, to Audrey's big, funny-looking tree. Harry patted the pocket containing her ribbons. Planting them would work—it just had to. Audrey would visit the clearing at some point. Truthfully, she could've been there many times without him knowing. Audrey would find a ribbon, realize he'd been the one to leave it, and curiosity would get the best of her. She would search around for another one. He would arrange a trail of ribbons for her, guiding her to his closest tunnel, then on to others that led to his fort. If the weather forced him out, Harry could even leave a note somewhere safe inside the fort for her.

Audrey was clever and would figure it out. Harry had nothing to lose.

Through scraggly branches ahead, Harry glimpsed the sprawling tree still a distance away. That was where the first ribbon would go, the one that would bring Audrey to him. Harry dodged thick, unearthed roots, consumed by his thoughts, pinning his hopes on the idea.

When a distinct sound reached his ears, he stopped cold and immediately squatted behind a tall, narrow tree. Harry heard the *crunch, crunch* of footsteps atop frozen leaves. His heart throbbed in his throat, echoing in his ears. His fast, uneven breathing steamed through his wool scarf.

Harry looked around and skittered toward his nearest tunnel to hide. It was not long or thick enough to cover him fully, thanks to recent harsh winds, but he would be safer there. He slipped into it. On his hands and knees, Harry crawled stealthily to the other end to peek through the sparse sticks and leaves.

A dark figure loomed behind Audrey's tree. For a second, he thought it was a black bear. He'd never heard of a bear in southern Illinois, but anything was possible. He stiffened when an angry voice pierced his ears.

"Where are they?"

Mother's voice. Harry's heart pounded harder. He flattened his body to the ground, face down.

"Jesus, Lord," his daddy would've said.

After a long minute, Harry forced himself to look up, and carefully, silently, he rolled onto his side to peek out. Mother was swinging an arm up and down in a stabbing motion. She was behind Audrey's tree, casting clumps of dirt every which way and grunting from the effort.

"I know you have them. You're the one who took them."

A cold chill ran down Harry's spine. Like she'd done in the parlor, Mother was talking as though a person was there with her. *But why is she digging?* Like a soldier slithering on the ground under barbed wire, he crept forward, eyes locked on the imposing black figure. At the end of his tunnel, Harry emerged and leapt like a frightened gazelle to hide behind a wide oak tree. From there, he watched

Mother chip, chip away with what looked like a long, sharp knife. She was definitely boring out a hole, using her hands then as well as the knife. Harry's toes and fingertips were numb, but he ignored the painful stinging, too hopped up to leave. He wondered if Mother had buried food underground to stay cold, just like he had in several spots around the woods. Harry made a sour face because that made no sense.

"I'll pull every inch of you out of there if I have to."

Harry shuddered, unnerved by her bizarre words, and waited for her to say more. Mother sounded ready for the booby hatch in Penshaw, and he might not need to show Audrey the letter burrowed inside his coat pocket after all. When she reached into the hole, half of her arm disappeared, then a skeleton's hand flew out and landed by her bent knee. His eyes went wider as Mother tugged on something. A long set of bones appeared then shattered into pieces in her hands. Harry's blood went cold.

She was digging in a grave, a damn grave.

"Stop fucking with me, Mrs. Hamilton. Where are my boots? My letter?"

Grandmother Hamilton? He heard a scream rise and escape from his throat, then Harry slapped a glove over his mouth.

Mother's head twisted to the side and targeted him with her eyes. She'd heard him. She stood. He gaped at her pale face, terrified by the hateful scorn, the wild, fiery eyes with a look Harry knew too well. He had to disappear, jump back into the tunnel, and move, move. Harry dropped to his hands and knees and darted into the tunnel. The leaves were sparse, not enough to truly shield him.

Without warning, his scarf tightened, and Harry's head snapped back, his body tumbling with it. He landed on the hard ground with a thud and looked up. Mother was towering over him, looking like the Grim Reaper in her black coat and hat.

"What have we here?" Mother said, holding the end of his scarf, knotting it around her knuckles. After she squatted before him, Mother bobbed her head like a curious rattlesnake. Harry half expected to hear the dangerous warning rattle. Mother hissed in his face.

"Sooo, son," she said. "How 'bout you tell me where you've been all this time? Been worrying about you, then come to find you out here snooping on me."

Harry tried to swallow. His heart was beating so hard that he thought it might explode. He yanked on the scarf to loosen her hold, but Mother held fast.

"Let's go, Harry," she said, pulling him up. "I think it's high time you came home for good."

They started to walk with Harry tethered to her. He looked toward the clearing, where fragments of his grandmother's bones lay scattered. She'd never moved away. She'd been dumped there like trash. That had to be why Mother had ordered them long ago to stay out of the woods. He fingered the letter in his pocket, wishing he'd never stolen her stupid boots, then he felt the satin strips. Harry moved them into his palm.

When he slowed his pace a little, Mother made a *harrumph* sound and marched ahead of him, pushing aside branches that crossed her path and tugging his scarf like he was her dog on a leash. If he could drop a few ribbons along their way, a trail would lead between the clearing and the house, and Audrey would find them and know to look for him. *Or will she?* Harry gulped. Snow might fall and cover them. Or a strong wind might blow them away.

He dropped the first one anyway. They were his only hope.

CHAPTER 58

Audrey

"I think I have the flu or something," Audrey told Bessie, slogging into their room after throwing up in the Shoe's bathroom. She went to their sink and brushed her teeth. "I've been tired for so long—feel like I can't ever get enough rest."

She dragged herself across the room and dropped wearily onto her bunk bed, smiling weakly at her older friend, who was pulling on socks while sitting in their chair. Bessie grinned back at her, but concern flickered in her eyes.

"I can't focus on my schoolwork. My head just seems so fuzzy lately. And I know I haven't been pulling my weight around here. You've been picking up the slack. Maybe it's not the flu. Could be that waiting to hear from Mrs. Littleton has got me so upset it's making me puke."

"You threw up just now?" Bessie rose and sat down beside her. Audrey nodded.

"And before today?"

"My stomach is off most mornings, it seems, ever since Mrs. Littleton was here." Audrey's lips slid into a pout. "Sorry, Bess. I'll do better. This will pass."

Bessie put her hand on Audrey's knee and patted it tenderly. "Honey, I don't want to pry, and you don't have to say," she said. "But when was your last period?"

Audrey's head bobbed. She turned frightened eyes to Bessie. "You don't think..."

"Ain't none of my business, but if—"

Audrey jumped off her bunk in a panic. "Oh, Bessie. Oh my God. I'm tired and feel sick all the time, and I haven't had my period since..." She hung her head and wept, covering her face with her hands.

Bessie stood and pulled her into her arms, and they huddled together until Audrey's sobs quieted.

"Before I came here, Bess... I-I was raped," she said haltingly.

Bessie's lips screwed up in anger, and her eyes moistened. She lowered her eyelids. "Did you know the bastard?" she asked in a hushed tone.

When Audrey continued to sniffle but did not respond, Bessie drew her closer. "Never mind, child. Bessie's not gonna let you go through this alone."

After wiping her eyes with the collar of her nightgown, Audrey stared at the floor in a locked gaze, breathing heavily, anxious and uncomprehending.

"I know nothing about being a mother, Bess," she mumbled. "Look how poorly I've done for Harry." Audrey sucked in a breath and turned wild eyes on Bessie. She grabbed her friend's forearms and shook them. "What if I'm just like my own mother, Bessie? I just can't do that to a child. I just can't."

CHAPTER 59

Edith

Light snow began to fall in the midafternoon.

Edith sipped hot water and watched through the kitchen window, scowling at the scene. She wrapped Red's old wool cardigan across her shoulders, wearing two large sweaters of her own underneath it, then cupped her mug to warm her fingers. Wood suitable for burning in the fireplace was gone. With so little coal left to burn, her shitty, drafty house was far too cold for any kind of comfort. At least she had electricity, but that would go away next if she didn't find that letter.

Damn the snow. Damn the frozen ground.

Damn it all.

Maybe she'd been too hasty, believing Mrs. Hamilton had removed the letter with her ghostly entrails. Edith mulled that thought over. She'd made an assumption, forgetting that Red was worse in death than he had been in life, which was really saying something. She nodded, agreeing with herself, and took another gulp of the unsatisfying water. The whole idea of working at the church again was revolting, but she desperately needed money to tide her over until she found the letter.

Edith slid her eyes to the locked basement door. Perhaps Harry could make himself useful. For some reason, Edith couldn't recall his birthday, but he might've been thirteen. A son had a sacred duty to take care of his mother, and many boys his age had jobs. She drummed her fingers on the table. Wherever her son had been holed up, he hadn't fared very well. The boy was stinky, skinny, and disheveled, although someone had given him a new coat, gloves, and hat. Eventually, she would force him to tell her who. So far, the boy hadn't spoken a word, had flat-out refused even after she smacked him but good.

Thinking about Harry, Edith grabbed the basement door key from a drawer and dropped it into her pants pocket. A car door slammed, and she wheeled around to peer through the kitchen door curtains. A taxi was idling in her driveway.

Who would...? Edith scrunched her eyes together and walked backward as croaking sounds bubbled up from her throat. She stumbled into a chair. She righted herself and seized the ice pick lying in the sink then slipped it in her pocket with the key.

That fucking woman was in the taxi.

The *tap*, *tap*, *tap* that came next was at the front door, polite but insistent. This time, Mrs. Somebody had seen fit to use manners to call upon another lady. Edith slunk down the hall in her baggy, layered clothes, flinging Red's sweater onto her bedroom floor as she passed. Through the door's lacy curtain, she could see Mrs. Somebody's face beaming under a festive holiday-red hat dotted by tiny white pebbles, probably pearls. She opened the door.

"Mrs. Scott. Hope I'm not disturbing too much?" Mrs. Somebody said. "May I please come in? This is for you."

Edith stepped back and put out her hands, accepting a loaf of perfectly wrapped, freshly baked bread. Mrs. Somebody strolled confidently past her before turning around with a questioning look.

"The parlor, to your right," Edith said, hiding her annoyance. "That's where we entertain guests."

She set the package on the counter, yearning to slice it up to eat, then followed Mrs. Somebody into the room, one hand behind her back, frantically shooing Red off her heels. She could feel him breathing down her neck.

Edith got right to the point. "What do you want?"

Mrs. Somebody cleared her throat. "I've come about Harry."

"What about Harry?" Edith lowered her eyelids.

"Mrs. Scott, your son came to see me a few days ago—well, not to see me, specifically, but to find his sister."

Edith remained stoic. "So what?"

"Couple of things. For instance, is he talking to you? I mean, using his voice? I simply couldn't get him to speak. He handed me a note asking for Audrey, seemed quite desperate to find her."

"Really? Did she come waltzing right through your parlor then?"

A puzzled look crossed Mrs. Somebody's face. "I don't know what you mean, Mrs. Scott. I told him I'd get a message to Audrey at the tavern. I didn't want to tell him she worked there. Then he left."

Edith's eyes tapered into slits. "Tavern? What are you talking about?"

"I assumed you knew where Audrey is working. Doing quite well, it seems." She faked a cough. "I believe Harry thought Audrey was living with my family."

Edith turned away. Mrs. Somebody sidled closer, and Edith could smell the woman's rosewater scent. A hand lightly touched her shoulder.

"I'm sorry if I've upset you. I just—"

Edith whirled around. "You just what? Keep stickin' your nose in where it's not wanted? You think I give a damn where Audrey is? I disowned her, that's what. Couldn't care less what she's doing or where she is."

Mrs. Somebody sidestepped a couple of feet away, her cheeks flaming high, making her even prettier. She cleared her throat.

"I actually came to talk about Harry," she said. "I... I learned he hasn't been in school, and I know his going is up to you. But..." Her eyes shifted to the floor. "I'm only a concerned parent, a friend of your family if you will allow."

Friend? Edith wanted to spit on her. The woman thought that her shit didn't stink, that she was somebody important, the queen bee, that it was just fine to come callin' without being invited, like the nosy bitch she was. Edith's hand found its way into her pocket to finger the blunt end of her small weapon, thinking as she rubbed it. The woman's eyes grew wide and curious, as if suddenly unsure of herself.

"Well, certainly, Mrs. Littleton. You'd like to see Harry, then? He's in the basement, shoveling coal to warm this place up. Would seeing him make you feel better? Since you took the trouble to come out here?"

"That's... well, that's just fine, Mrs. Scott." Mrs. Somebody's shoulders relaxed slightly. "I'd like to help you and your boy."

Edith stifled a laugh. "How kind," she said. "I see you came in a taxi? Such a luxury." She walked into the kitchen, waggling her palm to signal the woman to follow her.

"Yes, I asked him to come back in an hour."

Ah. Sending that cabbie away would be an easy matter, and she could say Mrs. Littleton had found another ride home.

Edith unlocked the basement door and glided it open, relieved that Harry was not squatting on the landing. "The bulb doesn't work up here, so watch your step," she said. That was a lie, of course.

She led the way down the stairs. When her eyes adjusted to the grayness, Edith spotted Harry sitting on the floor in the farthest corner of the large room, a dark bundle of ragged clothing. He was hunched over, his face hidden, motionless. Either he was asleep, or Harry hadn't heard them approaching.

"Harry?" Mrs. Somebody called out from behind Edith.

"Oh, he'll be in the furnace room right on the left."

"But there's no light on in there," she said then squealed. "Harry. My God."

Harry's head popped up, revealing the whites of his widened eyes. Mrs. Somebody pushed by Edith to get to him, then she was cooing and talking as though Harry was her own son.

Edith reversed course and marched back up the stairs.

Mrs. Somebody was shouting at Edith when she locked the door and would probably race back up the flight and pound on it, begging to be released. *No matter.* The key went back into the kitchen drawer, and the ice pick into the sink.

Edith settled into Red's rocker, considering what to do next and grinning at her own stupid luck. Mrs. Somebody was a fine substitute for that old letter.

CHAPTER 60

Harry

"Harry, what happened? Give me your hands."

Mrs. Littleton eased down beside him on the icy cement floor, rubbing his smaller palms in hers like they were sticks she was twisting to start a fire. Soon Harry's fingers were tingling as blood flowed through them. From the corner of his eye, Harry peered at her and considered how odd her fancy red hat looked in the dark, dreary basement. The long black coat she wore looked warm and would make a great addition to his fort. She'd tucked her bent knees into it, so only the toes of her boots stuck out.

Without asking, Mrs. Littleton put an arm around Harry and pulled him into what Daddy would've called a bear hug. Her sweetness was almost more than he could take, but he didn't want to cry like a baby. They snuggled like that, and he didn't pull away.

When she whispered to him, her breath moistened Harry's cheek. "Have you been living down here, Harry? Is this why you haven't been in school?"

Only a gurgling sound emerged from Harry's throat, so even trying to talk was utterly useless. He dropped his head. He needed to write a note as that was the only way he could tell her anything. He could use the back of the letter in his coat pocket, the one Mother was desperate to get back from her dead mother.

But he didn't have a pencil or pen.

After shaking his head no, Harry gestured toward the window well, where a fracture of light spilled through from the back side of the house.

"I don't understand, Harry, but that's okay. We need to figure out how to get out of here. I don't know why your mom locked me down here, but I'm glad because I've found you." She paused long enough that he looked at her. "I'm afraid she isn't well, Harry. She needs help."

When Harry nodded, Mrs. Littleton's eyes lit up. "I see you agree. Good. And I want you to know that I've seen Audrey. Talked to her. She's waiting to hear from me that you're okay."

Then Harry let himself cry, no longer able to act brave, and buried his head against her shoulder as throaty wails escaped his lips.

"Lord only knows what you've been through. Harry, we'll figure it all out once we're away from here. Promise."

As they held each other, snow pit-a-patted against the window, a comforting sound because Mrs. Littleton was by his side. Harry's eyelids grew heavy. He leaned into her, relieved that a grown-up could take charge and do the thinking while he slept.

When he awoke, Mother was moving about in the kitchen overhead. The room was much darker. Wanting to flip on the basement light, he pulled himself up, laden with his layers of clothing and heavy coat. Mrs. Littleton produced a small, tentative smile.

He wanted to trust her, needed to trust her.

At first, he hesitated, then Harry strode across the floor and clicked the string on the hanging bulb. A dingy glow spread around the room. He hurried to his grandfather's shelves and picked up the tin canister, carried it to Mrs. Littleton, and showed her the side with the skull and crossbones. In the shadows, her eyes toggled between Harry's face and the ghastly images.

"I don't know what you're trying to tell me, Harry," she said. "That's poison. Are you saying we should poison your mother?"

Harry shook his head no.

"Were you poisoned? Or maybe someone you know was?"

He nodded enthusiastically and returned the tin to its place just as the upstairs door scraped open, shooting a plume of light down the stairs. Harry darted to the corner under the stairway and pulled the top of his coat over his head. Pretending to be asleep had served him well in the past, and he could only hope Mrs. Littleton was watching him and would follow his lead.

Edith

When Edith saw pitiful Mrs. Somebody plunked down on the concrete, she couldn't help but grin. Even funnier, the woman was glaring at her while she descended. *Seriously,* she thought, rolling her eyes upward for a second. *Here I am, bringing down two bowls of chicken stock—the last in my cupboard—and this is the kind of thanks I get.*

At the foot of the stairs, she stopped and studied her pathetic prisoner, recalling the fancy Mrs. Somebody of fourteen years before.

Edith had just left Mac's Butcher Shop, holding a package of liver, when she overheard a man's deep voice then his distinctive guttural laugh. She withdrew inside the entrance, a hand on her throat, and calmed herself before slowly opening the door again to listen and step out. It had been him, all right, a dapper sight in a gray tailored jacket and fitted cuffed pants topped by a navy-blue Windsor hat tilted over one eye.

Even in the midst of the country's worst depression, the man liked to show off.

A beautiful blond woman was walking at his side. Together, they were pushing a baby stroller while exchanging glances, laughing with wide, open mouths, and waving to pedestrians like they were leading their own personal parade. Tucked inside that carriage was their son, about a year younger than her own little Audrey, who'd been almost two. Wanting to hide, Edith once again retreated inside the butcher shop, ignoring the questioning looks from a dozen or so turned heads.

Wearing a bloody apron and standing behind the counter, Mr. Hatcher signaled Edith to leave, but she turned her back to him and knelt behind the door. His patrons had lost interest in Edith by the time she peeled herself away and ran out the door. She'd overreacted and was furious with herself for days after that. Edith had a husband and a child, all respectably living with her mother in her parents' house, and she was a perfectly good mother, wife, and member of the Willowdale community.

That woman—that blonde—had thought she was better than Edith because she'd married *him*.

"Why do you hate me?"

Mrs. Somebody's question pulled Edith back to the dreary, cold basement. Edith set the tray on the floor and wiped her hands on her apron.

"All righty," she said. "You figured that out, huh? Honestly, it's simple. You ruined my life."

"What? Why, I hardly know you. What you're saying makes no sense. Surely you don't mean that?"

Across the room, Harry was snoring, and Edith glanced at him.

"Is... is that why you've locked me down here?" Mrs. Somebody asked.

"I'm keeping you until your husband pays up, gives back what he took from me. Because of you." She smirked. "Which he'll do to keep his dirty little secrets."

"What on earth? What secrets? We have no secrets."

"Now, that's funny. My guess is Wally will do anything to keep me quiet, to keep secrets that you say you don't know about."

"You call him Wally?"

"Let me lay it out for you. I used to care about keeping secrets, and your husband used that against me. But I've got nothing to lose now. But you two?" Her laugh was boisterous. "You've got everything to lose."

The look on Mrs. Somebody's face was priceless. Perhaps it was dawning on her that her husband was an asshole.

Edith clapped her hands to startle Harry, whom she suspected was only pretending to be asleep. "I brought you both hot—well, warm—soup. Get over here, Harry."

She refocused on her enemy. "Might as well plan to be here until I get the cash from him, then—"

"Cash? Like a ransom?" The woman had gone ashen. "You can't keep me here. The sheriff—"

"Will not be coming here, Mrs. Somebody, because—"

"Don't call me that."

"No, not ransom, you simpleton. It's money owed to me. Payment due. That's different. And Wally will come here soon because you're here."

"This is kidnapping. If I don't come home, Wally will notify the sheriff, and—"

"And you'll be dead before the sheriff sets one foot inside this house."

Mrs. Somebody swallowed so hard that Edith could swear she saw a big lump—like a bowling ball rolling down an alley—glide down her neck.

"So glad you stopped by today," Edith said.

Mrs. Somebody raised her head and tried to catch Edith's eyes. "I knew your husband, Red. A good man. He would never want—"

"Red? You knew Red?" Her voice was high-pitched. "Well, my, my, of course you did. Not enough to have one man—you had to have lots of them. Other women's too. Right?"

"No, it wasn't like that. Listen. I'm trying to tell you, he—"

"Oh, I saw you that day. At his grave." Edith spat on the concrete. "You whore."

She stuck her hand into her pocket and withdrew Mrs. Hamilton's ice pick then wielded it in front of the other woman's face.

Harry lunged at her, knocking Edith into Mrs. Somebody, who was trying to get her feet under herself to stand up. A chunky heel had caught in the hem of her coat, and she stumbled, unable to rise or to ward off the coming attack. Mother began to stab her in furious, quick thrusts.

"Jesus. Stop! Please stop!" Mrs. Somebody flailed her arms and legs to ward off the attack, attempting to shield her face from the tiny blade.

Harry managed to put his hands around his mother's forearm and jerked it back hard enough to loosen her grip. The bloody pick sailed through the air and rattled across the floor toward the stairway. She backhanded him as hard as she could, and Harry fell to the floor. He crawled to Mrs. Somebody, who was wheezing and caressing her leg. Harry huddled against her.

Edith wiped her nose with the hem of her apron, gaping at them. She turned, crossed the room, and seized her miniature weapon then ran a finger across its sharp, red-stained point. "Blood doesn't bother me, Annette. May I call you that?"

She kissed the ice pick then slid it into her pocket and started for the stairs, pleased with herself. Edith had not intended to hurt the woman, but she didn't regret it either. Everything about Mrs. Somebody brought out the beast in her. After flicking off the basement light, Edith slowly ascended the stairs, illuminated by the glow of the upper landing light bulb. Two pairs of eyes were following her. She smiled, happy to be in the spotlight, part of an unfolding drama where she was the star.

CHAPTER 61

Harry

"I'm going to be okay. It's just a flesh wound. I'm sure it looks worse than it is."

Despite her words, Mrs. Littleton's energy was waning, and her eyes fluttered while she wrapped then tied a rag Harry had found around the deep punctures in her thigh. Harry tried not to look at her exposed flesh, naked except for shredded nylons, or at the dark stain seeping through the cloth.

He wanted to say something to her and even opened his mouth to try, but the sound came out like a cough, or maybe as though he was about to retch. He couldn't help running a finger lightly across the rips in her coat, appreciating the fiber because it had shielded Mrs. Littleton.

Harry settled in front of her, cross-legged and wrapped in his coat. She smiled weakly.

"Your father was my friend a long time ago," she said softly. "I helped take care of him when he was injured. I had great respect for him."

Harry had already figured something like that, that Mother had wrongly accused Mrs. Littleton in a rage, so he bobbed his head, appreciating her honesty.

"And I don't know what secret your mother is talking about. I really don't." She clasped his hand in her palms and squeezed it. "But what I do know is we're not safe here."

Harry lifted a thumb and forefinger to form the image of a gun. He pointed at her and jerked his hand suddenly, pretending to shoot, and watched her face slowly contort as she grasped the meaning.

"She… Are you saying she has a gun, Harry?"

He nodded. Mrs. Littleton dropped her head and sucked on her lower lip. Harry studied her crumpled figure with a gnawing sense of guilt. She'd come to their house only because she was concerned for him. As a result, Mother had threatened to kill her if she didn't get money from her husband. Everything seemed to be about revenge. Somehow, Mother thought Mrs. Littleton and Daddy had been an item, so she wanted to get even.

Harry remembered the letter. Mother had wanted it badly enough that she'd torn into Grandmother Hamilton's grave like some frenzied animal. As a grown-up lady, Mrs. Littleton might understand how to use his mother's secret to help them get free.

Amazingly, Mother had not gone through his clothing. When Harry retrieved the crinkled letter from his coat pocket, Mrs. Littleton looked up with a question in her eyes. He handed it to her. She unfolded the paper to read it, visibly shaken and breathing rapidly. Afterward, she laid the letter in her lap and stared at it and, except for rubbing her leg, was still for a very long time.

Surprised by her continued silence, Harry gently nudged her. Mrs. Littleton blinked at him with soft blue eyes. He lifted his shoulders and spread his arms, miming his desire for her reaction. When she spoke, her voice had a touch of melancholy.

"I know the handwriting, Harry, in this letter. This awful…" She stopped, her mouth trembling while she fumbled for words. "I don't know how you got this, but thank you for showing me. It helps me understand what's going on with your mother."

She dropped her head, and her hat slipped then fell away to her side. He gazed at her, worried he'd done the wrong thing. Harry was listening to a maddening *drip, drip* somewhere in the room when

Mrs. Littleton's head lurched up, and she focused on him with big, glimmering pupils.

Harry pulled back.

"I think we're both in a dangerous situation, Harry." She snatched his hand and squeezed it until it hurt. "We need to get out of here as fast as we can. Whatever it takes."

Edith

Edith stuffed her newly penned letter to the almighty Wallace Littleton into an envelope. Her words would get his immediate, jaw-dropping attention. *Will he be angry?* She hoped so. *Worried?* He should be. She was in charge, and he would hate that. Wally would be the one to receive a threatening letter with the same level of compassion he'd previously shown her. "Pay up, dear Wally," she'd written, or the whole town—including his precious banking customers—would learn he had sired a child out of wedlock and heartlessly discarded a penniless woman, tossing her aside. Mrs. Somebody would be in the basement until he coughed up the dough, and she would not come home at all if he dared to contact the sheriff. Edith had made that clear in her letter.

Poor Wally. Losing a large amount of money was one thing, but Wally would realize his precious marriage was also ruined—the two of them would be forever locked in a perverse secret, desperate to avoid the condemnation of a critical Willowdale society.

Lazily swatting the air, Edith rose from the kitchen table. "Stop pesterin' me, Red," she said. "Talk all you want, but I ain't listenin'." Edith cackled like a witch delighted with the brew in her boiling cauldron. The taste of victory was sweet in her mouth. Wallace Littleton's jilted lover controlled his future. Even if Edith didn't have his letter in her possession, Wally didn't know that. And frankly, she'd realized her ace in the hole was that Audrey looked exactly like him.

She sealed the envelope and held it to her bosom. Harry must deliver it to the bank before dark, right at closing time, and Edith expected Wally to rush to her house like a knight galloping on his steed to save his fair princess. Once in her home, they would sip tea and come to terms. Mrs. Somebody would be set free without any backlash whatsoever on her.

It was perfect, finally perfect.

Edith was about to become a very wealthy woman.

Harry

Months before, when Mother locked him in the basement for several days, Harry had come up with an idea to escape but wasn't brave enough to try it.

Now, he was.

With Mrs. Littleton hobbling and leaning on him, Harry flipped the light bulb back on and coaxed her into the furnace room. They tiptoed around small stacks of scattered coal until Harry stopped and pointed at the black iron cover to the coal chute set into the wall.

She understood his intentions and said, "No, Harry. That's too dangerous. You could get stuck in there."

He shrugged and stripped off the coat, two sweaters, and a plaid wool shirt, keeping his waffled long-underwear top on.

"No, Harry, don't do this. I have an idea. Let's go up to the landing and wait there. We can tackle your mother when she opens the door, push her down the stairs if we must, and run away. That's a much better idea."

Harry didn't agree—Mother might have her gun with her the next time. Or a larger knife. If he escaped through the chute, Harry would run to his fort, where he'd stashed Daddy's gun. He'd return to rescue Mrs. Littleton. *Could I really aim, shoot, and fire at the woman*

I call Mother? Harry wasn't sure, but he was positive Mother would not hesitate to kill him.

He pulled off his shoes. Harry unzipped his corduroys and was down to his long underwear bottoms and socks. Hurriedly, he put his shoes back on, then his hat and gloves, and scooped up the pile of discarded clothing. He gestured that Mrs. Littleton should conceal them all under her coat.

"My God, Harry. You're so thin," she said.

Harry smiled at her, wishing she understood how that was the whole point. The chute was wide enough for him to crawl up because he was thin enough now to worm his way to the top. Harry did the gun thing with his fingers and pointed up toward the exterior wall.

"You know where a gun is?" Mrs. Littleton shook her head in disapproval.

Harry pointed at the wall then at himself several times, then he acted like he was shoving his finger gun into a hip holster.

"You have a gun out there somewhere and want to get it?" Mrs. Littleton shook her head more adamantly when he agreed. "Absolutely not. No. If you insist on crawling up that chute, run to Lucky's. You can write something down, tell them to call Wally Littleton or the sheriff."

He sighed, exasperated. If Mother saw the sheriff's car—or any car, for that matter—approach her house, he had zero doubt of what she would do. A gun was the only way he knew to scare her, holding her at bay so that Mrs. Littleton could escape. Harry's bigger fear was that he would freeze to death running to his fort almost naked.

Already shivering, he pried the chute lid open then turned to face her again. Harry tilted his head sideways and placed his palms under the low cheek, squished together like he was praying sideways.

"Sleep? Yes, I can pretend to be hurt, asleep, or something if your mother comes down. But Harry, you have to hurry. Get to Lucky's, okay? It will be dark soon."

Harry pushed his scrawny frame into the chute headfirst and started scooching up, using his hands, knees, and feet in a frog-like crawl. Frosty air skimmed his body, and his skin burned where it touched the cold chute. He focused on reaching the rectangle of light above, trembling from the shock of the frigid temperature and a heightened sense of fear.

CHAPTER 62

Audrey

Another wintry day. It will be dark soon.

"Maybe you should call that lady?" Bessie said, approaching Audrey at the bar. She reached out and tenderly patted Audrey's belly. "Or I could go with you tomorrow morning to your house."

Bessie wore her worry like a mink coat—a heavy shroud she wrapped herself in that was easy for others to recognize. But Audrey was pleased with how Bessie clucked over her like a mother hen.

"I promised to wait until I heard back from her," Audrey said with hesitation. "She's probably been busy." A hint of uncertainty flickered in her eyes, and Bessie didn't miss it.

"Tomorrow. We go. I'll be right beside you the whole time." Bessie raised her chin officiously.

Audrey went back to her work. Even with her back to the door, she knew when it opened again, shivering when a wintry blast chilled the room to shouts of "Shut the damn door!" Footsteps pounded on the floor, then a firm hand gripped her shoulder and whirled her around.

Freddie did not waste time with formalities or even pleasantries. "My dad's at work. I've got Johnny's car outside. This morning, my mom took a cab to see your mother, but she hasn't come home yet. The lady at the cab company said your mother, not mine, told the guy picking her up to leave because my mom had another ride. What other ride could she have had?"

Freddie's baritone voice had risen to a high-pitched squeal. Audrey stared at him open-mouthed, instantly gripped by his intensity and the terrified look on his face. She shot an alarmed glance at Bessie, who was scurrying toward them.

"Maybe a friend picked her up?" Audrey offered, but her heart was racing. She hurriedly untied her apron with jittery fingers.

"No. I'm worried she's still at your crazy mother's house."

"Shit, Freddie, shit!" Audrey shouted and threw her apron onto the counter. *Mother hates Mrs. Littleton.* Blood rushed through her ears, and for a moment, Audrey felt faint. Her hand instinctively flew to her abdomen, hoping her unborn baby couldn't feel the panic coursing through her body. "Let's go. I'll get my coat!"

CHAPTER 63

Edith

Silhouetted on the top landing, Edith bellowed down the stairway for Harry. In her fist she clutched an envelope with words scrawled on it: "Private. For Wallace Littleton."

"Harry, I said get up here now. You're going to town." When a heavy silence greeted her, a shiver of foreboding ran down Edith's spine. "Get your ass up here now, Harry. You won't like what happens if I have to come down there and get you."

Edith yanked the light on and trudged down the steps, muttering. In the corner, exactly where she'd left her, Mrs. Somebody was sitting bowed over and motionless on the floor, her face tucked under the collar of her coat. She clicked the second light bulb and scanned the room carefully. Not finding Harry, she tore into the furnace room to search the floor and shadowy space behind the furnace.

Back in the larger room, she peered under a rickety table and then pitched a chair across the room in a fit of anger. Mrs. Somebody stirred, apparently awakened, and Edith stormed over to her.

"Where is Harry?" she demanded. When she spoke, Edith jostled Mrs. Somebody's foot with her shoe. The woman winced and drew up that leg as if she were a child protecting a cherished stuffed animal.

"I have no idea."

"Speak up. That door up there was locked. There's no way he got out." Edith's neck prickled and itched. "Was he here?"

Mrs. Somebody raised her eyes to Edith. "Yes, Harry was here. But you know that."

"Not Harry, you idiot. Red."

At that, Mrs. Somebody shook her head slowly, perplexed.

"You're still here. Why didn't he take you?"

"I... I'm injured, Mrs. Scott. My leg has several deep cuts."

"Maybe he didn't want you. Maybe you and him weren't friends like you said, just a slut he'd used once."

"So, I mean, do... do you actually see him?"

"What a stupid question. I don't have to explain anything to you, of all people." Edith leaned down. "I didn't hurt you much. Could have, though. Are you thinking about breaking down that door up there? If I was you, I'd stay put until Wally gets here." She pressed her lips to Mrs. Somebody's ear and felt the other woman shiver. "You know, I have proof of your husband's secret that will ruin you both. You don't want to risk that, now do you?"

Edith flapped the envelope in front of the woman's nose and straightened.

"I'm goin' to take money from your pocketbook to get things rolling. All I have to do is walk to Lucky's and call for a taxi to deliver this letter to your hubby. Don't need Harry." No matter the problem, she'd always been able to think on her feet.

She might be able to milk Wally's secret for years.

"If you play nice, this will all work out. Especially for me." Edith laughed and turned her back on Mrs. Somebody.

Stupid Harry would be sorry he'd left—she would make sure of that—and she would have to get even with Red, too, for interfering in her business, taking her son away like that.

But she would never understand how the hell he'd managed it.

Harry

When Harry emerged from the chute, he dropped headfirst onto the driveway and scrambled to his feet, exposed like a vulnerable bunny in an open field. The cold air cut into his skin like needles, and snowflakes swirled around him, instantly peppering his face and hair. He wasted no time.

Harry raced toward the woods, heartened that soon the trees would block the wind he was battling. He was nearing the field—almost home free—when he heard Mother's shrill voice slice through the currents, calling his name.

Wheezing as he drank frosty breaths, Harry ran even faster, terrified of freezing to death and of what might happen to Mrs. Littleton, but more horrified by the predator behind him, who he was certain would hunt him down like a dog.

Edith

Edith was about to lock the back door behind herself, ready to walk to Lucky's, when a shimmer of movement caught her eye. She scuttled to the edge of the porch and looked into the snowy backyard. Far away, she spied a small figure moving speedily toward the woods, barely distinguishable from the color of the snow, apparently someone wearing all white.

Long underwear.

Red had set him loose, and he was running away—would get away, thanks to her fucking husband.

Twice, Edith screamed Harry's name. She jumped off the porch, angrily tossing her pocketbook and an envelope to the ground. Cloaked in heavy layers for her walk to Lucky's, she was snug inside a heavy coat, and her feet were nestled in new fur-lined boots. She growled. Edith began to run, a locomotive blowing steam, gaining traction.

Red had left the boy without his clothes. That was an unfortunate miscalculation on his part, for Harry, anyway—good for her.

Edith would outlast Harry in the frigid temperatures, sure enough.

CHAPTER 64

Audrey

Neither of them spoke on the short car ride out of town. Snowflakes swirled around their windows as they blew through them, driving too quickly.

Audrey's heart was pounding out of control. Months had passed since she'd ventured anywhere near her home. She might as well have been living on the other side of the state. Sitting in Johnny's car again was a nightmare come true, but she could never explain that to Freddie. Instead, she watched the town zip by behind a dizzying white curtain. Soon, they rounded the highway curve, and her house came into view.

As Freddie slowed the car to turn into the driveway, Audrey's eyes were drawn to its shabby exterior. The coating of snow somehow emphasized the lackluster gray underneath.

She was back in the belly of the beast too soon.

But before the car could roll to a stop, Audrey jumped out. She bounded into the front yard, her eyes fixed to the distance. Someone was running through the falling snow, followed by a much larger figure moving quickly across the field. Both of them were closing in on the tree line of the woods. When Freddie slammed his car door, Audrey jumped like a skittish dog who'd been kicked one too many times.

"Who's stupid enough to be outside in this weather?" he said, following her gaze. He tugged on her elbow. "Let's go. I can't stand not knowing if my mom's in there or not."

"No. I think that's my mother out there," Audrey said, pointing. "And she's chasing someone. It could be Harry. I don't know, but I need to help." She glanced back toward the porch. "Break a window if you have to." Before Freddie could stop her, Audrey went dashing through the yard. She ran as fast as possible in her boots, and once she gained some ground, Audrey recognized her mother's coat.

One after the other, they entered the woods.

Once in the trees, Audrey crouched low to the ground, advancing like a hunter, as quietly as possible—thrusting low-hanging branches aside; skirting mangled, rock-hard roots; and ducking behind tree trunks—her eyes continuously tracking her mother. She was catching up, getting closer, closer.

Then, *whack*—a limb cracked Audrey's forehead, and she reeled backward. Stunned by the sudden, urgent pain, she stumbled into brambles before toppling to the ground with a muffled thud.

Shit. Shit. Audrey's hands fought their way under her coat, cupping her stomach. Her first thought had been of the baby.

Audrey struggled to her feet and, although wobbly, pushed herself to go on, anxiously seeking signs of Mother through the maze of limbs. She worked her way through frozen underbrush, eyes darting ahead, searching, and not finding her. When Audrey caught sight of a speck of blue peeking out from under a bush, she stopped to examine it, frowning. It was a ribbon in tatters, like those she'd kept in her drawer at home. She moved on with her quest, finding her way and looking for signs of Mother, and stepped on a second ribbon, this one half buried in wintry powder. When Audrey found a third one, she sensed a path had been created and stared at the ribbons in her glove.

Neither Mother nor Harry was in sight anymore, but someone had clearly dropped ribbons on their way to the clearing, marking the path to her Indian Trail Tree. Deep down, she knew that someone just had to be her brother.

CHAPTER 65

Edith

Edith was on her hands and knees, clawing at the scattered bones she'd pulled from her mother's grave. "Which way did Harry go? I can tear this grave apart. I'll pull every bone out and throw them to the animals. What would you do then?"

The imp had managed to lose her. But Edith had always believed Mrs. Hamilton kept an eagle eye over the woods, so she would know where he was hiding.

"It's always on your terms, isn't it? You won't talk to me, Mrs. Hamilton? You're the same old wretched bitch."

She waited after that, gripping her sides and catching her breath, hoping Mrs. Hamilton would take her bait and speak. In the meantime, she listened carefully for sounds of Harry's feet swishing over dead leaves and snow, maybe the snaps of twigs breaking under his feet. But the only sound was the steady patter of snow thrumming the trees around her.

A growl rumbled in her throat.

She'd been a fool to go after Harry.

Dusk was near, and she still had to walk to Lucky's. Edith got to her feet and snarled at the bones littering the ground. She spat into the hole before she disappeared into the trees.

Audrey

Spying on her mother from behind a narrow tree, Audrey listened to her hair-raising conversation in the peaceful woods, her voice piercing through the wind like a zinging arrow. She was talking to Grandmother Hamilton as if she were there, in the ground. She was threatening her. The strange scene and the things Mother said upset her stomach.

Suddenly, Mother jumped to her feet and hurried away, off through the trees on the path back to their house. Audrey counted to sixty then rushed to her beloved Indian Trail Tree, her unrivaled symbol of courage, always strong when she was weak. That was the only place she'd belonged and felt secure as a child. If her arms had been long enough, she would've embraced the entire giant trunk. She clutched the bark, puzzling how Mother had known about the clearing, and angry that she'd violated her sacred memories.

Audrey rested her cheek against the low branch where she used to sit, momentarily forgetting about her brother. She suddenly wheeled in a half circle, panting.

Which way should I go?

She walked beside the sturdy limb, skimming the bark with loving fingers. The branch was like an arrow, her old teacher had told her, which pointed to a long-ago trail for Sauk Indians to find and follow, a symbol to help guide them on long journeys.

If only it could show the way to Harry.

She knew the woods well, and so did he. His fort was somewhere in that same direction. Audrey stared at the branch then moved with urgency, hopping across hardened roots and between trees so spartan that they looked like sad, insipid sticks. Soon, Audrey spotted rows of dormant saplings and bushes powdered by snow—normal enough—but large leaves and twine had been stretched over them to create a narrow canopy.

Harry's fort.

Audrey drew closer and knelt. It wasn't a fort but a tunnel of sorts. And she spied footprints in the snow, smaller than hers, and smushed together. Her heart skipped a beat.

She would find him.

Hands cupped around her mouth, Audrey lifted her head and called out their old signal, "Caw, caw, caw." Then she repeated it louder.

Snow rained down on her as she paced back and forth, mouthing under her breath, "Please answer, please answer."

Then it came. The distant call was faint, but it was a raspy, throaty cry that could only be human.

CHAPTER 66

Harry

The first thing Harry did after staggering into his fort was put on two flannel shirts even though they were ice-cold. With numb red fingers, he then yanked off his shoes and wet socks and pulled on dry ones before shimmying into a stiff pair of pants. His teeth were knocking uncontrollably as he threw a thick blanket on the ground and grabbed an armful of others off his improvised bed. Harry plopped onto the blanket and dropped their thick warmth over his body, his head holding them up like a tentpole.

Harry had made it to his fort intact, but he felt sick. He wanted to puke, and his body was buzzing with an overwhelming need to sleep. *If only my teeth would stop chattering...* Harry's jaw ached from jackhammering.

Strangely, Mother was the one who'd forced him onward. Harry's terror had been the engine propelling him through the woods. When she'd screamed his name, he kept running even though he'd already been cold to the depth of his bones, his lungs about to burst. When his mother had slowed near the clearing, Harry had needed only another minute to shoot into one of his tunnels, disappear from her view, then keep moving quickly.

A dark fog was floating through Harry's brain, and his thoughts were fuzzy, too muddled to understand what he should do next. He needed more clothing to warm up, but he couldn't remember where to find it in the fort. As he whimpered like a frightened puppy, Harry hugged himself, wondering if he was going to die right there, alone in the woods.

Then he heard a call from somewhere in the woods, an eerie *aww*, either sympathy from the departed souls of Indians who had once lived there, or his imagination was playing tricks on him.

With great effort, Harry pried his eyes open as a single thought made its way to the surface and broke through the murk. *Audrey.*

Harry moaned in agony then hushed himself to listen as hard as he could. When the cawing began again, he clumsily crawled to the fort's narrow entrance, half carrying and half dragging the blankets until he slumped over in despair, tears burning in his eyes. He pounded a palm on his forehead.

Even if his sister was truly out there, he had no voice and could not caw or shout to let her know where he was. And he needed help, badly.

With that realization, another memory came to him, and he struggled to make sense of it. *A woman. Injured. In the basement. The lady Mother hated so much.* He pulled the blankets aside to free his head and stretched his neck through the fort's opening, knowing he had to try, at least. His mouth formed a tight circle. Harry howled, baying with vocal cords he hadn't used in months, as loudly as he could. Then he tried once again. Exhausted, he slithered several feet to collapse, re-cover his head with blankets, and close his eyes.

Audrey

Harry's cries guided Audrey deeper into the thick woods, and she followed a unique system of aboveground tunnels with the belief she had to be headed toward her brother. When Audrey spied his fort ahead, nestled against a large tree, barely visible in the drab light and fast-falling snow, she was giddy with relief. She had to hand it to him—the fort was solid and bigger than she'd expected, the perfect place to escape Mother for a while.

Leaning against the tree, she poked her head inside the fort, hoping he'd run to this place. Audrey gasped then bolted toward a bulging pile of blankets. Finding an opening with jittery fingers, she moved underneath them. Within seconds, Audrey was folding Harry into the curve of her arm. She rubbed his back, his ears, and his legs with no response. So little of him seemed to be left, just a sack of bones. She continued to massage him all over, and his shaking subsided, the chattering of his teeth reduced to periodic spasms.

"Are you in pain?" Audrey asked, wiping tears that had sprung to her eyes.

Harry moved a little to cuddle into her shoulder. The simple act reminded Audrey of how young he was, and her heart nearly burst from her chest.

"Why was Mother chasing you?" She stopped. "Never mind. We have to get you to a doctor. Can you walk?"

When Harry didn't reply, Audrey removed her arm and lifted his head. "No, Harry, wake up," she said, patting his face tenderly at first, then briskly until he stirred. She didn't know much about exposure, but sleeping seemed like a very bad sign.

"I'm going to see what you have in here. I'll be right back," Audrey said.

She rolled out of his blankets and tucked them back around him, anxious to find more coverings to add warmth. Looking around, she saw her pillow on what looked like a bed, stacked cans of food, and some of Daddy's belongings, which curiously included his belt and shaving kit. Even Mother's chamber pot was propped in a corner.

A shockwave of understanding jolted Audrey's nervous system. Bile rose in her throat, which she choked back. The fort didn't seem temporary at all. She scooped up more of his clothes and bent forward, holding them to her chest and weeping quietly, holding back sobs that could alarm her brother.

She would not break down. She had to get him out of there.

CHAPTER 67

Edith

Edith plowed through the trees, the path back to her home still so familiar that she could've managed her way at midnight. And the sky was indeed getting dark. While forging on through the fast-falling snow, she screwed up her face, angry at herself, beating a fist in the air. Walking to Lucky's would be next to impossible. Fleeting sleet had changed back to snow, which was heavily falling in a hearty wind. Even though the trees currently protected her, she knew a blizzard was brewing.

Edith's thoughts turned to Wally. With luck, he was missing his loving wife right then, wondering where she'd gotten off to. Of course he was. Like the postman who pledged to endure rain, snow, and sleet to deliver the mail, Wally Littleton would show up at her house. He was a smart, determined guy. He would figure out where his wife had gone—Mrs. Somebody might've left him a note or told her ugly son her whereabouts.

Edith had made everything so complicated when really, it was all so simple.

She clapped her gloves together in a muffled celebration. She picked up her pace and recalled how her other great plans had fizzled out.

Not this time.

Too bad for Howard DeDecker, though. Edith had gone on to newer, maybe even better, options once he'd failed her, while he—of his own choosing—would have his life ruined. She wondered if his missus had received Edith's letter and kicked him out. Perhaps she was simply disgusted by him. Maybe she despised Howard's face, his breath, his very being but had chosen to stay with him for appearance's sake.

Edith hoped he'd been kicked out. He deserved to have people gossiping about him. After all, she'd threatened Howard over and over that if he didn't go along with their original deal, she would reveal his darkest secret. What a dolt that man had been. She was a woman of her word—everyone knew that.

Edith wasn't at fault for having seen him that long-ago night on Whiskey Row.

He'd been the one taking risks.

The pervert.

Edith was downtown around midnight on that hot July evening, fuming about Red frequenting the Wooden Shoe Tavern once again. By fetching him and dragging his ass out of there, she would save their family from yet another disgrace.

Strange sounds reached her ears as she approached the bar's entrance, and Edith thought a mugging might be going down right under the proprietor's nose in the alley next to his bar. With light footsteps, she reached the head of the narrow alley and strained to see what was happening in the darkness.

Two men were struggling less than ten yards away. Rather than running into the bar for help, Edith raised her pocketbook and charged at them, screaming and batting at the man who was standing, believing the other man, who was on his knees, had surrendered to the robber, giving up whatever drunks stored in their pockets.

Instead of being grateful, the man being robbed clambered to his feet and shouted profanities at her, and Edith abruptly halted her attack, wide-eyed and stunned by his reaction. She backed up.

"What the hell you doin', lady?" he slurred then staggered away faster than she would've predicted possible in his state.

She knew the voice was that of a harmless, strange man nick-named Poodles, and that calmed her somewhat. Edith remained there, stupefied and eagle-eyed. The tall man near her was hastily stuffing his pisser into his pants, head lowered and inching away.

But Edith had glimpsed his face.

"Hello, Howard," Edith said, folding her arms. "I gather this means you're a faggot? Been one since high school?"

He succeeded in relodging his noodle and zipped up. At first, Howard refused to look at her. He was swaying unsteadily on his feet. Edith decided that even when drunk, normal men would not do what she'd witnessed, no matter what he might claim.

More than the whiskey on his breath, Edith instantly smelled op-portunity. Howard's father was wealthy beyond her wildest dreams, and Howard would one day inherit the family business.

"Wasn't that Poodles Bellows you was with? The town fruit-cake?"

He looked at her then, eyes swimming in an alcoholic daze. "Please, Edith, keep this between us," he whined. Howard was behav-ing like a naughty child who'd been caught pinching penny candies. "I'll do anything, just name it."

"I'll think about it," she replied and had meant that far more than he could realize.

Days later, when they met near the swings in City Park, she de-manded that her daughter and his son marry one day, insisting that her silence could be bought only with the promise of a lifetime of riches for her daughter, one of respectability and wealth for herself. He readily agreed. Trusting him was a risk, and the deal would take time, but Howard didn't have much personal wealth of his own yet, not the kind she desired, anyway.

The money—the status—just had to be more than what Wallace Littleton's family had.

Admittedly, Howard was paying a big price for reneging on their deal.

The letter Edith had mailed to his wife had probably hit like a bomb, but on the other hand, Edith believed the revelation might not have been a total shock. She believed that down deep, women were suspect of their husbands' strange behaviors. More than likely, Howard had kept up his pastime over the years. She imagined he had many unexplained absences, displayed odd quirks, and had friends that didn't fit with his status—but not Poodles, because he'd moved away years before. Even if Edith's word had little credibility, her letter would confirm Howard's wife's deep-seated suspicions.

As she was nearing the rim of the woods, the tall light shining from Mr. Ritter's empty coop cut through the falling snow and trees to guide her way. Edith scuttled along, feeling optimistic.

Her new life would be grand indeed. For example, she would wear fashionable dresses in multiple colors, and hats—beautiful, smart hats—to elaborate parties on Victorian Row, her hair stylishly cut and permed. Edith would have money to buy a fine house, too, and she would fill it with the very best appliances and ornate Victorian furniture. She would bathe in a glorious indoor bathroom, enjoying tubs full of hot water.

She swung a gloved hand in the air, swatting something unseen, suddenly irritated. "Shut up, you," she said. It was just like Mrs. Hamilton to rudely interrupt her pleasurable thoughts. "Dammit all to hell. Now you talk?"

Another minute passed, and Edith emerged into the open field, immediately pummeled by a fierce, steady wind. She hunched over to brace against it and trudged on. Edith bypassed the shed and closed in on the porch, on the verge of a new life.

She looked up and scowled. In her haste to dash after Harry, she'd apparently forgotten to close the door.

CHAPTER 68

Audrey

Dressed in additional clothing, a hat, and wool socks, Harry had perked up some, but his strange bluish-gray skin tone hadn't changed at all.

"We have to leave now," Audrey said. "If Freddie's at our house, he'll drive us to a doctor or a hospital. If he's not, we'll go over to Mr. Ritter's and figure it out."

"Dane eh." Harry's voice was scratchy and weak.

"Harry! What did you say? Did you say, 'Danger'?"

They were both standing with blankets wrapped around them, Harry's the bulkier. He nodded and forced out a raspy "Try'n." Harry's eyes locked on his sister's before he pointed at what had been his bed, every covering now stripped away. He mouthed, "Gun."

Audrey's eyes followed his shaky finger. She moved to the long, thick pile of packed leaves that had served as his mattress and knelt there, thrusting her hand through them. When her fingers touched cold steel, her eyes zipped back to her brother as she lifted out a pistol.

"You have Daddy's gun," she said.

A fierce look flamed in Harry's eyes just before they flattened to slits. At first, she thought he was going to cough, but she quickly realized her brother was working hard to push words out. "Mis-uh Lit... t-t-ton."

"Mrs. Littleton? Freddie and I came home to find her. And you. Have you seen her?"

He nodded.

"Well then, don't worry. I'm sure Freddie's with her right now."

By crooking his lips, Harry showed her his skepticism, but Audrey ignored it and pushed the pistol into her boot as far as it would go.

"Loaded?" she asked, eyeballing her brother.

He nodded yes then croaked, "Leh-ter."

"A letter? I don't care about a stupid letter right now," Audrey shot back. "I care about getting you help. There's no more time to waste, so c'mon."

She coaxed Harry from the fort. Their walk was quiet except for the whisking of snow on rough bark. With blankets draping their bodies, Audrey and Harry zigzagged through trees, she prompting her brother forward when he slowed, worried that soon the woods would be too dark to see their way. She prayed like she thought Freddie would do if he were beside her, asking for guidance home and for Harry and Mrs. Littleton to be okay. Then Audrey thought of her baby and mouthed, "Please keep my baby safe," as she kept an eye on Harry's hunched-over form. She knew it would be wrong to pray that Mother was lost in the storm somehow, somewhere, so Audrey did not. But she hoped for it anyway.

If she had to face her mother, she would. And as they tromped over the snow, the cold gun rubbed roughly against her ankle.

Edith

Edith slammed the back door, annoyed that it had blown open in the storm, and tossed her hat and coat onto the table. Blowing snow had melted and left puddles on the floor, and the kitchen was as cold as the North Pole. She ticked the thermostat up a notch, hoping the furnace had enough coal to fire up.

Wally would be coming soon. She needed to tidy up, comb her hair, change her clothes, and dab on a little makeup. Edith had to relay her demand with words as perfect as what she'd written in the letter, which she'd foolishly thrown onto the ground in her haste to chase Harry. Given the storm, it would be buried under a pound of snow.

"Red? You here?" She wanted him around to watch the show. She wiped up the floor and tossed the soaked towel into the sink. "Stick around, dear. You'll be glad to know you didn't die for nothin'."

After that, she changed into a white sweater, topping it with a heavier red-and-green plaid one, then wiggled into gray woolen slacks. Edith combed her coarse hair and pinned it into a neat bun. She powdered her nose. Satisfied, she was eager to bring Mrs. Somebody upstairs, where they would await Wally.

Curiously, the basement door swung open too easily when she inserted the key. She had absolutely locked it, but it was not locked. Edith glanced around, flicked on the landing bulb, and barged down the stairs at cannonball speed.

"Mrs. Littleton?" she called out in her sweetest voice. The woman's real name tasted bitter on her tongue.

Edith's eyes scoured the dark room as she turned on the light, flitting across every shadow, stone, crack, and broken thing in sight. In the coal room next, she inspected every corner. *Where the hell is that woman?*

She folded her hands at the nape of her neck and rocked back and forth on her toes, puffing hot breath from her mouth. Rage was building inside her, burning her gut with hatred and exasperation. First, he'd taken Harry. Now, Red had helped Mrs. Somebody escape, even if she didn't understand how. The woman could already be home, unless Red had dropped her off in the yard like he'd done with Harry.

Edith paced around the sparse lumps of coal. She would write another letter and take it to Lucky's in the morning to be delivered. One more night waiting for Wally to show up would not kill her. She would state her terms. He would comply. Otherwise, Edith would shout Wally's indiscretions to the rooftops, and people would see Audrey and know it was true. Then all of Willowdale would shun him for what he'd done. Edith stopped and raised her head. No reason to fret about any of that. The phony baloney Mrs. Somebody would never, ever allow anything of the sort to happen.

What to do about Red and his shenanigans was another thing altogether. He'd gone too far this time, but Edith was clueless about how to get rid of him. Then a sly smile formed on her lips. She moved up the steps, gently releasing her full bladder as she glided. Streams of warm urine flowed down her pant legs, trickling into her shoes, and the distinctive odor penetrated the air around her. She would piss in every room of the damn house if that was what it took to keep Red away.

When she entered the kitchen, Edith rocketed one hand to her mouth, tongue-tied and stupid, just like her son. Her legs threatened to give way, and she fumbled for the doorknob to hold herself up.

He was standing by the sink, hat in his hands.

Wally cut a dashing figure in his tailored overcoat and matching pants, still debonair with a touch of gray peppering his short sideburns. He eyeballed Edith with the same piercing blue eyes she'd once been in love with. They still glimmered like aquamarine crystals.

"How'd you get in here?"

"Edith."

Edith was breathless, hearing him say her name. His throaty, booming voice had always made her toes curl.

"Hello, Wally," she said, looking up through her eyelashes.

His lips were pressed into a thin line, and his cheeks were red from the cold or rage—Edith couldn't discern. Rather than leaning casually against the sink, Wally was standing ramrod straight in a posture meant to intimidate, to show his authority. He unfolded a fist to reveal her ice pick, which she'd left on the counter.

"You stabbed my wife, you crazy bitch."

"Is it my fault your wife is a whore?"

A muscle twitched in his jaw, and one dark eyebrow rose. He was still quite handsome, but not like he'd been in their youth. One thing was the same, though: his need to be in charge. It was amusing that he thought he was.

"Give that back to me," she said, extending her palm. "It's mine."

The clock ticked off the seconds while the wind screamed around the corners of the house, rattling the windows. She lowered her hand.

"Won't you come into the parlor? Just give me a moment to freshen up." She was stunned at finding Wally in her kitchen and had been caught unprepared. She reeked of urine, and despite how much Red would hate that, changing clothing to avoid offending Wally was more important. The moment she'd long awaited had arrived.

His intense stare radiated heat, and she was drawn to it like a moth to a flame.

"So you've seen your wife?"

Edith jumped back, stunned when he soared across the room and waved her ice pick under her nose. The tip veered close to her chin.

"You stay away from her, goddammit," Wally said, his mouth quivering. "She's done nothing to you."

She used to appreciate Wally's fresh breath, but now it smelled stale and ashy. So, he'd become a smoker. Edith giggled like a schoolgirl.

"Oh, Wally, get that thing out of my face. Like you'd be man enough to use it. Did your wife give you my message?" She batted her eyes at him, but Wally's were flashing a warning. "Oh, put that thing down and listen. I want money, and you have it. You have what was supposed to be mine. You know it, and I know it. Otherwise..." She paused for the greatest impact. "I'll tell everybody in this town what you did to me."

"Stay away from Annette. I'm warning you."

Edith pushed by him, and just as she'd anticipated, Wally didn't do a thing about it. She strolled to the window side of the table, just in case he decided to get wise, but he'd already lowered the ice pick to his side.

"You? Warning me? Your chickens have come home to roost. About time, isn't it? You have an illegitimate daughter like some hill-billy hayseed. When word gets out, people will run from you and your bank like you got the plague."

"What? You really are insane. You think Audrey's mine?"

Edith's mouth fell open. "Don't you dare—"

"This is what you're accusing me of, to blackmail me for money? It's a lie, and you know it. You're jealous of Annette, and it's time you got over it."

Edith shivered inside her wet pants. "I kept your letter," she said, raising her eyebrows.

Wally crossed his arms, one hand holding the pick, and a glint of satisfaction shone in his eyes. "See, Edith, that's where you're wrong," he said. "Because I know where that letter is, and it's not with you."

CHAPTER 69

Audrey

"C'mon, Harry, you can make it," Audrey said. "I know you can." Her brother's movements had become ever more sluggish. Audrey nudged him on through the barren, winding trees, fearful that he might collapse at any time.

"We're close, aren't we? To the edge of the woods? Look up, Harry," she said.

Harry had pulled on her and pointed, his way of insisting they travel a path that he knew, and even though Audrey had agreed, she was apprehensive. When he weakly gestured ahead to their right, she was reassured, and when they rounded a particularly wide tree, Harry's speed picked up, his feet scuffling through the snow with renewed energy.

Minutes later, they walked into the open, only to be struck by a wind so strong that Harry lost his balance. Audrey helped to steady him, then they headed toward the flickering light above the pigeon coop. They marched side by side. Audrey's feet were numb even in her furry boots, and she glanced at Harry. His feet had to be frozen in those boots that were too big. She was ready to carry him the rest of the way if she had to.

Their house loomed ahead. Audrey squinted to see if a car was in the driveway, but visibility was so poor that she couldn't be sure. Soon, they were walking through their backyard, close enough that even in blinding snow, she could see the driveway was empty.

"Good job, Harry. Let's go to Mr. Ritter's. He may have hot soup. I bet—"

Harry jerked her arm, and Audrey stumbled forward. "Dammit, Harry. Why'd you do that?"

He gestured to their kitchen window. Two shadowy figures were moving inside, but it was impossible to make out their identities through the snow-plastered pane. Audrey frowned. If Freddie had left with Mrs. Littleton, someone else was with her mother.

"Never mind that," Audrey said. "C'mon."

Harry's eyes, barely visible below his hat and blankets, were big as an owl's.

"You think it's Mrs. Littleton? Still in there?"

A barely audible "yeah" squeaked out of him.

"It's not possible. The car is gone. But I'll find out, I promise." She was yelling at him now. "Let's go!"

She took Harry's hand and pulled him along, each step more difficult than the last. Her brother was like a car running out of fuel. At last, they reached Mr. Ritter's back door, and Audrey pounded furiously, wondering what the old man would think when he found the two of them on his doorstep in a raging blizzard.

CHAPTER 70

Edith

They sized each other up like fencing opponents, each preparing for the other's next jab. Edith couldn't help but be impressed by what a bluffer he'd turned out to be, but that wouldn't matter. Even though she didn't have his old letter in her possession at that moment, the esteemed Mr. Wallace Littleton surely didn't know where it was either.

Running her eyes over his smug face, Edith came up with a new tactic.

"Well, then. Let's forget about the letter. In this town, one look at Audrey is proof enough," Edith said. "She's the spittin' image of you."

"Red was Audrey's father, Edith. Trying to blackmail me is beneath even you. It will never work."

Edith's body stiffened. She screamed a bloodcurdling cry and tossed the table at the wall. Like a raging bull, she charged Wally with her head down and smashed into his stomach with all her might. He took the blow with a loud grunt, but the ice pick flew out of his hand and skittered across the floor close to the door. With brute force, he shoved Edith away, and she tumbled close to where it had landed.

Her eyes on Wally, Edith folded the pick into her palm as though it were a precious jewel then began slicing the air with it, taunting him. Bracing her shoulder against the door, she slid upward and to her feet.

"For God's sake," he whispered, "what the fuck has happened to you?"

Without warning, the door was flung open, striking Edith in the back and knocking her to her knees. A rush of air and snow blustered through the kitchen as Audrey slammed the door behind herself and stomped snow from her boots. Her eyes pivoted to Edith on the floor then up to Wally. Her mouth dropped open in surprise.

"Well, well. Look what the alley cat drug in. Wallace, say hello to your—"

"Shut up, Edith." Wally's voice was laced with venom.

Edith complied only because his expression had morphed from fury to one of bewilderment, which she found curious.

"Where's Freddie? Isn't he with you?" he asked.

Edith cocked her head to the side, keenly interested.

Audrey stepped around her mother and over to Wally. "He drove me here in Johnny's car to find his mom. But then I saw my mother chasing someone into the woods. So I... I went after them. Freddie was going to break in if he had to. I'm sure they're both home now. I mean, the car isn't here."

Wally's eyes nervously darted back and forth, and he gnawed on his lower lip.

"What's wrong? Why are you here?" Audrey's voice was tinged with panic.

"Freddie found her, all right. Locked in your basement." Wally shot Edith a hateful look. "Searched for the key and found it, thank God. But she drove herself home, not Freddie, and called our doctor, who called me. Your mother cut her leg up pretty bad. That's why I'm here."

Mortified, Audrey turned angry eyes on her mother, who smiled back at her daughter.

"You stabbed Mrs. Littleton?"

Edith wanted to hurt Audrey too.

"She'll be all right," Wally said, "but where is my son? My wife said he stayed here to help you."

"He's not with me. I've been at Mr. Ritter's house," Audrey said.

At exactly the same time, they swerved their heads to gape at the back door.

"What? You two think he's just gonna stroll through that door?" Edith asked.

"My God. If anything happens to that boy, I swear..." Wally stopped, sucked in his cheeks, and faced Audrey. "Where could he be?"

"I bet Red has him," Edith interjected. "No sense getting your britches in a knot about it. He let Harry go outside. Bet he let your slutty wife go too."

"Mr. Littleton, what if he tried to follow me into the woods?" Audrey asked.

The question hovered between them. Audrey and Wally exchanged distraught looks. "Do you have a phone here?" he asked, touching her shoulder.

She shook her head.

"I'm going for help. We need to gather men to check out Lucky's and any houses around here and to comb the woods. Flashlights. Blankets."

"I'll check the shed and the garage next door—"

"No, it's too dangerous." Wally popped his chin toward Edith. "But so is she. Get yourself next door to the Ritter house and stay there. Leave her here."

"So thoughtful as always," Edith said, sniffing her sour odor, then shrugging. "You can't go yet, Wallace. We have unfinished business."

"Where's your brother?" Wally asked suddenly.

"At the Ritters', safe," Audrey said.

When Edith heard Harry was next door, her eyes shot up. She slipped the ice pick into her pants pocket and glared at Wally, who was snatching his hat from the floor. He sprinted down the hallway. The front door slammed.

After so much time apart, being alone with Audrey felt strange. Edith ran her eyes over the girl.

Wally was denying she was his daughter, while his only acknowledged child might be lost in the blizzard, freezing to death.

Such a tragedy could work in her favor.

CHAPTER 71

Harry

Snuggled under several blankets on a couch near a crackling fire, Harry was plenty warm, but his head was pounding like someone had bashed it with a sledgehammer. His skin was tender, painful to the touch, like his body was one large bruise.

Mr. Ritter settled a cup of hot tea on the side table behind Harry's head. "Want anything else to eat?" he asked kindly. "You've hardly had a nibble. And I want you to drink some tea, Harry. I'll help lift your head."

Harry did not want tea, but he was so grateful for Mr. Ritter's compassion that he smiled weakly and nodded then let the man cup his head to take several sips. His teeth felt filmy, and he hoped the tea might cleanse them somewhat.

"I'm sorry, Harry," Mr. Ritter whispered, settling Harry back onto a small green pillow. The old man sat down in a worn armchair next to the couch.

Turning to look into Mr. Ritter's bespectacled eyes, Harry wasn't sure what the old man was apologizing for. All he could think about was the food and milk Mr. Ritter had regularly left for him in his garage. Without that help, he likely would've been starving and would've let himself be taken to jail.

"I should've done more—told you to stay with me here, hidden you from your mother for as long as it took." Mr. Ritter's face contorted as if he, too, was in pain. He removed his eyeglasses and wiped them with the hem of his shirt. His eyes were moist. "I was afraid of her, Harry. I believed you. I mean, I do believe that your mother poisoned your father and, I'm quite sure, my birds. Can't prove any of it, though."

Harry wormed his arm out of the covers and patted Mr. Ritter's arm affectionately.

"If I'd only known you were living in the woods," Mr. Ritter said.

Overcome with fatigue, Harry was too weary to think about that or what would happen next to him. He just wanted to sleep.

"We'll get you to a doctor tomorrow," Mr. Ritter added, rolling Harry's arm under the blanket. "We'd never make it to Penshaw in my old car in this storm." He leaned in closer. "But I will take good care of you."

Together, they listened to the popping and snapping fire, occasionally interrupted by the turbulent blasts of wind slapping the house and shaking the windows. Even though Mr. Ritter's table lamps flickered as the storm pelted power lines, Harry was grateful to have any lights at all.

"I'm so glad you're able to speak a little again, Harry," Mr. Ritter said. "Talking comes in pretty handy."

Harry couldn't tell him how much his throat burned or how difficult eking out even the simplest word was. But his brain had connected with his mouth again, if only a little. When Mr. Ritter glanced toward the doorway into his kitchen, Harry knew he was worrying about Audrey, just like he was.

"I don't know what's keeping her. I'm an old man, Harry. I'd never make it over there to check on her in this storm." Then Mr. Ritter's face brightened, and he patted the top of Harry's head. "I've got something to show you while we wait."

Harry forced his heavy eyelids to stay open, watching as Mr. Ritter hobbled into another room then reappeared with a Folgers coffee can in his hands.

"There's more than twenty of them, Harry. I dug them all up to keep for Audrey. I have that notebook of hers you gave me, too, still in the same bag—all of them safe and sound."

Harry smiled weakly and let his eyelids slide down. It felt so long ago when he'd given Mr. Ritter the notebook he'd found under Audrey's bed after explaining his mother's tirades to the old man. And they'd almost been caught making the exchange. Mr. Ritter had confided then that he knew Audrey had been burying things next to his garage but hadn't interfered because of his fondness for her.

"It's okay to go to sleep now, Harry. I'll wait right here for your sister," Mr. Ritter said.

Harry drifted into unconsciousness, confident his ordeal was finally over.

CHAPTER 72

Audrey

"Don't you even think of coming near me," Audrey said, standing by the hallway.

Mother turned her back and walked around the overturned table to look out the window. "It's a shame your friend is out there in the dark. It's so cold. Do you think he might be dead?" She shrugged a shoulder. "That's sad. And all because of you."

Mother had always known just how to poke her and twist, twist, twist until she couldn't breathe.

"You caused all of this," Audrey snapped back. She could feel the gun in her boot.

Everything about her mother revolted Audrey. The malicious arrogance made her blood boil. Ending all the torment would be easy. She could claim Mother had attacked her and that she'd reacted in self-defense. If she waited long enough, that would likely be true.

"If you'd just done what you were supposed to do, we'd be—"

"Are you serious? Sacrifice me so you could be rich? That's all you ever cared about. Not me. Daddy. Or Harry."

"You're wrong. I cared about Harry."

"You always wanted to use me."

"And you let me down."

"Guess what, Mother," Audrey said, clapping her gloves together. "Exciting news for you. I've been with the DeDeckers. Nice people. And they liked me, too, and Johnny was wooing me. Yep. It could have worked out, even. Too bad it's you they hate so much." She sa-

347

vored her next words. "Without your threats to Mr. DeDecker, they would've accepted me as his wife. You ruined it for yourself. But you came close, Mother, so close."

The overhead light flickered, steadied, then blinked on and off repeatedly. The storm was playing with their electric lines, tossing them around, toying with anyone who was afraid of the dark. Mother turned around to face Audrey when she drew closer.

"Know what else, Mother? I'm pregnant, and it's Freddie's. He's no Johnny DeDecker, I'll grant you, but I'll be well enough off." Audrey sighed. "Of course, you won't."

Mother shrank against the windowpane, the whites of her eyes enormous, a horrified look replacing her previously smug expression. "Do you know what you've done?" she screeched. Mother lurched to the upturned table, putting Audrey only a few feet away.

"I wish to God my father was here," Audrey said. "I loved him. But you took care of that, didn't you?"

"Your father?" Her eyes sparkled with some strange, evil joy. "He's never even acknowledged you."

Audrey knitted her brows, assuming Mother was lying as usual to confuse her. She was doing the same thing, playing tit for tat. Lying about Freddie being the father of her baby just to rile her up had been a split-second decision.

"Nice try, but that won't—"

"He was standing right there. Caring more about his son than you, his own daughter." Mother crossed her arms over her chest. "You went to bed with Freddie? Disgusting. He's your half-brother, you stupid girl. How many times did I tell you to stay away from him?"

Audrey blanched. Since the previous Christmas, she'd known about being conceived out of wedlock by her daddy. *But Freddie's dad is my actual father?* Mother could've been trying to trick her, but she didn't look or sound like she was lying.

"Don't for a second think it's not true," Mother went on. "You think you're so much better than me. Now, you've made a bastard child just like I did. Seems the apple don't fall far from the tree. But I never did something like incest, little girl. You're ruined forever."

Audrey was a bastard. So was her child.

Heat crackled through Audrey's body, so lightning hot that her flesh burned. She was *not* worse than her mother—she was not. Mother had always lied, schemed. She didn't care whom she hurt, only cared about her own needs. She'd probably killed Audrey's daddy—murdered him.

Audrey needed to end this.

End her.

She could shoot her, blow a big hole in her head and watch her pathetic excuse for a mother sputter backward.

See her body crumple onto a floor she rarely cleaned.

Witness the fixed stare of disbelief in her cold, dead eyes.

All Audrey had to do was reach inside her boot. Grab the handle. Lift the gun out quickly.

See sweet recognition cross her mother's face.

Aim.

Fire.

Audrey looked up.

A few feet away, Mother was eyeing her closely, waiting for Audrey to fall apart, to show signs of breaking down, of despair. When the overhead light again blinked wildly, Mother glanced at it, distracted. Audrey lowered her quivering fingers, their tips itching to feel the steel.

After a final flash of the light, they were suddenly shrouded in inky darkness.

She pulled the gun out, aimed where Mother had been standing, and waited for her eyes to adjust. Mother shuffled a few feet.

"Go ahead." She was silhouetted at the window, where moonlight reflected off the fast-falling snow and the pristine ground cover.

"I hate you," Audrey said.

"So what? I hated my mother too."

"Why? I have a million reasons for hating you."

"What do you care? She deserved what she got in the end." Mother's outline blended with the frosty pane. "She's out there, where she belongs."

Holding the gun, Audrey's hand trembled. She, too, gazed out the window at the beautiful snowfall. *But the complexity of Mother Nature was such that she could delight you or kill you.*

"What does that mean?" Audrey's eyes widened. "I saw you in the woods, heard you talking to her. I-Is my grandmother buried out there? That's why you refused to let Harry and me play in the woods all those years, isn't it?"

"She's around."

"How did you know about my clearing?"

"I used to hide from Mrs. Hamilton there." Her head tilted sideways. "For years, Wally and I met there. I used to love that tree."

"My Indian Trail tree?" Audrey's tone was incredulous.

"Yes, Mother, she wants to shoot me." Mother's warm breath fogged a round area of the backlit pane. "You and Red must be awful proud."

Audrey's eyes darted from her mother to the door. "Are you talking to Grandmother Hamilton? Cut it out. I know what you're doing."

Mother's shadow moved quickly and blended with the dark.

The table careened to one side, and Audrey ducked, but not in time. Mother's hands enveloped her neck, and the gun dropped to the floor. Audrey kneed her mother in the groin, and the woman loosened her grip. They fell to the floor, hammering each other with fists and elbows. When Audrey punched her mother in the nose, the woman fell backward toward the door. Freed from her tentacles, Audrey scrambled across the linoleum, sweeping her hands over the floor to find the gun.

"Stay there," Audrey commanded. Kneeling near the oven, she aimed the gun at her mother's outline and cocked the hammer.

Mother's words snipped the darkness like sharp scissors. "Look at her now, Red. Your perfect little Audrey."

"You just want me to think you're crazy so I don't kill you."

"Don't you understand? He won't leave me be. But I keep him away with piss. Remember how much he hated that smell? He's only here now because you're here. Always his Audrey. Audrey. Audrey. Audrey." Her body slumped against the door with a thump. "He was a bad man. He threatened me once that he could ruin me. Like he knew about Mrs. Hamilton. I never forgave him for doing that."

The irony. Mother was saying she refused to forgive her daddy after everything she'd done to him. But the woman must have gone insane, sitting on the floor talking to her dead husband and mother.

She lowered the gun and loudly whispered, "Hello, Daddy."

Audrey could feel Mother's eyes shift to her from across the room.

"You hear him too?"

"He's talking to me now, Mother. Said you have to stop this. That it's over."

"Of course he'd say that. He never understood anything."

"He loved you."

"I never loved him. My mother made me marry him. Because of you." A pause, then, "Hope you're in hell, Red."

Overwhelmed, Audrey closed her eyes and tried to catch her breath. She didn't feel sorry for her mother, but she no longer wanted to kill her either. Murder was something Mother would readily do—had already done, she silently corrected herself—because of relentless greed and the self-pity she'd harbored her whole life.

"Did your mother love you?" Audrey asked.

"Mrs. Hamilton never thought I was worthy of anyone, not even Red."

Audrey fell silent, on alert for her mother's movements, but the anger had drained out of her. She had come close to doing the unthinkable.

The gun went back into her boot. Audrey pulled her pants leg down to cover it and pulled herself up onto unsteady legs. Her eyes had adjusted to the dark, and moonlight filtered in through the windows. Audrey found her hat and turned to look at her mother again. The woman was holding something that glinted in front of her face. The sight of the ice pick might've terrified Audrey months before. It was Mother's tiny sword, and she was looking for a final contest that could prove her superiority.

"I'm done with the fight," Audrey said flatly. She headed down the dark hallway, her fingertips running along the wall to steady herself.

"Get back here! We're not done. Don't you dare leave."

Audrey slipped out the front and slammed the door with a bang. Instantly, a brutal gale swept her down the steps and into the storm, blessedly drowning out Mother's screams from inside the house.

CHAPTER 73

Audrey

Slumped on Mr. Ritter's couch with Harry's head on her lap, Audrey swished hot tea in her mouth and stroked her brother's hair. His future was in her hands, and she had no idea what to do. But at least he was safe, and they were both away from Mother. The volunteers outside just had to find Freddie. Her heart raced while she worried, terrified that something bad had happened to him.

She heard shouting just then, and Mr. Littleton burst through Mr. Ritter's front door. Outside, a dozen men were barking at each other as cars started and engines revved.

"We found Freddie. Taking him to Penshaw Hospital," Mr. Littleton said excitedly, out of breath. His hat looked frozen solid to his head. "We have to take the drive, even in this blizzard, or he might not make it."

Mr. Ritter jumped from his chair, no small feat given his difficulties, and limped to the open door, oblivious to the frigid air rushing in. Audrey eased Harry's head onto the armrest and bolted after him in her stocking feet, intent on going outside to see Freddie. Mr. Littleton stopped her.

His long arms folded her into an embrace that planted her against his wet wool coat.

"Your brother needs to come too," he said in her ear.

Within minutes, Harry was carried to a waiting car, and the sounds of footsteps and men shouting waned as, one by one, vehicles pulled away.

Audrey clicked the door closed and moved to stand before the fireplace, where Mr. Ritter joined her in quiet solitude.

They'd been sitting for an hour in silence.

Mr. Ritter carefully placed another log onto the shrinking fire, and it sparked and licked the fireplace opening, flushing their faces with heat. "You will sleep here, of course."

She smiled and sipped a small gulp of hot tea, looking over at her neighbor. Deep lines crisscrossed his complexion, etched far deeper than she'd remembered, and his cheeks were sallow. He returned her gaze. Behind his glasses, Mr. Ritter's eyes had become glassy with compassion and something else.

Audrey knew the telltale signs of guilt—knew them too well.

"We both did some things wrong, Mr. Ritter, made some bad decisions," she began. "We can't change that. For what it's worth, I think you're a wonderful, caring man."

A hand covered his mouth, then Mr. Ritter nodded. He hobbled away and headed for the hall space separating his two bedrooms, motioning she should follow.

"Well, I know a good decision you made," he said.

Audrey nearly dropped her cup upon entering his guest bedroom. Coffee cans and her notebooks from the farm had been neatly stacked against the far wall, long-lost treasures that she'd assumed Mother had destroyed. She'd given them up for gone.

Smiling gamely at her, Mr. Ritter looked as though he had just revealed a long-kept secret and was quite proud of himself.

"Thank you." Audrey threw her arms around him.

Her mother had called Mr. Ritter an old geezer, a dirty Kraut, a worthless human being. So much malice had been lobbed at one kind man. He was both a neighbor and her friend, an American citizen whom her mother had never bothered to know.

CHAPTER 74

Edith

The day after the blizzard was sunny and calm.

Edith squinted at the scene outside her kitchen window. Audrey and the Kraut were sitting in his old car, no doubt talking about her, laughing at her, while they apparently waited for the motor to warm up. Silently, Edith dared them to look her way.

She would give them the finger.

That needle-nosed Nazi fucker was taking Audrey somewhere. *Where?* And Edith had yet to see Harry emerge from his house, although she was uncertain whether he was inside.

She was their mother and had a right to know.

The snow sparkled with such brilliance that Edith winced and briefly looked away. Her stomach growled. Then she spotted exhaust puffing out the muffler and glared at the sight of Mr. Ritter's car backing down the driveway before turning away.

CHAPTER 75

Audrey

Freddie slurped a spoonful of chicken soup then fell back onto his pillow, depleted by the effort of eating. His bedroom was warmed by sunshine streaming through his window, yet he was snuggled under a heavy comforter as though he were cold.

"I'm glad you're here," he said, yawning, then closed his eyes.

Out of Penshaw Hospital for a week, Freddie had been at home, continuing to recover from "hypothermia," a word Audrey had never heard before though she understood the condition. He didn't seem to recall his ordeal much, if at all, and once he felt strong enough to talk, he asked questions about what had happened to him. Patches of red skin still blotched his arms and legs, and frostbite had nipped most of his toes. He'd lost two of them.

Leaving him momentarily, Audrey crossed the hall and stood on the threshold of the bedroom she and Harry were sharing. Her brother was sleeping soundly. She smiled, grateful he was doing better and gaining strength. Harry had suffered much the same as Freddie, but his exposed skin had been more seriously damaged, and the lasting effects would not be known for some time. She wished he would try to talk more. So far, he'd said very little.

Mr. Littleton breezed past, and she followed him back to Freddie's room.

"How's the patient doing?" he asked after a few seconds of watching his son sleep.

The question was directed at Audrey, who'd taken a seat at Freddie's bedside, but at the sound of his father's voice, Freddie's eyes fluttered. Mr. Littleton touched Audrey's shoulder, a sign of his newfound ease with her. They both gazed fondly at Freddie as he floated away again.

Audrey stroked the young man's cheek. Freddie had risked his life to help her find Harry, and she would be forever grateful. He was, after all, her half-brother. Mr. Littleton had told her the truth, that Mother was not lying, but Freddie didn't know that yet. He was too frail to hear such shocking news, according to Mrs. Littleton, who'd been adamant they not speak of it even though Audrey silently disagreed.

"Mrs. Littleton wants to see you downstairs," Freddie's father said in a hushed tone. "Go on. I'll check on Harry before I come down."

Audrey jumped up. Freddie's mom was still limping from the wounds Mother had inflicted on her and probably needed her help. She trotted down the winding staircase, her hand covering her slightly swollen belly, keenly aware that a baby would further complicate her—and Harry's—uncertain future.

Two days after Mr. Ritter had driven Audrey to the Littletons' home to stay, she'd tearfully shared with Freddie's mom that she was expecting and had steadfastly refused to identify the father.

Ambling into the living room, Audrey was surprised to find Mrs. Littleton stoking the logs in the fireplace. The woman turned and smiled at her. With her flowing blond hair, lace-trimmed white blouse, and glowing pink skin, she looked like an angel on earth.

"Here goes," she said, folding her hands. She inhaled sharply. "I've known for some time that Wally was your biological father."

Audrey's jaw dropped.

"I'm sure you've figured out by now that's why Mr. Littleton was so against you and Freddie hanging out, being friends. Possibly becoming more."

Mother had tried to prevent the same thing for the same reason. *Secrets.* How tired Audrey was of secrets, even if she had a big one of her own.

"Anyway, you know I was trapped in your basement with Harry for a while. But..." She stalled then sought Audrey's eyes. "What you don't know is that Harry had a letter your mother has kept for many years."

"A letter?" She recalled Harry trying to tell her something about a letter when they were in his fort. "Who wrote it?"

"My husband. In it... well, frankly, he's quite loathsome in jilting your mother, saying he planned to marry someone else even though she was pregnant with his child. Of course, he never makes an outright admission to being the father."

A gasp escaped Audrey's lips. She started to ask a question, but Mrs. Littleton stopped her with a waggling finger.

"I have the letter. It was in the coat Harry left behind when he stripped down to crawl up the coal chute."

"What? He crawled up our coal chute?"

"Yes, to save us from your mother. I told him to run to Lucky's for help, but he wouldn't listen. He wanted to get a gun he'd hidden in the woods. I wasn't certain about all of that. It was hard to communicate since he couldn't talk." She lifted a poker and jabbed a log. "He's a brave little boy. Turned out the timing was bad since she saw him in the yard."

They both stared into the orange-and-yellow flames. Audrey was waiting to hear more, wanting badly to read that letter. At last, Mrs. Littleton reached into her skirt pocket and removed a folded piece of stationery.

"This is the letter, Audrey. As I indicated, it's not very flattering for Wally. He didn't seem to care a whit about your mother's feelings. In some ways, Audrey, I understand what happened to your mother after that. From the pain he caused her."

"May I... I'd like to read it now, please." Audrey put out her hand.

"That's not really necessary, is it? Harry has read it and can tell you what he remembers."

With deft fingers, Mrs. Littleton unfolded the paper and flung it onto the smoking logs. Audrey's hand flew to her mouth, and she cried out as the paper caught fire, its edges blazing in orange before the letter ignited into a large yellow flame. Within seconds, only crispy black ashes remained.

Audrey stared at the ashes then looked at Mrs. Littleton open-mouthed and incredulous, wondering what possible explanation she could have for destroying the letter.

"You see, even though unsigned, that letter was in Wally's own hand. We simply can't take a risk like that. I'm sure you understand." She tossed her hair as they locked eyes.

Audrey blurted, "But you didn't need to destroy it. I would have kept it to myself, kept the secret. That letter could've explained so much to me about my mother." She blinked back tears. "People in town don't give a shit about what happened a long time ago."

"Nonsense. Of course they do. But everyone already knows your mother is crazy. So was your grandmother. Spreading this type of vicious gossip could only hurt your and your brother's future."

Audrey recoiled. She abruptly turned her back to Mrs. Littleton and walked toward the staircase. After a moment's hesitation, she started up.

Mrs. Littleton's voice rose behind her. "The good news is that you and Harry will be staying right here until he's well, then I've made acceptable arrangements for you both. You certainly can't go home or back to work downtown in your condition."

In my condition. Audrey had considered asking the Littletons to adopt her child, but the sanctimonious mother she'd admired was sending them away. Spinning around from halfway up the stairs, Audrey eyed Mrs. Littleton up and down. She still looked like an angel, but that was just a clever disguise.

Freddie's mom had always been kind to her. She'd given Audrey clothing, advice, and a ride home from the farm. She'd cared enough about Harry to get involved, too, risking her safety. She had a good heart.

But the other side of Mrs. Littleton made Audrey's spine curl. She put a hand over her stomach, suddenly understanding that no such thing as a perfect mother existed.

Audrey didn't utter a word. She turned and ran up the rest of the way to see her little brother, leaving Mrs. Littleton to pluck away at the logs, aggravating a perfectly fine fire.

CHAPTER 76

Edith

With a foot of snow covering the frozen earth, Edith had been trapped in her house for a week. She had rationed the last of her canned fruits, nuts, and stale crackers. Luckily, the electricity had turned on the other day even though she'd neglected to pay a light bill for months.

The last of the snow had finally melted to a few inches, so she dressed warmly and wrapped herself in her heavy coat, scarf, and hat. The time had come to take care of unfinished business. Edith would make Mrs. Somebody listen to her. She would say something like *"Remember our conversation in the basement? How you ruined my life? Well, let me tell you what you're going to do now."*

Okay, sure. Edith had stabbed Mrs. Somebody a few times, but she'd only used a tiny ice pick.

She was owed the money. It was her due. Those facts had not changed.

Edith opened the front door only to stumble backward, practically keeling over from the shock of seeing Mrs. Somebody, once again out of the blue, standing on her stoop. Decked out in a canary-yellow hat and matching coat, her lips painted strawberry red, the woman had poised one hand to knock, her ruby nails still dangling in midair.

"Sorry to bother," Mrs. Somebody said, smiling. "I was hoping we could talk."

It was too good to be true. Either Mrs. Somebody was a glutton for punishment, or her appearance was sheer luck. Edith eyed her as though she were the big bad wolf sizing up one of the three little pigs, the dumbest one.

"I was on my way out. Got no food left in the house," Edith murmured but motioned for the woman to step inside.

"I was worried about that, so I brought you something." Mrs. Somebody hoisted a grocery sack off the stoop. "You haven't been by the church in some time. What with the storm, I thought you might not be able to get out."

The sweet aroma of baked bread wafted into Edith's nostrils. Mrs. Somebody brushed by her as though she owned the place and headed for the kitchen. Edith followed her like an eager puppy, panting. Her visitor unloaded a loaf of fresh bread, a large covered bowl of soup, and a pan of brownies.

Edith slipped out of her coat and dropped it on the floor even though the house was cold. Mrs. Somebody kept her own frock buttoned up but set her hat on the counter.

"That's for me?" Edith said with delight. Then she drew back. "Wait a minute. Why you bringing me that stuff? I ain't exactly your friend."

"I'd like to be yours" was the reply. "I think I can help you. I'd like to, if you'll let me."

Edith kneaded her fingers like a spider rubbing its legs together. *Help me?* That was exactly what Edith had had in mind, but with much, much more than food. She said, "Wally know you're here?"

"No."

"Ain't you mad I hurt you the last time you was here?" Edith had noticed her limp but didn't feel bad about it.

"Not mad. I think you've been through a lot, and so, regrettably, you lash out at people."

"Oh, regrettably," Edith mocked then added, "I appreciate the food and all, but I want to talk about what I really want. If you—" She interrupted herself to bat at the air as though a mosquito had buzzed her. "Shut up, Red. Dammit, go away. This is between me and her."

The muscles in Mrs. Somebody's face twitched, but she did not otherwise move or indicate any surprise. "Please sit, Mrs. Scott, while the soup is still hot. And the bread just came out of the oven, made just for you. I hope you like it."

Searching the cupboards after Edith sat down, Mrs. Somebody found a plate, bowl, and utensils, and placed them in front of Edith, who was drooling with hunger. She served her with a cheerful air then pulled a chair alongside Edith as though they were already friends.

"I think the bread is best dunked in the soup," she said.

Edith shredded pieces into bits and dunked them with one hand while spooning soup into her mouth with the other. *Potato cream, delicious.* The bread was moist, even fluffy, until she drenched it thoroughly.

"I'm glad you like it," Mrs. Somebody said. "Let's get you more. You certainly deserve it."

She obliged Edith with two more thick slices of bread and another ladle of soup. Edith devoured all of it then stuffed several brownies into her mouth and chewed them noisily. Mrs. Somebody looked at the clock then back at Edith.

"Let's have a chat. May I call you Edith?"

Edith smacked her lips and licked off the remaining brownie crumbs. She didn't appreciate such familiarity, but the money deal hadn't been sealed, so she said, "Okay. And I'll call you Annette." Stuffed like a turkey at Thanksgiving, she sat back in her chair, satiated.

"I thought you would want to know that Audrey and Harry have been staying with us," Mrs. Somebody said. "They're both doing fine."

"Audrey isn't fine. She's knocked up."

"I'm aware. And I'm going to help her."

"Because your son is the father? The kid will be ugly and retarded."

Mrs. Somebody's brow twitched. She uncrossed her slender legs and tucked them around a chair leg.

"Actually, that's not true," she said. "We don't know who the father is."

Edith arched her eyebrows.

"I believe your daughter fibbed to you. She's simply not telling who it is." She sighed then folded a soft hand over Edith's clenched fist. "It's like how you kept quiet for all these years. I expect your daughter will do the same."

"So, you know about Wally and me, then. I expect he had to tell you, finally. And I want—no, deserve—a payoff to continue keeping my mouth shut." Edith slid her tongue along her gums. "And that's how you're going to help me, Annette."

The chair squeaked as Mrs. Somebody scooted it back and stood up. "I did say I was here to help you. But not that way."

Edith's burgeoning grin morphed into a frown. She didn't like the sound of that. While she was thinking about how to reply, Mrs. Somebody got busy rinsing and drying her few dishes, moving maddeningly slow, as though they were fine bone china.

"You know, my Freddie almost died because of you," she said, keeping her back to Edith.

"Me?" Edith scoffed. "I never made him run after that stupid girl."

"And Harry, he barely made it. Nearly froze to death, trying to save me."

Edith shrugged. "If you want to blame someone, blame yourself. And that husband of yours."

"You've hurt a lot of people, Edith. Badly. I could list them."

"Got my reasons."

Mrs. Somebody turned and faced Edith again. "Did you have a good one for killing Red? And your own mother?"

Edith's heart leaped into her throat, and adrenaline gushed through her body. She glared at Mrs. Somebody. "Did Red tell you that?"

"No. Audrey told me everything that's happened. It just all came together for me. Then there were your sweet neighbor's pigeons."

"Try proving anything about anything," Edith said stubbornly. She rubbed her stomach, suddenly feeling too full. "See, you can't. But I can. I have a letter from your husband admitting he's Audrey's father, and she's my Wally-look-alike daughter."

Mrs. Somebody's expression was placid. Then her eyebrows arched, and her chin sank until she looked like the cat who'd secretly swallowed the canary, not at all the reaction Edith had expected.

"Two thousand dollars for now," Edith said.

Apparently contemplating the offer, Mrs. Somebody smoothed her hair, pushing several strands behind her ears. Edith's stomach was gurgling, and she was starting to sweat. Her hands felt clammy.

"Red had been my friend, Edith. A sweet man," Mrs. Somebody said. "We were never lovers, you know. Just dear friends despite our stations."

"I don't want to talk about that." Edith tapped her foot on the linoleum, agitated that Mrs. Somebody had glanced at the clock again. "In a hurry, Annette? Got plans? You won't be going anywhere until we finish this."

"I'll be leaving soon enough," she said, twirling a wavy lock around one finger. Her eyes bored into Edith. "I'm afraid your plans will be changing, though."

Edith spied her ice pick on the counter and lunged from her chair to nab it, but a severe cramp toppled her back to her seat. She grasped her stomach, aware that Mrs. Somebody's eyes were fixed on her. Shooting pains, sharp and unrelenting, racked Edith's midsection, and her abdomen seemed to be hardening into a rock. She doubled over. A strong spasm seized Edith with such force that she could not breathe, or maybe she was holding her breath. Wave after wave of cramps followed until Edith forgot where she was. She could only wail from the pain.

"What's wrong, Edith?"

"I have to use the outhouse. Don't leave," she gasped. Beads of sweat smattered Edith's face, smearing her white flesh like the freckles on ugly Freddie's face. Pleading with her eyes, Edith silently implored Mrs. Somebody to help her, but the room was swaying and out of focus, and she had to close them.

"You don't have to use the outhouse, silly. I actually do know what's wrong. You've been poisoned."

At the counter, Mrs. Somebody started to pack leftover food into the sack. The bread. Soup. Brownies.

"You did this," Edith panted. "With Red, to get even." She let out a long wail.

"Nope. Just me. Takes about thirty minutes from the time you ingest. Definitely lethal for someone who ate as much as you did." She sighed and caressed Edith's shoulder. "This is how I'm helping you, Edith. We'll be putting an end to all this misery."

Every cell in Edith's body crackled like hot cinders, and she was sweating profusely. Attempting to move off her chair, she fell over, crumpling to the floor at Mrs. Somebody's feet. She curled up on her side. Just then, relief came as a torrent of diarrhea exploded into her pants.

"Oh my God, that smell." Pinching her nose with her thumb and forefinger, Mrs. Somebody caught Edith's barely open eyes. "Nasty business, this. But then, you'd know about that."

Edith moaned more loudly as tears streamed down her cheeks. She needed the ice pick. She had to get it.

"Shush now and listen. Here's what you don't know, Edith. And it's a lot." Mrs. Somebody prodded Edith's shoulder with the toe of her pump, nudging her back down to the floor. "Nobody hears Red but you, probably because you're the only one guilty of killing him. Which, I assume, is why you hear your deceased mother too." She clicked her tongue on the roof of her mouth. "Guilt is a terrible thing."

Edith's eyes darted upward.

Mrs. Somebody followed Edith's gaze and turned slightly. "This? You want this?" She tossed the small weapon into the sink. "It's just crazy that you think Red rescued Harry—or me, for that matter—from that god-awful basement. It's not reality, Edith. Harry escaped through the coal chute, and Freddie helped me out of the basement. That's the truth."

Edith retched, puking her stomach's contents until they flowed like lava up to Mrs. Somebody's shoes. Her pain briefly subsided. She lay there breathless, helpless.

"So here it is, why you're down there and I'm up here. My God, so many reasons. You killed Red, someone I cared about. Your daughter hates you, and for good reason, mind you." Her voice dripped with disdain.

Edith moaned. Mrs. Somebody tut-tutted and stepped closer, avoiding the vomit.

"I can't believe your own little boy has suffered so much because of you. Then my son nearly died, which of course I can't let stand. But the final straw?" She tapped her knuckles on the counter, counting each of the next six words. "You wanted to ruin my life." Her voice rose. "You are threatening Wally and me, hoping to ruin our marriage, tarnish our family's reputation. For *money*." She spat the last word. "But I would do anything, and I mean anything, to keep that from happening. Except to pay you money."

Mrs. Somebody squatted and spoke into Edith's ear. "Can you hear me, Edith? This is the very same poison you used on Red. Had it tucked inside my coat with Harry's clothing when you came to the basement and realized he was gone."

Somehow, Edith pulled herself onto her hands and knees, wobbling and dizzy. A distant memory of Red played through her mind, a sickly, sniveling, puking man shaking on all fours like a dog. That this was happening to her wasn't fair. Too weak to stay upright any longer, she dropped to the floor, splayed out in a stinking stew of her own vomit and shit.

"Might as well stay down, Edith. Oh, and one last thing before I go. You asked if Wally had told me about Audrey. The answer is yes, but it was a very long time ago. I've known, Edith, since before Wally and I got married."

Edith gagged.

"At first, I felt sorry for you being pregnant and all. But when I heard you were getting married to Red, I thought you could be happy together, that you'd accept him, help him. Such a kind man, Red. After all, you grew up poor too. And all along, I've tried to help you and your family from behind the scenes. But that wasn't enough for you." She pressed her palms together. "So here we are."

Edith shut her eyes again and moaned.

Then *click, click, click*. Mrs. Somebody's heels marched across the linoleum, so cold it soothed Edith's hot cheek, and the sack rustled as she grunted to pick it up. After more heel clicks, the back door squeaked open, and a current of frigid air blew across Edith's body.

"Understand now? I only did what was necessary," she said in a small voice that seemed far away. "So, goodbye. Enjoy hell."

The door snicked shut, and just like that, the respectable Mrs. Annette Littleton was gone.

It would have been funny if Edith hadn't been on the floor, dying. She'd been right about that woman from the start, right to hate her guts, to distrust her. She bellowed Red's name but only in her head as she drooled and rolled herself into a ball, blubbering. Dry heaves overtook her and stole her breath.

Red would come. He would save her. He'd loved her once.

But good God, it wasn't Red who answered Edith's pleas.

Mrs. Hamilton, who'd only ever visited Edith on her own terms, saw fit to come just then and hover over her, but not to comfort her—Edith would never have expected that anyway—she came to gloat. Edith could smell her stale breath laced with the odor of cigarettes, then she felt her mother's lips pressing against her ear. She was hissing, laughing.

Defenseless, Edith tried to scream, but her throat was dry and swollen. The image of Mr. Ritter's wrinkled face floated into her mind then burst like a soap bubble. Her neighbor was her only chance.

Edith coaxed her arms to move even though they were as heavy as black kettles. She had to get to the door and open it. She managed to scooch several inches to one side. Her mother's hissing revved up, and Edith tried unsuccessfully to cover her ears, tucking her elbows in close, desperate to drown out the taunts she knew would come next.

Stabbing her mother to death had never truly silenced her.

Searing pain overcame Edith, and she writhed, a human log immersed in feces and puke, and she silently begged for mercy from a God she'd never believed in, for a miracle to come instead of this undeserved retribution.

The clock ticked off the seconds—unbearably slow, sluggish, and interminable—then stopped.

Epilogue

Audrey
1950

From the living room's picture window, Audrey watched Harry jump out of the Wantaka school bus and race up the long dirt driveway. His bus lurched and kicked up dust as it went on its way. Within minutes, her brother busted through the kitchen's screen door and skipped into the living room, throwing his books onto the couch with his usual "Guess what happened today?"

Turning to smile at him, Audrey observed how much he'd grown and filled out, how talkative he'd become. As a teenager of thirteen, Harry was full of boisterous ideas and boundless energy. She tousled his short hair, and he pretended to dislike it, slapping the air around her.

"I thought I heard Clara stirring," Gladys said from her knitting chair. "Want me to go?"

"I'll get her," Audrey said just as the baby cried out, fully awake. As she stood and set aside the *Look* magazine she'd been reading, they smiled at each other. Audrey felt her heart squeeze. Gratitude and happiness were new emotions she was embracing.

The room Audrey had occupied that first sizzling summer was hers again, but a crib was butting up against her bed. All her papers and journals were stacked against the far wall, and a half-filled notebook lay open on her desk, containing a story she'd started about the difficult, crazy relationship between a fictional mother and a daughter. One day, maybe, she would be a published author.

Audrey tenderly picked up four-month-old Clara, whom she'd named in honor of her daddy, and snuggled the warm baby against her chest before she changed her diaper. With deep-blue eyes, a pug nose, and dark, wavy strands of hair, Clara was the spitting image of her mama.

She carried her baby to the kitchen, where Harry and Gladys were talking at the table about his day. Audrey beamed at both of them. The Trents were planning to adopt Harry, and she felt giddy whenever she thought about it. Audrey lowered Clara into Gladys's outstretched arms.

After she poured a can of Carnation evaporated milk into a pan to heat for Clara's feeding, she turned the flame on low and swiveled at the sound of tapping on the back door. She grinned as Freddie darted over the threshold.

"Greetings, all you good people," Freddie said, plucking multi-colored leaves from the soles of his shoes and flipping them back outside. "Am I in time to help with supper?" He swooped down on Clara, lifting the child from Gladys's arms and swinging her into the air. Freddie had become a welcome fixture in the Trent household. He was, after all, both friend and family.

Two days before she and Harry moved to the Trents', Audrey had told Freddie the truth about their father.

They'd been sitting together on the living room couch, and with twilight falling, she confided what Mother had revealed the night of the blizzard. At first, Freddie was stunned to hear Audrey's mother and his father had been involved in a secret affair. He scoffed at the very notion of his father forsaking a pregnant woman and refusing to marry her. She told him about the letter written in his father's own hand, which Harry had found and read, but that it had since been lost. She suggested that when Harry recovered his physical ability to talk, they would better understand its contents.

When Audrey reached for Freddie's hand, he pushed her away and clambered to his feet in an explosive fury, ranting that nothing she said could be true.

"Why would I make up something like this!" she exclaimed. "Doesn't it explain why they tried so hard to keep us apart? Why my mother hated your folks so much? It was about more than money or status. We're related, Freddie. They had to keep it a secret. I'm not even supposed to be telling you this now. Your parents forbade it."

Freddie was aggressively pacing, but he slowed down then, becoming more thoughtful with each step. She tugged him back onto the couch, and they sat quietly in the shadows for a long time, Freddie holding his head in his hands. Audrey watched his expressions morph from bewilderment to anguish to shoulder-drooping sadness. In her mind's eye, she'd witnessed Wallace Littleton's fall from grace as clearly as if she'd watched him tumble from a skyscraper.

When at last Freddie turned to her, his eyes were glassy and swollen. "Now that I look at you, I can see the resemblance." His smile was weak.

"Deep down, we both must have known something was off, that romantic feelings didn't feel quite right," Audrey said softly.

He put up an index finger. "I think you're right. I developed a strong connection with you but always thought we were best friends. I wanted to protect you, I guess. Hoped you'd feel special, learn how you should be treated by a guy. But even I let you down several times." Freddie's voice caught, and he lowered his chin.

As they sat without speaking, twilight merged into evening, and the room grew dark. When at last Audrey stood to excuse herself, Freddie, too, rose while avoiding her eyes.

"I need some time," he mumbled. "I hate my father so much right now. And I'm afraid I might hate you for telling me all of this."

When Ed Trent picked Audrey and Harry up days later, Freddie was nowhere in sight.

A month later, on a frosty Saturday morning, Freddie paid Audrey a visit. Arms linked, bundled warmly in hats and coats, they walked down the Trents' long driveway and strolled together along the washboard country road.

Freddie explained that once his shock and anger had worn off, he thought long and hard about the mess—the "tragic circumstances"—that his father's decisions had caused.

Freddie hadn't yet forgiven him.

Looking remorseful, Freddie said he missed Audrey terribly and felt awful about their parting. They both cried with relief, hugging in the middle of the empty road, and vowed to stay in each other's lives. To Audrey's surprise, Freddie hadn't told either of his parents what he'd learned.

"One day, I want Harry to tell me what he read in that letter," he said, "what pathetic excuse my dad gave for abandoning your mother. But I'm not ready for that conversation. In the meantime, there's nothing they can do to stop me from seeing you."

Audrey knew the reason—the pathetic excuse— but she held her tongue.

Freddie was forthright and honest. Even though Audrey was worried about his reaction, she unbuttoned her coat and put his gloved hand on her hard, slightly swollen belly.

"I'm going to be a mom," she said hurriedly, her eyes big and begging for his acceptance. "Your mother knew I was pregnant and contacted the Trents. Gladys is going to help me until I can manage myself. I-It's a new start here."

Freddie hugged her again so tightly that Audrey thought the baby would pop out right then.

"I'll do anything I can to help," he promised, letting her go.

Audrey saw the sparks of curiosity in Freddie's eyes. As they walked side by side, she sensed he was biting his tongue, too polite to ask what he wanted to know. But she wanted him to know too.

"This is going to be hard to hear, Freddie."

He stopped and turned to her, his face scrunched up with worry.

"The night I ran away from home and stayed at the DeDeckers', Johnny got drunk and came into my room. He raped me."

Freddie's mouth dropped open then closed with a snap. The muscles in his jaw bulged as he clenched and unclenched his teeth. The freckles on Freddie's face melded into a flaming red.

"He hurt you." Freddie's tone was frighteningly calm yet filled with an underlying rage. His hands were trembling with anger.

"Yes." Audrey touched her brother's arm. "But he can never know, Freddie."

They stared at each other. Wisps of white vapor clouded the space between them, their warm breaths colliding and mingling as one. Audrey saw his damp eyes and wanted to cry too. He pulled her against his chest, and their heads intertwined.

"He will never know. Not from me, Audrey. I promise," he'd said close to her ear. "That guy is dead to me."

A squeal of delight from Clara brought Audrey's thoughts back into the kitchen. She turned off the low heat on the stovetop and removed the pan, smiling at Freddie as he mimed his desire to feed Clara. He was a good uncle.

As the room filled with chatter, Ed's truck rolled into view, shortly after which he joined them in the kitchen. He smiled lopsidedly at Freddie and the baby in his arms, hung his cowboy hat on a peg, then kissed his wife on one cheek.

"Hello, Freddie," he said, tickling Clara under her chin. "Would you hold the baby for a bit longer? I need to talk to Audrey."

Audrey handed Clara's bottle to Gladys to fill after the milk cooled and glibly followed him into the living room. She plopped onto the couch. When Ed sat beside her—a rare gesture—the hair on the back of her neck stood up.

"What's wrong, Ed?"

"Bad news, I'm afraid. Mr. Ritter's gone, Audrey. Died yesterday. Peaceful, though, in his own bed."

Audrey's eyes filled with tears for the sweet old man, and her shoulders quivered as she tried to hold back her sobs. Harry would be devastated. After giving her a minute to compose herself, Ed cleared his throat.

"Sherriff rang me up early today about it, so I been in Willowdale for a bit. Seems that you and Harry are the only people he named in his will."

She tilted her head and blinked. Mr. Ritter had truly little to his name, but the sentiment warmed her heart. "That was kind of him." She was unsure what else to say.

"Audrey, it's not a lot of money, but he left enough that you could go to college. If you want to, I mean. And we could save Harry's portion until he's older." Ed stared at his shoes then said, "I think he loved you and Harry very much."

Audrey nodded then returned to the kitchen, where she lifted the baby from Freddie's arms. She twirled with Clara as the baby giggled, and Freddie's eyes twinkled at the sight. Harry joined in after that, jumping and clapping his hands, and Freddie whooped and hollered as he tried to make Harry square dance with him. Ed and Gladys watched them, their eyes crinkling with amusement, smiles plastered across their faces.

Later, Audrey would tell Harry about Mr. Ritter.

Right then, her little brother was laughing and dancing, filled to his brim with hope and joy, feasting on the love and family surrounding him.

Acknowledgments

My deepest thanks to family, friends, and coworkers who knew my heart's desire and encouraged me to write a novel after I retired from a career in corporate communications.

Foremost, thank you to my husband, Mark, who championed me during long days and evenings when I was writing or researching, for his ongoing, honest feedback. Mostly, you've been the voice in my head saying, "You can do this," when I desperately needed a cheerleader who believed in me.

I'd like to thank my parents, Ernest and Shirley George, who supported my goal to become a journalist and to follow my dreams always. Dad, I feel your pride beaming down on me from heaven and wish I could get a hug. To Mom, thank you for demonstrating courage, faith, and optimism no matter what life throws at you. Several scenes in the book will be familiar because they were derived from your stories about family and life in the 1940s. The setting in *Somebody Knows* is based on the small Illinois town where you both grew up.

Thanks to Stacia Wiess, my daughter, for your frank and helpful advice on the story as it developed and, later, for the beautiful creative design and development of pamelaungashick.com. And to Troy Blase, my son, who never fails to show enthusiastic interest in my work. You help me believe I can do anything.

Thank you, Kate Chaney, my dear friend, for the countless hours of conversation about writing in general and the development of *Somebody Knows*. You've been with me every step, every page.

Hugs and thanks to my dear friend Linda Cather Johnson, a talented shutterbug with a keen eye, for her artistic photos of me.

For the early readers who gave awesome feedback, your time and interest are appreciated more than I can say.

Last but not least, I am forever indebted to Red Adept Publishing for taking on a debut novelist who eats from senior menus. Thank you to Lynn McNamee, RAP's owner, for calling me when Mark and I were in Jerusalem to express your interest in *Somebody Knows*. That was the biggest and best surprise of my life. To the editorial team at RAP who made my book shine, a world of thanks for showing me the ropes with your expertise, candor, and guidance.

About the Author

A self-professed grammar geek, Pamela Ungashick has spent a lifetime in love with words. After graduating with a degree in Journalism from the University of Nebraska, she built a successful career as a journalist and corporate communications executive in Wyoming, Nebraska, and Missouri.

When she's not writing, Pamela is thinking about writing. As a quiet observer, she draws inspiration from real people and events and is especially intrigued by dark characters. Pamela enjoys dinners and cabernets with her husband, Mark, and hikes with their dogs, Dublin and Keeley. An avid reader and explorer, Pamela believes that books, like travel, open our minds and hearts to new and different worlds.

She and Mark are at home in both Missouri and Montana, where she's working on her next novel.

Read more at https://www.pamelaungashick.com/.

About the Publisher

Dear Reader,

We hope you enjoyed this book. Please consider leaving a review on your favorite book site.

Visit https://RedAdeptPublishing.com to see our entire catalogue.

Check out our app for short stories, articles, and interviews. You'll also be notified of future releases and special sales.

www.ingramcontent.com/pod-product-compliance
Lightning Source LLC
Chambersburg PA
CBHW030143200726
48285CB00004BC/1405